I0650203

WHO HAS BURIED THE DEAD?

Also by K.G.E. Konkel

The Glorious East Wind
Evil Never Sleeps

WHO HAS BURIED THE DEAD?

AN INTERNATIONAL THRILLER—BASED
ON TRUE EVENTS

K.G.E. KONKEL

Who Has Buried the Dead, From Stalin to Putin….The Last Great Secret of the Second World War

©Ottawa, 2022, Optimum Publishing International and Chuck Konkel

First Edition

Published by Optimum Publishing International. All rights reserved. No part of this publication may be reproduced in any form or by any means whatsoever or stored in a data base without permission in writing from the publisher, except by a reviewer who may quote passages of customary brevity in review.

Library and archives Canada cataloguing in publication

Chuck Konkel

Who Has Buried the Dead, From Stalin to Putin….The Last Great Secret of the Second World War
    I.   Title
ISBN: 978-0-88890-339-6 (Paperback)
ISBN: 978-0-88890-342-6 (E-Book)

For information on rights or any submissions, please e-mail to Optimum: deanb@opibooks.com
Optimum Publishing International
Dean Baxendale, President
www.optimumpublishinginternational.com

www.opibooks.com

Twitter @opibooks | Instagram @opibooks

Printed in the USA This book can not be sold into Canada

To all those who have been there

AUTHOR'S NOTE

This book turns on secrets. One secret is buried in the deep, dark forest of Katyn, Poland. The other in the pages of a notebook kept in a modest café in Lwów, an ancient Polish city.

The principal contributors to the Scottish Book, as the notebook was called, were professors and several pure mathematicians from the nearby university. While the mathematicians' musings were dismissed by some as esoteric scribblings, when the Nazis overran Poland in 1939, the book mysteriously vanished from its hiding place in the café. Some of its authors vanished too, fleeing to America to avoid certain death. With their arrival in America came recruitment for the Manhattan Project.

Also very real are little-known places like Bad Nenndorf, the British interrogation center for hardcore Nazis before they were sent to the London Cage, a manor house located in Kensington Palace Gardens, for a three-dimensional—and certainly more aggressive—"debriefing." Also mentioned are Wünsdorf, the principal oversight warren for the *Wehrmacht* OKW during the Second World War and the victorious Soviet Occupation forces in the Cold War Era, and the Hill of Goats, located in the chilling forest of lost souls—a place called Katyn.

A thought, then, to keep uppermost in your mind as you read this story: If the Scottish Book was of little importance, then why, as a ruthless world war reached its ugly end, did the NKVD, the Gestapo, and yes, even the Allies, desperately seek to find and secure its contents? Why has its existence not factored into the telling of Second World War history? After years of in-depth research, I believe I have discovered an extremely plausible insight into what might have been, and in all probability was, one of the last great secrets of the Second World War. Until now.

CAST OF CHARACTERS

Alexander Sergeyevich Fedin: A senior member of the Comintern—the international organization of Communist Party—and one-time close friend of Josef Stalin's.

Nadia Fedin: Alexander's daughter. She becomes an elite investigator with the NKVD.

Paulus Heinrich Henschell: An *UntersturmFührer* posted to the *Hauptamt SS Gericht*, the headquarters of the SS court. He is ultimately assigned to command the German field investigation of the bodies found at the Katyn Forest.

John Paul (Johnny) Callison: A Kansas sharecropper's son and former China Marine, he joins the Royal Canadian Air Force and becomes a fighter pilot before the US enters the war.

Robert Jacquinot de Besange: A Jesuit priest in Shanghai who created the concept of civilian free zones to protect people caught between warring armies.

Antony Eskenzi: A Shanghai Municipal Police superintendent involved in a top-secret British Special Operations Executive (SOE) project.

Ryszard Manel: A barkeeper at the Scottish Café and a Polish reserve army officer (intelligence).

Stanley Ulam: A Polish-American scientist specializing in pure mathematics who helps fund the Scottish Café. He knows of the Scottish Book, teaches at Harvard, and has returned to Poland to help his younger brother, Adam, flee the imminent German–Polish battle.

Georgy Konstantinovich Zhukov: A marshal of the Red Army, skillful Russian military commander, and Hero of the Soviet Union.

Charles Tiberius Vickery: Originally the director of Central Intelligence for the Imperial Indian Police, he is sent home to the UK to take charge of intelligence-gathering for Central Europe

Simon Goldkind: A pure mathematician at the University of Lwów, investor in the Scottish Café, and contributor to the Scottish Book.

Fritz Knöchlein: An *Obersturmbannführer* and the commanding officer of the 14th Company, SS Division Totenkopf (Brandenburg). He served in France during the 1940 Blitzkrieg against the British French defenders.

Maximilian Maria Kolbe: A Polish Catholic Franciscan friar, he founded and supervised the monastery of Niepokalanów, operated an amateur radio station, and ran several international religious organizations. He subsequently volunteered to die in place of another man in Auschwitz.

Oskar Dirlewanger: The German officer in charge of the infamous SS Penal Unit active in Poland, Ukraine, and Russia.

Wladyslaw Sikorski: A Polish general and statesman who took part in the 1920 War of Independence against the Russians. In 1939, he escaped the German invasion and fled to France and later to the UK. In London, he was prime minister of the Polish government-in-exile and commander in chief of the armed forces. He died in a suspicious plane crash off Gibraltar on July 4, 1943.

Harold Adrian Russell (Kim) Philby: A high-ranking British intelligence officer and double agent working for the Soviet Union.

Klaus Fuchs: A theoretical physicist who fled Germany for the UK as war approached and his Communist allegiance became known to the Gestapo. He was part of the British delegation at the Manhattan Project, where he was responsible for significant calculations relating to the first nuclear weapons and early models of the hydrogen bomb.

Doctor Werner Beck: The director of the *Staatliches Institut für*

Gerichtsmedizin im Geneneralgouvernement (State Institute for Medical Jurisprudence and Criminology) in Kraków, Poland. Beck was responsible for the storage and security of the Katyn evidence.

Patrick Aiden Flaherty: A commissioned officer in US Army Counterintelligence and a New York City police detective. One of the new breed of military intelligence officers brought into the Office of Strategic Services (OSS), the precursor of the CIA, he was assigned by his superiors to seek out the location and establish the importance of the Scottish Book.

William Joseph (Wild Bill) Donovan: A decorated American veteran of the First World War, he founded and took command of the OSS, modelling it on the British SOE.

Fabian Lis, aka Dzik (Wild Boar): A colonel in the Polish underground, he worked cooperatively with MI6 and the SOE to combat the German occupation of Poland.

Wilfred Bowes: The officer in charge of the Special Investigation Branch, RAF Police, Bowes was tasked with investigating the German execution of fifty Allied airmen who were captured after escaping from *Stalag Luft* III in what became known as the Great Escape.

Robin (Tin Eye) Stephens: An intellectual and a multilinguist, he served in the First World War and spent years as an officer in the Gurkhas, the elite Nepalese regiment of the British Army. Stephens lost an eye in an Italian mustard gas attack while volunteering for the British Red Cross in Abyssinia. In 1940, he was seconded to MI5, where he commanded Latchmere House, one of the London Cages for holding Nazi officers. He favored psychology over violence to break prisoners. At the end of the war, he commanded the holding cells at Bad Nenndorf.

CHAPTER 1

Moscow,
Soyuz Sovetskikh Sotsialisticheskikh Respublik
(Union of Soviet Socialist Republics)
8 July 1937

Before 1917, Aleksander Fedin had been a key activist in the Marxist Underground, personally in charge of smuggling illegal literature between Russia and Europe. After the Revolution, his close friendship with Lenin had propelled him to become secretary to the influential Moscow Party Central Committee and after that, to a lofty post within the Comintern, the international organization of the Communist Party.

As befitting his status, the Fedins were provided an apartment on the top floor of the House on the Embankment, the principal residence for Party elite, located as it was on the tadpole-shaped island of Balchug, a mere stone's throw from the Kremlin and the ominous lair of the Supreme Leader.

Perhaps what ultimately doomed Fedin had been his speech at the most recent plenum of Central Committee, where he accused the *Narodnyi Komissariat Vnutrennikh Del* (NKVD) (People's Commissariat for Internal Affairs) of fabricating evidence. He called for a commission to review its overseas work. Perhaps it was the private comments he had made to a close circle of friends as he entered the conference hall of the Supreme Soviet for the 1936 Comintern—boldly honest words about the failure of the State to adequately support the struggling comrades of the Republic in the Spanish Civil War at a time when Franco's Nationalists triumphantly advanced on Madrid. *Perhaps.*

Aleksander Fedin, also known as "Batya," was a trusted comrade and senior member of the Politburo. It had initially been hard to think of him as an "Enemy of the People and a Trotskyite," but it was now The Truth, and The Only Truth, in the land.

They came for him near midnight, seven hard-faced men arriving simultaneously in a matching set of ZIS-101s, the black-lacquered saloon car so shamelessly modeled on the American Buick Roadmaster, and so capriciously favored by the sinister flying squads of the NKVD.

Ironically, the arrest, when it came, did not shock Batya. He had prepared for it. He had transferred his savings book and valuables to his wife Lara and destroyed some private notebooks. Escorted by the burly agents of the State, he carried with him only a small suitcase containing a dressing gown and toothbrush. The next day, the NKVD broke into the apartment and took away family valuables, cash, and savings books, a radio, a bicycle, coats, sheets, linen, even teacups. They then sealed the door to Batya's private study with wax.

On Tuesday, August 3, 1937, Aleksander Sergeyevich Fedin, along with 126 other prisoners, was tried by a military tribunal of the Supreme Soviet. He was charged with being a leader of a Fascist spy ring of Trotskyists covertly operating within the Comintern.

The death certificate, which contained the names of the convicted, had been officially signed before the trial began. At the top of the document there was a brief handwritten note: "*Za*—'in favor'—Shoot all 127. J. Stalin."

In the end, it was a slip of paper allegedly found tucked into a seam of his writing bureau that had doomed him to such an ignoble death. The text, in handwriting that did not even remotely resemble his, had implicated him in a palace plot against The Leader. The obvious forgery hadn't been necessary, but it had given the arresting team a sense of pious legitimacy as they ransacked the flat looking for additional incriminating evidence. Batya hadn't challenged its authenticity at the twenty-minute hearing. What good would it do? They would only have manufactured another "authentic" piece of incrimination.

Fedin never found out who had planted the paper in the seam of the desk. He never knew who'd informed on him for those presumably private comments in the foyer of the Supreme Soviet that muggy August afternoon. The informant? It was one and the same person.

And she, Nadia Alexandrovich Fedin, was his one and only dutiful daughter.

Three days after she was advised of her father's death sentence, Nadia took a streetcar to Lubjanskaja Ploschadj, an imposing neo-Baroque structure with a facade of dirty yellow brick located in the northern corner of Dzerzhinsky Square, a fearful place for certain enemies of the State destined to make their journey across the River Styx. But not so for Nadia Fedin.

Once inside, after identifying herself and having her purse and person thoroughly searched by a sullen matron, Nadia was escorted to an office at one end of the ninth floor. There, for the first and only time, she met her handler.

A week later, a twenty-year-old Nadia Fedin commenced her training as an NKVD recruit at the Gorodok Chekistov housing for secret police, the top-secret *Cheka* enclave in Sverdlovsk, 1,500 kilometers east of Moscow on the very border of Europe and Asia.

She was never to see her mother again.

**Munich, Bavaria,
Third German Reich
17 October 1937**

He'd graduated from the University of Heidelberg in the spring of 1936 at the top of his class in law. In so doing, Paulus Henschell had surely followed in the footsteps of his father Wolfgang, a fourth-generation Berliner, renowned jurist, and veteran of the Great War, where he'd served as a *Hauptmann* on the Somme in the 5th Guard Regiment of Foot—the White Devils—before he was invalided out after being wounded in a night-time artillery barrage. His mother, Maria, was descended from an old and respected Prussian landed family that had resided on the outskirts of the ancient town of Marienburg, an ancestral lineage whose impressive roots went back to the time of the Teutonic Knights. Paulus Henschell had no brothers or sisters, but he did possess a strong sense of history, a stronger one of destiny, and a filial loyalty to his parents' pedigree that was uncompromising. He was twenty-five and a fit Aryan male specimen with refined Nordic features who was obviously intelligent and extremely idealistic.

3

Because of his father's close relationship with an old comrade from the White Devils, who'd become commandant of the Junker Cadet Officer candidate school at Bad Tölz in Bavaria, it was a given that Paulus Henschell would serve the Fatherland.

While at Bad Tölz, Henschell had been selected for training in the *Shutzstaffel*, the uber-elite black-shirted SS. After a strenuous program that tested him physically, mentally, and morally, on the morning of October 17, 1937, the very same day when orchestrated pro-German riots took place in Sudetenland, Czechoslovakia, SS *UntersturmFührer* Paulus Heinrich Henschell was posted to the *Hauptamt SS Gericht*, the headquarters of the SS Court at *Wagmüllerstrasse* 16, an imposing Gothic structure located in the old city center of Munich.

In the manner of the internal affairs units of disciplined services from time immemorial, the *Hauptamnt* was responsible for formulating the laws and codes for the SS, conducting its own investigations and trials, and administering the SS and German Police Court and penal system. Its headquarters at Number 16 administered thirty-eight regional courts throughout the Third Reich with a legal jurisdiction that fully superseded civilian authority. Over time, its laws would extend to all SS and German Kripo—*Kriminalpolizei*—operating in Germany and elsewhere in what would become, through hostile occupation, the Greater Germanic Reich of the German Nation.

With over five hundred highly qualified lawyers, the *SS Gericht* was the only authority that could try SS personnel for criminal behavior, and Paulus Henschell, ever loyal, was assigned to that very section: *Ampt II—the Disziplinaramt*. There he dealt with special cases calling for the intervention of the higher moral authority of that august inner circle, one that was ultimately answerable to one man—the Machiavellian Heinrich Himmler.

After the Great War, the elder Henschell had contributed financially to the *Friekorps*, the renegade paramilitary units that fought the Communists and Spartacists in bloody street battles for control of German cities in the immediate postwar period. It was inevitable that Paulus would espouse his father's ideals, a rabid fear of the Red Menace, an unmitigated love of the Fatherland, and a blind trust in Prussian discipline. It made him a perfect fit for the jet-black SS uniform and equally jet-black ideals of the inner sanctum of the Third Reich.

Shanghai Center,
National Government of the Republic of China
29 October 1937

The rider sat astride the sleek Indian Scout motorbike on a lay-by leading up to the Tibet Road Bridge. His olive campaign cover was tipped aggressively forward over a tanned brow. A Thompson submachine gun was slung tautly across his athletic back.

Corporal Johnny Callison was twenty-two years old, and yet after less than two years, he was already a seasoned veteran of the 4th USMC Regiment—a China Marine—in starched khakis and tightly wrapped leggings, and proud of it. The only child of a widowed sharecropper raised just outside the Dustbowl hamlet of Elkhart, Kansas, Callison still felt overwhelmed by it all. Being here in the epicenter of a seething Asian metropolis that enveloped him on all sides was as darkly bewitching as the scent of opium in a Shanghai alley.

The Bund.

Twenty-six magnificent edifices commanded the west bank of the Huangpu River, a massive fortress-like arrangement of buildings gauzed with pollution, even at this early hour of the day and, representing in vainglorious splendor, the domination of Foreign Devils over a subjugated China.

The Park Hotel, where a pharmaceutical giant had originally distilled opium into morphine, the Bayer neon sign still resting brazen as a triumphant battle flag at its apex. The Astor House, Shanghai's first grand hotel, had hosted countless luminaries, among them Will Rogers, Charlie Chaplin, and Guglielmo Marconi. The English Renaissance structure of Jardine Matheson and Company, the largest and most powerful trading house extant, constructed in 1920 with grand Romanesque arches, huge blocks of stone, and giant pillars. The Cathay Hotel, a manor housing the offices and private residence of Victor Sassoon, the richest and most influential landowner in the City. Beneath its sea-green pyramid roof was rumored to be Sassoon's sumptuous penthouse apartment. The Shanghai Customs House, distinguished by four colossal Roman granite columns, topped by a bell tower and clock face visible up and down the river, tangibly reminding ships it would soon be time to pay. The Hong Kong and Shanghai Bank, the second largest financial edifice in the world, sporting a Grecian dome looming above

5

its exterior columns and archways and decorated panels that saluted the financial capitals of their day. And finally, the Shanghai Club, home to the world-renowned black-and-white marble Long Bar, measuring over one hundred feet and reputed to be the longest in the world.

The Bund had received its unique name from expats who'd come to Shanghai after serving the British Raj in what was then called Hindustan and would one day become the nation of India. Literally translated, Bund meant "muddy embankment," evoking the flood barriers that used to line the shore of the lazy mud-brown river when Shanghai was but a small seaside town and the levee merely a low sandy hill laced with reeds.

Over time, the levee and the lands surrounding it had developed in a most remarkable fashion until the Bund stretched for over 1,500 meters along the west bank of the Huangpu River. The river, which meandered like a sated dragon until it found its way into the financial capital of China, a sprawling, sweltering city of more than three million and, in 1937, one of the most densely populated metropolises in the world.

Yet on this steamy October morning, for all its puffed-up Western pretense, the Bund might as well have been nestled millions of kilometers away along an arterial canal on the red planet, Mars.

Not that he was a bleeding heart. Far from it. For any red-blooded Yank, Shanghai was a veritable garden of earthly delights. Nubile White Russian women at his beck and call. Teak, jade, and ivory of the highest quality bartered for a few packs of Camels. Full-dress uniform blues, custom-tailored in a day. Free-flowing booze by the barrel and, for the more daring, the shrouded enticements of the Triad-protected opium divans located in the French Concession just south of Avenue Edward VII.

With all its extravagance and debauchery, and perhaps more intriguingly because of it, the China Station had become the premier overseas posting of the Corps. It was certainly much more attractive than what the Marines had been tasked with in the past, dealing with the *Cacos* resistance in poverty-stricken Haiti or rallying round to protect the interests of Old Glory and the United Fruit Company during the Central American Banana Wars. It was better even than the soft pastel Pacific touches of a sanguine tour in the Philippines or Hawaii.

Compounding Shanghai's earthy profligacy, the 4th Marines Club on West Nanjing Road was surely the finest enlisted men's destination in the world. "The Club" included an NCO and enlisted men's bar, a grand ballroom, several dining rooms, accommodation for sleepovers—with or without escort—a library and billiards room, bowling alley, gymnasium, movie theater, and a ninety-six-seat restaurant. NCOs like Callison were comfortably housed in luxurious expat mansions rented from the Shanghai Municipal Council. Chinese room-boys performed the drudge work—spit-shining boots, ironing uniforms, doing laundry, making beds with sheets so tightly hospital-cornered that the most exacting top-kick sergeant could briskly flip a quarter on them, and running Joe-boy errands of all kinds, from securing wheels to wines to whores. In Shanghai, anything and everything could be bought. And cheaply. Even life.

No, it wasn't that Callison didn't enjoy Shanghai for all its sumptuous decadence It was just that he had this nagging notion about common decency being inherently important, even in times of war, and especially for occupying armies confronting a terrified civilian population. And in the last few weeks, in Callison's mind, that concept had been rudely shattered.

A distinct nuance had been added to the odor of human waste and garbage that habitually emanated from the ancient river a few meters beyond where he was poised on his bike—the rancid stench of putrefying flesh. For the past few days, bloated bodies had begun to float down the murky Whangpoa. On the surrounding mudflats, helpless infants wailed beside the mute corpses of their mothers. Everywhere around him, the battleground inched relentlessly nearer as Imperial Japanese troops aggressively challenged Chinese Nationalist defenders for complete possession of Shanghai.

The young corporal had never grown accustomed to the humiliations he'd seen inflicted daily on the local populace by the Japanese military in their ongoing expansion into the city, but as a disciplined Marine he had no choice. While the American government publicly opposed Japanese aggression, the Shanghai garrison was partnered with Japan and the other treaty powers to defend the International Settlement against any incursions by Chinese Nationalist forces. There was no provision in this agreement for dealing with a situation when one of the treaty-governing cohorts itself attacked Chinese citizenry. The Japanese had shrewdly agreed to withdraw from the actual Settlement, leaving the 4th Marines, along with the British North Lancashire Regiment, with no option but to remain neutral in the bloody battle for the city that now raged beyond the Settlement proper and all around them.

The imminent evacuation of what remained of the Kuomintang defenders from Greater Shanghai would leave the International Settlement and adjacent French Concession as perilously exposed islands of Western authority in a hostile Japanese sea. The Allied forces were sparse when compared to the Japanese army of occupation engulfing the city. The Soldiers of the Sun numbered 300,000.

Facing them, Great Britain had 2,500 troops, and the French some 4,000—and most of those a poorly trained, and largely corrupt, municipal police force located in the French Concession. The Americans were represented by the 4th Marines, with fewer than 1,000 armed personnel.

Callison was not reassured by such off-putting statistics and how he might fit into it all. But he knew in the long run that it wouldn't be pretty.

Mere minutes earlier, Brigade Headquarters had dispatched him from the Haiphong Road barracks to attend the American Consulate on the edges of the Bund to rendezvous with a Mr. Hiram Billingsgate of the State Department. Pronto, if not sooner.

As Callison arrived outside the massive consular gates, a middle-aged man stood petulantly waiting. Patrician, and wearing a finely cut suit and sporting a regulation Ivy League tie, the functionary handed over a sealed courier pouch, pronouncing his orders in a clipped Vermont accent as he did so. He seemed only too happy to slam the portals shut in the Marine's face with a loud clang when he was done.

Callison's task had been straightforward. He was to take the pouch, "post haste," to the one-armed padre in the Free Zone and not let it out of his sight. The padre—Robert Jacquinot—was well-known in the foreign concessions. Tall, robust and square-bearded, the French Jesuit was a favorite with the Chinese and European communities. Unorthodox in his ways, he was a worker-priest who liberally quoted Kant and Marx as often as Augustine and Ignatius, the saintly luminaries of his avowed calling. He was also a skilled mathematician and taught adults who professed an interest.

Like all Shanghai expats, Callison was familiar with the Free Zone, a unique enclave created by Jacquinot in the Old City for Chinese refugees fleeing the brutal fighting between the Nationalist and Japanese military. It was supervised by an international committee to ensure its neutrality and continued existence in the face of the horrors of a savage and unforgiving battleground.

Callison also knew Jacquinot personally.

The padre was a fine athlete, spoke excellent English, and had impartially refereed several friendly—and some not-so-friendly— sporting events between the 4th Marines and the resident British garrison, including a rugby match on a Sports Day just after Callison arrived at the station. He had found himself gang-tackled by a swarm of squaddies from a place called Haslington, a rough and ready Lancashire mill town fallen on hard times in much the same manner as his Kansas homestead. After the game, Callison had nursed his bruises and downed cold Pilsners with his newfound English friends and a rather surprising table mate, the French padre who enjoyed his hops and semi-ribald jokes with equal aplomb.

Callison wasn't religious by any stretch of the imagination. His faith began and ended with the Good Book and an infrequent hymn sing in the garrison chapel, but he understood human dignity, and Padre Jacquinot clearly exuded it. When he wasn't on duty, Callison gradually found he was dropping by the Padre's to help where he could. It didn't hurt that the padre also had a modest library. Callison devoured the books, particularly those involving mathematics, for which he discovered he had a natural aptitude.

He glanced at his wristwatch, a sleek Hamilton Winslow he'd picked up for chump change from a street hawker on Yuen Ming Road a month before. Ten minutes to ten. Soon it would be time for the artillery barrage.

If nothing else, the Japs were extremely methodical. Five minutes of ear-blasting hell interspersed with twenty minutes of echoing silence. Callison peered across Soochow Creek toward the crumbling Sihang Joint Savings Godown.

Ochre clouds curled from a semi-collapsed roof and gutted windows. Japanese tankettes jitterbugged close to the building, their pillbox turrets spewing forth tongues of crimson flame. Squads of caramel-garbed infantry scrambled behind them like crazed ants. What little remained of Chiang Kai-shek's units in Shanghai was being mercilessly attacked by the Third Division of the Japanese Imperial Army. The deadly vise-grip strangling the remaining Chinese forces was growing ever tighter. Callison cursed softly in Mandarin.

Cào. Plain and simple. Fuck. Shanghai had become the Gateway to Hell.

For the past three days, the Sihang Godown, and the area surrounding it, had withstood withering fire, much of it from 81mm Japanese mortars and heavy field artillery located to the north and west of the river. Horrific as it was, Callison appreciated that the barrage could have been much worse. The location of the warehouse, resting as it did near the Foreign Concessions, had proved a fortunate choice for the defenders. The Japanese didn't dare call in artillery strikes from the *Izumo*, the ancient three-stacked armored cruiser moored at the Nippon Yusen Kaisha wharf, for fear that a stray shell might land in the Concessions and provoke a serious international incident with the European and American governments.

Still, two months of intense fighting had perilously depleted the original core of German-trained KMT troops. Rumor had it that most of the KMT battalion defending what was left of the Godown was made up of lowly garrison troops from the surrounding provinces.

At daybreak, the residents of Shanghai awoke to discover a four-meter-wide flag of the Republic of China hoisted onto a makeshift pole atop the warehouse ruin. A large crowd had gathered by the river shouting "Long live the Republic!" while furious Japanese commanders had sent naval aircraft to dive bomb the building.

It's a Chinese Alamo, Callison thought ruefully. Only there's no Davy Crockett to fight on the side of the good guys. He feverishly gunned the motorbike and contemplated the quickest route to his objective.

Suddenly, a Jap Navy biplane darted by overhead, unleashing staccato machine-gun bursts at the pockmarked warehouse facade. Instinctively, Callison dove off the motorcycle and into the nearest gulley, drenching himself with fetid water. He caught a momentary glimpse of the Jap pilot—leather-helmeted, insect-goggled, and wearing a flourishing white scarf wrapped around his neck and shoulders as if he were jockeying some Waco crop duster in a flypast at the Morton County Fair.

Abruptly, the stubby aircraft canted to the northwest toward newly occupied Japanese airfields along the city outskirts, growing smaller by the second until it faded to a speck on the dusty horizon.

Callison remounted the motorcycle, fumbling with the submachine gun and leather courier packet. Thankfully, both were still dry. He paused for a moment and wondered what it would be like up there in an airplane, free from the confines of rank gullies, scurrying rats, and decaying bodies that seemed to be his destiny as a Shanghai Marine.

He revved the motor of the Indian Scout, then pushed off zig-zagging through teaming crowds until he approached the Old City. There, he was forced to slow to a turtle's pace by a conga line of anxious Chinese peasants shuffling toward the sandbag-barricaded entrance at Min Goa Road. He jostled the bike relentlessly forward until confronted by harried municipal police constables who, at the sight of a burly foreigner armed with a Thompson, prudently waved him through.

Located as they were on the third floor of the Fire Brigade building, the offices of the Free Zone were not too difficult to find.

The room itself was postage-stamp small and as dismal as the inside of a Hakka farmer's coffin. It reeked of camphor and cooking grease. Boxes of canned carrots crept up to a sagging stucco ceiling, itself smudged toffee brown by water stains. Feeble light trickled through a peephole window on the west wall. A table stood in one corner. A foreigner of indeterminate nationality was seated at it, pecking laboriously at a dilapidated Underwood typewriter. Next to him stood another European, garbed in a shabby pea jacket, threadbare cassock, and blue beret resting atop a scarecrow-angular face.

The clergyman instantly recognized Callison and gestured for him to enter. The young Marine stumbled over stacked bags of rice in the semi-darkness, opening the clasps of the courier pouch as he handed the man a sealed manila packet. "I was ordered to deliver this to you."

The priest deftly opened it. After a moment's perusal, he handed it to the seated stranger who removed two items from the packet.

Callison quickly recognized them from his stints on the embassy guard detail. An American passport, black cover, the kind reserved for diplomatically protected persons. The second item appeared to be a travel ticket.

The cleric seemed genuinely relieved. "I want you to meet Professor Mendelsohn. Joshua has been in Shanghai one week. He's been helping us with administration."

Callison mumbled a greeting.

The priest gestured to a chair. "Tea? Perhaps something stronger?"

"Tea will be fine."

The Jesuit rummaged about until he found a kettle. He filled it with water drawn from a rusty spigot and placed it on a boiler plate. Once heated, he poured the contents into a stoneware pot, unearthed three cups of uneven size and placed them before his guests. Then he sat down. So very proficient was the priest at this mundane task that Callison had to remind himself his host had the use of only one hand.

The conversation began gradually. The stranger was in his forties, a slight, stoop-shouldered man wearing a wrinkled suit and horn-rimmed spectacles that framed the wearied countenance of someone much older. He spoke English haltingly and with a pronounced accent. He had been a senior researcher at the Kaiser Wilhelm Institute for Chemistry in Berlin. "Before I had my privileges removed."

Callison's quizzical expression did not go unanswered.

"You do not know of the Nuremburg Laws?"

Callison met the query with an uncomprehending stare.

"Perhaps then of Albert Einstein?"

"Sort of. Isn't he a scientist? Won a big award a little while back?"

"The Nobel," the stranger responded patiently. "Albert won the Nobel."

"That's the one," Callison beamed, openly pleased with himself.

The stranger continued unpretentiously. "Albert is a good friend. He has invited me to join him at Columbia University. You have heard of it?"

"Yeah, who hasn't? They beat Stanford in a great football game. The '34 Rose Bowl. Seven to zip."

Now it was the professor's turn to be perplexed. "Seven to nothing? That seems a rather one-sided score for a football match."

"No, no . . ." Callison chided with a knowing smile. "Wrong kind of football."

As he began to explain the difference, a shadow appeared in the doorway. A Shanghai Municipal Police official entered the room whistling tunelessly and garbed in muted khaki. Of stocky build and sporting a deep tan, his eyes were his most striking feature—they were cerulean blue. A Webley revolver was tucked neatly into the polished holster of his Sam Browne. He was unescorted.

The intruder introduced himself. "Superintendent Eskenzi." He looked at the stranger for the longest time before he spoke, and when he did, his voice was toneless.

"You know this is part of the Safe Zone, Padre. Except for members of your committee, it's meant for the Chinese refugee population only."

"I'm afraid that I must remind you that you are not in your jurisdiction, superintendent," the priest countered.

Eskenzi raised a hand in silent admonition. He might have been doing a traffic point on Oxford Street for all the calmness he displayed. "Only doing my job, Padre." The slight suggestion of a human emotion flitted across the policeman's features, then quickly disappeared. "I have a duty to ensure the law is maintained in Shanghai in these troubled times, particularly in the Safe Zone. After all, those were the rules you made when you created this place, were they not?"

He paused to let the impact of his words sink in, then matter-of-factly turned his attention to the professor. "Your name?"

"Joshua Mendelsohn."

"You are a German citizen?"

"Yes."

"And you taught at the Kaiser Wilhelm Institute?"

"You seem to know the answer to that already," Jacquinot interjected.

The newcomer glanced dispassionately at the cleric.

"Yes," the professor answered meekly. "Yes, I did."

Eskenzi pressed the point. "You are, or were, friends with a Simon Goldkind?"

Silence.

"I take it that means yes. And Edward Teller? I believe he now resides in the United States?"

"I know Teller," the professor allowed grudgingly. "We sometimes correspond on matters of physics and pure mathematics."

The impassive expression on Eskenzi's face did not change. He appeared to ponder the response as he would a complex algebraic equation that he was on the verge of solving.

"May I see your passport?"

Mendelsohn nervously handed over the document.

The policeman looked at it in silence. His gaze returned to the man named Mendelsohn. He moved as if to say something, and then appeared to think better of it. He returned the document.

"Good luck, Herr Doctor." His comment had all the warmth of night winds on the Gobi Desert. "It appears you'll be busy tomorrow. A first-class berth to Manila on the steamship *Matsonia*. A China Clipper to San Francisco and then a DC-2 to your final destination—New York City."

"How do you know this?" Mendelsohn stammered.

The Englishman shrugged. "You forget. It *is* my business." He tipped the shiny visor of his forage cap. "Gentlemen."

"Oh, superintendent?" Callison blurted. "What did you say your name was?"

The policeman paused in the doorway. His smile ended as it left his eyes. It was as if he were seeing the Marine for the first time. "Eskenzi. Antony Eskenzi."

He turned back to Mendelsohn and his eyes softened imperceptibly. "You'll like Broadway, Professor. Lots of lights, color, excitement. They tell me that in many ways it's just as Shanghai was. Once." He paused and shook off the moment as one would the memory of all precious things lost to time. "A pity, isn't it? But then such things always are."

And then he was gone.

CHAPTER 2

Lwów,
Second Commonwealth of Poland
31 January 1939

Kawiarnia Szkocka—the Scottish Café—that was the common name everyone in Lwów knew the place by. And never thought twice about the odd juxtaposition of something Scottish so deep in the heart of an ancient Polish city.

The *Kawiarnia* sat on *Ulica Akademicka*—the Avenue of the Academics—near the Grand Theatre, a short block away from the famed medieval University of Jan Kazimierz. The best mathematicians met there informally to discuss and debate solutions to mathematical puzzles, functional analysis, probability theory—it mattered not. The co-owner of the restaurant and the group's founder was Stefan Banach, a superb scholar and chair of the university's department of mathematics.

The academics usually began arriving at dinnertime; occasionally, they would stay far into the formless winter night. With the drab regularity of an immutable equation, they invariably occupied the same tables and, in the ensuing hours toiled, both collegially and alone, through a virtual infinity of numerical equations with remarkable intensity while dining on the house specialty—*bigos*, a delicious combination of cabbage, mushrooms, venison and sausage, served with crusty rye bread and steaming mountains of plump potatoes. Their appetites were whetted by copious bottles of Żywiec lager, capped with the occasional malt whiskey or jigger of buffalo grass vodka.

Initially, they scribbled theorems onto the marble tops of the café tables in pencil. But then, as much as to ensure that the results of such remarkable deliberations might not be lost as from annoyance at their scrawls, Banach's wife Zosia had purchased a black binder specifically for their use.

The binder contained an eclectic mix of calculations—some already solved, some not, some which perhaps never could be. The proper solution to any one of the puzzles was rewarded with what were sometimes absurd, even exotic, prizes. A live duck, a box of expensive Cuban cigars, a bottle of rare liquor, 100 grams of caviar, a cheese fondue to be consumed only in Geneva, and even, on one special occasion, a full-course meal at Kendrick's, an established gentleman's club located off the High Street in Edinburgh (for many of the professors had been educated at the coldly rigorous universities of Scotland). Of late, the prizes had become curiously valuable. A rare silver sketch portrait of an unnamed woman, allegedly done by a seventeenth-century Flemish artist was the prize for this month. Donated by Krzysztof Rykiel, a dour scientist from Poznań with an aptitude for radiochemistry, it was rumored to be of great value.

The binder could be borrowed by any one of the guests. When not in use, it was retained by an angular-featured man named Ryszard Manel who, when asked, would bring it forth from a secure hiding place. Each night, without fail, after the diners had departed, he would return it to its secret location.

Ryszard was Stefan Banach's junior business partner. He was aptly suited for the day-to-day operations of the Scottish Café, for he admired everything about the United Kingdom, from strawberry trifle to the movies of Laurence Olivier, bangers and mash, and the writings of Somerset Maugham. He loved Shakespeare and the *Tempest,* with its principal character Prospero, a master of illusion, adrift in tumultuous seas where he has been exiled by his brother. And he loved adventure movies, especially those featuring the Tasmanian devil, Errol Flynn. He'd even affected Flynn's pencil-thin mustache, a look that suited his finely sculpted face.

But Ryszard's personal leanings were not solely artistic. He was also adept at electronics. It was said he had spent time at the Electrolux factory in Luton, sent there by an ill-fated consortium of investors from Kraków who wanted to make British appliances in Poland under contract. Their ultimate investment was never realized. Still, Manel did travel to Britain and became quite fluent in English—lightly accented as it was by the Pomeranian dialect of his ancestors. By that same quirk of familial geography that bedeviled many of his fellow citizens, his German was more than adequate, yet Manel considered himself a Pole and a patriot through and through.

There was no challenging such patriotism. As a young subaltern in the waning days of August 1920, Ryszard Manel had ridden in a saber squadron as it took part in the successful defense of Warsaw against the threat posed by an invading Red Army. The subsequent Russian defeat had been so great and unexpected that the battle became known forever after as the Miracle on the Vistula.

Tragically for Manel, the Miracle had a singularly bittersweet result. Amid close combat with a retreating Bolshevik mounted unit near a ramshackle village too tiny to deserve a name, a determined Cossack *shashka* slash to his right calf had sent him toppling from his steed onto the hard clay soil. He lay there for hours, helpless and bleeding as the battle swirled around him, until a team of Polish medics chanced upon him.

The subsequent six-hour surgery he underwent at the ultra-modern Jewish Hospital in the *Czyste* district of Warsaw had been successful in containing the gangrene, but the cost had been profound. Manel had lost much of his right limb below the knee to be replaced by a cruelly functional prosthesis. Over time, he had grown accustomed to the device, so much so that he barely noticed it in his everyday life. Yet, it was on bitterly cold nights such as this that the ache became barely tolerable.

On the avenue beyond the café, a solitary street light cast a bluish glow onto a bleak streetscape. Mounds of snow blocked the doorway and swirled dervish-like around frosted windowpanes. Lwów had become a maddening Sahara of snow.

It was a few minutes after 10 p.m., and most of the university dons had retired to the arid silence of their tiny lodgings. Only a handful remained in the café at this late hour, seated snugly near a smoldering fireplace, sipping *krupnik* as they whispered confidences in muffled tones. Their voices were lost amid the beams in the fire-honeyed light.

Manel puffed on a Cuban cigar as he hunched on a bar stool intently reading the daily paper. In Tunisia, French troops were held in barracks while others moved to fortifications near the Libyan border. Submarines patrolled the Tunisian Coast as the French fleet moved into the naval base at Bizerte, the narrowest part of the Mediterranean opposite Sicily. Carrying out "spring exercises" not far away from them were ninety-two men-of-war of the British Mediterranean and Home Fleets.

In Hamburg, the Germans were methodically putting the finishing touches to a new battleship, the sleek and aggressively gunned *Bismarck,* while at Newcastle upon Tyne, the British countered by christening their own dreadnought, the regal *King George V.* A correspondent from *The Guardian* wrote that German air mobilization was 95 percent complete, while on the Moselle River along the German border, France was planning the biggest air-raid drill it had ever held. Adding to the tension in America and to better balance the rising threat posed by Nazi Germany, President Roosevelt had approved the sale of Curtiss Hawk fighters to France.

According to related reports, huge shipments of European gold had arrived in America earmarked for "foreign accounts," and purportedly deposited there by the French, Dutch, and British governments. Their probable purpose, the writer posited, was to buy food and to meet American "cash-and-carry" laws governing armament sales.

In a final irony, an obscure member of the Swedish Parliament had allegedly nominated Adolf Hitler for the Nobel Peace Prize. This was a patent absurdity, as the paper's editorial astutely viewed it, a tongue-in-cheek protest against the recent nomination of Neville Chamberlain, the foppish and ineffective British prime minister who'd boasted he had secured "peace for our time" by giving Hitler the Sudetenland and, with it, carte blanche entrée into a defenseless Czechoslovakia.

The innkeeper absorbed the news with rising agitation, took a last aggressive puff, then mashed the cigar into an ashtray. The world was spinning into madness.

Suddenly, the oak door of the café was thrown open, letting in a torrent of wind-churned ice pellets. A chill Siberian blizzard roared in to envelop the chamber.

A solitary figure, garbed in a snow-buffed greatcoat, dominated the room. An ample scarf, knitted in the school colors of an Ivy League university, was draped mummy-like around the lower portion of his face. His forehead was burnished beet red from the buffeting winter wind. A man's eyebrows were visible, heavily tufted in white powder. Beneath them, his hazel eyes glimmered.

"Well? Wake up!" the stranger boomed in a rich baritone. "Will no one say hello to a weary traveler?"

Manel warmly greeted the man as the patrons looked on with bemusement. He moved awkwardly. The storm raging outside the café had not treated his bad leg kindly. "Stasiu! My friend!" he beamed. "It's so good to see you! I never expected you here! A whiskey to warm the bones?"

The newcomer unraveled his scarf and brushed dollops of caked snow from the tops of his shoulders. He removed his gloves and rubbed his hands briskly together, blowing hot breath into them. "Yes! A wonderful idea! It's more bitter outside than a Siberian icebox."

Stanislaus Ulam tossed his outer clothing onto a vacant chair, pulled up a bar stool, and sat down as his host poured a generous shot of cognac. He downed the amber liquid in one gulp and shivered deliciously at the burning sensation. He glanced around the room. "They've gone already?"

"Yes." Manel's face bore a bemused expression. "I'm afraid a talk about Kwiatkowski's *Boundedness of Polynomial Functions* can't trump an old-fashioned Polish blizzard."

Ulam shrugged. "So? What was the recent prize? If it was any good, I'll kick myself for not returning to Warsaw sooner."

"Don't worry. It was only a bottle of Russian vodka of mediocre quality."

"Thank goodness." Ulam thrust the empty tumbler outward. "A top-up?"

Manel complied, then poured one for himself. He offered up a toast. The glasses clinked together. A cough echoed from a far corner. Ragged laughter rippled from the punch line to a twice-told joke.

"Are you enjoying your time in America?"

"Tolerating my time in America might be a better choice of words. I miss Poland."

"But they treat you well there, no?"

A wry smile. "As well as can be expected in the circumstances."

"Stasiu. Stasiu," Manel chided. "Surely a research grant to Harvard University deserves better than 'as well as can be expected.'"

With his index finger, Ulam tapped a faint rhythm on the drinking glass. "I'm a Polish Jew and not exactly the most popular newcomer to an Ivy League faculty club."

"And since when did a lack of popularity stop you from conducting research?"

The innkeeper disappeared into the pantry and returned with a large tray. Several plates were on it. One held a loaf of rye bread, the others, a block of churned butter and a heaping mound of sausage. He placed the tray on the bar and sliced the loaf with precise motions before he offered a piece to his guest.

"So, Ryszard." Ulam buttered the offering with practiced sweeps of his knife, took a healthy bite, then another. "How is your English friend?" he asked between mouthfuls.

"He's fine," the innkeeper responded guardedly.

Ulam turned to the innkeeper. "Don't worry," he tut-tutted. "It's not as if I'm accusing you of spying for the Tommies." He pointed to an empty glass. "I truly appreciate where you get your liquor. It certainly isn't from that *Kraut* bastard Zimmer."

"Zimmer," the innkeeper replied with a chuckle. "That German would charge his own mother for a thimble-full of potato vodka."

The two ate and drank for a time in silence as the winter storm raged outside.

When they had finished, Ulam wandered over to the fireplace. A row of hardcover books filled the mantle. His index finger traced along the gold-leafed titles. The finger stopped.

"Ah, what's this?" he turned to his seated companion as he took a book from its resting place. "I thought you only collected scientific tomes."

The innkeeper raised his eyebrows. "I'm sorry?"

"This one here," Ulam remarked tapping the book in his hand. "*The Trumpeter of Kraków*," written by that American chap who taught at the Jagiellonian University. Kelly, his name was. I understand it's quite popular in London and New York. But it's a young person's novel, not a serious work like the other books you have here."

The innkeeper smiled cautiously. "It's a gift from a friend."

Ulam opened the book. He softly translated the written English words he found on the face page into Polish. "*Remember there is always another note . . . E.*"

"What a curious dedication." He returned the book to its place. "You know the legend, don't you?"

"Of course," the innkeeper replied. "All Poles do. During a Mongol invasion of Poland, their troops threatened Kraków. A sentry on the tower of St. Mary's Church sounded the alarm by playing the *Hejnał*, and the city gates were sealed before the Tartars could enter. Sadly, the trumpeter was shot in the throat as he sounded a warning, and, so dying, he did not finish the anthem. And that is why throughout history, the tune at St. Mary's tower has ended abruptly before completion."

"Correct," Ulam nodded. "Yet the story in the book you hold is far more romantic. Forced to abandon their farm to invading Tartars, a young boy and his parents flee to Kraków with the only thing they have managed to salvage—a family heirloom called the Great Tarnov Crystal. Alleged to have magical powers that guarantee victory to anyone who possesses it, the crystal must be delivered to the Polish king before it falls into the wrong hands.

"His father teaches the boy the *Hejnał*. Someone must be left to trumpet the song on the hour, even when facing enemies. One evening, the boy and a friend are confronted by bandits who demand to be taken to the gem. They order the boy to trumpet the *Hejnał* since it's nearing the appointed time, and its absence will be noticed. The boy thinks quickly and plays the tune in entirety, not stopping at the broken note. His friends recognize the finished tune as a warning sign—head to the tower and free the boy while saving the crystal for the Polish King."

Sparks burst out of the fireplace flitting like errant fireflies. The faces of the two friends shone a serene gold in the fire glow. The few patrons still in the dining room were blissfully silent, retreating into anonymous shadows. The wind outside grew fiercer, howling relentlessly as thick fusillades of snow pummeled the abandoned street.

Manel spoke first. "Hitler's on the warpath over the Corridor, Stasiu. This time I believe he's after Poland."

Ulam pondered the notion. "I disagree. Now that he occupies the Sudetenland, he'll devour what's left of Czechoslovakia. It will end there. Józef Beck believes Poland can negotiate a long-term settlement with Germany to avoid direct confrontation."

Manel grimaced. "Beck? The Polish foreign minister is a vainglorious fool."

"Yet the German foreign minister likes him," Ulam countered.

The innkeeper cut a healthy piece of sausage from a link and took a bite chewing vigorously. "I hear Göring calls Ribbentrop 'the little champagne salesman.'" He brushed a grimy hand across his mouth.

"That's precisely why I said what I did of Beck. Face it, Stasiu. You can't make a deal with the devil, even if he tries to sell you champagne." He jabbed his knife toward a newspaper on the counter. "Look at today's headline. The Führer is actually talking war."

Ulam picked up the paper and began to read aloud: "Appearing before the Reichstag on the sixth anniversary of his rise to power, German Chancellor Adolf Hitler stated that:

"Europe cannot find peace until the Jewish question has been solved. Today I will once more be a prophet. If the international Jewish financiers in and outside Europe should succeed in plunging the nations once more into a world war, then the result will not be the Bolshevization of the Earth and thus the victory of Jewry, but the annihilation of the Jewish race in Europe.'"

Ulam's features paled. "So, it's us again. The Jews."

"I'm sorry," the innkeeper remonstrated. "For Hitler, it is always the Jews." He paused. "You worry about Adam, don't you?"

"A little." Ulam's face turned melancholy. "My father has made arrangements for him to join me in America by late September, but I fear by then that it may be too late."

"How old is Adam? Seventeen, isn't it?"

"Yes."

Manel paused thoughtfully. "Perhaps something can be done for you to speed up the process . . ."

Ulam was perplexed. "What do you mean?"

"Leave that to me." Manel stood and languorously stretched to his full height. "For now, you must relax! I have a bottle of buffalo grass vodka in the cellar, and I know they don't serve sausages like this at Harvard."

A glass or two later, Ulam asked if he could see the book, "for old time's sake."

Manel disappeared for a moment into a small antechamber beside the bar, then returned. In his hand he held a black hard-covered book, the kind favored by grumpy ledger clerks and impecunious solicitors starting on the first rung of their profession.

Ulam opened it slowly, perusing each page with either an approving nod or quizzical expression, depending on the alphanumeric tabulations presented and their ultimate resolution, if any.

Then, abruptly, he stopped. The formula on the page was very lengthy and written in green ink with a broad-nibbed fountain pen as if its author wanted to be recognized, not only for his mental prowess but for his obvious flair and audacity.

Pointing to the page, he looked up at Manel. "Can I assume there is a solution to this one elsewhere in the book?"

"No," Manel shook his head. "And the prize for the correct answer is quite handsome. A bottle of 1931 Veuve champagne."

"Who prepared the question?"

Manel glanced down at the page as if for verification. "A young mathematician teaching at the university—Simon Goldkind."

"I don't believe I've ever met him."

"No, I don't think you have." Manel offered. "He joined our group after you left for America. Has a wife and two children. Likes to keep to himself. He studied under Kwiatkowski. Does quite well with fusion—fission—whatever the blasted thing is called!"

Manel nodded to the corner of the room where an Austrian-made Fliegen Schweighofer Baby Grand dominated the space. "Plays the piano too. Very well, I must say."

Ulam seemed not to have heard the bartender. He was transfixed by the complex formula on the page before him, as if he were committing it to memory. "It has boundless possibilities—some good, some inherently evil. Fusion, you say?" he remarked finally. "Then we can only hope that it is never used for the latter, and especially not now, with so much evil all around us. For the world will come to dread that outcome."

Manel topped up Ulam's glass. They were the only two persons still remaining in the café, for it was well past closing time. Outside, the snow piled steadily higher as the night devoured Lwów, shrouding the two friends in their shared thoughts and memories.

Warsaw,
Second Commonwealth of Poland
12 August 1939

It had been a truly remarkable European summer, one that clung endless and swirling as a butterfly in a gentle August breeze. A deep cerulean sky canopied Warsaw. Here and there, high wispy clouds dappled overhead, teased by a hot-breath breeze.

The boulevards were awash with people—well-dressed men in three-piece suits, bowlers and spats; stylishly attired women in colorful Parisian prints; society matrons strolling arm in arm with their latest paramour. Children played hoop the hoop, hide and seek, and tag. Pensioners sat wistfully alone on a multitude of benches that flanked the park.

In spite of the outward bravado of its citizenry, the talk everywhere was of only one thing—the uneasy possibility that peace was coming to an end and that the twenty-year-old Republic of Poland, formed in part in a victorious struggle with the brooding Bolshevik giant to the east, was on the verge of another, more ominous conflict. This time with a menacing jackbooted western neighbor, Nazi Germany.

On August 10, the Polish government had formally warned the German Reich that further encroachment on the Free City of Danzig, the ancient Hanseatic port situated on the Baltic created by the *Versailles Treaty*, which currently functioned in a tense customs union with Poland, would be considered by the Polish Republic to be an act of war.

The officer cut a striking figure as he wove his way down the Boulevard General Haller, his leather boots gleaming and tawny brown dress tunic and riding jodhpurs fitting just so. On his uniform, he displayed two combat ribbons—one commemorating his involvement in the 1920 Russo-Polish campaign and alongside it, the dusky crimson and virgin white of the martial Cross of Valor for "demonstrating deeds of courage on the field of battle." He moved gracefully, albeit with a noticeable limp, tapping the brim of his *rogatywka*, the four-pointed garrison cap that had been worn by the Polish military from the time of Napoleon, as he returned the crisp salutes of passing soldiers.

His walking companion was slighter and possessed the natural tweed and tobacco demeanor of a career academic. "I never knew you were in the army." He gestured to the officer's lapel. "And a captain no less!"

The soldier shrugged "It's merely a title. All the reserves are gradually being called to active duty. Don't worry—I'm still the same person."

They entered the park proper. A soccer ball bounced across their path. The officer skillfully kicked it back to a waiting youngster. The match continued.

"Do you really think there will be hostilities with Germany?" the professor asked.

"Yes," the officer responded grimly. "We've been left no room to maneuver. Look around you. Poland has become a nation of military uniforms. Our pride won't allow for anything else but the Grand Battle."

"There's no other choice?"

"None," the officer sighed. "We will fight because it is a principle. And sadly, we are a principled people."

They went on for a few more minutes until they reached the northern boundary of the park. A geometric bow of gray-stone apartments loomed before them, separated by a broad roadway *Aleje Jerozolimskie*—Jerusalem Avenue, one of Warsaw's main streets. The ground floor of the apartment complex was liberally sprinkled with chic cafes and confectionaries. A photo studio occupied a gallery entrance and a freshly painted window sign offered reasonably priced custom portraits and same-day service.

"Come, Stasiu," the officer gestured. "Let's get a photo taken of the two of us. It will be something to remember for the ages."

They trotted across the broad thoroughfare, narrowly avoiding a municipal tram cannonading toward them. A harried conductor clanged a bell with the exaggerated alarm of a fretful spinster confronting an unwelcome suitor.

The photographer was a sour-faced septuagenarian from Poznań, who had honed his craft under strict Prussian instructors at the Stettin Polytechnic before Poland had achieved its most recent reunification and he had returned to his homeland. With intense eyes and fidgety hand motions, the old man directed them through various poses clicking relentlessly away with a boxy Linhof Technika camera as he did so. After ten minutes, he was finished.

The shopkeeper painstakingly entered their particulars on the order form. The professor offered to pay, but the officer would have none of it. After asking for duplicates, he placed the *zloty* notes on the countertop and provided a mailing address.

Outside, Warsawians were enjoying the day, perhaps heading for a cheesecake pastry at the luxurious Hotel Bristol or an espresso at the chic coffee shop at the *Europejski*, overlooking the capital's grand avenue of palaces, the Royal Way—the *Trakt Krolewski*. A hot wind drifted lazily in from the west, originating somewhere over the Great

Polish Plain. The sky was without a hint of the abundant rains that usually cascaded from the heavens at this time of year. The remains of the afternoon were glorious. The August of 1939 would certainly be remembered in Poland, the officer thought to himself.

"I sense things are closing in," the professor commented as he squinted in the golden sunlight.

"As do I." The officer unbuttoned the breast pocket of his tunic. "Here, I have something for you." He handed over a Polish passport.

The professor's eyes widened. "How did you . . . ?"

"Don't ask, my friend," the officer remarked softly. "Don't ask. You will have need of this item very soon."

They strolled wordlessly down the Boulevard General Haller. A handshake. A bittersweet smile. That was all. They parted a short time after.

The officer waited until the professor was out of sight, then flagged a taxi. He had less than an hour before his train left for the eastern frontier, and there was something important that he had to do.

En route to the central station, he directed the cabbie to a taxi queue outside the main office of the Polish Telegraphic Agency—PAST—located on *Marszałkowska* Street. Motioning for the driver to await his return, he handed over a ten-*złoty* tip to cement the arrangement.

Inside the lobby, the officer faced a fortress-like wall of telephone booths. He entered one, picked up the receiver, and dropped the required coinage into a slot. He dialed five digits. The phone rang several times, then was picked up. The call, to someone at the Ministry of Defense, was short, pointed, and necessary.

The communication complete, the officer made his way to a marble counter to one side of the chamber. An enamel cup filled with pencil stubs and a pad of cheap plain paper rested atop the counter. He nimbly reached for a hard-nub pencil. With aggressive strokes he wrote: "Closing Sunday 12 August. Dwindling supplies. Stock cannot be replenished. Remaining items will be stored for safekeeping."

He signed it "*M.*"

He took the completed sheet and joined a lineup of querulous persons advancing toward a bank of wickets. After what seemed to be an interminable wait, his turn came.

The telegraph clerk was a mousy, older man with coke-bottle thick spectacles and a nervous tick affecting his left eyelid.

"Who shall I send it to?" the clerk inquired in a laconic voice.

The officer patiently spelled the name and then provided a London address—an odd-numbered apartment flat in a nondescript brownstone on Erasmus Street near Vauxhall Bridge.

"That will be twenty-six *zloty*," the clerk sniffed.

The officer fumbled about his pockets until he found some coins. He tossed them onto the counter. "Keep the change."

"Any idea when it should arrive there?" he asked, as the clerk perused the paperwork one last time.

The man looked up with a world-weary face, his manner suddenly quite sincere. "God willing it will arrive at all, *Pan Kapitan*. God willing it will arrive at all."

On the banks of the Khalkhyn Gol River,
Near the town of Bayan Tu'men,
Dornod Aimag (Province), Mongolia
19 August 1939

Junior Lieutenant of State Security Nadia Fedin stood before the ragged platoon of conscripts and grimly contemplated the spidery twists of fortune that had landed her here on the desolate outer fringes of the Mongolian People's Republic, eons away from the world she had known in Moscow.

It was devastatingly hot. A merciless noon-day sun beat down on the arid desert like an unrelenting sledgehammer onto a leaden anvil and she was tired. Oh so tired, of the mosquitoes swarming from the dense marshlands along the nearby Khalkhyn Gol. Tired of the lingering stink of death. Tired of the constant stupidity of the randomly armed serfs lounging before her masquerading as infantry soldiers in the glorious *Raboche-Krest'yanskaya Krasnaya Armiya*—the Workers' and Peasants' Red Army of the USSR.

Her first two years in the NKVD had been spent as a cadet officer, a ciphered "go-for" toiling in the drearier lower echelons of a now-unfamiliar Moscow, a place known derisively to all who mattered as the "Third Rome." At first, she'd driven experienced arrest teams around the gloomy capital like a hack cabby—assigned the mundane task of piloting sleek black ZIL limousines for sinister snatch squads engaged in what was known as *mokrie dela*—wet affairs—for the inevitable spilling of blood that flowed in their murderous wake. She had gamely endured the tediously long hours, rampant chauvinism, and cheap come-ons. She had lost her virginity to a section head in a vodka-induced encounter atop a cluttered desktop within a month of her arrival at the *Lubyanka*, but it had been worthwhile, for that loveless coupling had enabled her to leave the paperwork to become operational.

"Why are we here again? Comrade Commissar?" The boy called Stepan piped up with that foolish lopsided grin that had at first amused and now so thoroughly annoyed her. He was the youngest member of the platoon, a Ukrainian peasant who should have been herding sway-backed cattle on dusty back roads instead of lugging an ancient Mosin-Nagant rifle in this pestilent backwater.

Nadia sighed and, for what must have been the tenth time, patiently outlined the volatile situation they were facing.

As she explained it, to their immediate east and looming just beyond the front lines lay the army of their principal adversary, the Manchu State known as *Manchukuo*, a blundering puppet regime propped up by Imperial Japan. Where they now stood was Mongolia, a true communist worker-nation loyal to the proletarian values of the Soviet Union and, as such, worthy of their military assistance. The Japanese imperialists had fraudulently maintained that the border between Manchukuo and Mongolia was the Khalkhyn Gol. In contrast, the Mongolians and Soviet people rightly asserted that the border ran 16 kilometers east of the river, near a village called Nomonhan, and had dispatched units to show the flag.

What she didn't tell her naive charges was that the principal lifeline of the Soviet position in the Far East and Siberia, and in fact, the only link between those regions and European Russia, was the Trans-Siberian Railroad. Outer Mongolia was essential to the strategic control of that railroad, and it was largely to protect that vital artery that the Soviets had established the puppet Mongolian People's Republic.

The recent incident had begun in May when a small Mongolian cavalry unit entered the disputed area in search of grazing for their horses. They were attacked by Manchuokan cavalry and driven back across the Khalkhyn Gol. Two days later, the Mongolian force returned in greater numbers. The Manchuokans were unable to dislodge them.

For the next two months, the opposing sides had traded desultory blows along a desolate landscape to test each other's resolve as they gradually built up their respective forces for the definitive battle that they both knew was coming.

On June 5, the Soviet high command—the *Stavka*—had dispatched a new corps commander, Georgy Konstantinovich Zhukov, to lead an expanded army group that included armor and air support. Zhukov was a close confidant of Comrade Stalin and a strict, even brutal, military disciplinarian who sought victory at any price, even when it meant the blood—and copious quantities of it—of ordinary Ivans. To foster the proper Spirit of the Revolution and ensure complete fealty to the State *apparatchik*, Zukhov had brought with him a contingent of twenty NKVD officers.

The initial battles along the Khalkhyn Gol had been Soviet victories, but with the boundaries shifting only infinitesimally as a result. A victory ending in such a stalemate was, as Commissar Galiaskarov was wont to remark, like making love to your sister—somewhat satisfying but irrelevant in the greater scheme of things. Galiaskarov had also liked to toss back *chut-chuts*—quick gulps of vodka—and in such copious quantities that he was staggering drunk for most of the day. And it was that weakness while engaged in yet another ill-advised fireside toast to the Party that had caused his decapitation on July 24 at the receiving end of Japanese howitzer shrapnel—a night on which the two sides engaged in brisk artillery duels. The drunken fool's brain splatter had ruined Nadia's best uniform but had also made her the senior NKVD official in the 5th Rifle and Machine Gun Brigade.

And that was precisely why Nadia Fedin was brashly perched atop the ammo flatbed of a mottled-toffee *Betushka*, a sturdy Russian BT-7 tank, hectoring and cajoling what was little more than a group of moon-faced peasant rabble to fulfill their sworn duty for Communism, for Mother Russia, and for Stalin.

"Tomorrow will be a day of victory for the workers," she shouted hoarsely. "A day to break through the Fascist lines and to reclaim those lands that rightfully belong to our brothers and sisters in the Mongolian People's Republic!"

She glanced down at a sea of apathetic faces.

A truck horn sounded shrilly in the distance. A horse neighed. The soldiers arrayed before her nervously shuffled their feet.

"Comrades?" she repeated ominously. "Tonight, you may rest in the knowledge that when you go into battle at dawn you will write a glorious chapter in our beloved nation's history. Each and every one of you." Nadia couldn't restrain herself as she gestured to the young soldier. "Even you, Stepan Ivanovich."

The men guffawed. The youth named Stepan blushed. Nadia spread her hands triumphantly in benediction. "Comrades . . ."

The song began slowly from the rear ranks, helped along no doubt by the strong baritone of an anonymous NKVD operative—*The Internationale*:

> Stand up, you who are branded by the curse,
> All the world's starving and enslaved
> And ready to fight to the death.
> We will destroy this whole world of violence
> To the foundations and then
> We will build a new world.
> He who has nothing—will become everything!

Nadia looked over at the boy; he was singing timidly at first but with ever-increasing vigor. She wondered for a moment what it was like to have such blind trust in anything, then banished the thought. The Party demanded loyalty, not trust. They were two different commodities and separated the true leaders of the proletariat from the common rabble spread before her. Loyalty was hard to find. Trust was easy to lose.

The next morning at daybreak, Zhukov, ever the chess master, broke the stalemate. A massive Soviet force consisting of reinforced rifle and tank divisions and over 550 fighter aircraft and bombers vigorously attacked the Japanese Kwantung Army 23rd Division along a common front, while an armored force of five tank brigades pinched in the suddenly vulnerable Japanese flanks, covered as they were by unreliable Manchuokan cavalry. The attack was lightning swift and brutally successful, for Japanese intelligence had somehow failed to detect both the scale of the Soviet buildup or the scope of the imminent offensive. In fact, the Japanese headquarters proved to be an ineffective and paralytic 150 kilometers away from the fighting.

It was early that afternoon, just outside Nomonhan village, that the 5th Rifle and Machine Gun Brigade first engaged their foe, taking on a

Japanese medium tank that inched dumbly toward them in a low-lying fog of sun-gilded dust accompanied by a ragged line of infantry.

The third platoon, officers and all, had sheepishly sought cover cowering in a nearby gully. Nadia, who had followed them there, furiously urged them forward with a barrage of curses and pistol whippings, but the terrified men did not move.

Then Nadia Fedin did something instinctive—she drew her Nagant revolver and fired three short bursts into the head of the nearest soldier.

Stepan Ivanovich's skull burst like a ripe melon showering his horrified comrades with viscous brain and bits of bone. What was left of him slumped forward like a deflated potato sack. She kept her revolver drawn on the remaining soldiers, coldly staring down their shocked looks until, one by one, they stumbled numbly out of the gulley and onto the battlefield.

Above her and beyond, she heard the raspy cacophony of gunfire; conflicted shouts in Russian and a foreign babble; the hollow blasts of several grenades; and then, a huge explosion that sent clods of heated metal, dirt, and human tissue sprinkling about her in an ungodly benediction.

Nadia paused before clambering up onto the field of battle. She summoned a precious few seconds to be surprised at how little emotion she felt in killing another human being in cold blood. But she knew that it was essential for the good order of the attack—it was the duty of the proletariat that they sacrifice selflessly. She glanced over at the limp remains of what had once been a seventeen-year-old farm boy. The will of the people was surely a curious thing.

That evening during the military mopping-up operations, Nadia was ordered to General Zhukov's headquarters for a briefing. The Command compound proved to be a cascading series of field tents resting along a sheer-edged gulley. Its perimeter was patrolled by stern-featured automatons in stiffly pressed uniforms operating in lockstep pairs.

The general's orderly demurely ushered her into the largest tent. The air inside was close and stank of filthy canvas, garlic, and prolonged tension. She gradually grew accustomed to the faint light from a hurricane lamp that was its only illumination. On one side was a camp bed, sheets tousled. At another, a flimsy campaign desk sat corralled by five butterfly chairs. In another corner stood a full-length dress mirror.

Before it lay rumpled officer tunics and several pairs of muddied cavalry boots and trousers, all haphazardly strewn about the packed earthen floors. Various operation maps were incongruously stuck on the tent walls by huge hair pins. A collapsible table held an unfinished meal for one—meat, potatoes, rye bread and a half-empty bottle of expensive vodka.

Nadia sat alone by the table. For a moment, she caught sight of herself in the mirror. Tall, lithe, even in the formless NKVD uniform, she had always carried herself well. Her facial features were quite compelling, accented by high cheekbones and slightly slanted eyes, a Tartar legacy reaching back to the invading hordes of Tamerlane the Great. Jade-green eyes that held all in their thrall. Straw-blonde hair, her late father's pride and joy, tied tightly in a proletarian bun, framed her face.

The general entered, a stocky pillbox of a man with a reputation for being foul-mouthed, demanding, and brutally cut-throat. All in all, a man commanding respect—by fear if necessary. Nadia wondered why she was there.

He was uncommonly polite. He asked if she had eaten. She had. He then gallantly offered her fruit from a bowl full of Mongolian wild strawberries and a glass of vodka, which she politely accepted. Then he poured one for himself. They sat down at the table. They talked of family and home and Mother Russia and their great leader *Tovarishch*—Comrade Stalin. But only for so long.

Zhukov had heard of the incident with the boy soldier. He complimented Nadia on her strength of will—something that he admired in a person.

"Blood is power, comrade. You will make many more of these decisions in your life. It is good that you made this first one correctly. The others will not prove to be as difficult."

He paused and peered into her face.

"How old are you, girl?"

"Twenty-two, Comrade General," Nadia responded with a mixture of temerity and pride. "I am twenty-two."

Georgy Zhukov smiled. There was a vague sadness in his eyes, perhaps the fading memory of a callow youth anxiously facing combat and the specter of death for the first time.

"This is your first such action?"

Nadia averted her gaze from the general.

"There will be more . . . many more," Zhukov responded. "If you proceed in life in the path you have chosen, you will have to build your career on corpses."

"Sir?"

"Trust me, child," the general remarked quietly. "There is no other way for those like us," he paused. "I know."

He reached forward and gently brought his hands together over hers. Nadia let them remain there. A gentle breeze wafted into the tent. The light in the hurricane lamp flickered briefly in protest but held its intensity.

The world outside faded to nothingness.

Nadia left the general's tent three hours later. It had been an eminently more satisfying foray than her first intimate encounter with the Party and power.

On August 26, 1939, a Japanese counterattack to relieve Lieutenant General Michitaro Komatsubara's 23rd Division grandiosely named (旭兵団) *Kyokuhei-dan*—the Sunrise Division—failed. The 23rd then attempted to break out of its encirclement, but could not. By August 31, the Japanese presence on the Soviet side of the border had ceased to exist.

As a result of the Battle of Khalkhyn Gol, Georgy Konstantinovich Zhukov received the prestigious title "Hero of the Soviet Union" and began to acquire a reputation for combat skills and, more particularly, for the pioneering use of tanks.

The following week, Nadia Alexandrovich Fedin was promoted to Captain of State Security. Her reputation for other more sublime strategies and conquests was also well on the way to being made.

CHAPTER 3

Gdynia,
Second Commonwealth of Poland
20 August 1939

Shortly after 10 a.m. on the muggy morning of Sunday, August 20, 1939, the Italian-built ocean liner *Batory*, a 14,287-ton vessel and the pride and joy of a nascent Polish nation, departed the harbor at Gdynia, outward bound for the great oceanic port of New York.

Twenty minutes into her voyage, the *Batory* slipped passed the Hel Peninsula and swung nimbly westwards into a surprisingly placid Baltic Sea. Two men stood alone on her forecastle. Not a word passed between them. It was a moment to be savored—almost too good to be true.

The immigration visa officer had been skeptical when he first viewed the documents. It was rare indeed to see inside a seemingly ordinary Polish passport the stamp *Posiadacz podróżuje za specjialna zgoda Ministra*—"Bearer especially approved to travel by Minister"—and below that approval, the graceful departmental seal of the Polish crowned eagle and a signature that looked remarkably as if it belonged to the Polish Minister of Foreign Affairs, the enigmatic Colonel Józef Beck.

The official called his supervisor. Together they had seriously considered forgery. After all, there weren't many Jews fleeing Poland anymore, not at this late juncture and not without greasing someone's palms in a big way. And these two specimens, even the one bearing the American passport, didn't look like they had either the money or the contacts.

An urgent phone call to the regional immigration office in Gdynia. From there, a hasty telex to Warsaw to an anonymous mandarin sitting in an obscure office of Division II—the Department of Intelligence and Counterintelligence—in the *Saski* Palace at Pilsudski Square.

Yes," their answer came back within minutes via Gdynia. "Adam Ulam? Is he with his brother?" A laconic affirmative, and the reply equally curt. "Then they both have special permission to exit Poland."

"Permission? From whom?" The query, a mixture of impudence and naivety dangled in space like the note of an unfinished Mazurka. For a moment, all the exit officer at dockside could hear on the phone line was a man's exasperated breathing, and then it came—a barrage of curses like nothing he had ever heard, summoning all the ancient Mongol demons that ever populated the vast Polish steppes to rest in the inner sanctum of the poor immigration officer's Christian soul.

"Don't you *ever* question an order from Warsaw!" the anonymous immigration superintendent at the regional office stormed. "Not if you truly value your current position! Just be thankful that they are going." A tinny click and the line went dead.

The Ulam brothers were free.

Gdynia,
Second Commonwealth of Poland
1 September 1939

SMS *Seiner Majestät Schiff Schleswig-Holstein* was a Deutschland-class battleship and the last pre-dreadnought vessel built for the Imperial German Navy of then-Kaiser Wilhelm. By 1936, she was considered creakingly ancient and had been relegated to the rather prosaic role of cadet training ship in the new Nazi *Kriegsmarine*.

On August 25, 1939, the 13,000-ton warship arrived at the ancient Hanseatic port of Danzig at the mouth of the River Vistula. Her visit was supposedly to honor sailors lost on the cruiser *Magdeburg* which, after being accidentally grounded by its own captain on the Estonian coast near the Odensholm lighthouse at the very beginning of the First World War, was demolished by Tsarist Russian naval vessels that arrived on scene. Some of the German mariners who had died on board the ill-fated cruiser had been buried in Danzig.

The *Schleswig-Holstein* was anchored 164 yards from Westerplatte, a military transit depot manned by a Polish garrison of 182 soldiers and 27 civilian reservists. Unknown to the Poles, 500 combat marines, under the command of *Leutnant* Wilhelm Henningsen, waited expectantly in the battleship's hold. The troops had been smuggled aboard during an open-sea rendezvous in the Baltic with a flotilla of whippet-like torpedo boats.

At 0430 hours on Friday, September 1, 1939, the ancient warship creaked slowly down the Port Canal and took up a confrontational position in an area that contained munitions storage and workshops in addition to a camouflaged Polish troop barracks.

At 0448 hours, the *Schleswig-Holstein* opened fire at point-blank range on Polish defense positions. Within five minutes, eight 280mm heavy artillery shells and fifty-nine 150mm light artillery shells had struck the southwestern section of the depot wall. Several harbor buildings were hit and swiftly set ablaze.

The battleship inched steadily closer, the Kriegsmarine tug *Danzig* at her stern, until her bow touched the slope of the docks. The shelling caused serious breaches in the defense wall, and the Nazi assault company scrambled ashore from the *Schleswig-Holstein* to commence its ground attack.

Twenty years, nine months, nineteen days and eighteen hours after the last shot of "The War to End All Wars" had been fired, the Second World War had begun.

Somewhere in Poland
11 September 1939

By the second week of the fearsome German blitzkrieg, the Polish Army commander-in-chief, Marshal Edward Rydz-Śmigły, had ordered a general retreat, prudently directing that all troops fighting east of the Vistula River—more than twenty armed divisions—withdraw toward Lwów and then up into the hills along the borders with Romania and the Soviet Union.

His plan presumed that the Polish military would be able to organize a successful defense until winter and hold out until the promised French offensive on the Western Front commenced. Rydz-Śmigły believed the rough terrain, the Stryj and Dniestr rivers and the numerous valleys, hills, and swamps that defined them, would provide natural lines of resistance against any German advance. The area he had selected was home to ammunition dumps that were fully stocked and awaiting the third wave of Polish troops. The area was also providentially linked to the Romanian port of Constanța, which could be used to resupply the retrenched Poles.

At this crucial stage, Rydz-Śmigły would not even consider the thought of conceding.

Lwów,
Second Commonwealth of Poland
12 September 1939

Initially Lwów was not to be defended by the Polish army as it was considered too deep behind the Polish lines and too important to that nation's culture for urban warfare. However, the speed of the Nazi invasion and the almost-complete disintegration of Polish reserves in the first stage of the battle left the city in imminent danger of collapse in the face of a direct German assault.

For the next week, heavy fighting see-sawed back and forth. Several times, the Germans broke into the city center, but were repelled each time after intense street fighting by makeshift infantry units formed of local volunteers and refugees.

The German command then decided to play a waiting game, capturing the surrounding hills and placing heavy artillery there to shell the defenders, both combatant and civilian. In addition, the city was constantly bombed by the *Luftwaffe*, which specifically targeted churches, hospitals, and water and power plants.

Somewhere in Poland
17 September 1939

At daybreak on the morning of Sunday, September 17, 1939, the Polish government still administered six eastern *voivodeships*, plus significant parts of another five. Rail connections still operated in one-third

37

of the country, and passenger and cargo traffic was still carried out at the borders with five neighboring nations. In the Polish city of Pińsk, workers labored feverishly to assemble PZL.37 Łoś bombers at a site some distance from Warsaw. A French naval ship transporting Renault R35 tanks for Poland was approaching Constanţa, while another vessel with artillery equipment had just left Marseilles for the same harbor. Altogether, seventeen French ships headed toward Romania carrying aircraft, tanks, and large quantities of ammunition.

More critically, the Poles still held onto the major cities of Warsaw, Lwów, Wilno, Grodno, Tarnopol, and Lublin. In total, more than 750,000 soldiers remained in the ranks of the active Polish Army, including two motorized brigades and twenty-six infantry divisions, making it larger than most European armies extant. Though decimated by two weeks of fighting, the Polish army—the *Wojsko Polskie*—was still a formidable force.

Under the Plan West defensive strategy, Poland assumed that the Soviet Union would remain neutral during a conflict with Germany. Therefore, Polish commanders had deployed most of their troops to the west to face the Nazi invasion. At the same time, fewer than twenty understrength battalions, some 20,000 troops of the Borderland Protection Corps—a military formation created in 1924 to protect against armed Soviet incursions and local bandit gangs—were all that could be mustered to defend Poland's eastern frontiers.

Suddenly, at 0600 hours on Tuesday, September 19, 1939, seven field armies, comprising nearly one million soldiers of the Workers' and Peasants' Red Army, swarmed over the Russian border into the eastern region of the Republic of Poland.

Rydz-Śmigły ordered Polish units to fall back, directing that they only engage the advancing Russians in self-defense, but violent clashes between individual Polish and Soviet units began to occur along the entire border.

At 1115 hours that same day, the Royal Castle of Warsaw, once the official residence of Polish kings and, more recently, the home of the president of the nascent Second Republic of Poland, was heavily shelled by German artillery. Its roof and turrets were engulfed in flames. In the principal ballroom, Bacciarelli's beautiful ceiling fresco, *The Creation of the World*, was completely destroyed.

Tarnopol,
Eastern Poland
19 September 1939

The Polish word *Kresy* means "borderlands." It was used to define the eastern frontier of the Republic of Poland in the interwar period from independence until 1939 and reflected the sweeping domain occupied in the once-grandiose Polish-Lithuanian Commonwealth.

Founded in the fifteenth century as a Polish stronghold to repel Tartar attacks from the east, the old town of Tarnopol lay at the very heart of the Kresy and was the command center for the Polish 12th Infantry Division and home to the 54th Kresy Rifles Infantry Regiment.

In 1939, Tarnopol had a population of 40,000. Located on a pleasantly undulating plain, it was a regional transport hub with several railway lines running through it, the most significant being the Lwów to Odessa route, the only link through the Carpathians between the two cities. The River Seret and a marsh-bordered lake separated the western section of the town from its center.

The garrison of Tarnopol operated in relative obscurity, located as it was far from the western zone of combat. It was made up of a Polish Border Protection Corps battalion (in reality, little more than light infantry), with a scattering of regular infantry officers tasked to liaise with General Kazimierz Sosnkowski, the commander of the rapidly crumbling Polish southern front. As the blitzkrieg thundered ever nearer, the garrison's numbers were depleted as troops were sent to reinforce Polish units in their advance to assist in the defense of the beleaguered city of Lwów.

The first Polish soldiers guarding the access to Tarnopol encountered vague silhouettes sauntering in casual files lightly haloed in pollen-sprinkled morning light. For Private Ignace Nowak of Borderland Protection Corps Czortków, posted at the bridgehead, his carbine cautiously held at cross-port, to guard the dusty roadway that meandered into Tarnopol from the nearby town of Skalat, it was all quite confusing. For these figures were arriving from the wrong direction—from the east—and not from the western battlegrounds. Floppy campaign hats, quilted bedding, and bulky bandoliers over patch-worked uniforms. Ivans. Lots of them. But what a sorry lot they were to look at.

Nowak's partner—Wojtek Pruszinski—in his young nineteen-year-old life had never seen such a ragtag assortment of misshapen humanity, bony mules and total lack of discipline—not even in his own boot camp days at Legionowo.

Soon a long column of bedraggled Red Army infantry was shambling down the road into Tarnopol. A clanking tank appeared in the bend and grew larger as it inched forward with them, a giant beetle caught in a swarm of ants. Another tank followed. And another. The road was soon awash with men attired in filthy mustard-colored uniforms.

Iggie Nowak glanced at his equally bewildered partner. There had been no orders to cover this unexpected intrusion. But then they looked friendly enough in an open-faced peasant sort of way. Perhaps the Ivans had arrived to help defend their fellow Slavic countrymen against the common Nazi enemy.

Young Nowak knew a few words in Russian. His father had been one of the cavalrymen who fought the bastards to glorious defeat at the Miracle of the Vistula, the culmination of the 1920 conflict when the belligerent Russian forces almost reached Warsaw before being turned back in the rout that ultimately ensued. "Tovarischchi," he shouted boldly. "Comrades! *Privet*! Greetings!"

They would be the last two words that Ignace Nowak, beloved second son of Wladyslaw and Irena from the Baltic fishing village of Leba, would ever speak as a spray of bullets from the nearest tank split his skull open.

It took Russian advance units a brisk twenty minutes to enter the center of Tarnopol. In that time, the aggressors had captured 143 Polish Border Corpsmen, cold-bloodedly killing eleven who had actually surrendered and one Polish soldier who returned fire and was decapitated by the splatter-burst of a PPD submachine gun.

The four Polish officers found scattered about the battlefield were treated as bourgeois oddities by the Russian peasant soldiers. They were rounded up at bayonet point and roughly herded to the rear where they were placed under "protective custody" in an abandoned-goods warehouse.

Miraculously, as all this was happening, the Polish captain in charge of the defense force was able to send a last message from the confines of his makeshift command post—a convent school—using the fragile landline in the office of the Mother Superior that still linked Tarnopol to Kraków.

The phrases he used would not have meant much to the uninitiated. They weren't meant to. "I'll aim to be at The Cesare on Friday, but I may be delayed. Tell Uncle I've got his present with me. I know he loves books with riddles." He signed it simply "*T.*"

When the captain opened an adjoining door to the secretary's office, he was greeted by a blunt-nosed Nagant pistol held in the outstretched hand of a determined Russian wearing a red star on his tunic sleeve that marked him as a commissar—a political officer. A single shot was fired from the Nagant, narrowly missing the Pole and shattering a nearby windowpane. It appeared that "Uncle" would have to wait.

The captain's message from Tarnopol made its way to the British embassy in Paris, where it was stamped "Top Secret," translated into military code, and sent "accelerated dispatch" to London, landing on Antony Eskenzi's desk three hours later. The Special Branch superintendent had transferred from the Far East and had recently spent over a month in Poland with his principal Polish contact. Reading it, Eskenzi quickly determined the high-risk stakes in play. He promptly sought out his mentor who resided in a plush apartment at Dolphin Square in the fashionable central London district of Pimlico.

The man who answered his knock was trim and fit as only an ambitious career soldier could be. A smidgen under six feet, with jet-black hair combed back to highlight his patrician features, he carried himself with the confidence of one accustomed to giving orders and not receiving them. Dressed in a crimson smoking jacket with gold Chinese dragons scampering about it, Commander Charles Vickery, Companion of the Most Distinguished Order of St Michael and St George, and Companion of the British Empire, had entered middle age comfortable in the knowledge that he was at the peak of his faculties and perhaps the very pinnacle of his career at the Secret Intelligence Service, more commonly known as MI6—Military Intelligence, Section 6.

Vickery, or simply "V" as he was known in the trade, had served as a young subaltern seconded to the Australian 3rd Light Horse in the Dardanelles and Palestine during the First World War. There he had earned the grudging respect of the 3rd's crusty Outback troopers for his singular bravery under fire.

He had followed that with a stint in the Imperial Indian Police as Chief Superintendent for the State of Madras. Finally, in 1930, he had achieved the much-sought-after posting of Director of Central

Intelligence for all of India, operating from a gauche Tudor-style head-quarters located in the mountain city of Simla.

Originally a tiny hill station located in the remote northwestern Himalayas known only for its sanatorium and chill winter snowfalls, Simla had become the summer capital of British India, the place where Rudyard Kipling had brought *Kim* and the *Jungle Book* to life on the printed page and where the very best soldiers, merchants, and civil servants and their families moved each year to escape the heat of the Indo-Gangetic plain.

For Charles Tiberius Vickery, Simla was where he first discovered his knack for ruthless cloak-and-dagger intrigue and acquired full fluency in Russian and a smattering of Slavic tongues, thanks in no small part to the ongoing concerns about the ominous Russian bear and her cubs looming beyond the Afghan Hindu Kush mountain range. In Simla, he had not only checkmated the internecine squabbles that were the essence of ruling Imperial India but had also managed to become an integral chess piece in the "Great Game." And he had loved every blessed minute of it.

Then, in the autumn of 1935, the call came for him to return to London and take over a moribund military intelligence section dealing with the newly minted pseudo-states that made up Central Europe as they careened wildly between the serpentine demands of a bourgeoning Red Peril emanating from the Soviet Union and the jackbooted menace of Hitler's Germany.

With the discreet whisk of an outstretched arm, the Commander bade Eskenzi enter, directing him into the reading room and one of the plush leather armchairs that framed an onyx-mantled fireplace. Dispensing with formalities, as any true British gentleman would, he offered his young protégé a drink.

Over Booth's Gin, served two fingers-neat in Bohemian cut-crystal glasses, their conversation was short and to the point.

It could not have been otherwise. It was in Eskenzi's very nature. And that is what made him invaluable to the ultimate mission Vickery now outlined. "V" had recruited his guest right out of Cambridge where he had languished, an earnest young academic who had read the classics but possessed a seeming gift for Slavic languages. In 1936, he had dispatched Eskenzi to a seemingly mundane colonial police posting in Shanghai—there to commence the tortuous journey to a truth that

Vickery suspected existed deep within a complex labyrinth halfway around the world.

It didn't hurt that Eskenzi's father had served with Vickery in 1916, riding with the 3rd Light Horse in the imperial victory at Magdhaba, an obscure village located in the northeastern Sinai desert, as they effectively blocked the road to the Suez Canal to Ottoman forces. The Old Boys' network did have value after all, if only to perpetuate its lineage.

Eskenzi patiently laid out his plan. Vickery merely nodded agreement. It was enough; the clinking ice punctuated the deal. Vickery loved presents—even belated ones from Poland.

* * *

To avoid suspicion, the route Eskenzi chose had been circuitous. Hop and skip on a KLM DC-2 from Croydon to Amsterdam-Schiphol, then switching onto a connector flight to Milan, followed by a mind-numbing milk run to Bucharest on board a dilapidated *Dragon Rapide* passenger liner sporting the colors of LARES, the Romanian state-owned airline. Just short of two travel-tortured days to cover 2,600 kilometers.

Then, when Eskenzi had thought it could not have gotten more tedious, it did. And with a vengeance.

It took him a further six maddening hours riding on the grandiosely named *Caile Ferate Romane,* the Romanian national railroad, seated within a rickety carriage in what passed for first class before he reached the ancient Moldavian capital of Siret—though "capital" might be too pretentious a term. The town was a gypsy armpit, squalid by even local standards.

And that is where Eskenzi now rested, atop a creaky bed in a shoddy hotel room overlooking a horse stable and not much else, frantically attempting to place telephone calls to someone, anyone, in the tortured heart of what remained of the Second Polish Republic.

Finally, he succumbed to the inevitable and tried a confidential number in Bucharest. After several fevered attempts, he succeeded in reaching a thoroughly disinterested human voice that barely understood his poor attempts at French and seemed to care even less.

Help when it came arrived grudgingly, over thirty minutes past the agreed time. A grimy plum-on-gray Renault Celtaquatre salon auto and a trio of gruff trench-coated figures transported Eskenzi to the border closed area a kilometer north and across the river from the hotel. It was a stiff courtesy that they offered, a transparently banal ritual, as one would offer a tray of stale cookies and lukewarm coffee to an unwanted guest.

It began to drizzle. Worn windshield wipers squeaked ineffectively as the Renault stuttered to a halt. A candy-cane metal pole blocked the frontier passage between neutral Romania and beleaguered Poland. An armed guard on the Romanian side eyed the vehicle warily beneath a Dutch-manufactured tear-drop helmet several sizes too large. Acned, with the faint shadow of a mustache inching across a feeble upper lip, he could not have been more than eighteen. If he'd been in a more generous mood, Eskenzi might have pitied him for his dismal future.

The Englishman alighted from the Renault and walked cautiously toward the crossing, leaving his sullen escorts leaning against the sedan, glumly sharing a pack of Gitanes, their coat collars turned up as the air misted tendril-like about them. The rain began to spiral downward in heavy drops.

Across the border, there was little evidence of the fleeing soldiers and terrified citizenry Eskenzi had expected to confront as the Polish nation hovered near death. At a nearby junction, black-shawled women shuffled along, stubbornly defying the downpour as they carried wicker baskets filled with produce to a makeshift street market. An abandoned Polish Army lorry squatted on the roadway; hood up and doors ajar. Nearby were other derelicts—deserted command sedans, shell-blackened TK-3 tankettes, a Fiat ambulance vacated in hurried disarray. A swaybacked mare pulled the remains of a rusting car chassis. Seated behind the steering wheel was a young boy, whose shouted abuse made no impression on the animal.

A concrete pillbox hunched amid foliage on the Polish side of the boundary. A figure loomed vaguely in its entrance. Tall. Uniformed. Wearing a helmet and brandishing a weapon. Eskenzi hesitated. The clothing was wrong—sloppy peasant's shirt, ill-made trousers, filthy boots. And, under the helmet, the broad-blank features of a peasant.

Eskenzi knew then that he had been too late. He had no option but to return to the room in the Hotel Cesare above the horse stable, alone. There would be no present—no book with riddles—for "Uncle."

* * *

The news of the Russian advance into Eastern Poland in fulfillment of the recent *Molotov-Ribbentrop Treaty* resulted in the mass exodus to the west of Lwów's Polish population. A flat in a modern apartment building on Nabielaka Street, one of the city's choicest neighborhoods, became available at one-tenth of its true market value. It came complete with draperies, bedding, and pictures, and much to Simon Goldkind's joy, a Baby Grand piano. The Goldkinds quickly moved in and anxiously awaited the future of their city and their family.

**Elkhart,
Morton County, Kansas
30 September 1939**

It was a balmy dusk, the open prairie sky awash in peach and lavender hues. It was the kind of evening made for farmhands who drove Chevy pickups to the county crossroads where they would sit together on work-crumpled truck hoods, chug beer, and gossip about high school football and the frisky town gals they wanted and could not have.

On this night, Johnny Callison was not at the junction with his friends. Instead, he sat inside a theater on the main street of Elkhart alongside 173 popcorn-munching neighbors waiting to watch *Five Came Back*, a nail-biting melodrama about surviving a plane crash in the Amazon jungle and starring Lucille Ball and Chester Morris.

Before the main feature began, a Pathé newsreel exploded on the screen to show German Stukas mercilessly raining bombs down onto a besieged Warsaw and its defenseless inhabitants. For Callison, the grainy action footage struck home.

It was Shanghai all over again. The bottle of Sarsaparilla that he had been quietly sipping suddenly lost its tang.

Callison packed a few belongings and then headed north, following the county roads through Nebraska and the Dakotas toward his destination. He walked a lot and thumbed a ride whenever he could. He was lucky. The weather wasn't bad, and he was used to the exercise.

He arrived at the United States-Canada border crossing at daybreak on a placid Sunday morning. He looked across the golden flat lands to the horizon, a prairie eternity away. It was as if trees hadn't been invented.

The Stars and Stripes and the Canadian Red Ensign flapped benignly in a light breeze.

The American guardpost was a sturdy brick pillbox. A string bean of a man in pressed tunic and sporting a high-peaked Stetson came to the doorway, greeted him with a friendly "Mornin'," and nonchalantly waved him past.

The Canadian presence 50 yards north of the boundary line was a modest, albeit tidy, wooden shack. Inside, a solitary immigration officer sitting behind a desk awaited his arrival. He looked smart in bottle-green serge; a thin line of campaign ribbons festooned his tunic. The Canadian silently inspected the Yankee farm boy standing before him then, seemingly satisfied, got up from the desk and moved to the countertop, walking with a pronounced limp.

The official took out a ledger and opened it. "Purpose of your visit?"

"To fight Mr. Hitler."

The official peered closely at Callison, incredulity on his face. "Repeat that, son."

Callison was nonplussed by the reaction. "I was in Shanghai when the Japs destroyed it. A few days back, I saw newsreels of Nazis bombing Warsaw. You folks are getting involved, and it looks like we're going to sit on the fence like we did in the Big War. Well, I'm one American who isn't going to sit by and do nothing. I came up here to help you fight."

The immigration officer patiently beat a slow tattoo on the ledger page with his pencil. "Shanghai, you say?"

"Yes sir. Fourth Marines."

"You have papers to prove that?"

Callison fumbled through his knapsack. He clumsily handed over the crumpled parchment. "My honorable discharge."

The official scanned the document intently, then looked up. His eyes met Callison's. "Why did you leave the Corps?"

"I came home to help my daddy on the farm. But he doesn't need my help anymore."

The border agent walked over to a desk phone and dialed. After a long pause, "Clete?" he spoke in a dreary monotone. We got a volunteer here for you." He returned the receiver to its cradle "Sit down, lad." He motioned to one of two hard-backed chairs in the austere office.

The minutes stretched into an hour. Callison began to wonder what might be happening to him. Finally, a rickety blue pickup with an RCMP crest stenciled on its doors pulled up outside the guardhouse. A Mountie corporal got out, brushing a faint layer of prairie dust from his riding boots.

He quietly apologized to the Immigration officer for the delay. He had driven down from the Boissevain detachment and had stopped to serve a court summons on the way. Clearly John Callison was not the center of the universe for government officials of the Dominion of Canada. They took the road to Brandon, Manitoba, motoring the 62 miles into town in a leisurely one and three-quarter hours. If he and the Mountie had said more than a dozen words in that time, Callison would have been mighty surprised.

Two days later, suitably papered up and vetted, Johnny Callison was on his way to the Royal Canadian Air Force Number Two Manning Depot located at the Canadian National Exhibition fairgrounds in Toronto. His war with Mr. Hitler had begun.

**Lwów,
Soviet-occupied Poland
October 1939**

After the Soviet invasion, Simon Goldkind had returned to his teaching position in the pure mathematics department of Jan Kazimierz University. Under the Russian occupiers, education was free, but his salary had now become negligible. Simon supplemented his family's meager income by playing piano at the Scottish Café, surviving on loose change dropped into a beer tankard strategically placed near the music rack.

The remaining inhabitants of Lwów began learning Russian in cramped classroom settings, interspersed with grainy 16-millimeter histories of the Communist Party projected on paint-peeled walls. In every household, family radios incessantly blared Russian music and Soviet hymns. And nothing else.

The first wave of Soviet soldiers was naively friendly, freely handing out pamphlets praising communism and life in the Soviet Union. This aspect of the occupation ended abruptly with the arrival of the Party leadership—its political commissars and their underlings—and with them, the NKVD.

Lwów's streets were immediately festooned with huge hammer-and-sickle flags. Pictures of the current Soviet leadership and the founding saints of Communism—Marx and Lenin—were to be found in every storefront window. Street names were changed from Polish to Russian.

Monuments and statues evoking Poland's historic presence in Lwów were knocked down, except for one of the Polish poet, Mickiewicz, exalted as a poet of the proletariat.

In short order, all typewriters were seized and mere possession of personal radios and radio devices was made illegal. All clocks were moved two hours back to Moscow time, and the Polish *zloty* was replaced by the Russian *ruble*.

Within days, every building in the city received a registration book in which all residents were to be listed. And, in addition, to ensure the unwavering loyalty of all their occupants to the will of the political commissars, in each building, a tenant committee made up of trustworthy NKVD stooges was set up.

Gniezdowo, Belarus,
Белорусской Советской Социалистической Республике
(Byelorussian Soviet Socialist Republic)
12 April 1940

Gniezdowo lay due west of the venerable city of Smolensk, eighteen minutes away by automobile—a mode of transport available only to Party members—and more than three hours for those using the two legs that everyone who was a member of the proletariat possessed. Located as it was on a trading route between the Greeks and the Varangians—the much-feared Viking ancestors of the Rus—the village had once been a place of some importance. But long before 1940, Gniezdowo had dwindled into a sleepy farming hamlet, easily supplanted in scope and size by the relative grandeur of nearby Smolensk, time-honored as one of the oldest Russian settlements.

A meager twin-rail line joined the two communities, providing local farmers the basic means to market their wares and connect to civilization, or at least what passed for it under Comrade Stalin. The rickety city commuter arrived daily and at the usual time and stopped as always on an isolated track on the north side of the station house.

But something had recently changed. Something was now profoundly different. A strange new train began to visit Gniezdowo four times a day with uncommon promptness and little fanfare. It generally consisted of a filthy steam engine and four chunky carriages—once milky cream in color—now weather-bleached to bone-white. The carriages seemed to carry the same cargo on their journey inbound and were always empty when they departed for points west. It was that daily cargo, made up of unarmed foreign soldiers, whom the villagers furtively eyed but dared not acknowledge, lest heavily armed escorts standing guard on the station platform indelibly mark them for future "corrective intervention."

Many of the foreigners wore flopping russet-colored greatcoats, four-cornered hats, and high-cut cavalry-style boots, their faces mostly grizzle-bearded and wan. Snatches of muted conversation in a Slavic tongue wafted in the air, a language similar to, but not quite that of, the Ruthenian dialect spoken in the village. Each batch of strangers was herded into chunky prison buses painted a matte black with their windows smeared with cement to block the view. Inside the buses were cages, one person per cage, thirty per bus. The doors slammed shut.

The convoy set off at a staggered pace, led by a rumbling lorry carrying what passed for the prisoners' effects. This was followed by the buses dubbed "Black Ravens;" a phalanx of utilitarian GAZ trucks loaded with stern-faced guards holding Tokarjev rifles. And finally, at the tail end, a mud-splattered ZIL limousine carrying anonymous men in broad-brimmed fedoras and cheap gabardine trench coats.

The grim cavalcade headed due west and, at a given point, disappeared on a deeply rutted trail set among towering stands of fir. Villagers brave enough to track its route knew that the nearby forest was a sealed area used by the NKVD as a killing ground. As early as 1929, the secret police had built a large dacha among the trees—a luxurious habitation surrounded by coiled barbed wire and armed guards. To keep any curious villagers at bay, the NKVD deployed half-mad Alsatian dogs to patrol the perimeter.

The Polish captain was exhausted as were his compatriots. The 250-kilometer journey had drained them of everything but their dignity.

The close air in the crowded cattle wagon reeked of human waste and fear. They had received a few maggoty loaves of rye bread on their initial departure, tossed through small square holes in the roofs of the wagons by indifferent hands, as one would toss to doomed livestock. There had been rest breaks every six hours, where they were marshalled out of the wagons, but widespread dysentery had punctuated these intermittent ventures with far greater frequency, and the wagons soon stank of feces.

In the late afternoon of the first day, the captain had provided his greatcoat to a young cavalry subaltern hunkered down in a corner of carriage. Marek Piotrowski, nineteen years old, was from a small farming town near Torun. A mere boy, he should have been drinking Krupnick, studying *Quo Vadis*, and gazing into the eyes of his first true love, instead of lying there in abject squalor, hovering near death from a toxic combination of virulent pneumonia and NKVD beatings.

For a fleeting moment, the captain thought back to the prison camp they had left two days before, a rundown monastery outside Kozelsk known as the Optyn Hermitage, a place where Gogol, Dostoevsky, and Tolstoy had written some of their greatest works, and where he and the other officers had been interrogated.

He bleakly remembered Gogol's words: "They don't listen to me, they don't hear me, they don't see me." And then he recalled the book he had found them in so many years before at the Jagiellonian University— *The Diary of a Madman*. He glanced about him at the weary, tormented, futilely defiant faces of defeat. How fitting, how superbly fitting. His right leg ached horribly; the prosthesis was exacting its revenge on the body.

The journey was mercifully short, less than fifteen minutes. The buses shuddered to a stop. Brusque, shouted orders in Russian. The sound of shuffling feet. Vulgarity. Curses. The dull thwack of cudgel on bone. In the vague afternoon light of a drizzly April day, 143 Polish army officers were awkwardly debussed under armed guard and stumble-marched over the still-frozen earth toward an opening in the forest.

The Poles were commanded to stop at a pit edge and ordered to turn to face into the abyss. Pistol shots began to resonate briskly in the dusk. Cold. Methodical. One by one. One. One. The deadly reports came ever closer to him. A fiendish metronome. A repetitive cavalcade of death. Badly slurring the words to *Katusha*, a Russian folk song, the shooter assigned to his section of the pit area was stone drunk.

In the brief few seconds before the bullet from the executioner's Walther 7.65mm pistol would take his life, Ryszard Franciczek Manel did something he had not done in years—he bowed his head and began to pray: "Zdrowaś Maryjo, łaski pełna, Pan z Tobą."

"Hail Mary, full of grace. The Lord is with thee."

He did not look up. His body crumpled forward, propelled into the pit. He gasped mightily for air. He heard death throes and felt bodies twitching. Gasping. Hacking. Gasping. Then, cold. Cold. Nothing.

It was nearing twilight when two farmhands ambled onto the burial site leading a brood mare harnessed to a cart heaped to the brim with mounds of white lime powder. The two men, who were brothers, advanced slowly along the pits, their horse and cart trailing, as they indifferently shoveled the slaked lime powder over the stacked corpses. They wore broad strips of cloth over their faces to mask the stench and averted their eyes whenever possible from the foul contents in the pit.

* * *

Peasant stock was an overly generous term to describe them, because it had been assumed that they were competent to perform rudimentary farm chores. But much to the dismay of their parents, Stefan and Anastasia, even that had proved taxing for the brothers. The mundane repetitiveness of their detail in the forest quickly replaced shock with a robotic tedium.

Ostensibly, Vladimir Rudecki and his younger brother Cyril had been chosen by a surly young NKVD lieutenant out of the male population of the village because they appeared and acted simple-minded. Yet, there was another very practical reason for their selection.

Albeit gruesome, the work provided the Rudecki family with additional food rations courtesy of the resident NKVD garrison. It was the commandant's perverse way of thanking the family for their patriotic sacrifice. The elder Rudecki brother, Mieczek, had met his death in 1939 during the first months of the disastrous Winter War against neighboring Finland. The second-oldest brother, Edmund, had been ill and bedridden with pneumonia at the time or he, too, would have been sent forth to battle for Mother Russia.

The Rudeckis had occupied the isolated farm near the Katyn forest since the end of the First World War. While serving as a blacksmith in the Tsar's Polish Uhlan cavalry, their Polish-born father Stefan had discovered Anastasia, a pretty local girl, when he had been stationed in the village on extended maneuvers. He instantly fell in love and, at war's end, returned to make Anastasia his bride and the tidy farmstead near the Katyn woods, newly purchased with her dowry, their home.

The village was initially reluctant to accept a foreigner, certainly not a Pole, but over time, their hostility lessened. After the village blacksmith died of a heart attack, it helped that Stefan could competently shoe the villagers' horses and did so for little or no recompense. In this manner, he gradually became an accepted member of the community.

In addition to being a very competent farrier, Stefan Rudecki was also a devout Catholic. For the first months in his new home, he took his wife every Sunday by buggy on the three-hour journey to the Roman Catholic parish of the Immaculate Conception in Smolensk and back.

And when the church was shut down, as it often was, in grim accordance with the anti-religious edicts that sporadically emanated from the Kremlin, Rudecki would organize furtive prayer meetings for the smattering of Catholics who lived in the neighboring villages. At these, his wife and four young sons took an active part.

In 1937, thanks to the good will that they had evoked over time in their tiny village, the Rudecki men survived NKVD Order 00485—the State-sanctioned campaign of mass murder that largely wiped out what Stalin contemptuously termed all "Polish filth" resident along the western borders of the Soviet Union. Anastasia was miraculously spared deportation to Kazakhstan, the plight of most women who were Polish by birth or marriage. A humble rural village had somehow trumped the steel will of a monolithic socialist state.

The pastor of the Immaculate Conception Church in Smolensk, and many in his parishioners, were not nearly as fortunate. They were summarily shot in the churchyard and their place of worship abruptly converted into an NKVD armory.

For the next three years, brave priests journeyed from towns in neighboring Poland to provide the sacraments to a clandestine circuit of believers throughout western Belarus, including the few remaining in the tiny settlement of Katyn. They wisely traveled incognito, using barns and cowsheds and the rank, cluttered kitchens of village inns as their meeting places.

Occasionally, the priests and their minuscule congregations were caught and murdered by roving NKVD squads. But the Rudeckis, along with a small circle of like-minded believers and their visiting clerical soul catchers, somehow survived.

On November 26, 1939, an incident had occurred near the remote Russian hamlet of Mainila on the frontier with Finland. According to Soviet reports, a customs post had been shelled by parties unknown, resulting in the deaths of four and injuries to nine border guards. Moscow claimed that the bombardment was a premeditated Finnish artillery attack. The situation quickly intensified.

On November 30, 1939, without even the pretense of a formal declaration of war, twenty-one Soviet divisions, totaling more than half a million troops, crossed the Nordic border and invaded Finland. Three hours later, a fleet of Russian Tupolev twin-engine aircraft darkened the skies over Helsinki as they mercilessly bombed it. The brutal Soviet onslaught of Finland, the Winter War, had commenced.

The Rudeckis' eldest son, Mieczek, was summarily impressed into a lackluster rifle regiment—arbitrarily numbered—an inconsequential micro-cipher in the complex algorithm of the Soviet military machine. His regiment saw its first action in early December close to the shore of Lake Ladoga at the eastern end of the Mannerheim Line, a Finnish defense fortification that stretched along the Karelian Isthmus facing Leningrad. The Line used 221 strongpoints and enhanced natural terrain, strategically complemented by trenches and obstacles, to repel any prospective invader from the east.

Rudecki was one of the first Soviet soldiers killed on the regiment's opening day of battle, slain at a desolate place so raw and ill-defined that it bore no name. Attempting to save a wounded comrade caught in open ground in the face of a Finnish machine-gun nest, Mieczek Rudecki forfeited his life. He was posthumously awarded the Medal for Bravery, ostensibly for his heroism, but more for the fact that the regime desperately needed a martyr to the cause.

"He died for Mother Russia" was the shabby platitude evoked by the hatchet-faced Red Army operative who visited the Rudecki farm a week later with the tragic news. The elder Rudecki had asked for the name of the wounded man who'd been saved by their son's fatal act of heroism. The curt response lent itself to self-righteous allegory. "It should be enough to know that Comrade Rudecki died for the nation.

The name of the soldier is not important."

Stefan Rudecki knew better than to push the matter.

The brothers Rudecki were slow and methodical in their work. They had become inured to the sickly stench of death that pervaded the forest of Katyn. The ghastly bodily contortions of the recent dead lying scant feet beyond their gaze came to mean nothing. Work brought money, and money fed their family.

The normal circuit around the graves took the two men the better part of an hour. Twilight gave way to darkness. The brothers kept a kerosene lantern on the cart for just that purpose.

As they completed their grim task, they heard moaning at the edge of the burial site. They steeled themselves for the inevitable death rattle that would follow as it so often had in the past, for the dying in these pits did not always go quietly. But on this occasion, the moaning became ever stronger, more persistent.

The two brothers were simple-minded, but not lacking in compassion. It was a trait their father had drilled into them; something they had acquired attending the clandestine Catholic services with their parents. Perhaps it reflected the true reason their brother, trying to save a wounded comrade in battle, had perished.

The brothers neared the origin of the sound and looked nervously about. No one else had heard it. The lure of beetroot vodka had proved too strong for the death squad. Shouts, drunken laughter. Then a gentle stillness punctuated only by the melancholy strains of an accordion—the ballad of *Katyusha.*

Vladimir looked down into the pit and nudged his younger brother. "There," he whispered, gesturing apprehensively. "There! It's alive!"

The chest of the figure nearest to them showed slight movement. Then a sound, a low lingering moan. The man's face was badly bloodied. He had a large gash on the right side of the temple. Feeble chest movements. The feathery, reflexive twitching of a hand.

The brothers scurried into the pit, trampling on inert corpses. The two furtively lifted the limp body onto level ground and then carried it to the back of the cart.

A cold wind murmured through the trees like an insistent remorseful hymn. A twig snapped. A fox scurried past in the underbrush.

The horse snorted uneasily at such sounds. Wooden wagon wheels squeaked in protest as the animal began to inch forward, and the cart

54

moved off into the enveloping evening mist.

When they arrived back at the farmhouse minutes later and told their father, he went out to the cart to see for himself.

High-cut military boots made from the finest leather. Well-tailored trousers and tunic opened at the collar. A fine sculpted gold cross hanging from a chain around the man's neck. Yet the body carried no identification beyond the silver collar patches and a trio of stars on the uniform epaulets, denoting a Polish army captain. Stefan knew instinctively what he and his family had to do.

For the next few weeks, Anastasia cared for the gravely wounded soldier in a spare room adjoining the kitchen. For much of that time, the man was comatose. By the third week, he began to stir, but only barely. His speech was slurred, his pupils dilated. He had no idea who he was or why he was in this condition. Whatever initial head injury the stranger might have suffered, his concussion was truly severe.

Discovery was a real and present danger. None of the neighbors could know they were harboring a survivor of the dark happenings at Goat Hill. Yet Stefan was quite aware that the presence of the Polish soldier could remain a secret for only so long. His discovery would mean the certain elimination of the entire village, even for those rabid few loyal to the People's Proletariat.

For some time, Father Pawel, a parish priest from a Polish border town, had bravely chanced the long trek into Belarus to bring comfort to the few Catholics remaining in and around Katyn village. He dressed for his solitary journey as a woodsman; his means of transportation, a lethargic chestnut mare inexplicably named Lightning that pulled a ramshackle cart. His Russian was fluent, as befitting a youth spent growing up in the Tsarist Partition of Poland. He had no love for the successors of the last Tsar—Comrades Lenin and Stalin and their pestilential ideology.

The personal papers he carried with him were exquisite forgeries. But then, the documentation required of citizenry in the nascent Soviet state was rudimentary at best—a hodgepodge of bastardized Tsarist seals and immature scribbled signatures. Paper begetting paper ad infinitum, with little rhyme or reason and with no central core as its genesis. It didn't help the new Soviet hierarchy in Moscow that few of the *lumpenproletariat* charged with reviewing such documents in the field could neither read nor write.

Pawel Olszewski was a diminutive man who had trained for

medicine in Warsaw before entering the priesthood as a Franciscan monk. He had served as a battalion chaplain in the bloodiest, most bitter clash of the entire 1939 campaign—the Battle of the Bzura River. The action began with very real potential for a Polish military victory and ended tragically in utter defeat. The Polish Army Pomorze was completely destroyed, while the fractured Army Poznań, with no ammunition or food rations remaining, barely managed to break through eastwards to the besieged Polish capital of Warsaw.

The Battle of the Bzura would become the army's final defining moment, one which would poignantly resonate for the Polish Second Republic like the closing notes of Chopin's *Funeral March*.

For Father Pawel, the defeat meant he would fade into priestly anonymity in a small parish church in the quaint border town of Sokolka located along the busy Warsaw–Białystok–Grodno rail line.

After a short service held in the respectful presence of the Rudeckis and nine like-minded believers brave enough to risk discovery by Communist officials, they led the priest into a tiny room. It stank of sweat and decay. The form lying in the straw bed was mere skin and bone. The head injury and the man's acute lack of awareness were something Pawel had seen before among the Polish wounded brought into the overworked field hospitals along the edges of the Bzura battlefield. The military doctors had a term for it: "blunt force amnesia." At the field station, he had observed a combat surgeon, a crusty Warsawian named Valery Michalski, who seemed uniquely aware of its symptoms and what appeared to be successful long-term treatment. The doctor had been chief of surgery at the prestigious Hospital of the Holy Spirit on Elektoralna Street in the Polish capital before volunteering to become a senior combat medico in the Polish Army.

The options Pawel considered were slim. Either surreptitiously remove the man on the straw cot to Warsaw to seek out the learned doctor or let him lie here and die. Removal would entail a four-week trek over enemy territory, yet Pawel knew he had no choice. He had heard too many tales of how the Soviets had cold-bloodedly murdered scores of clergy, military, and intelligentsia to believe that the man would be safe if he remained in this farmhouse. And then there was his small flock to consider—could they continue to safely hide this Polish officer?

The Rudeckis provided Pawel with suitable identification documents—government papers of their late son, Mieczek. In addition, they prepared three baskets filled with loaves of rye bread, salted lard, sticks of pork sausage, dried mushrooms, ripe apples, and two goat-skins of potable water. They also offered goose-down quilts to allay night chills.

Pawel set off on a pink-misted weekday morning, heading due west on the feeble two-lane roadway that connected the two social polarities of Soviet-strident Moscow and Nazi-occupied Warsaw. This was the beginning of a risky journey that would involve travel along several hundred kilometers of patchy macadam, randomly patrolled by illiterate hostile soldiers with guns, few directives and even fewer inhibitions as to their use.

He urged his horse along the soft shoulder at a steady pace. There was little traffic, other than a smattering of unexceptional carts, lackadaisically guided by brooding farm folk, and the occasional Soviet military transports that sucked the air from their throats as they roared past, bound on self-important missions to nowhere in particular.

At night, they slept in forest lay-bys or in the darkened recesses of remote village squares when they chanced upon them. By day, they were just unexceptional farm folk going about their business at plodding speed.

They were stopped only once on their journey by a roving Soviet military patrol downstream from the ancient city of Grodno. It was raining heavily, and a treacly ground fog rose from nearby stubble fields of winter rye. The young corporal who headed the group asked stock questions and received apparently satisfactory stock answers.

Pawel could speak reasonably fluent Russian, and the vacant gaze of the traveling companion seated next to him was quickly explained by his involvement in the recent and successfully concluded Winter War with neighboring Finland. The paperwork that Pawel handed over somehow passed muster. To the corporal it looked official, and therefore it must be for he, like all the members of his patrol, was illiterate. He waved Pawel to move along.

The border crossing—the artificial line that officially demarcated Nazi and Soviet spheres of influence over what had once been the Polish sovereign state—was a benign one, a crumbling concrete bridge stretching over the muddy Niemen River. A trio of *Wehrmacht* regulars and a corresponding trinity of Soviet *militsiya* shared a smoke at the bridge's center.

Superficially perusing Pawel's documentation and the crude validating initials made by the overzealous patrol corporal a few hours before, the group dismissively allowed the wagon on and into Nazi-occupied Poland.

Their immediate destination—Pawel's church, the rural parish of St. Antony of Padua—was located in the village of Sokolka, some 200 kilometers northeast of Warsaw. For the time being, the mute stranger would be safe in the dusky rectory. Father Michal, the other resident priest, was elderly and indifferent to anything but the salvation of his immortal soul and the after-dinner card games he enjoyed with Florek, the parish sacristan, and two elderly widows who ran the rosary society. Florek was a gentle sort who did a passable job maintaining the church interior and surrounding properties. And Pawel didn't pressure him for more than he could do.

A man with no name and no history was, for the time being at least, surely the safest human alive in all of occupied Poland.

Time passed, and as the stranger regained strength and an awareness of his surroundings, Pawel pondered the lifeline to Warsaw and the good doctor who would cure him. His attempts toward that end had been intentionally vague. A whispered query here, and another there.

Ultimately, it proved to be Florek who knew someone, who knew someone else.

On Friday mornings, Pawel routinely heard confessions after the last Mass. The parade of old women with ridiculously amplified petty indiscretions soon mercifully died out until, in the end, he found himself alone in the silence of the darkened confessional. Then, a cough on the other side of the tawdry cloth screen. Without prompting, the anonymous penitent began to speak in a gruff, yet muffled, voice. He had heard that Father needed assistance to reach Warsaw. Pawel wavered. "Yes," he finally answered. Yes, he did.

The man wasted no words. A wagon would be waiting adjacent to the rectory at six on Saturday morning. A food basket and relevant instructions would be found on its front seat. This should satisfy all the priest's needs and those of his passenger, including concerns about lodgings on the journey. Did Father Pawel understand?

Before Pawel could reply, the anonymous penitent was gone.

The journey from Sololka to a village west of Warsaw took the better part of a week, resting as they did at a number of desolate farms where few questions were asked and none were answered.

The Franciscan monastery that was Pawel's destination was named

Niepokalanów—or the City of Our Mary Immaculate. Located in the village of Teresin, 40 kilometers west of Warsaw, it was there Pawel was ordained to the priesthood. At the outbreak of the recent conflict, Niepokalanów was the largest monastery in the world, but since then, its religious membership had been brutally decimated by the invaders.

The Abbot of Niepokalanów was well traveled. In the early 1930s, he had undertaken missions to the Far East, founding a monastery on a mountainside overlooking Nagasaki. He had journeyed to India, establishing another abbey in Malabar. Poor health had forced him to return to Niepokalanów, where he had pioneered a radio station and newspaper—both of which came to have huge followings throughout fervently Catholic Poland.

The Abbot was astute. He knew too well the deadly risks he would face if the mysterious Polish officer brought to him by Father Pawel was to be subsequently linked in any way to the Monastery of Niepokalanów. Several monks had already been taken into custody by the Gestapo, disappearing without a trace for far less grievous transgressions against the Occupying Authority than for what he was now being asked to do. But the bespectacled clergyman was also a proud Pole.

After Teresin was captured by German infantry, the Abbot had been briefly arrested, held in detention, and, ever defiant, released after three months. Even then, he had unflinchingly refused to sign the *Deutsche Volksliste*, which would have given him rights similar to German citizens in exchange for his acknowledgment of ethnic German ancestry.

The Abbot possessed many sterling qualities. Surprisingly, for Father Pawel, the most critical of these was not an attribute of character, but rather one of relationships—for the Abbot, Maximilian Maria Kolbe, was a personal friend of Dr. Valery Michalski.

The good doctor responded quickly to the Abbot's call, arriving at the priory that very night and well past the strict Nazi-imposed curfew. He was promptly taken into a whitewashed cubicle in the basement of the monastery where he confronted an emaciated creature lying on a crisp-sheeted hospital bed.

Despite his wan expression and sunken eyes, the man who Michalski beheld still suggested an iron will to live that the doctor knew from experience could only have been gained from surviving on a battlefield.

Wordlessly, Michalski opened his physician's bag and began his preliminary examination. As all good doctors do, he began at the head and finished at what remained of his extremities. Throughout it all, when questioned his patient uttered only monosyllables.

The doctor then turned to two monks hovering expectantly at the entrance to the room and patiently provided his diagnosis. He concurred with Father Pawel. This was more than shell shock. The man's slow-healing head wound confirmed it. A bullet graze, but no puncture. The vacant stare. The listless response to straightforward questioning. The complete lack of awareness. He had seen such symptoms all too often among military casualties arriving at Polish field stations during the recent Nazi blitzkrieg. The man required rest and silence. Here, hidden in the depths of the Franciscan monastery, he would have both.

Somewhere on the rue de la Grande Voie,
Le Paradis, 10 kilometers north-northwest of Bethune,
Pas-de-Calais Sous-Préfecture, France
29 May 1940

The Nazi invasion of France, begun on May 10, 1940, using the convenient back door of a naively neutral Netherlands and a hopelessly outflanked Belgium, was nearing its predictably successful conclusion. On May 12, *Wehrmacht* forces had pushed what remained of a demoralized French army and an equally dispirited British Expeditionary Force to the Meuse River, crossing it themselves that same evening. From that point onward, German formations rapidly advanced toward the English Channel. The British Expeditionary Force and its bewildered allies attempted in vain to retreat through the Pas-de-Calais region to the weakened evacuation salient that remained open at an ancient fishing port whose name derived from its original West Flemish origins—*dun* or "dune" and *kerke* or "church," which together mean "church in the dunes"—Dunkirk.

The stubby *Kubelwagen* punched its way through a querulous traffic jam of Panzer II tanks, petulantly inching forward along a narrow country road jammed with other military traffic and homeless French civilians salvaging what little was left of their lives. It carried one SS driver and one passenger—and that passenger was late for an appointment.

After what seemed an interminable wait, the vehicle finally reached an intersection where the road widened a bit. The driver feverishly honked a tinny horn; refugees tumbled out of their path. Gradually, the *Kubelwagen* began to pass the clanking metal behemoths of the *Panzercorps* that lumbered clumsily along beside it.

Just past a hairpin bend, the driver turned sharply right onto a dirt lane. A figure suddenly loomed—a grim-faced *Feldgendarmerie* corporal wearing the dull silver gorget or *ringkragen* of the German military police. An outstretched hand holding a traffic paddle rigidly punched the humid air. The *Kubelwagen* screeched to a stop. The military policeman approached the vehicle.

"Your papers sir," he remarked curtly. "The road beyond here is sealed, *UntersturmFührer* Henschell," he remarked as he began to peruse the documents. "No unauthorized personnel allowed entry. By direct orders of General Hoepner, General Officer Commanding XVI Corps."

The SS officer was nonplussed. "I know who your general is, corporal," he sniffed, "And it does not matter. My authority comes from Ampt II—the SS Court Head office."

The policeman's expression changed noticeably. "The *Disziplinaramt*? But . . . but," he stammered. "It is not here among your papers."

Henschell reached into the breast pocket of his tunic with a black-gloved hand and presented the flustered soldier with a folded document. The man's features blanched visibly as he unfolded it and spied the authorization. Spidery as the individual who wrote it, there was little difficulty in identifying the writing and authorization as belonging to *ReichsFührer* Heinrich Himmler.

"I'm sorry, corporal." Henschell purred. "I thought you knew. But then again, perhaps I presumed too much."

The chastened gendarme snapped to rigid attention, his self-esteem dissolving to vapored nothingness. "Sir."

"So, my good man." Henschell sniffed, all pretense of civility gone. "Could you now direct me to the site?"

"*Yawohl, UntersturmFührer*," the corporal barked robotically. He jabbed the traffic paddle down the road. "It is there, *UntersturmFührer*. Less than a kilometer away. The locals call it Cornet Farm," he added all too quickly, fumbling over himself in a failed attempt to regain a modicum of respectability. "There is an officer already waiting for you."

"I know." With two words, Henschell condemned the oaf to his proper place among the great unwashed. He shot his right hand upward. "Heil Hitler."

As the *Feldgendarme*, martinet-like, returned the Nazi salute, the *Kubelwagen* jerked into gear. A shower of cobblestones flew into the air and splattered onto the policeman's boots.

The man stood beside what was left of a stone barn. A study in Prussian elegance—tall, aristocratic-featured and confident—he wore the same jet-black uniform and glistening leathers as Henschell, but without the holstered Luger pistol. Instead, a Leica camera hung around his neck. An infantry platoon stood nearby, spaced at regular intervals, their weapons at the ready, guarding something within an enclosure.

As the *Kubelwagen* glided to a halt, the man beckoned Henschell over.

Waffen SS Hauptsturmführer der Reserve Gunter d'Alquen was known to all who mattered in the Nazi cosmos. He was well respected and comfortable in his craft as the commanding officer of *SS-Kriegsberichter-Kompanie*—the SS War Reporter Company—and, more importantly, as principal editor of *Das Schwarze Korps*—*The Black Corps*—the official SS newspaper.

The War Reporter Company was formed in January 1940 at the personal behest of *ReichsFührer* Himmler. D'Alquen had been placed at its head, guided by a terse set of orders. The company comprised four platoons of war correspondents and support staff operating independently of one another. Each platoon was equipped with both still and motion cameras to enable them to visually document the courageous actions of *Waffen SS* formations in combat. That was to be their mission. That was to be their life.

So, when the discreet call came from d'Alquen the day before, asking Henschell to rush to this obscure site in the French countryside, he had not wasted a second hitching a ride on a Junkers 52 trimotor ferrying supplies to the front lines from Oberwiesenfeld, a *Luftwaffe* airfield located on the leafy outskirts of Munich.

Henschell had known d'Alquen since 1937 when they'd first met as young comrades-in-training at *SS-Junkerschule* Bad Tölz. They had shared a love of opera and art, fencing, and fine wines and, of course, the high-sounding pan-Germanic ideals of the Reich. He could tell by the solemn expression on his friend's face that today was not going to provide one of those sought-after cinematographic opportunities.

D'Alquen wordlessly led him to a break in the fence line, but there was no need. The stench of sudden and violent death assailed their nostrils before their eyes confirmed it.

He peered inside the enclosure and involuntarily grimaced. Khaki-garbed corpses lay strewn along the length of a pockmarked wall like so many forsaken rag dolls. Most had suffered head wounds from shots fired at close range. Others had their skulls smashed in. Fatal injuries, he surmised, that could only have been caused by rifle butts. None of the dead wore helmets, nor were any discarded weapons near the bodies.

Silently Henschell began to count, his lips subconsciously moving as he tabulated the numbers.

"As I told you over the telephone," D'Alquen offered, "there are more than ninety. And they are all Britishers."

Henschell turned to his compatriot. "Do you know which unit did this?"

D'Alquen sighed then responded. "*SS Division Totenkopf*, commanded by *Hauptsturmführer* Fritz Knöchlein."

A cow bellowed in a distant field. Henschell mulled over the options available to him. At the mere mention of *Totenkopf*, one of the Führer's prized units, he knew they were dwindling rapidly. He sensed the *Wehrmacht* sentries eyeing him with guarded looks.

"And the victims?"

"Their shoulder flashes are from the Royal Norfolk Regiment."

The two officers began to walk back from the enclosure in virtual lockstep. For a time neither said a word.

It was D'Alquen who broke the silence. "Did you know that Edith Cavell was from Norfolk?"

"Who?"

"Edith Cavell. The British nurse. Units of the Imperial Army executed her in 1915 for helping Tommies escape to neutral Holland. The powers-that-be had charged her with treason and then held a show trial that led to an inevitable conviction and an equally inevitable death by firing squad."

D'Alquen lowered his voice. "As you can well appreciate, the execution of Cavell did not play well in the international court of public opinion."

He turned to his companion. "I accept that war is war. But this eminently stupid action in a farmyard that reeks of cow manure?" He sighed. "Especially in light of what happened to Cavell, a woman who

63

our enemies even now consider a martyr. The Führer himself will not be pleased."

Henschell's eyes narrowed. "So, what is it that you would have me do?"

"I don't know." D'Alquen shrugged. "I was hoping you might commence an investigation, even if it has no final resolution. After all, you are in the *Hauptamnt Gericht*."

Henschell laughed aloud. "An *actual* investigation of the SS? Gunter, you are quite priceless!" The laughter abruptly ended. "And you are also quite mad."

They arrived back at the *Kubelwagen*. The driver deferentially clicked his heels together and awaited his next instructions.

D'Alquen turned to his associate. He discreetly nodded in the direction of the infantry officer lurking nearby. He began to speak—a prudent whisper. "I suspect the young *leutnant* reflects the feelings of his rank and file. They must despise this intemperate act, in no small measure, because it opens the door to retaliation against them at any time in the distant and not-so-distant future."

"Despise the deaths of enemy soldiers?" Henschell sniffed, curtly dismissing the very concept. "My dear D'Alquen, killing the enemy is what we pay the men to do! Moreover, I don't believe for a single second that our great leader gives a rat's ass as to how these fine young people do their jobs. They are German soldiers, my good man. *Landsers*. The ultimate truth in our profession is that an infantryman of the Third Reich must either kill or be killed. It is in his very nature and training."

"And what of us, Paul?" D'Alquen countered. "What are we if we allow this act to go unpunished? Are we still officers and gentlemen?"

"Yes, we are," Henschell answered with steely assurance. "We are indeed officers and always—I repeat, *always*—gentlemen.

"Hear me out, my dear D'Alquen," he confided in a more subdued tone. "This act will certainly be repeated by us and by the Tommies many times over before this damned war ends. Ultimately, the act itself matters not in the grand scheme of things. The victor will write the history, not the vanquished."

Henschell pursed his lips, as he appeared to collect his thoughts. Then, seemingly satisfied, he turned to his friend and began to speak calmly, as if he were dictating an office memo on how best to impart regimental spirit to a troop of unwitting new recruits.

"Gunter, in your article, you will write something to this effect—that on this date, a troop of *SS Division Totenkopf* commanded by *Hauptsturmführer* Fritz Knöchlein was ambushed by a company of British soldiers near the town of Bethune France while they were engaged in the removal of wounded *soldaten* from a field hospital under a flag of truce. The SS bravely defended their helpless comrades and, in the ensuing struggle, soundly defeated the enemy without the loss of German life. It has been determined from their shoulder flashes that the involved British criminals were members of the Royal Norfolk Regiment. End it with something to the effect that, unlike the principled actions of the German soldier both in combat and in reserve, this is not the first time that the British and their so-called Allies have broken the articles of the Geneva Convention. Is that clear?"

Silence. Then the slightest nod.

Henschell motioned the infantry *leutnant* to his side. The man jogged over and instinctively saluted in the traditional German army fashion, not the Nazi salute increasingly used by the *Wehrmacht* in Hitler's Reich. Henschell let the not-so-subtle insult to the Führer and Party pass. "Your name?"

"Zimmerman," the officer responded nervously.

Henschell eased himself into the back seat of the *Kubelwagen*. "Leutnant Zimmerman, prior to my arrival, I requested the presence of Doctor Werner Beck, who commands an SS team extensively trained in approved forensics, to bring prompt closure to this distraction. They should arrive shortly. I strongly suspect their findings will confirm the cause of death of the Britishers in all instances as being combat-related. After Doctor Beck's inquiries are complete, you will dispose of those bodies as you see fit," he directed matter-of-factly. "There's a war on, and your *Landsers* have better things to do than to guard a morgue."

The order given, he turned back to his new traveling companion. "Beck is a good man and loyal party member. He comes highly recommended."

"So, you had already made up your mind when I called you yesterday," D'Alquen commented accusingly. "Before you could even view for yourself the clear evidence of this—this atrocity."

Henschell shrugged, a slight smile crossing his face. The smile disappeared all too quickly, replaced by a sterner look. "We are at war, D'Alquen. And in war and in the heat of combat, such things will happen."

Henschell gestured to the vacant seat beside him. "Come, Gunter. Let us leave this place and see if there is a proper café in town—one that serves a decent French *crêpe*. Battlefield decisions give one such an appetite. And, as our *vino*-loving Italian allies would say, *que sera, sera*."

CHAPTER 4

Niepokalanów Abbey
57 kilometers west of Warsaw,
Generalgouvernement für die besetzten polnischen Gebiete
(General Governorate for the Occupied Polish Region)
18 July 1940

For the next while, Dr. Valery Michalski visited the abbey regularly and treated his anonymous patient with a consummate skill born of experience. His diagnosis? It appeared that the man had suffered serious damage to the hippocampus area of his brain. His memory loss involved facts rather than skills, leaving him with the inability to recall persons, faces, and places, and most of the general knowledge he may have acquired before the onset of amnesia.

The unknown male became known to the monks as "Bratumil"—an unusual first name derived from the Slavic words *bratu* (brother) and *milu* (dear)—and *Brat* for short. His presence there and the circumstances leading up to it were a fog-bound mystery.

Members of the Underground knew all too well of the summary executions of captive Polish officers by the Soviets. It was the norm and not the exception in the Russian partition. Bratumil would rest in the very womb of the German section of occupied Poland until he had recovered. Silence. Here, hidden in the heart of the Franciscan monastery, he would have both.

In the world outside the abbey, the budding Polish Secret Army—the *Tajna Armie Polska*—had moved quickly. By the late summer, the

Secret Army had launched sabotage attacks on railways, ammunition dumps, and weapons factories throughout Poland. Military arms buried after the recent defeat were dug up and made ready for use. Hand grenades and other weaponry were manufactured in secret underground workshops laboriously burrowed out beneath city cellars. For its part, the Polish nation would not disappear without a fight, for that was a gamble well worth taking.

A special section of artists and printers forged identity papers of excellent quality in a print shop excavated below a luxurious abandoned Warsaw mansion. The illicit shop was situated near the Belvedere Palace in the very center of the so-called German Police District and within walking distance of Gestapo Headquarters with its dreaded detention facility on Szucha Avenue. Next door to the HQ, the SS had incongruously created a twenty-four-hour members-only casino.

* * *

Three months after the mysterious Pole was safely delivered to the abbey, Father Pawel made another stealthy visit to his tiny flock in the village of Katyn. Only this time, as he entered the Rudecki farmhouse, he did not receive the expected greeting.

Stefan Rudecki and the three members of his family who were present with him were arrested by a Party commissar for grievous crimes against the Proletariat, in that they had hidden a bourgeois fugitive believed to be a Polish officer, his actual identity yet to be established.

After undergoing painful NKVD tortures lasting for three days and nights, the priest, the elder Rudecki and his two middle sons were summarily dispatched in a desolate cow pasture to meet their Maker.

As to the identity of the mysterious Pole who had been their guest? Even after the beatings, the doomed men couldn't—or wouldn't—break their silence.

The youngest son—Edmund—had been away in the nearby village pub when the NKVD raided the farmhouse. Unlike the rest of his family, he was not at all religious. When soldiers subsequently ransacked the Rudecki farmstead and the area around it searching for him, he was nowhere to be found.

Number 2 Ulitsa Bolshaya Lubyanka,
Aka Dom Dva (House Number 2),
Meshchansky District of Moscow,
Soyuz Sovetskikh Sotsialisticheskikh Respublik
10 September 1940

Following specific orders emanating from "the highest authority," the salient facts concerning the raid were swiftly Telexed to a sophisticated Communications Room located in the gloomy underground maze of rooms and corridors of Number 2 Ulitsa Bolshaya Lubyanka, a caramel layer cake of a building strategically situated in the center of Moscow near the Kremlin. The imposing structure at Number 2 had been designed by the famed Russian architect Alexander Ivanov in 1897 and completed the following year. It was originally the headquarters of the All-Russia Insurance Company and had remained so until the Revolution when the Supreme Soviet seized it to house their new intelligence service—the NKVD.

The building was a sobering labyrinth of pea-green walls, waxed parquet floors, and ominously silent corridors. Over time, it had become infamous for the gloomy prison nestled deep within in its cellars. Here, suspected enemies of the state were routinely tortured before being sentenced to forced labor camps. Or worse. Either way, they were destined to become Lenin's dead men on parole. A dark joke told by Muscovites had it that the building was the tallest structure in Moscow, for from it one could see Siberia.

A harried orderly immediately took the message to a third-floor office with a polished nameplate on its oak door: Captain N. Fedin.

He knocked three times. Then wisely awaited permission to enter, for he knew all too well the temperament of the occupant of the office. He knew her unwavering demands for minutiae and a hypersensitive belief in rank and the respectful privacy it bestowed on her and the select few in this ominous building.

A monotone voice from somewhere within. Permission granted. He entered the room.

In spite of her emerging stature in the firm, the workplace of Captain Nadia Fedin was not lavishly decorated. She sat behind a functional desk perusing a document, her face barely illuminated by a single goose-necked lamp. An Underwood upright typewriter, a bank of three phones—one Revolutionary red, the other two standard bourgeois black—and the institutionally obligatory companion set of olive-colored in-and-out trays.

Blood-red crimson drapes shielded the desk from harsh streetlights, which stretched like brooding sentinels in the massive square below. Stirring portraits of Comrades Stalin, Lenin, and Marx glowered imperiously from battleship-gray walls. A polished brass *samovar* rested on a tea *poy* directly under the windows. The sturdy teak table was a gift from an unknown admirer. She had many of them within the Lubyanka and beyond. She wasn't completely certain whether the present of a table was motivated by fear, lust, or a genuine admiration for her professional skill as a rising star within the organization. Nor did she care.

Unlike her uniformly stout female compatriots who looked and acted like Kazakh tractors after a particularly brutal plow match, Nadia Fedin was outwardly modest as a virtuous Socialist maiden, yet as cunningly feline as a prowling Ural tiger in her every thought and movement.

Without raising her head, Nadia motioned for the orderly to place the document he was carrying in the in-tray. With the same hand, she tersely dismissed him. He obediently removed himself from her presence, meekly closing the door as he left.

She waited a respectable period of time, listening vigilantly as the young man's footsteps receded down the corridor. She heard the elevator open, the concertina doors creak shut. Silence. Nadia was alone once more.

Nadia reached for the document. It contained what she had expected. She read the report carefully and considered her options. Then she opened a diary on her desk and started a fresh page. She reached across her desk to the finely crafted black marble slab and withdrew one of the two fountain pens nestled there.

With short, sharp strokes, she sketched four boxes onto the page, one in each corner. Then she labelled them clockwise: #1 Edmund Rudecki—son. #2 Anastasia Rudecki—mother. #3 Pawel Olszewski—village priest. And, finally, #4 Polish soldier—beside which she placed a question mark.

Next, she deftly connected the boxes with a series of open dashes. Nadia Fedin was shrewd, dispassionately so. She allowed her thought processes to flow freely as she began to make cursory comments in each cube, beginning with the first.

"#1 Edmund Rudecki. He would not travel far from his home village. A simple peasant, it was against his very nature. He knew no other place.

"#2 Anastasia Rudecki. Mother. Probably a mere peasant, she would be no more than a passive participant in her husband's dealings, however dangerous they might be to the State or her family's well-being. A true wild card to be played."

Fulfilling Fedin's longstanding directive regarding families and their customary place on the NKVD chessboard, she would dispatch the mother to a nameless *gulag* in the furthermost eastern regions of the Soviet empire. At a future date, she would inevitably become a fading whisper in the cold Siberian wind. But for now, Anastasia Rudecki might prove more useful to the System as a live pawn.

She reflected that once the son discovered his mother had been spared death, the youth might attempt to seek her out, even to communicate with her. Though it was certainly a foreign concept to Fedin, it was something all good children did. The premise was open to interpretation until proven either way. Was Edmund Rudecki a loyal Christian son or a socialist survivor?

Which brought her to #3. The priest. "Did not possess the intellect to orchestrate anything beyond the ritualistic blather that backward Polish peasants understood. Still, as with others of his ilk, a potentially dangerous specimen spewing forth Vatican vomit to the few who still bothered to listen. Eliminated."

She placed the fountain pen back in its stand and meticulously considered the options confronting her. Then, her course of action determined, she pressed the buzzer on the desk intercom. A tinny voice answered.

"Comrade Bulganin. Ensure all activity involving the female prisoner Rudecki is monitored. That includes all movements and any attempts made for external communication. This task must commence from the moment she is removed from the custodial train until she stops breathing, wherever in Siberia that might be. Second, obtain a list of all missing persons and suspicious deaths that have occurred within an 80-kilometer radius of Katyn, effective immediately. Include a brief daily summary detailing each circumstance. Third, open a file on a village priest, Pawel Olszewski, and await further orders."

"Yes, yes," she muttered petulantly at the obviously redundant question that followed her orders. "Continue this in a comprehensive fashion until I tell you otherwise."

Her gaze drifted behind her desk to the portrait of Comrade Stalin as she critically pondered her next move—#4, with a question mark.

She knew she would soon need to report to the People's Commissar for Internal Affairs and First Rank Commissar of State Security, Lavrentiy Pavlovich Beria, on the Katyn matter. Great faith in her abilities to handle such a sensitive and utterly confidential item had resulted in her promotion, which came as a direct and personal recommendation from General Zhukov to the People's Commissar. She also suspected that the recommendation came with unspoken and as-yet-unrealized consequences, for Comrade Beria had a well-deserved reputation as a sexual predator.

It was whispered that at night he would cruise the streets of Moscow alone in a jet-black Lincoln Zephyr seeking out teenage girls. When he saw one who captured his fancy, he would have a team of bodyguards deliver her to his residence. Sometimes he would have his people bring five, six, or even seven girls to him. He would make them strip, except for their shoes, then force them into a circle on their hands and knees with their heads together. He would dispassionately walk around in his Chinese silk dressing gown, inspecting them as he would field cattle. Then he would pull one out by her leg and haul her off to rape her. He called it his "flower raffle."

In Nadia's mind, Beria was lecherous but also shrewd. She strongly suspected that her protector, Zhukov, had given the People's Commissar pause to act in his usual predatory fashion, but even the great man could only do so much from his new assignment: a promotion taking over the Military District of Kiev, more than 1,300 kilometers away.

She knew that Beria would bide his time and then, without warning, spring upon her. Yet to date, the People's Commissar had not called in "the consequence" salaciously implicit in her accelerated appointment. Still, the manner by which she had received the promotion, and even the sullied outcomes that might flow from it, mattered not. Captain Nadia Fedin NKVD truly had a wonderful ring to it. Captain.

Kirkdale Railway Station, 1 Marsh Street,
Liverpool, United Kingdom
5 June 1941

"Pilot Officer Callison!" Johnny stirred from a fitful sleep. Filigreed dust particles dancing in the dank gray air. Around him, a rolling landscape of blue serge filled the waiting room. The plaintive sound of a steam whistle; the huff-puff of a weary locomotive, harsh screeching of brakes. His mouth felt cottony. His head ached. He vaguely remembered the night before. One too many bottles of India Pale Ale, smuggled on board a crowded troop train rolling up from the RAF Operational Training Unit at Aston Down. There, he had qualified on battle-weary Mark I Hurricanes, before heading forth from the ancient Cotswold market town of Minchinhampton on a route made necessarily circuitous by the latest spate of *Luftwaffe* bombings of the Mersey wharves.

"*Callison?*" Once more, the irascible, hectoring voice intruding on his thoughts.

"Sir!"

The beetle-browed RAF sergeant glared over at him. Squat as a fireplug, he was a thoroughly unpleasant specimen of manhood. Even a razor-creased tunic and trousers could not disguise the fact that he was as unattractive as the industrial Midlands that had spawned him.

"I would prefer that you don't call me 'sir,' Mr. Callison," the NCO bellowed. "I'm not a blooming duke! And I'm not your bloomin' FATHER!! I'm Flight Sergeant Death. D-E-A-T-H. Pronounced '*DEEETH*,' in case any of you misbegotten sods are interested in learning how to speak the King's English!"

A nervous titter trickled through the hall. Flight Sergeant Death's laser-like stare swiftly silenced it. The little man pursed his lips and snorted.

"Now listen up, people! I will only say this once. The Gerry blitz has hit Liverpool hard, so this is as close as the train will take you to His Majesty's docks. My job is to get you sorry lot the rest of the way to your troop convoy, and to do so quickly."

"Pilot Officer Callison? If you would be so kind as to gather your kit, sir," he remarked sardonically. "There's a car waiting for you outside. Now, get a move on! In case you haven't heard, there's a war on!"

73

Callison briskly brushed himself off, straightened his uniform and tie, and, tossing his duffle bag over a shoulder, hurried out into the moist Liverpool dawn.

The "car" turned out to be a battered Bedford three-ton lorry. Callison deftly flipped his kit bag over the raised tailgate and hopped on board. Several aircrew were already seated. Thirteen others followed. The truck motor turned over a few times, then kicked in with a nervous spasm. Soon the Bedford was making its way in a faux-gold Liverpool dawn to the Mersey dockyards.

Over the course of the next two hours, Callison and 211 other military personnel would shuffle on board the Yeoward Line passenger vessel SS *Aguila*. At 0809 hours, the venerable ship would cast off to become part of a convoy comprising thirty-five merchantmen and fifteen escorts, all outbound for Gibraltar. The journey would take fourteen days, on a route around the north of Ireland. And then well out into the Atlantic, before the anxiously shepherded ships altered course to the south and then due east to vector back onto their final destination—the Rock.

Somewhere along the shared frontier between the Deutsches Reich (German Reich) and the Soyuz Sovetskikh Sotsialisticheskikh Respublik
22 June 1941

In the moist predawn of the summer solstice of 1941, three million battle-hardened soldiers of the German *Wehrmacht*, accompanied by 250,000 Romanian troops and half a million Finns, struck an ill-prepared Soviet army along a 2,900-kilometer front, initiating one of the most titanic struggles in history. A line of 3,712 German tanks relentlessly rumbled toward their respective goals of Leningrad, Moscow, and Kiev as 47,260 field guns and mortars, and 4,950 aircraft blasted anything that stood in their way. In the month when the peonies and green willows blossomed, on a northern White Night, Operation Barbarossa, the ambitious Nazi invasion of Comrade Josef Stalin's Russia, had begun.

CHAPTER 5

Lwów,
Arbitrarily renamed Lemberg by the
occupying German Army
29 June 1941–30 June 1941

In the early morning of Sunday, June 29, 1941, advancing German troops entered the outskirts of Lwów, capturing it one day later. Within hours of the Nazi occupation, Jewish men were press-ganged into removing hundreds of corpses from three local jails, allegedly the victims of a vengeful retribution on enemies of the State, whether real or imagined, by the evacuating NKVD.

That night, Simon Goldkind braved the curfew to go to the Scottish Café and play the piano. The place was filled to the rafters with a new breed of clientele, a depressing landscape of *Wehrmacht* gray and SS black, all profoundly drunk as they congratulated each other on their sudden conquest of the city. A few even came over to the piano to compliment Simon on his playing, particularly when he focused on the works of Beethoven and Wagner, pieces coincidentally favored by Hitler himself.

After a time, a tall, ruddy-faced SS officer sidled over to the bar, a large glass of cognac in a beefy left hand. He toasted Simon. "You play very well, young man. What is your name?"

Simon hesitated.

"Come, come," the SS officer pressed. "I know you are a Jew, you foolish boy. The fear is written all over your face. Now, let us try again. What is your full name?"

"Simon," he stuttered. "Simon Goldkind."

The German officer extended his hand and smiled. "Mine is Gustaf

Altmann. Don't worry, Simon Goldkind," the German gently admonished. "I am more formally known as SS-*Oberführer* Altmann, and"—a sly wink—"I am by far the most senior and important person in this room." He downed his drink and then, in an almost wistful voice, continued. "In another life, I was the alternate pianist in the Bavarian State Orchestra."

His open smile returned. "Nothing will happen to you. Nothing. So, I repeat, Simon Goldkind, do you know any works of Count Basie perhaps? Or Fats Waller?"

"Yes, sir. But they are . . ." Goldkind hesitated.

"Black? And that means what?" The *Oberführer* was now plainly toying with him. "Look at your piano keys. There are fifty-two white and thirty-six black. Are there not?"

A meek nod.

"Has anyone ever said to you that you can't touch the black keys because of what the Führer may think?"

"No sir," Goldkind admitted after some hesitation. "No, they have not."

"Then play."

Simon Goldkind began, hesitantly at first, then gradually with more vigor. Count Basie's *Swingin' the Blues*, followed by Fats Wallers's *Got to Cool My Doggies Now* and *Birmingham Blues*, and many, many others, nonstop, by the two artists.

The uniformed occupants in the room, at first hesitating, one by one, then in groups, turned to face this audacious pianist. Here and there, a foot started tapping. A head nodded in time with the rhythm—a cautious smile—then many more. When he finished his set, there were slurred shouts of "Encore! Encore!"

Before the evening was over, the *SS-Oberführer* handed the pianist his business card. He paused, then sheepishly fumbled around in his tunic pocket. "You wouldn't happen to have a pen, would you, Goldkind?"

Simon leaned over and took an onyx fountain pen from his jacket pocket. He handed it to the German officer. Altmann scribbled something on the back of the business card and signed it with a flourish. "If you ever get stopped by a roving patrol, hand them this. It is as good as a pass."

He paused, admiring the pen.

"A fine writing instrument, Goldkind. An Osmia Supra. German made, is it not? Very rare, I'm told. I always wanted one."

Simon nodded. "A gift from my late father. He too was a musician and played first piano in the Warsaw Symphony."

"And the green ink? Your personal touch, I assume."

"Yes, *Oberführer*." Goldkind replied with perhaps slightly too much enthusiasm. "We must always possess something unique that marks our time on this earth, mustn't we? After all, life is too short."

The smile abruptly disappeared from the German's face. "Acch so. It is short. Very short." Then without another word, he strode away to join his uniformed SS friends at a nearby table.

On the very next day, Simon and his family were ordered to vacate their apartment and find housing in a northern suburb of the city, Zamarstynów, in what would become the Jewish ghetto. They quickly fled to their destination, carrying what belongings they could, daring not to look as Jewish men were arbitrarily snatched from the fleeing throngs and made to clean streets on their hands and knees with scrub brushes until their hands were bleeding and raw. Every so often, one of them was whisked away under armed guard. Simon was later to learn that they were taken to the same prisons that had recently held Polish intellectuals, including professors from the university, and there to be tortured and shot.

Within the week, *SS Einsatzgruppe C* units arrived in Lwów, and the violence escalated as the paramilitary death squads engaged in mass killings. The SS informed the population that such executions inexplicably were in retribution for the arrest and execution of "Ukrainian patriots," which had been carried out in the city's prisons by the NKVD during the last days of Soviet occupation.

Shortly thereafter, all of Lwów's Jews were ordered to wear a badge with a blue Star of David.

Katyn Forest,
12 kilometers west of Smolensk,
Soyuz Sovetskikh Sotsialisticheskikh Respublik
23 December 1941

The forest was dark. Its *pushkas*—those large unpopulated tracts of birch and alder etched relentlessly into the Russian sky—were dappled in charcoal hues. A lone grizzled timber wolf emerged from the murk, padding cautiously over a mantle of new-fallen snow. It sniffed apprehensively about the uneven winterscape, trying to scent the pack's absent Alpha leader.

Its nostrils dilated and expanded. Its feral eyes narrowed and salivary glands involuntarily began to function. There seemed to be another odor distinct in the chill night air coming from somewhere beneath the blanket of moon-sparkled snow. It was the faint, yet persistent, stench of blood and rotting flesh.

The wolf moved to the source of the scent and pawed the ground, timidly at first and then with increasing ferocity. The soil began to break up and give way. The animal's paws started to bleed, but its instinct proved to be greater than the pain it must have felt. The animal dug and dug until it had unearthed what it sought—a long femur-like bone. Bits of rank flesh and decaying gristle dangled from it as did tattered bits of thick khaki fabric.

The wolf wrenched the item out of the hard earth. The bone was human, but the predator would not have known, nor would it have had the capacity to care. On such a bitter night, the discovery would extend its life perhaps a week. But for the wolf, that week was an eternity.

The animal skulked away with its find and disappeared into the shadows. The ancient forest was left once more to the cold and the dead.

**Lwów,
Arbitrarily renamed Lemberg by the
occupying German Army
March–April 1942**

The Lwów ghetto was one of the first to transport Jews to death camps as part of *Aktion Reinhard*, a plan to systematically murder all Juden in the *Generalgouvernement* of Poland. Between March 16 and April 1, 1942, approximately 15,000 Jews were taken to the Kleparów railway station and deported to the Belzec extermination camp. Following the initial deportations, death by disease, and random shootings, 86,000 Jews officially remained, although unofficially, there were many more.

Yet Simon Goldkind and his family were allowed to stay in their modest quarters in the ghetto and, carrying the *Oberführer*'s calling card, he was still able to frequent the Scottish Café. For he was one of the lucky ones.

It was on an unusually quiet Wednesday night during one of the few breaks in his evening repertoire that *Oberführer* Altmann approached him. As always, he carried a full glass of spirits in his hand.

"You have fine hands. Goldkind," his smile was pencil thin. Insincere. "They will be put to good use serving the Reich. Accordingly, you will report promptly at seven o'clock tomorrow morning to the German Armament Works just up the way at 134 Janowska Road. They are expecting you. You will be paid and fed. And most importantly, you may return home to your family every night."

"And of course," the senior SS officer continued as if it were to be taken for granted, "You will continue to entertain myself and my comrades at the café."

The smile once again, now verging on brittle. "It is good?"

"Yes, *Oberführer*," Simon replied meekly. "It is good."

Sevastopol Peninsula, within the Crimea,
Soyuz Sovetskikh Sotsialisticheskikh Respublik
17 June 1942

The Soviet naval base at Sevastopol lay at the southwestern tip of the Crimea along a deeply fissured limestone promontory. Its strategic location made any approach by hostile ground forces virtually impossible. Steep cliffs overlooking Severnaya Bay made an amphibious landing equally dangerous.

Significant military fortifications had initially been constructed there in the two decades between 1806 and 1825. Later in the ensuing Crimean War, the battlements had valiantly defied an army made up of British, French, Italians, and Turks for nine months, until finally succumbing to the vastly greater numbers of a resolute attacking force.

In the late nineteenth century, the ancient forts were retrofitted with concrete encasements and armored cupolas housing cannon that could fire 12-inch shells both inland and far out to sea. The biggest of these, Number 30 battery, was 275 meters long and 40 meters deep, with a thousand defenders housed within its three stories.

Before the Nazi onslaught that commenced at the end of October

1941, the base had housed the entire Soviet Black Sea fleet, comprising six cruisers, two of them modern, twenty-seven destroyers and torpedo boats, and fifty-one submarines, in addition to a decrepit First World War dreadnought-class fittingly christened *Sevastopol*.

Land defenses now encircled the city of Sevastopol to a distance of 15 kilometers, with a hardened inner defense belt commencing at 5 kilometers. This belt was interlaced with hundreds of timber bunkers strategically punctuated by machine-gun nests and anti-tank artillery. Each was fed by a rabbit warren of supply stores. Enhancing it all was the heavily forested, rugged terrain that encircled the entire peninsula. A menacing landscape, the entire belt was also liberally peppered with thousands of anti-tank and anti-personnel mines and seemingly interminable barbed-wire obstacle belts.

Next to the British fortress at Gibraltar, Sevastopol was reputedly one of the strongest military fortifications on the globe. Adolf Hitler had enviously described it as a "floating aircraft carrier." He firmly believed that the capture of Sevastopol would enable the Axis armies to conduct far-ranging operations against Soviet targets lying far beyond the Caucasus Mountains. And this he commanded his loyal charges to do.

General Erich von Manstein, the Führer's personal choice, had amassed a massive assault force for the task, including 208 artillery batteries, totaling some 1,300 guns in all, and these solely dedicated to turning the formidable fortress city into socialist rubble. Von Manstein's crowning glory was a gigantic rail cannon nicknamed *Schwerer Gustav*, which required a complement of 4,120 soldiers to assemble and situate the weapon in proper firing position, and a 500-man crew to operate it. Astoundingly, it took twenty minutes per salvo to load the monster so that it might discharge a carefully selected assortment of five-ton high-explosive shells and nine-ton armor-piercing shells at its hapless target from a colossal 31-inch barrel.

When Nadia Fedin came ashore in one of the four rickety landing craft that ferried two platoons of raw replacements for the beleaguered 95th Guards Regiment, the Nazi siege had been ongoing for 223 days.

The anxious riflemen in the landing craft with her had been sent to reinforce the northern perimeter of the Soviet defenses. Nadia, meanwhile, had been tasked to be the regiment's political and moral minder, replacing the third in a tenuous line of NKVD overseers who had died during the lengthy siege. She also had a second mission, one that she did not share with her peers or immediate superiors—one that came directly from an office located within the very heart of the Kremlin.

They had landed under cover of darkness at the mouth of the Belbek River, assiduously avoiding the scavenging Italian motor torpedo boats that lurked in the maritime gloom like voracious tiger sharks. Their faces masked in charcoal camouflage, the newcomers warily made their way under a cloud-scudded moon toward a rendezvous, accompanied by a guide sent out from Number 30 Battery.

The man who met them offered no last name and wore no rank, though what lay behind the scraggly beard and tatters that were once a uniform was anyone's guess. He would be their escort.

He nimbly led the newcomers up a rough-hewn path generously littered with the detritus of the most recent German assault: Mauser rifles, cast-off coal-scuttle helmets, still-smoldering remains and, in the air, the overpowering stench of decomposing human flesh.

They halted before what appeared to be a sheer cliff side. As Nadia's eyes grew accustomed to the formation, she realized she was confronting the gargantuan silhouette of a gun battery. The guard gestured to a nearby steel door guarded by two bedraggled sentries who appeared to be sleepwalking and an emaciated Alsatian guard dog that was more dead than alive. She had arrived at her destination. Her taciturn guide stumbled off with the relief column before she could thank him.

She was informed by one of the guards that the lieutenant she requested to see would arrive shortly.

The man who finally met her at the battery entrance was gaunt-faced, hollow-eyed, and filthy with the stench and stain of battle. He may have been in his late twenties, but the intensity of combat had aged him beyond comprehension.

With brusque motions, he wordlessly directed her into a chamber that wound its way, serpent-like, for several hundred meters. As they moved through the subterranean maze, ground water dripped relentlessly off the curved ceiling as the stark wall lighting cruelly etched their features.

The lieutenant offered Nadia a *Belomorkanal*. She politely declined. The man jabbed the proletarian cigarette into his mouth and scraped a wooden match against the dank concrete wall. It struck. A faint flicker danced about the room and momentarily bathed their faces in a ghostly blue light. The lieutenant drew deeply, slowly inhaled, then brushed a hand wearily across his face.

Nadia noted that her host was much younger than she had first imagined. And he was quite handsome, though his slate-gray eyes were eerily expressionless.

The lieutenant apologized for his seeming lack of courtesy. The officers' quarters were located some distance away, tucked between the two principal gun turrets in the very heart of the battery. The battery commander and his retinue were asleep. They had just endured twenty-six hours of shelling without rest, so he was the official greeting party. Her bedchamber was there if she wanted it, but perhaps she would like a snack.

Nadia agreed. She had not eaten in more than twelve hours.

They made their way gingerly down the constricted corridor to the galley. It was spottily lit by a string of naked bulbs hanging from the arched ceiling and powered by an emergency generator that coughed and roared intermittently in a darkened crevice of the room. As they sat on iron benches, the lieutenant outlined their current situation over slices of rough-cut sausage and cups of bitter chicory coffee served lukewarm.

Originally, Number 30 Coastal Battery was designed to defend the sea approaches to Sevastopol on the west and northwest. Though it currently faced a determined German enemy advancing from the east, Number 30 was still an exceedingly formidable weapon, armed as it was with two 305mm twin-tower installations, each capable of rotating 360 degrees and each with a range more than 40 kilometers.

Protected by a concrete shell four meters thick, the battery compartments housed ammunition cellars, a power station, living quarters, and service rooms on two levels. Outside of the battlements of Number 30, the Russians confronted a daunting number of heavy-caliber German mortars and a fearsome railway gun—*Schwerer Gustav*.

"And do you know what the enemy calls this battery?" the soldier continued with a weary smile.

"No."

"Maxim Gorky."

Nadia smiled grimly. "Somehow I never pictured Fritz honoring a great Socialist writer in this manner."

The soldier gave an indifferent shrug. "I don't believe they've ever read *The Life of a Useless Man* nor any of Comrade Gorky's other works. Still, no matter what name they chose, the bastards have learned to respect us."

Hearing this, Nadia could not help herself. "You must be so proud to do this for the nation."

The soldier took a crumpled pack from his breast pocket, flipped out a cigarette and jabbed it into the side of his mouth, unlit. "We do what we must to survive inside this filthy tomb, Comrade Captain."

"Not for Mother Russia?"

"When you see your friends blown to what passes for eternity, you discover how little a slogan means. In the end, all such words are hollow. Meaningless. On the battlefield, we just do it for each other, Comrade Captain. For each other. Nothing more. Nothing less."

She noticed the lieutenant's wedding ring. It seemed ill-fitting, resting loosely on the right ring finger in the fashion of the religious Orthodox. It was a gesture that still had a tenuous hold over many Russian peasantry in what was seemingly a transparently atheist state.

"You are married?" she chose her words carefully. "Your wife must be terribly concerned for your safety."

The young man hesitated. "Vera was killed by shrapnel several months ago. She was a military nurse at a forward dressing station at Kharkov."

Fedin nodded perceptively. "Yet you still wear the ring?"

The lieutenant stubbed the unlit cigarette against the wall. "At least Vera was not a slogan." The words trickled uneasily into the darkness.

Fedin allowed the black silence to envelop them. She could sense the soldier's shallow breathing. There was a hurried rhythm to it.

The lieutenant sighed and then turned to peer at Fedin. "Let's get to the point, Comrade Captain," he challenged, tightening his hand around the rifle grip of his weapon. "You specifically asked to see me on your arrival here and not the battery commandant. Why?"

Fedin was happy to do as the lieutenant asked. "What village did you live in before you entered the Patriotic War against fascism, Comrade?"

"Katyn."

"I know you as Lieutenant Zyk, initial N. And your middle name?"

A silence which lengthened.

"It wouldn't be Nikolayevich, would it? Your father being Nikolay with the same surname as you possess?"

The lieutenant's eyes narrowed. Nadia thought she caught a glint of guarded awareness in them. Or was it a groundswell of fear?

An uneasy nod. "That is correct."

"If that is true, Comrade Zyk, army records indicate that you entered active service in July 1940 in a feeder battalion at Smolensk and were ultimately posted to the Ninety-Fifth Rifle Division here at Sevastopol."

"Yes."

"Which is very curious," Fedin commented. "Several months after you were impressed into the Red Army at Smolensk, a local militiaman found a corpse that had drifted ashore along the Dnieper River just outside the village of Katyn. What remained of the body was severely bloated, face and hands and feet nibbled away by catfish, carp and who knows whatever other distasteful creatures lurk in the Dnieper. The cadaver carried no papers and proved impossible to identify."

"An accidental death," the soldier interjected. "Perhaps a suicide. They aren't that uncommon in this day and age, you know."

Fedin played her next card. "Not in this case, Comrade. The deceased had been stabbed several times."

She waited for a reaction. None came.

"I must be candid. The hamlet of Katyn isn't the homicide capital of our glorious nation. In fact, there has only been one previous murder since the Revolution, and it was as the direct consequence of a vodka-induced brawl between two pathetic drunkards. You wouldn't happen to know any information about this cadaver, would you?"

"No," he answered steely-eyed. "No. I don't."

"Curious. Because the death was a forgotten afterthought on the militia blotter until a woman came forward claiming her husband had disappeared around the time you went off to enlist."

No reply.

"It's ironic, isn't it?" Fedin continued in a hushed voice. "The dead man had the same name as you. Zyk."

"Ironic," he countered guardedly. "But not impossible. It is a common enough name in our area."

Fedin could sense the lieutenant's hurried breathing.

"What caused you to join the Red Army when you did?" she asked.

"I don't know what you mean, Comrade."

"Edmund," Fedin challenged the lieutenant with his real name. "I know who you are. I believe you weren't involved with your parents' crimes against the State."

The man's eyes darted to hers. Fedin detected a glimmer of what passed for socialist humanity in them.

"Why do you say that, Captain?" he rasped.

Fedin sighed. "My officers have thoroughly investigated your past. You and your family weren't close. More critically, you've made no attempt to contact your mother. Why is that?"

The lieutenant hesitated then spoke. It was if a burden had been lifted from his shoulders.

"What purpose would that serve?" he began, gathering strength as he continued. "I am certain she is dead. And if not dead, she might as well be. My father was a religious zealot. My mother, a weakling. Her priest was a fool spouting claptrap. The future for our nation is through the Party, Comrade Captain, and not through witchcraft."

"Then why assume another identity?" Fedin pressed.

The lieutenant turned to face her, once more unemotional and in control. "Your bulls would have beaten me senseless if I had remained a Rudecki," he countered. "And what would they have ultimately discovered after such torture? That they were mistaken, and a dying man can actually be telling the truth—even if it isn't their version of it.

"As to Zyk?" The lieutenant smirked, and then suddenly became quite somber. "Tell me that you have not killed someone in furtherance of the Socialist cause. Zyk was a drunk, Comrade. He would never have taken up our cause against Fascism. My brother died for the proletariat. I wished to revenge his memory with a bayonet. I wasn't going to hide in a farmhouse spouting mumbo jumbo like my parents did to some mysterious being who doesn't give a damn about me or anyone else.

"Truth be told, Comrade Captain, I had to decide who was the greater evil. Your people? The bastards who eliminated my so-called family? Or the Nazis who, as we speak, are cold-bloodedly killing my comrades in this hellhole. It was an easy decision to make, and I have made it. This is my place. These men and women are my family. If I must die, this is the way I choose to do so."

A barrage of German artillery suddenly shook the massive battery, filling the passageway with clouds of dust. A solitary bulb blinked in hectic synergy with the salvos. After a minute or so, the barrage ceased.

Fedin knew that somewhere above ground, Russian defenders were probably dying, yet here inside Number 30 they were reasonably safe. For now.

The lieutenant sensed her unease. "After a while you get used to it, Comrade Captain," he remarked reassuringly. "The walls are quite thick. We've withstood countless direct hits and are still operational." "Come," he motioned to a far-off chamber. "I'll take you to your sleeping quarters. The dawn comes all too soon here in Sevastopol, and we have no guarantee it will be followed by another."

The lieutenant escorted Nadia to a vacant cubicle at the rear of the fortifications. Inside was an iron bed; upon it, a coarse military blanket and straw-filled pillow. The room was dimly lit by a single tapered candle resting on the earthen floor. Nadia sat on the bed and surveyed her surroundings.

Faded markings seamed the walls—names, ranks, units, dates. Poignant epitaphs to the previous occupants, etched for eternity in a doomed sepulcher. She wanted to ask more questions of the lieutenant, but he had departed in the manner he had first met her, without a word. She blew out the candle and, in the concrete-encased gloom, she fell into a troubled sleep.

Over the next few hours, the Soviet defenses began to crumble outside the rock-hard confines of Maxim Gorky. Two German infantry divisions advanced steadily from the northeast, deploying remote-control demolition vehicles against the rough-timbered Russian bunkers that dared to block their passage. One of the miniature-tracked units, called Goliaths, exploded prematurely and two others were knocked out in a minefield. But the remaining Goliaths continued onward, crab-like, until they succeeded in carving out a huge opening in the Soviet line.

At daybreak, when Nadia awoke from a restive sleep, Number 30 found itself completely encircled. By mid-morning, the one communication landline connecting the battery to Russian headquarters in the city of Sevastopol was cut. However, 200 soldiers of the 95th Rifle Division still remained inside the smoke-filled compartments of Maxim Gorky. They were completely enveloped by German infantry units with stuttering Nazi machine guns strategically positioned to control all the exits as they battled for their very lives.

By noon, German pioneer battalions had crawled up to reach the damaged outer series of battery turrets. They began to lob hand grenades inside the position, and quickly discovered the exhaust pipes of the diesel generators that provided electrical power to the beleaguered Soviet troops inside. They poured countless liters of gasoline into the pipes and then torched the oozing ochre-hued liquid. Soon the internal gun compartments were engulfed in flames from the burning fluid. In spite of this, the sturdy steel doors and what remained of the battery's air-ventilation system managed to somehow contain the blaze.

For the remainder of that day, as German infantry troopers furiously scrambled about its granite carcass like so many ravenous ants, the Maxim Gorky battery fired the remaining live shells it held in its cavernous armories. When they ran out of primed projectiles, the Russian gunners began to use archaic whole shot, which had been stored before the war for training purposes. When those were fully depleted, the battery fired 70-kilogram powder charges in batches of three.

During much of that time, Nadia sat in her quarters, every so often wandering the tunnels as shadowy figures scurried ferret-like past her. There was nothing for her to do and no one who would listen. Yet she had somehow accomplished her mission if not her objective. An errant piece of the puzzle was now firmly in place.

That night, in inky darkness, she boarded a Malyutka-class submarine in the company of the few senior military commanders and party officials who yet remained in Sevastopol. On Stalin's personal order, they were all to be removed to relative safety, immediately.

Just before dawn, as the submarine safely surfaced somewhere in the Black Sea, Nadia was handed a radio transmission by the vessel's commander, a morose Muscovite named Koltypin. The flimsy sheet held but a few words:

"There are twenty-six of us left. We are preparing to blow ourselves up. No more messages will be sent. Farewell."

It was authorized by Lieutenant Edmund Rudecki.

Within the hour, Nadia Fedin had sent a top-secret ship-to-shore telex to the communications center in the Lubyanka. Her specific instructions were that it be immediately forwarded to the personal attention of the commandant of a certain tin mine, one of the many unremarkable Gulag pits that proliferated like malignant cancer cells in the bleak far eastern regions of the Soviet Union.

Her orders to that commandant were crystal clear. The project concerning "Rudecki, Anastasia" was to be terminated immediately.

Moreover, the subject was to be returned to the general labor pool and used therein until she had become redundant—wherever or whenever that might be.

Anastasia Rudecki had finally become just a fading whisper in the wind.

Landing Ground (LG) 91, RAF El Amiriya, Approximately 40 miles east of Alamein and 20 miles south of Alexandria, Aka somewhere in the North African Desert 3 July 1942

On June 20, 1942, after launching a massive land and air assault that totally humiliated the South African divisions charged with its inner defenses, the Axis forces recaptured the vital Libyan port of Tobruk. After two years in secure Allied hands, the harbor fortress had fallen in just two days.

Yet on July 1, a scant ten days later, the British Eighth Army had begun what history would come to know forever after as the first battle of El Alamein, effectively ending forever Rommel's advance into Egypt and the ultimate Axis victory prize, the Suez Canal.

For the tank crews and lowly infantry of the two dueling armies, the North African desert war had become as harsh and unpredictable as a whirling sandstorm. But for Johnny Callison (RCAF), the Sahara battle arena had acquired an almost leisurely, devil-may-care rhythm. He'd been with 112 Squadron for the better part of nine months, had completed thirty-nine sorties with 126 hours flying time, and had stenciled five and a half swastikas onto the side of his kite. He'd even found himself promoted to flight lieutenant. Whether it was because of his flying prowess, or rather because of a never-ending need to fill the many vacancies higher up the operational ladder created by those killed, missing in action, captured or hospitalized with life-altering injuries, Callison could only guess. What he did know, and could plainly see, was that he now had two thin robin's-egg-blue stripes on each shoulder epaulet instead of one, as well as a bit of a bump in his pay packet.

Callison rose each morning precisely at dawn, ritually enduring a water-rationed "wash 'n shave" out of the battered jerry can that he shared with his tent mate, a perpetually tipsy Englishman from Croydon aptly surnamed Pimms. Ablutions complete, he donned a rumpled pair of drill shorts and well-worn desert boots before nonchalantly making his way down the "officers' promenade"—a neat pathway trimmed by white-wash on stone, to eat what passed for breakfast at the mess.

The mess was actually a moth-eaten marquee that had seen service in the encampment of an Italian general before its ignominious capture by a marauding Long-Range Desert Group patrol and subsequent barter to the fighter squadron for a crate of Black and White blended whiskey, purloined by an opportunist from the Alexandria wharves.

Callison entered the tent. This morning there was only one person present—holding a plate of slim pickings, a tousle-haired Englishman named Crampton who'd been grounded by a broken arm suffered when his kite crashed while attempting to land at the base two months ago. Before that time, he'd been Callison's steady wingman on every mission that Johnny had flown. Forever there. Forever watchful.

Jubal Crampton was a Londoner, an insurance salesman by trade, an optimist by nature. He once proudly bragged to Callison that he could sell iceboxes to Eskimos. When told that there were no Eskimos where his mate came from, but rather Cheyenne and Apaches, he pretended disappointment. "But they do buy insurance, don't they?" Callison didn't let on that he saw the line coming.

Callison wandered over to a blackboard sitting on an otherwise vacant camp chair. Raggedly scribbled in chalk, the "breakfast menu" never changed—tinned bully-beef and hardtack biscuit with a rationed spoonful of Rhodesian marmalade, washed down with tepid Barkley and Sons tea.

Suddenly a tiny red spotted lizard peeked out from behind the blackboard. "Toto?" Callison turned to his mess companion with an impish look. "Somehow I don't think we're in Kansas anymore."

The Englishman looked up quizzically.

"Sorry, Jubal. You don't go to the movies much, do you?"

Crampton absently scratched himself in the groin. "*Au contraire*, old sport. I see Formby's flicks at the NAAFI whenever I'm in Cairo."

"Formby? You mean that ukulele-playing guy with the toothy grin?"

"Yessiree, Bob! Leaning on the lamppost his bloody self! Here"— he gestured to an empty seat. "Care to join me? They say the food in this five-star hotel is bloody marvelous!"

Crampton had been reading a copy of *Stars and Stripes* he'd recently pinched from a NAAFI barbershop in Cairo on a rare leave grudgingly given when the medical officer had declared him once more fit for flight duty. Over slurps of tea, Crampton shared the headline story with Callison about a "real Captain America." A US Army Air Force officer, Charles Kegelman, flying in a mission with twelve Boston light bombers to attack a marshalling yard in France on the twenty-ninth of June, 1942 became the first member of the Eighth USAAF to drop bombs on enemy-occupied territory.

The story went on to state that more recently Kegelman had led Boston light bombers joining an RAF squadron on a successful low-level attack on Nazi airfields in the Netherlands. His twin-engine aircraft was severely damaged by enemy fire, yet Kegelman succeeded in bringing it back to base on only one engine.

"It says here he received the Distinguished Service Cross." Crampton gestured to a newspaper photo of the ceremony. "Jolly good show, eh wot, Johnny?" he smirked.

Callison languidly stirred his teacup. The tinkling sound of metal on cheap crockery. "Yes . . . yes, it was."

"A DSC? How high is that?"

Callison paused. "Just below the Medal of Honor."

Crampton whistled. "Bloody hell."

They ate for a time in silence.

It was Crampton who spoke first. "Johnny, why do you still stay with us? I mean, a Yank serving with Brits in North Africa?" He brushed a hand over his mouth to catch a loose crumb. "Your lads are in the war now. Ever thought of joining them?

"No," Callison replied earnestly. "I joined up with what you call 'the Colonials.' The Canadians accepted me, and I'll stay loyal to them."

Crampton considered the response. Finally, he jabbed his fork at Callison in mock derision. "You are a funny one, Yank. You're the only Canadian in this squadron, and you're not even that."

Callison smiled. "But I am here with you, Jubal. Of that you can be certain. I'm here with you guys for the long haul."

"Bloody marvelous," the Englishman responded, nodding his head in open admiration. "Bloody flippin' marvelous. Pass us the marmalade, would you mate? I need a taste of 'ome in me stomach."

An orderly came and placed Callison's breakfast before him. He grudgingly picked at the bully-beef, then nibbled idly on the hardtack as if begrudgingly picking his poison. The biscuit and overly sweet marmalade won, as did a tepid cup of tea.

"Come up with me on today's sortie, Jubal? I miss your eyes in the sky."

Crampton sniffed, roughly running a free hand across his nose. "Sorry, mate. The MO says perhaps by the end of the week I'll be fully cleared. As far as he's concerned, this 'ere sniffling is the start of a bleedin' head cold. Which could affect me in altitude flying." He chortled cheerfully as he rambled on. "Me? I say it's because I'm totally allergic to this flippin' war."

Callison joined in the laughter. After struggling a few minutes with a bit of the beef, he placed the plate to one side and excused himself. Crampton gave his friend a thumbs-up, which Callison jauntily returned.

He made his way to the morning briefing, delivered, as was customary, from the rear of a three-ton Humber lorry. His section was flying today, so he listened intently to the details: ops officer, the intellwallah, and the latest weather outlook. Callison neatly scripted their words into his logbook before tucking it into the pocket of his KDs. The session ended.

The flight line was less than 100 yards from the lorry. His aircraft, a slim desert-camouflaged Curtis P40, rested elegantly with the others. The 112 Squadron signature—a leering shark's mouth and his personal logo "Johnny on the Spot"—were emblazoned in brash script on its metal, semi-monocoque structure.

The 112 "Shark" Squadron had been posted only a few weeks ago to RAF El Amiriya, an arid wasteland of depressing anonymity that passed for a military airfield located a few kilometers south-southwest of Alexandria. The base was little more than a patchwork of barely serviceable packed-sand runways clawed out of the hard desert floor by a trio of determined RAF bulldozers.

Settling into the cockpit, Callison shared a joke with the flight crew. His "erks" had performed miracles on his Kittyhawk fighter. Their motto was faux Latin—*Ubendum Wemendum*—and Scotty, the ground tradesman responsible for the P40's Allison engine, had ensured that it had been upheld.

Right foot into the stirrup step, left foot on the port wing, one short step along, right foot on the step inset in the fuselage, into the cockpit. Callison's rigger deftly passed parachute straps across his shoulders, then secured the harness straps—pin through and tighten the adjusting pieces—mask clipped across and finally, oxygen on. He primed the engine, adjusted the switches. His thumb went up in signal to the mechanics. The chocks slipped away all round, frisky fighter engines roared into life, raising dervish whirlpools of desert sand with their slip-stream, and Callison was on his way, taxiing out behind "Jumbo" Gracie.

Kittyhawk took off at 0945 hours and headed due west using the faint azure trim of the Mediterranean shoreline as a reference point. Their mission was to escort a squadron of Beaufort twin-engine bombers targeting the Axis supply line running from the harbor at Benghazi eastwards along the coastal road to the strategic *Luftwaffe* air base of Martuba.

He glanced out of the Perspex cockpit. The Sahara spread below was a rich buff hue beneath an electric blue sky. A Connecticut Yankee in King Arthur's Court. No, he smiled inwardly, it was more like a Kansas drifter in the ancient land of Saladin. In the end, it didn't matter, for he was airborne and being airborne made him happy. He allowed his mind to drift to a far-off place and time. To Shanghai and the Bund. The young China Marine he once was seemed an eternity away.

Fifteen minutes into their mission, they rendezvoused with the Beauforts at angels nine—nine thousand feet above the arid Sahara floor. The sky all around was clear of bandits.

Suddenly, a slew of enemy fighters—Italian MC200 Saettas—descended out of a white-hot sun. Machine-gun fire laced the air as they closed rapidly on the Allied formation. A Beaufort burst like a Mexican piñata, sending shards of metal, Perspex, and eviscerated humanity into an uncaring infinity. A Saetta fell away in flames, and then another with a severed wing cartwheeled toward earth.

Callison found himself right on the tail of an Axis fighter. His Kittyhawk shuddered visibly as he fired several bursts at the Saetta. The enemy pilot feverishly swerved to the right, then left. He banked wildly skywards as Callison coolly followed his tracer fire lacing the sky. The Saetta disappeared from his line of sight. Another enemy fighter approached, then veered away. Then another. A Kittyhawk wildly jit-terbugged in front of him, flames gushing from its engine cowling. An enemy aircraft approached head-on, closing rapidly. Callison instinctively pressed the firing button and a torrent of Browning machine-gun rounds spewed forth until the aggressor canted away, enveloped in smoke. Out of the corner of his eye, Callison could see aircraft darting about in the frenzied craziness of air combat. Then, an ethereal stillness.

Callison peered warily about the vast sky. Wafting contrails were all that remained of the recent air battle. He gave a chipper thumbs-up to his two wingmen, then briskly motioned to the bomber flow rapidly melding into the far-off western horizon.

But tranquility proved to be short-lived.

Suddenly a flock of tawny-beige MC 202s descended out of the sun. The air was once more laced with a fusillade of white tracer shells, converging on the Kittyhawks from Italian Breda machine guns.

A thunderclap explosion tore at Callison's eardrums. His first reaction was "I can't have been hit. It just is not possible. It can happen to others, but not me. Never to me . . ." Then the fuel tank exploded and flames engulfed the cockpit.

His head instinctively reared back from the licking flames as he desperately grappled with his shoulder harness. He watched dumbly as the exposed skin of his hands shriveled like burning parchment in the blast-furnace heat. Struggling, he screamed and screamed again. And again.

Clear of the cockpit, he was tumbling madly through the air as if gravity did not exist. Then something from inside him spoke, echoing down a long, tapered tunnel. "The ripcord . . . pull the bloody ripcord, you idiot!" In a daze, he fumbled for the ring, but each time his hand made tentative contact, an intense stinging pain shot from his fingers and caused the hand to jerk away.

Callison continued in free fall. Instinctively, he curled his fingertips once more round the parachute ring. He screamed aloud into the howling wind. He felt the parachute webbing tightening underneath his armpits, the silk canopy above him unfolding to form an elegant umbrella as he began to slow to a graceful, gentle glide to earth, like a leaf falling from a tree.

Brutal pain shot through his arms as he tried to grasp the harness straps. He could not comprehend what remained of his hands.

Callison hit the desert floor. Hard. With raw, blistered hands, he tried to unbuckle the harness. His skin peeled away he battled to free himself. The strap of the flying helmet had tightened like a noose around his chin. The intense heat had fused the buckle and the strap together, making its removal impossible. His face was beginning to explode in pure agony. As the horrific realization of what he had become sank in, he lapsed into merciful unconsciousness.

When he awoke, through an anguished haze, he vaguely sensed someone looming over him. The stranger wore a tan pith helmet with black grouse plumes adorned to one side of it. His taupe shirt and shorts were soiled and ill-fitting.

"*Hey! Inglese! Attenzione! Mettere le mani su!*" The stranger waved a stubby burp gun in Callison's general direction and spoke a language he vaguely understood. But Callison knew him to be an Italian and member of the elite Bersaglieri—the one Italian unit that Rommel, the feared Desert Fox, had come to admire. Callison was not conscious for long.

CHAPTER 6

Lwów,
Arbitrarily renamed Lemberg by the
occupying German Army
1 August 1942

In midsummer 1942, the Great Lemberg Aktion was carried out by the SS and their underlings. Almost 50,000 Jews were rounded up, gathered together at a transit point in Janowska camp, and sent to their deaths at Belzec. Others were executed on the "Sands" behind Janowska. Local orphans and hospital inpatients were merely shot on sight. Around 65,000 Jews remained as winter approached, and deprivation and typhus waited in the wings.

Simon Goldkind was growing ever more weary. His once-sharp eyesight and delicate touch led to an assignment making adjustments to the intricate scopes on rifles used by snipers. But his natural gifts gradually began to diminish.

The table he was at every day always had three other occupants. They were all afforded safe passage nightly to their homes in the ghetto, and an ever-dwindling sum of nearly worthless occupation currency as a stipend and incentive to continue their work. They were allowed the meager luxury of wearing their own clothing and not the striped prisoner garb worn by most factory workers.

But there was an ominous and dreaded catch. No mistakes were tolerated. Goldkind had seen many returned to the general population for work that did not meet a nearly impossible standard.

Goldkind was determined to stay alive and provide for his family, even if it meant discreetly switching others' good workmanship for his own slipshod efforts. Survival came at a price, even if it meant sacrificing one's integrity and self-respect.

Over time, Goldkind's ever-changing compatriots became mere nameless shadows, appearing for a moment then disappearing forever.

Until one morning Boddo Fetchner, the SS sergeant and formerly a boorish factory worker from the Ruhr, came to speak to him in private. Fetchner was never kind, but on this occasion the man's words and body language bordered on combative belligerence.

"Goldkind," the SS sergeant barked. "I have something for you." He tossed Goldkind the standard-issue factory garb. "From now on, you will be staying here at the factory with the rest of these vermin."

"But my family?" Simon sputtered in shock.

"They are no longer your concern."

"And the business card from *Oberführer* Altmann? The one granting me safe passage?"

"Right." Fetchner nodded in agreement, as if he'd forgotten something important. "Hand it over to me. Now!"

Goldkind, meekly taking the card from his coat pocket, did as he was told.

The SS sergeant looked at the card momentarily before tearing it into tiny pieces. "The *Oberführer* is gone. He has been reassigned."

Goldkind felt a cold hard fear grip him.

Katyn Forest,
12 kilometers west of Smolensk, Belarus,
Wehrmacht-Occupied Zone
8 February 1943

Swathed in rags against a cutting-cold northern wind, four men feebly began to dig a shallow pit for garbage and, perhaps in time, their own graves. After eight months in brutal captivity, they were left unguarded. And not out of kindness, for there was no way to escape. Malevolent Ukrainian guards who hated anything Russian manned watchtowers that defined a kill zone.

The forest around the four captives was an eerie place of rumor and shadow. It had only recently become headquarters for the *Wehrmacht* 537th Signal Regiment. Before that, it had been an NKVD compound—a place where those unfortunate souls deemed to be enemies of the People's Proletariat disappeared forever.

As Russian prisoners of war, the four were all too aware of their own inevitable fate. In such matters, their Nazi captors were as pragmatic and savagely unforgiving as their Soviet predecessors had been.

The first bone they unearthed was quite unusual—no animal appendage was as long nor was it as sculpted as this one. And after a few shovelfuls, there were many bones and all found in one general location, as if some unknown giant's hand had scrambled ivory into bundled toothpicks and stuffed them into the frozen earth.

Still, four more weeks would pass before the Russians told one of the Nazi guards what they had discovered.

When it became obvious that there was no alternative but to investigate what appeared to be mass murders by "suspects unknown," German field police teams were summoned from nearby Smolensk. With Teutonic efficiency, they commenced their inquiry. Within five hours, the first forensic report was in the hands of a senior identification officer. Human remains—those of a Polish officer—had been located in the frozen ground and appeared to be those of an artillery captain. A full report was rushed to the headquarters of Army Group Center by a relay of motorcycle dispatch riders.

Katyn Forest,
9 April 1943

The frozen field where the bodies were buried was near a place called Katyn. The German military swiftly created a mini city to aid in identification of the remains, complete with morgues and corpse-dissection tents. A barn-like structure was built on site for post-mortem work, and the rudimentary undergraduate laboratory situated at the nearby Smolensk Polytechnic was expanded to cope with the inherent rigors of enhanced pathology identification. The local field police commander quickly organized a labor gang of thirty-five villagers to take care of the initial digging and recruited seven Russian civil guards as night watchmen to protect the remains from being disturbed by looters.

On this early spring morning. Paulus Henschell was listening to Brahms's symphony *Number 1*, *Opus 68*, playing softly in the far corner of an office partially warmed by a coal stove. Henschell loved such music passionately, and for that reason, he trundled his gramophone and record collection everywhere he went. Beethoven. Wagner. Bach. Mozart. Haydn. But only Party-approved composers; nothing else would do. The very best of Reich Kultur to fill the martial tedium of his working world.

He glanced over at the framed photo of Astrid, the perfectly pretty young thing from the perfectly prosaic village in Thuringia, who possessed an unbridled loyalty for all things Nazi, including him. For a brief moment, he missed her.

But he would not have her here at this heinous place, this depraved killing field. She was far better off with his parents, sharing their large red-brick home and gazing serenely across at Spandau, the massive medieval citadel strategically situated on an island where the Havel and Spree rivers met.

Henschell had anticipated a knock at the door. He bade his adjutant enter.

Wehrmacht Hauptmann Dirk Schneider had been at the camp for less than two months, the final chapter of his last battle—the spectacular storming of the Stalingrad Tractor Factory, where he had single-handedly attacked a Russian machine-gun nest before being seriously wounded in the shoulder and hospitalized for a month.

Awarded the Iron Cross for such a brash effort, he was sent to Warsaw for a time. There, his command of Slavic languages—acquired in undergraduate studies at the prestigious and conservative University of Gottingen—stood him in good stead as he worked in close concert with a strangely anonymous colonel who reported directly to the *Oberkommando des Heeres* (OKH—the German Army High Command). His subsequent move to Katyn appeared to be part of the shrewd maneuver by the OKW to have someone with both rank and fluency who could win the confidence of the Poles.

By dint of his rank and outgoing personality, Schneider had quickly become Henschell's confidant and right-hand man. The *Hauptmann* was a seasoned infantryman, with combat experience in the relatively easy battles of Poland, France, the Balkans, and Yugoslavia and, most recently, the rugged trials of the Eastern Front.

He was young, strident, and, for all intents and purposes, a true Aryan who would shrewdly calculate his path to greater promotion using the bleached bones of his rivals and challengers as markers.

In Henschell's eyes, he was almost too perfect, with the fabricated sincerity of a Bavarian hamlet bank manager. Schneider, for all his bravado and bonhomie, was a quick study. It took an evening over schnapps in the ramshackle hut near the main gate that passed for the officers' mess to make his own measure of the man. As a consequence, Henschell was always on his guard.

Schneider delivered a thick folio, then retired. Henschell, with typical efficiency, began to review the documents. With confident pen strokes, he jotted notes onto a blank sheet of paper affixed to it. Through a grime-smeared window, he could make out the excavation site. He watched dispassionately as POWs toiled drone-like under the harsh supervision of black-uniformed Gestapo NCOs. In addition to their striped prison garb, the workers wore masks, heavy rubber gloves and hip-wader boots. Time and time again, they would awkwardly raise contorted muddy husks out of the massive pit and stack them in a long martial line. A foul odor of putrefaction seeped tendril-like under the office door into the room. Henschell did his best not to think about it.

He had heard the cutting gossip, seen the openly resentful stares darting dagger-like from his contemporaries at *Wagmüllerstrasse* 16, but his firm decision-making in France had obviously not gone unnoticed by his superiors. It was for that reason, he believed he'd been assigned this unique task, one which he deemed aptly befitted his rising station in the shrouded hierarchy of the *Shutzstaffel*. Certainly, his recent promotion to *Obersturmführer* seemed to validate that view.

In great secrecy, Henschell had been briefed about the grisly discovery in the nearby woods, an area that stretched from the main road to an abandoned NKVD dacha overlooking river marshland. As a result, he had made the audacious determination to affect the course of history rather than waiting for it to reveal itself to him. Given the degree of operational latitude he possessed, Henschell had arranged for an encounter with an individual who could carry out a plan he had drawn up.

Another knock on the door. Henschell glanced at the wall clock. It had just gone ten o'clock.

"Open."

An individual attired in the remnants of a Royal Canadian Air Force uniform entered the room, escorted by Schneider. The newcomer walked awkwardly with a cane and had a noticeable limp. His face was hidden by tear-drop sunglasses and a puffed-up paisley ascot. In the gaps of the ascot, Henschell could see a lattice scar of badly stitched skin. His hands, partially covered in bandages, were red and raw and terribly blistered in areas where they were exposed.

Henschell looked up and involuntarily gasped, then caught himself and curtly motioned to the high-backed chair. "Please, sit down."

The airman fumbled in obvious discomfort as he struggled to comply.

"*Hauptmann*, would you kindly help the flight lieutenant?" Henschell extended his hand in greeting. Schneider did so, and then discreetly hovered in the background.

The last strains of the Brahms piece gave way to the repetitive clicking of the gramophone needle. Henschell rose, strode over, and lifted the playing arm. The room was still but for the dull, metronome ticking of the clock.

He turned to face his guest. "My name is Paulus Henschell." A thin, contrived smile. "*Obersturmführer* Paulus Henschell. I am with the *Shutzstaffel*. The SS."

Callison's body tensed. Henschell relished this instant of recognition. He always did.

"I'm certain that you have heard many exaggerated things about us," he purred. "I can assure you, however, that we are quite cultured." He gestured to the *Luftwaffe* officer. "You may wait outside, Dirk."

Schneider closed the door firmly behind him.

"Coffee, Flight Lieutenant?"

Callison declined.

"But you won't mind if I have one? In a war as dreary as this one, a warm cup of coffee is always welcome, even if it's made from chicory."

The German began to pour the coffee substitute from the decanter into a porcelain cup, then glanced at his visitor. The benign look on his face evaporated.

"You wear the uniform of a Royal Canadian Air Force officer. Yet you are an American."

"My name is John Paul Callison. My rank is flight lieutenant. My date of birth is 27 August 1914. My service number is J-102564. I currently serve in the Royal Canadian Air Force."

"You are an American," Henschell repeated more forcefully.

"My name is John Paul Callison. My rank is flight—"

With a terse wave, Henschell stilled him. "Frankly, I must say that how you respond Mr. Callison matters little to me." He gracefully steepled his well-manicured fingers. "Do you not wonder why you have been brought here? Flown eight hundred kilometers from a POW camp in Silesia to this godforsaken place on the Russian plain?" Henschell stood up, the coffee untouched. "Come to the window," he commanded tersely, though well aware of his guest's limitations.

The American didn't move.

"No?" Henschell sniffed. "Suit yourself. But let me tell you what exists out there less than one kilometer from this hut. Two months ago, village laborers came upon a burial ground. In it, our criminal investigators have discovered several hundred bodies. On the twenty-ninth of March, by special order of the German High Command, we commenced an excavation. So far, three hundred corpses have been unearthed and identified." Henschell turned to face his visitor. "Are you not intrigued to know who these dead men might be?"

Callison rocked back and forth in his seat. Outside, a dog barked; a transport lorry angrily ground through gears. Somewhere in an adjacent office, a male voice shouted for someone called Heinz.

"Come, come, Flight Lieutenant Callison," Henschell pressed. "You are not even slightly interested?"

Callison remained silent, fighting pain that felt like his very nerves were on fire. He had spent nine months in captivity, much of it in a heavily guarded POW hospital located deep within the Silesian spine of the Nazi Reich. There he had been methodically cared for by a flock of sour-faced Dominican nuns and an overworked Welsh Guards medical officer who'd been captured at Dunkirk.

And for much of that time, because the proper medicines were not available, he had endured unrelenting pain. There was no plastic surgeon available, certainly not one who could be spared for an enemy of the Reich, so Callison had to rely on the kindly medico who, through the intervention of the Red Cross, was given permission to receive instructional articles on how to preform interim surgery on the disfigured Allied airman.

Henschell shrugged. "Very well then, I will tell you. The uniforms in which the dead were clothed are those of the Polish Army. Fur coats, leather jackets, pullovers, and caps—winter-issue items worn only by commissioned officers. Cavalry boots on the corpses are well-fitting and, similarly, of a shape worn only by the Polish officer corps."

The German returned to his chair. Seated, he took a languorous sip of coffee before he continued. "The highest awards for gallantry were found on many of the dead: Silver Cross. *Virtuti Militari*. Polish Cross of Merit. Cross of Valor. There are even the remains of Catholic priests. Most critically, the documents, diaries, correspondence, and newspapers found on the bodies prove conclusively that the victims were murdered during the months of March, April, and May of 1940."

Henschell paused. "Do you wish to know who the killers of your gallant Allies are?"

"No," Callison replied, sensing a trap. "No, I do not."

Henschell opened a cerise folder on his desk and continued as if he hadn't heard. "I have here before me the summation of an autopsy conducted on one of the corpses by Doctor Ference Orsos. The man is an eminent pathologist and currently director of the Department of Forensic Medicine at the University of Budapest. Until we can properly confirm its identity, we've assigned this cadaver an arbitrary number. Corpse 72."

He looked up matter-of-factly. "I've taken the liberty of having the good doctor's notes translated into English. I will provide you a copy if you wish."

Silence.

Stolidly, in near-perfect English, Henschell began reading the notes:

The bodies are packed together, cemented in a way by fluids from the process of decay. The heads are face down. One body facing one way, the next the other, the next back again for the entire width of the grave for twelve layers down, then multiplied by its length. I estimate approximately 2,870 corpses in the one gravesite alone. It is a solid mass in which I saw just skulls.

I went into the graves and studied which one would give me the best information, what a single dead body could tell us of its companions. With the help of two Russian peasants I picked a body, and gradually—it took them close to an hour—they exhumed it.

During my autopsy, I examined this body very carefully

to determine two main points. First, what the cause of death was. Second, the period of time this individual had been buried. The third salient issue—who he actually was—will take some time to determine. For now, the corpse has been assigned a number: 246.

Numerous stab-marks were discovered on deceased number 246. These appear to be inflicted by a dagger-like weapon corresponding to the fluted Russian bayonet, yet the actual cause of death is a pistol shot to the head. The entry point of the bullet is below the protrusion at the back of the skull. The exit is in the forehead above the eye. The nature of fissures of cranial bones and the fact that traces of powder were found at the entry orifice prove the shot was fired point-blank. Correlation of the point of entry and bullet exit show the shot was made from behind with the head bent forward. The bullet pierced vital parts of the brain, and death was caused by destruction of brain tissue.

Henschell stopped to observe Callison. He turned to a new page.

None of the bodies I observed is in a condition of decay or disintegration. All of the 925 bodies we have exposed thus far are in a state of preservation. Corpse 246 is in the initial phase of body desiccation. This is clearly expressed in the thorax region and abdomen. It is also in the initial stages of adipocere.

Especially noteworthy is the fact that muscles of the trunk and extremities are fully preserved in their macroscopic structure. Color almost normal. The internal organs of thorax and peritoneal cavity have preserved their configuration. Sections of heart muscle in Corpse 246 have a clearly discernible structure and specific coloration, while the brain presented characteristic structural peculiarities with a distinctly discernible border between the gray and white matter.

A crust, composed of layers of necrotic structure, has formed around the surface of this man's brain. It has turned into uniform clay-like pulp. I note especially that bodies that have been in graves less than three years do not exhibit this condition."

Henschell closed the file. "We are done here. It is time for you to go."

"Go?" Callison answered, visibly confused by the abrupt dismissal.

Henschell sighed. "Flight Lieutenant Callison. You have been acutely injured in combat. Accordingly, once you leave this office, you will be escorted to a waiting aircraft and flown to Portugal in a manner befitting an officer and gentleman. In Lisbon, you will board an Allied hospital ship bound for England as part of an exchange involving Italian and British prisoners of war."

"And then?"

"Well . . ." The German smiled disingenuously. "Upon arrival in the United Kingdom, I naturally assume you would report to your superiors what you have seen and heard here at Katyn."

Callison remained silent.

"You see, four days from now Radio Berlin will broadcast a critical communication to the world. An announcer will state that German authorities have made a shocking discovery here at Katyn—a 28-meter-long by 16-meter-wide grave containing the corpses of three thousand Polish military officers. Each buried in full military uniform. Each with a fatal wound caused by a single shot to the back of the head. It will not be terribly difficult to identify the nationality and martial profession of the dead since they have been mummified through unique properties residing in the local soil. Moreover, the Ivans foolishly did not confiscate their personal papers. And, most critically, the total number of corpses unearthed is about ten thousand, which roughly approximates the size of the Polish officer corps taken prisoner by the NKVD in 1939."

Callison sat up in his seat. "Your press release will prove nothing," he protested. "Nothing but that you have committed these murders yourselves and are now attempting to cover them up!"

"Do you really think that Mr. Callison? You can plainly see the evidence. It is just as the great Sherlock Holmes once so aptly observed: 'When you have eliminated the impossible, whatever remains, *however improbable*, must be the truth.' And you, Flight Lieutenant, are confronting it."

Henschell's tone changed perceptively. "Think about what I have told you. Think about it very carefully. When your superiors hear the Radio Berlin broadcast, you will be questioned about what you witnessed here. Will you deny you were here? That you did not receive this briefing? That these pitiful corpses don't exist?"

Henschell reached for the phone. "Norbert," he barked, "Advise the *Hauptmann* that our guest is ready to leave. Yes, now. Oh, and Corporal, contact the air base. Ensure that the Condor is fueled and ready for take-off within the hour. It will have only two passengers—*Hauptmann* Schneider and the American."

* * *

After a meal served in the officers' mess, Henschell religiously visited the diggings daily, including on Sundays. Arriving at a timbered viewing gallery located at the edge of the pits, he would stare vacantly down at press gangs of gypsies mechanically prying each rotting skeleton out of its frozen earthen sepulcher. The stench nauseated him, but he dared not show it. It was unbecoming for a member of the *Shutzstaffel* to exhibit such weakness—particularly before *Untermensch*.

Nearby, beneath open tents, skilled forensic experts carried out the gruesome task of determining the individual causes of death. Each body was placed on an examining table and assessed. After a time, the verdict became ominously repetitive. Bullet to the back of the head. Bullet to the back of the head. Bullet after bullet. And each one, nine grams of unforgiving lead.

The individual identifications followed a similarly monotonous pattern. Pockets and boots were cut open and their contents meticulously placed into drab manila envelopes. All envelopes were then placed in large wooden crates for long-term storage. In the end, there would be nine crates in total, each sequentially numbered. After this material separation process was complete, the violated cadavers were reburied in huge common graves to share for all eternity.

**Katyn Forest,
14 April 1943**

It was late afternoon when the stranger arrived at the Katyn site. Meticulously escorted by two leather-coated Gestapo officials, the man entered the room, walking with a pronounced limp. He was tall, dressed in a scruffy army greatcoat and patchy homburg, yet he had a disciplined presence about him that Henschell sensed. A threadbare turtleneck sweater exposed an ugly scar just behind the right ear and down the man's neck. He tersely introduced himself in flawless German as Kazimierz Matuszek, a senior official of the Polish Red Cross.

Henschell was fully aware that the humanitarian agency had studiously avoided being in the first delegation of prominent Poles who had visited the site on the tenth of April, ever so careful not to be perceived as being party to an elaborate Nazi propaganda stunt. He also knew that the evidence was damning. After examining two pits containing 250 mummified corpses, in addition to being allowed to examine documents taken from the bodies, the Polish delegation had reluctantly come to accept that, ostensibly, it was their Russian allies and not the hated Germans who had committed this atrocity. Berlin had also determined through neutral diplomatic channels that the Polish government-in-exile in London had accepted the evidence and convinced the Polish Red Cross to co-operate in the investigation. Their British and American Allies were not nearly as supportive.

Their initial conversation was stilted. Matuszek's reticence extended to personal information about himself. When pressed, he acknowledged that he had been a commissioned officer on Poland's eastern frontiers in 1939 and that he had been captured by the Russians. But for the grace of God, he would have been found here in this bleak lingering expanse of violent death.

He offered no more information about himself, and Henschell did not press.

In the end, Matuszek allowed that he would provide a ten-member technical group to view the Katyn dead, but that its role was to be confined to the identification and reburial of bodies and the return of the victims' possessions to their families. And nothing more.

For his part, Henschell was accommodating. Arrangements would be made for Herr Matuszek and members of the Polish Red Cross to return to the site for inspections in the next two days. German air and ground transport would be provided from Warsaw, where the Red Cross had its headquarters. His second-in-command, Schneider, would be the Polish group's traveling companion on this mission to ensure that all went well.

The Pole's eyes betrayed little, yet Henschell detected a flash of anger in them. "We do not require the close intervention of the *Wehrmacht* to visit the final resting place of our fallen brothers," he bristled.

Henschell was momentarily taken aback, but quickly recovered himself. He was, after all the victor and this utterly useless cripple, the vanquished.

"But you do require the means to get here, Matuszek—transportation that only the Third Reich can provide. After all, you cannot call on your famed Polish cavalry anymore now, can you?"

A weary flick of the wrist and the Pole was hurried out, dismissed like a troublesome gnat. The Führer was right. They were indeed a pestilence.

Aboard *Luftwaffe* Junkers 52, identification letters A-RX, Departed Warsaw, arriving near Katyn Village, Belarus, German-Occupied Zone
17 April 1943

The Junkers trimotor labored though pea-soup fog before bouncing to a careening stop at the very edge of a frozen-mud runway recently built in a cutaway forest by German army engineers. On board the transport was a Polish Red Cross team comprised of forensic specialists and lab assistants who'd worked at Jagiellonian University prior to its arbitrary closure by the Nazis in November 1939. The specialists were a grab bag of experts from lesser-known universities and polytechnics. The lab assistants were the lucky ones, for most of the 184 faculty of the Jagiellonian had been arrested and deported to *Sachsenhausen* concentration camp, where many languished and some died. Also included in the ensemble were individuals representing the Catholic *Caritas* charity.

Kazimierz Matuszek headed the Polish group. Accompanying them was the ever-present Schneider. Arrangements for their involvement in the macabre project had carried with it several hard and fast conditions. The undertakings had been readily agreed to by the German High Command, which exploited the propaganda value of its deference to a haplessly defeated nation.

During the two-and-a-half-hour flight from Warsaw, Schneider made a point of attempting to befriend the Polish team, but he soon found out that he was wasting his breath. The Poles were understandably reluctant to communicate in any way, shape, or form with their Aryan conquerors. The only individual who would even speak to him was Matuszek.

Their initial conversations on that first meeting had been strained at best, but they had gradually reached an understanding, as battleweary enemies sometimes do. While they hated each other, it was apparent that they hated the Ivans more.

After a tour of the site, the Red Cross team was escorted to a wooden barracks block, guarded day and night by heavily armed *Wehrmacht* personnel "to protect the distinguished Polish visitors from packs of wolves lurking in the forest." This was to be their home for the precious few weeks they were to be at Katyn.

At daybreak, after a hearty breakfast largely left untouched, the team was taken to one of the excavated pits—Grave #1—where they began what would soon become a gruesomely repetitive regimen.

Commission members climbed into the pit to select individual bodies for removal at random. Russian peasants used picks and hooks to pry the corpses loose. Because of the great compression caused by the collective mass, the removal of a single body might take more than hour.

Once a corpse was separated from the putrid mass, it was taken on a stretcher and laid in a clearing with other decaying cadavers. Then, in as much of a sequence as could be followed, it was placed on a makeshift examination table for the attending Poles to conduct their due diligence under the ever-watchful eyes of German military personnel.

The corpse was first given a sequential identification number. Next, an inspection was conducted to retrieve documents and personal objects. The corpse's pockets were cut open and searched; knee-length cavalry boots were slit open. All rings, medals, military passes and identification cards, Polish *zloty*, newspaper clippings, diaries, religious items, and personal effects were placed in evidence bags with markings that matched the corpse's body identification number. All possessions of the deceased that could be identified were securely stored for immediate transfer to a lab, where they would undergo a more detailed analysis that might assist in determining the actual time of death.

Schneider stood to at the edge of the site for the entire day, hidden by a stand of fir, studiously observing everything that the Polish team did.

At one point, he saw Matuszek walk to a spot somewhere behind the resection table, where he had a rather animated discussion with a *Wehrmacht* corporal who was itemizing the evidence bags before placing them into larger receptacles. It was the only time Matuszek had moved from his original station to one side of the examination area. The discussion piqued Schneider's interest. After a respectable interlude, he sauntered over to the resection table.

"Corporal?" he asked quietly. "What did that Pole want?"

"He was rather curious about Body 865, sir," the enlisted man offered. "He asked if there was any identifiable clothing that we could salvage from the cadaver. He seemed particularly interested in a greatcoat."

"And?"

The corporal shrugged. "I told him, yes, Body 865 had worn a greatcoat."

"Did that satisfy him?"

The corporal appeared genuinely perplexed. "Well, somewhat, *Herr Hauptmann*. The Pole then asked to see the evidence packet for Body 865 as I was preparing it. The coat and other personal effects had been inspected by the Polish forensic team and were to be included in the items I was readying for evidential review."

The corporal paused awkwardly, and then continued, carefully parroting the exact words from the briefing he'd been given earlier in the day. "There appear to be discrepancies in the evidence we found that will require further analysis."

"Those are our instructions, *Hauptmann*," he lamely ended the justification for his actions.

"Body 865 has a name?"

The corporal glanced over his tally sheet. "Yes, *Hauptmann*. Ryszard Franciczek Manel."

Schneider discreetly walked to the Red Cross observer team and gently tapped Matuszek on the shoulder. "May I speak to you, sir? Privately?"

The Pole's eyes glazed over. After a time, he nodded and followed the German back to the anonymous copse of firs where they lingered for a time, side by side.

After a theatrical pause that appeared only to heighten the tension, Schneider spoke. "You are interested in Body 865, Matuszek. An individual who appears to bear the name Manel." A lengthy silence ensued as the German observed the Pole's reaction. Seeing only a blank stare, he probed further. "I believe his rank has been determined as captain."

Matuszek appeared nonplussed. "Yes," he responded. "Ryszard. I saw the name on the list when I went over to the desk to do a routine check. The name is familiar. I believe I know his family from Warsaw."

"You asked to see his greatcoat." The German delved deeper. "May I ask you why?"

Matuszek shrugged it off. "A natural enough request given these circumstances, *Hauptmann*. I was hoping to find something to confirm that Ryszard Manel was murdered here at Katyn. I owe it to the family, don't you think?"

"Is that all?"

Matuszek suddenly snapped. "Yes," he bristled. "Compassion is my motive. An officer's compassion for a fallen comrade. Is that not enough? Or is our presence here merely a propaganda coup for Goebbels and your Ministry of Public Enlightenment?"

"No," the German astutely caught himself. "I can assure you that my interests here go beyond a mere propaganda victory. Please accept my sincere apologies."

He moved to leave, then turned gracefully. "Oh, and one last thing. As one participant in this unholy war to another, where did you say you were wounded? I don't believe you ever told either me or *Obersturmführer* Henschell."

"On the Eastern Front," the Pole countered dryly. "Fighting the Ivans. But you would already know that. Else I would never have been allowed to be here."

"The exact location?" Schneider pressed.

"Tarnopol. The seventeenth of September 1941. The day the Soviet army came calling, uninvited, on Poland."

"Oh, yes," Schneider responded smoothly. "Once more, I profusely apologize for my tactlessness. That fact must have slipped my mind. More importantly, I just want you to know that you and I—we are both on the same side here. I am not your enemy, Matuszek. I mean you no harm." The German hesitated. "You might actually be surprised about my true intent," he paused and caught himself.

"Am I free to go, *Hauptmann*?" the Pole responded coldly.

"Certainly. You may return to the observation station. To watch and to learn."

As agreed in the protocol, the Condor left for Warsaw after dusk on the fourth week, with its full complement of Polish Red Cross officials, its sleek pencil-thin form soon to be undistinguishable in a moonless night.

For the return journey to the Polish capital, Schneider had shrewdly delegated the task of custodians to a duo of ambitious German lieutenants with ready familiarity of the Polish language, inasmuch as they were *Volksdeutsche* from Danzig. He was certain their innate hatred for all things Polish would be tempered by a greater and realistic fear of his wrath if they did not follow his explicit instructions.

Lip service to the term "diplomatic courtesy" would always be extended to their "Polish guests" but, as with all such unwritten nuances of "diplomacy," it would be duplicitous and self-serving. Accordingly, he expected extensive reports on the flight by noon on the date of their return. Of interest would be anything they could discover about the enigmatic Kazimierz Matuszek.

The two lieutenants entered his office three days later with a comprehensive report of what they had found. The Poles on the Condor had been understandably reluctant to reveal anything of import. Still, somehow the two were able to industriously piece together the semblance of a credible paper trail.

Their conclusion?

Kazimierz Matuszek had been a very recent addition to the Polish Red Cross team, parachuted into Poland and assigned a mission of some consequence by the Polish Underground.

This nugget of information dovetailed nicely with what Schneider had already unearthed. Records of the short-lived Battle of Tarnopol, with the names, ranks, and serial numbers of all Polish soldiers captured, killed, or missing during the defense of that city were readily provided in 1939 by the Russians to their then-German allies.

Yet the name Kazimierz Matuszek was nowhere to be found in the records.

So, who was this man Matuszek? Why was he so interested in Body 865—Ryszard Franciczek Manel—if that was even the corpse's identity? And then there was the question of the officer's greatcoat? What made that item of clothing so important?

111

Schneider resolved to contact his clandestine mentor in Warsaw with his findings rather than report to Henschell. His message was entrusted to a *Wehrmacht* sergeant scheduled to board a Junkers courier plane to Warsaw.

As were most communications from the German camp at Katyn, the item was intercepted by the NKVD, and a copy of its contents was soon on the desk of Captain Nadia Fedin, who reviewed the document before her. There was a key element missing. For safety's sake, the compromised piece was still being "hand delivered" by the *Wehrmacht* sergeant. It was an old trick in spy craft that she herself had used. Two elements were never joined to form a whole until they reached their principal recipient.

* * *

In 1917, Ludwig Schneider, a Ruhr coal miner and humble eighteen-year-old youth, was gassed at Cambrai while obeying the bizarre orders of a fanatical Prussian *Hauptmann,* who ranted and raved about cowardice. Ludwig Schneider survived the war, but not the gas that sent him to an early grave.

Still, he had been fortunate enough to see his wife Trudy give birth to a healthy son Dirk three years after the Armistice, and to have been with Dirk for five years before his lungs rotted to the core.

His mother's good looks and quiet desperation in the face of widowed poverty had ensured her remarriage in short order to Gustaf Bach, a middle-aged shopkeeper in the small market town of Berchum, a mouse of a man who was afraid of his own shadow. Yet for such a timid individual, Bach turned into a raging lion when he donned the brown shirt of the fledgling *Sturmabteilung*—the storm detachment of an unknown street orator named Adolf Hitler. And from that point onward, Dirk Schneider's gradual arc into the ironclad arms of National Socialism began.

Young and impressionable, Dirk effortlessly followed the path of millions of like-minded German *volk.* As he grew into adulthood, he qualified and became a *Wehrmacht* officer naively loyal to the Führer and all that he had come to represent for the future well-being of the resurgent German people and emerging Third Reich. In tribute to his late father, he had petitioned for, and been allowed to retain, his birth surname of Schneider. Neither his mother nor stepfather had seen fit to complain.

Upon graduation, Schneider was posted to an armored reconnaissance squadron commanding rifle troops, their firepower complemented by several MG 34s. To ensure total mobility, the squadron employed sidecar mounts on all its motorcycles.

But with dizzying familiarity, and before he had even gotten to know the first names of many of his NCOs, a global war began again.

From the vainglorious crushing of an upstart Poland to the adrenalin-inducing victory dash across France and equally satisfying enslavement of the Balkans and Yugoslavia, Dirk Schneider's combat skills and those of the men in his reconnaissance battalion were rarely tested. Throughout this relentless onslaught, German army morale was remarkably high, casualty figures, correspondingly low.

Until Russia.

Even then, Schneider and his reconnaissance battalion seemed to live a charmed life. They originally began as part of the wasp-like swarm that crushed Poland and then went on to operate in a policing action to counter Polish Underground activity in the area of Dzików Stary in southeast Poland.

Then, on the summer solstice of 1941, when the Operation Barbarossa, the Nazi invasion of Soviet Russia, began, they became part of the Army Group South tasked with advancing through Galicia and into the Ukraine. With lightning speed, the ancient city of Kiev surrendered, and 400,000 Soviet prisoners were taken.

Army Group South next advanced relentlessly through Kharkov, Kursk, and Stalino and thence into the Crimea, where they were engaged in the bloody siege of Sevastopol. In November, they took Rostov, the gateway to the Caucasus. Elsewhere, Hitler's determined drive to capture the Russian capital city of Moscow failed. To Schneider and his colleagues, it mattered little. They were intent only on staying alive.

Army Group South's next goal was the oilfields of Baku, capital of the Soviet Republic of Azerbaijan, which Hitler mistakenly assumed would quench the thirst of his massive *Panzer* armada.

But then, in an ominous change of fortune, Schneider and his recce unit were ordered to leave their motorcycles idling behind to become one of many feeder units into the emerging meat grinder that was

Stalingrad. And Dirk Schneider's world changed forever.

In less than three weeks, he had lost two-thirds of his men—killed, wounded, or missing. Those that remained were hollow-eyed shadows; nothing more than walking dead in tattered *Feldgrau* uniform. Of the wounded, only those who had lost an arm or a leg, were blinded, or had gone mad were not forced to return to their decimated unit inside *der Kessel*—the Stalingrad Cauldron.

On what should have been a placid Sunday morning stroll through his home village of Berchum, Schneider was instead elsewhere, lying badly wounded after single-handedly attacking a brutally efficient machine-gun post in the blood-drenched rubble of the Stalingrad Tank Plant. Left for dead, his life was saved by a fleet-footed young *soldat*, a private named Weber. A shy, unassuming eighteen-year-old who avidly played chess and lived with his parents, Weber's father had also been a coal miner. The boy had been with the battalion for only eight months. He hadn't even begun to properly shave.

Schneider was extremely fortunate to be evacuated from the Cauldron. He was surprised to see Weber on the same dilapidated Junkers trimotor as it ferried them 250 kilometers from the raging battle to Tatsinskaya airfield and the relative safety of the German lines.

After the briefest of stops in a *Luftwaffe* field infirmary, Schneider was swiftly moved to a military hospital at Wünsdorf in the leafy eastern suburbs of the German capital, where he was treated as a conquering hero and not the fortunate escapee from the Cauldron that he was.

After a month, he was deemed fit to be presented to a naive and fawning public. At a set-piece military ceremony on the massive parade square, Schneider, along with nine other officers representing various theaters of war, was publicly awarded an Iron Cross—Second Class—presented by an ancient tone-deaf Brigadier-General Judiciary who proclaimed the young man to be one of the true heroes of the Battle of Stalingrad. Young *Landser* Wolfgang Weber, standing ramrod straight behind the officers among two dozen rank and file recipients, received the same medal for saving Schneider's life, but without similar laudatory comments.

Their movement orders arrived the next morning. Schneider was to be posted to Warsaw to work for a colonel on a special project, while Weber, a mere "Other Rank," was being sent back to the wretched killing field that Stalingrad had become.

That night, Schneider took the ordinary soldier who had saved his life to dinner at Berlin's legendary Hotel Adlon. With its sustained air of decadence, its famed elephant fountain, gold-leaf coffered ceilings, and stained-glass cupola, and located, as it was, on the Unter den Linden adjacent to the Brandenburg Gate, the Adlon was the premier choice for Nazi Party dignitaries and high-ranking military.

The maître d' in the hotel's Grande Restaurante was initially somewhat indifferent to the young officer's request for seating. However, the thickset Swabian had learned long ago to treat each "visitor" with superficial respect until he had a final determination as to their suitability for admission. As such, he astutely sized up his two prospective guests.

Iron Crosses within the hallowed spaces of the Adlon were as numerous as the linden trees blooming each June on the celebrated thoroughfare outside. But the maître d' could see that the medal the lieutenant wore was newly minted and his *feldgrau* uniform was well worn, not "wedding-cake ornamental" as were those sported by many other military types in the sheltered German capital. The man standing politely before him was therefore in all probability a real soldier of the Reich, compared to the pretenders who populated his illustrious dining room. The boy soldier with the inquiring officer was scarcely worth a passing glance, until the maître d' had noticed a similar Iron Cross on the lad's shabby, but neatly pressed, tunic. He nodded politely for them to follow. They had passed muster.

Heads discreetly turned to look as the two soldiers made their way into the dining room. Staff officers cast looks of studied dismay at the presence of an inconsequential infantry *Leutnant* trailed by an enlisted man—and a callow youth at that—within their closely guarded preserve. But they were judiciously tempered by the sight of the medals dangling from their chests. Party functionaries were not nearly as kind or discerning, as a rippled muttering continued to follow their progress through the room.

Schneider and his subordinate were shepherded to a small, two-place setting in a quiet raised corner, far from the orchestra. This spot was not too ostentatious to offend the various well-placed members of the General Staff and not too demeaning to belittle the right of passage that the Iron Cross ostensibly afforded these low-ranking intruders.

As Theo Reuter and his thirty-five-piece orchestra romanced the diners with lush big-band pieces approved by the Propaganda Ministry, white-jacketed waiters flitted about the tables.

Weber seemed overwhelmed by the grandeur of it all, so Schneider ordered for them. A bottle of Kronenburg Reisling circa 1933, a platter of cheeses, and a main course of roast beef, baked potatoes, and vegetables, à la carte. Then they sat back to enjoy the fine wine, lavish music, and ambience of the place.

A heated discussion was developing by the dance floor just below their table—an after-dinner disagreement about the ongoing battle of Stalingrad, aggressively fueled by profuse quantities of schnapps and vodka. Tellingly, the six members at the table all wore the raven-black uniforms of the *Waffen SS*. And the more they drank, the louder their disagreement became.

One individual, a rat-featured *Obersturmführer*, ruled the table. The fawning responses to his utterances only seemed to stimulate his mounting rage.

The drunken SS officer became louder and more obnoxious by the minute until the orchestra stopped playing and much of the room turned in his direction. No one attempted to silence him. He did not appear overly tall, but there was palpable menace in his voice. Finally, the man stood up and addressed the room, swaying slightly as he did so.

"Ladies and gentlemen," the *Obersturmführer* slurred, holding a half-filled glass of vodka in an outstretched hand. "My comrades and I were just having a discussion, and I wish to know your opinion. I believe that the moral degenerates who serve with Paulus and his Sixth Army at Stalingrad are not worthy of wearing the uniform of the Third Reich. They are incompetently led cowards. The Sixth Army should have been victorious months ago!" He brushed a sloppy hand over his mouth before continuing. "Is there anyone present in the High Command who disagrees with me?"

An awkward hush filled the dining room, the kind that in polite company permeates a place when someone loudly relates a deplorably rude joke. No one breathed a word.

"Good." The SS officer swayed slightly as his bloodshot eyes moved lazily about. "Any *Wehrmacht* toadies who dare to differ with me?"

An unnerving silence.

The drunk's eyes scanned the dining room and seized upon Schneider and Weber, both sitting calmly at the table behind him.

"You." He pointed a wavering finger at Schneider. "I see that you wear an Iron Cross. Just as I do. In fact"—he gestured arrogantly to his heavily medaled chest—"I appear to have a number of them. Nonetheless," he raised his glass in mock honor, "I salute you."

He drew the glass up into an exaggerated toast, downed the vodka, and poured himself another, spilling most of its contents onto the table as his drunken comrades laughed uproariously. "May I ask where you received this prestigious award?"

Schneider stood up and faced his superior officer. "Stalingrad," he remarked with unruffled pride.

The *Obersturmführer's* fixed smile abruptly disappeared. "Then you are a cowardly swine," he hissed. "You and your men should have defeated those bastard Ivans long ago. I know my unit would have done so and danced on their graves."

Young Weber rose from his chair and moved to Schneider's side.

The *Obersturmführer's* mood abruptly changed as he seemed to assess the two soldiers. "Is this young boy your 'friend?'" he remarked slyly. "Boy-friend?" he repeated for emphasis as he scanned the audience. "Now, we all know what that means *Hauptmann,* don't we?"

Schneider's gaze was steady and direct, and bore no sign of acknowledgment.

"Don't you know who I am, son?" he thundered. "I am Oskar Dirlewanger. *Obersturmführer* Dirlewanger to you, *Hauptmann!* You have not heard of me?"

The room turned deathly still. Anxious eyes jumped from table to table. Chairs shuffled awkwardly. Dropped dinnerware clinked on porcelain. An uneasy cough from the far end of the dining room.

"Oh, rest assured, I know of you," Schneider responded calmly. "Perhaps more than any decent human should. When my unit made its way through Poland and into Ukraine to join the Army of General Paulus, we passed through a town called Stary Dzików. There we learned of you and your toadies, that pathetic bunch of *Sonderkommando* thugs that you dare to call soldiers. It is common knowledge that you were commandant of a labor camp in that town. Moreover, while in command, you were the subject of an abuse investigation by Judge Morgen of the *Hauptamnt SS Gericht.* You stood accused of murder, corruption, and other detestable acts by the SS Court Head Office, indictments besmirching the dignity and honor of all true officers of the Reich.

Ultimately, the only thing that appears to have saved your sorry soul from an SS trial was a late-night phone call from some spineless uniformed Berlin mandarin intervening on your behalf."

On hearing those words, something inside the SS *Obersturmführer* snapped. He charged toward the two soldiers with the fury of someone possessed, tripped over his chair, and fell awkwardly to the floor.

Schneider and the young private stood their ground. They had confronted the enemy before but never seen it in their own ranks.

"Why you little bastard!" Dirlewanger screamed in frustration as he crawled drunkenly forward on all fours. "You Jew-loving pig!"

Swiftly, three of his dinner companions grabbed their commander by the arms and forcefully started to remove the struggling SS officer to the exit. They realized, even in their drunken fog, that in a room full of high-ranking Nazis bosses, even one as feared as Dirlewanger, could not benefit from such an attention-drawing incident.

He struggled vainly to break their hold and, for a moment at the main entrance, he achieved his goal. He turned back to face the room. "You think you can preach to me you sniveling little kike kisser!" he shrieked. "Beware, *Hauptmann*. I will get you for this insult to my honor. And in ways that you cannot begin to imagine."

And then without any further assistance, the SS officer marched out the door, his black riding boots thundering in a parade cadence on the tiled floor.

Schneider awoke at daybreak the next morning and, after a light breakfast in the officers' mess, he returned to his quarters and prepared his kit for travel. When he finished, he sat down in a leather armchair and luxuriated in a Turkish cigarette. Then feeling drowsy, he drifted off to asleep. Schneider was not overly concerned; he was packed, and his flight was not due till late afternoon when he would hitch a ride on the *Wehrmacht* mail run to Warsaw.

At around three o'clock in the afternoon, there was a knock on his door. Schneider opened it, expecting a driver to take him to the *Luftwaffe* airfield situated in the Wünsdorf military complex. Instead, he confronted the building orderly, who saluted primly, handed him a plain envelope addressed to "*Hauptmann* Dirk Schneider," smartly about-faced. and then departed.

Inside the envelope was a note written in a childlike scrawl.

My dear Dirk,

As a small token of my "esteem" for your foolhardy attempt to challenge me at the Hotel Adlon last night, I am pleased to inform you of the following.

Your boy soldat: For an act of transparent insubordination, he has been reassigned from the suicide mission that the Paulus Sixth Army has become at Stalingrad. Instead, he has been sent to a Strafbatallion in Montenegro. As you must surely acknowledge, he insolently challenged my rank by actively taking your side in what was clearly a professional disagreement between two officers.

The Strafbatallion in question is currently engaged in anti-partisan patrols with a mortality rate of 40 per cent. If the boy serves well, he will certainly receive more medals, as well as experience in proper discipline. If not, there is always someone to take his place.

Understandably you must wonder why this transfer does not apply to you, my young "friend."

It is, as I told you during our discussions, you are the recipient of an Iron Cross and I will respect that, if not the person wearing it.

Did you know Dirk, that in the autumn of 1914, the Sixteenth Bavarian Reserve was one of hundreds of German units decimated in the month-long Battle of Ypres? The Sixteenth marched into action with 3,600 men; by the end, fewer than 600 were still standing.

One soldier, a twenty-five-year-old volunteer who'd enlisted in the Sixteenth only three months before had received the Iron Cross, Second Class, for his part in that battle. His name was Adolf Hitler! When I met the Führer for breakfast this morning, he told me that receiving that medal was the happiest day of his life. Of course, we had other more discreet discussions, as we always do when we meet. I certainly mentioned you.

A word of warning. Be careful, mein kleines kamerad. Be very careful. Rest assured that my respect for an officer of the Wehrmacht is non-existent. Two inches of iron on your chest is all that is keeping you from the same fate as your young soldat.

Oskar P. Dirlewanger,
Obersturmführer-SS
Sonderkommando Dirlewanger

PS: If I am not mistaken, your mother lives in the village of Ber-
chum just south of Dortmund. I certainly hope she will be safe. It
would be truly regrettable if something happened to her because of
some ill-chosen words by members of her family, don't you think?

Schneider paused a moment, then put the note back in the envelope and placed it in the breast pocket of his tunic. He recalled his
dead father's words about men such as Dirlewanger. Once they were
allowed to indulge in actions accorded that style of leadership, and
with impunity, they were extremely dangerous. His father had been
damned to an early death by such a fool. Schneider had already seen
the writing on the wall in Stalingrad. But now as he saw that a creature
like Dirlewanger had been given such liberties that even the dreaded
SS Court could not touch him, the rot had reached the very top, and
an honorable German was no longer safe.

CHAPTER 7

Grand Square of Kraków—Adolf Hitler Platz,
Generalgouvernement für die besetzten
polnischen Gebiete
19 April 1943

Sister Maria Elzbieta moved unsteadily in the pre-dawn darkness, her starched veil buffeted by a harsh east wind. She was old, four years past seventy, and the cobblestones wore hard on her high-laced boots. She ached from the ever-present dampness within the convent she had just left. A cold April drizzle bit relentlessly into her exposed skin. In these, the blackest hours of the Nazi occupation, her Mother Superior had wisely rationed the meager lumps of heating coal that remained, but at a truly exacting price for the older nuns. She offered up her suffering as a penance. There was much greater misery in the world of late than an old woman's afflictions.

The coming dawn proved to be but cheerless gauze on a formless horizon. Steely clouds draped the ancient tower that loomed before her. A cyclist struggled past, legs stubbornly churning in the blustery weather.

The Grand Square of Kraków—the *Rynek Glowny*—spread out before the elderly nun. At ten acres, it was the largest of its kind in all of Europe's medieval cities and, as with all things involving grandeur under the Nazi occupation, it was renamed Adolf Hitler Platz. Sister Maria Elzbieta glanced furtively about. There was not a creature in sight, save for the rock pigeons and the ever-present pairs of Nazi troopers.

The ancient square, designed in 1257, once hosted merchant caravans traveling from the German principalities in the west to points east at Kiev and Marienburg, and flourishing communities along the Danube basin. Located on the coronation route between the Barbican of Kraków and Wawel Castle, the square was considered the center of the city and its social life from its very inception. Among the square's landmarks were a sixteenth-century cloth-trading hall and St. Mary's Basilica, a fourteenth-century brick Gothic church. A number of aristocratic palaces formed a dusty pastel boundary. They were now inhabited by German officers serving on the administrative staff of the Occupation Directorate. In the southern corner, squatting like a stone turtle, stood the tiny eleventh-century church of Saint Wojciech.

Sister Elzbieta was a Felician. Her order had provided devoted service to Saint Wojciech's, preparing its altar for daily Mass since 1855. And today would be no exception. She peered up at the tower—thirty-five minutes past seven. Ample time for the eight o'clock morning service—the earliest public event allowed under the rules of Nazi occupation. A German guard nodded brusquely as she passed by. She did not return the terse acknowledgment.

The sound, when it first came, was a dull booming base, strangely insistent. Utterances emanating from huge speakers located along the perimeter of the venerable square. Name after name began to fill the chill dawn air. First in German then in perfect Polish, a litany played out in slow and measured cadence: "Body number 789, Juliusz Arkady Maliszewski. Body number 790, Ignace Stephan Malys . . ."

The public address system was utilized by the Nazi General Government to assert its iron will over the citizens of Kraków. Daily, it parroted vitriol against Poles, Christians, and Jews alike, deriding their culture, race and, more ominously, in the case of Jews, their very existence. The remaining time was filled with Nazi propaganda that no one gave any credence to and the music of Wagner, which all had come to soundly detest. And there was no escaping it. On occasion, the speaker system would announce persons killed by the occupiers for any number of imagined transgressions. And often for none at all. Symbolic shootings. Ritual killings. Ten here. Fifty there. One hundred elsewhere in the hollow city. Put to death without trial, machine-gunned en masse in the cobbled streets of Warsaw. All to ensure that the strict order and blind discipline of the hated Nazi governor general, Hans Frank, were maintained.

But today there were more names than at other times. Many more.

Sister Elzbieta paused to adjust her rosary. She listened attentively, holding her breath. "Body number 863, Czesław Damien Maciejewski. Body number 865, Ryszard Franciczek Manel."

Manel? The elderly nun gasped, then discreetly crossed herself before scuttling into the church. The nave was dark and cold. There were only a few chairs remaining intact for the congregation, as most had been appropriated for firewood. A blood-red light danced frantically about the far wall. A votive candle in the sanctuary, it denoted the presence of Christ in the tabernacle. Her feet echoed on the uneven stone floor. Two spinsters slouched on their knees in the front pew loudly muttering ritual prayers to the Black Madonna. A man lurked in a darkened corner; crutches scratching the concrete, a pant leg pinned above the knee where a healthy limb had once existed. A Polish veteran of the 1939 invasion or a survivor of the current Nazi occupation? Elzbieta bit her lip. It was increasingly hard to tell.

She went into the sacristy, asked for, and received confession. The elderly priest was uncommonly attentive. When the nun left the cubicle, the priest returned to his living quarters having heard only one penitent. Later that morning, the priest re-entered the darkened sacristy and made his way haltingly to the altar. He mounted the marble steps and genuflected before the tabernacle where the hosts were stored. Inside, somewhere behind the chalices, he found the dog-eared notebook he sought. Tucking it into his cassock, he shuffled back to the rectory, his footsteps echoing hollowly through the now-deserted building.

Entering his sparse chamber, he drew the drapes so that the room was suitably dark. He shambled over to the Victrola gramophone that sat on a table by the door and placed a recording on the turntable. He patiently wound the mainspring, then took the needle and lowered it onto the outer rim of the record until it slid into the playing groove.

The sound was timid at first, then more pervasive, filling the room with melody. Chopin. The *Opus 58 Sonata*, something he knew the Nazi occupiers of Kraków would tolerate, if not actually approve of, inasmuch as it held the not-too-subtle overtones of Brahms in its structure.

The priest then removed a shabby suitcase from a corner of his wardrobe and gingerly opened it. He carefully arranged the contents—a BP-3 valve-based radio transceiver. With this, he could communicate with another Pole a thousand miles away at Station Number Eight, the top-secret Polish Military Wireless Unit located at Barnes Lodge, an estate in the village of King's Langley, a short train journey from London.

In the next seven minutes, the identity and whereabouts of Body 865 would be quickly forwarded with the usual efficiency from Station Eight via a fifty-six-strand cable to dedicated transmitters a few miles away at Chipperfield House. From there, it would travel through 50 miles of landline to a team of MI6 intelligence experts operating out of an imposing Edwardian house in secluded grounds in the English cathedral city of St. Albans, Hartfordshire.

* * *

For some time, the Polish government-in-exile had sensed a major rift developing between itself and its British and American counterparts. It certainly wasn't that Allied troops in the field and most of their commanders were not to be trusted; they were good and loyal comrades-in-arms. It was their political masters who were the source of increasing suspicion and unease in the Polish war room, located in the basement of 43 Eaton Place in the Belgravia district of London.

In early April, with that express concern in mind, General Wladislaw Sikorski, leader of the Polish government-in-exile and commander-in-chief of its armed forces, attended a private luncheon at Number 10 Downing Street with outright proof for his cigar-chomping British counterpart that the Soviets had murdered thousands of Polish officers and other prisoners in their custody. And, furthermore, that the dead had been buried in mass graves in the forests around Katyn.

Although the general had a wealth of evidence, Churchill's blunt reply was cruelly telling: "If they are dead, nothing you can do will bring them back."

As for the President of the United States? Sikorski's eyes in Washington observed that Roosevelt believed he could come to some understanding with Stalin. The President was convinced that he was a natural charmer whose consummate manipulative skills would prevail with "Uncle Joe" Stalin, thereby guaranteeing the British and Americans a favorable outcome in all matters of importance with the formidable Man of Steel. The incident at Katyn—whatever credence one could ascribe to it—was a potential spanner in the works. Tragically, for the Poles, the American President didn't know the real Josef Stalin. Or if he did, he didn't care to hear the truth. Katyn and the calculated murders of thousands of Poland's best and bravest? For the West, they had become regrettable collateral damage.

For the East, the real game had begun.

**University of Wisconsin,
Madison, Wisconsin
23 April 1943**

The staff reading room reeked of ancient books and stale pipe tobacco. It was a place where grown men could hide from the realities of a world torn asunder by war while they contemplated Plato and The Republic. Outside, an angry rain lashed at tidy mullioned windows, while inside, the slightly seedy chamber held the mildewed musk of irrelevant ideas shared by a brace of irrelevant middle-aged academics. The Madison campus of the University of Wisconsin in mid-April could be quite a dreary place.

The man sat in a sagging leather chair situated in a far corner of the room. Hunched over a recent *New York Times*, he read each article attentively. An item about Franklin Roosevelt dedicating the Jefferson Memorial in Washington on the 200th anniversary of the third American President's birth, complete with photo. A strategic piece about Montgomery's Eighth Army breaking through the Mareth Line in Tunisia. An article about the new wonder drug, penicillin.

He folded the newspaper and placed it on a side table. A few months before, he had begged a close friend—a theoretical physicist—to find him suitable war work. He knew he couldn't stand idly by any longer and not use his talent to actively confront the tyranny that was Nazism.

And then in the past week, out of nowhere, he had received a written invitation from a US Army general named Groves to join an unidentified government project in the American Southwest. He reached for a book he had just taken from the library to research the location—Santa Fe—and on the checkout card, he found the names of his Wisconsin colleagues Joan Hinton, David Frisch, and Joseph McKibben—all physicists whose sudden absence from campus had caused some remarks. He decided then and there, to accept the invitation. Stanislaus Ulam was finally going to war.

HM Hospital Ship *Newfoundland,*
Avonmouth Docks,
Bristol, Southwest England
23 April 1943

The hospital ship repatriating them from Lisbon in the prisoner exchange had landed in Avonmouth, a dreary port tucked in the nether regions of the Bristol Channel, on Good Friday. Callison had disembarked with 448 other wounded Allied personnel. He had gone through an intelligence debriefing managed by a puffy-cheeked, remustered artillery major who appeared indifferent to Callison's claims that he had personally seen damning evidence at Katyn that directly implicated the Soviets in mass murder.

"Impossible to confirm, old boy," the major had remonstrated breezily. "Certainly not by our trusted allies. Remember, lad," he cautioned, "Uncle Joe is on our side and he's lost millions fighting the Nazis while we stand by and twiddle our thumbs. For those at Whitehall, a few dead Poles are nothing by comparison."

"So, you aren't including my observations in your report?"

The eyes of the intelligence officer narrowed. "I will certainly forward this item up through proper channels as I would any observations made by returning POWs."

The major put his pen down and folded his hands across his chest, all good humor gone. "And strictly off the record as it relates to this Katyn thing," he offered sympathetically, "I'm not at all hopeful that anything I do commit to paper will be appreciated by our political masters. It just isn't in the cards. Sorry."

A kindly smile appeared on the portly major's face. "Now why don't you just go along and get yourself fixed up. Lord knows there's a lot to do to make you look right again. Or hadn't you noticed yourself in a mirror?"

En route to the main Katyn–Kraków Highway,
Belarus, German-Occupied Zone
9 June 1943

Shortly before ten o'clock on the morning of June 9, 1943, a small *Luftwaffe* land convoy departed from Katyn to begin a top-secret two-day journey to its destination, the State Institute of Forensic Medicine and Criminalistics, located at 7 Kopernik Street in Kraków. A pair of cargo vehicles held fourteen large plywood chests containing over 3,000 numbered envelopes, each involving items found on the corpses, as well as specific clothing remnants that could be positively identified and connected to a dead Polish officer.

Three lorries accompanied the acutely sensitive transport. Each sprouted a menacing MG42 machine gun above the driver's cabin, while another high-velocity weapon loomed viper-like from the tailgate. Each vehicle carried a contingent of weary and cramped SS soldiers. The tiny caravan was escorted by a phalanx of Puma armored cars.

Holding command position in the secure middle of the formation was a sleek gray Horch Phaeton, the opulent vehicle much favored by German staff officers. Inside it, *Obersturmführer* Paulus Henschell fidgeted impatiently with a pair of tan kid leather gloves he had purchased during a recent weekend in Budapest. A locked strongbox resting firmly at his side contained the tattered dairies of twenty-two murdered Polish officers, specially selected for their relative completeness and relevance.

His traveling companion had arrived under protest from Warsaw mere hours before, but Paulus Henschell was indifferent to the man's feelings. The leather gloves had captured his full and undivided attention. It was Berlin's wish that Kazimierz Matuszek, as a senior official of the Polish Red Cross, bear witness to all that was about to transpire in this burgeoning windfall of inculpatory evidence. And it would be so.

The convoy took a security-conscious fourteen hours to travel to its destination, arriving on Thursday in the late afternoon. They had stopped overnight in mid-journey at a relatively safe traveler's inn frequented by personnel from a nearby bomber base at Biala Podlaska.

Throughout the lengthy journey, Matuszek and Henschell shared no more than thirty words, until the major gave up trying to be even remotely civil to his tight-lipped guest. For his part, Matuszek seemed content with the stony silence. He was there as the principal representative of the Polish Red Cross to ensure that the evidence of Katyn was securely maintained. But, unbeknownst to his traveling companion, he had a second and equally important motive—to ensure that he knew exactly where the chests were to be stored within the labyrinth of rooms in the Institute of Forensic Medicine and Criminalistics prior to his departure.

It had been a grueling two-day trek to Kraków, and the cargo carried in the lorries had emitted a truly nauseating odor, which only intensified and necessitated a constant rotation of SS guards.

Nearer to five in the evening, they approached the center of the ancient city. Founded in the year 400 A.D. and dominated by the magnificence of Wawel Castle, Kraków had surrendered to surging German armed forces without a fight on Wednesday, September 6, 1939. Less than a week later, it was made the capital of the new General Government. A territorial entity created and ruled by Nazi Germany, the Government was ordained by Hitler to become the principal base for his eastern thrust into Ukraine and Soviet Russia.

Matuszek gazed numbly out of the car's back seat at what was once the thriving heart of Kraków. It was, for all intents and purposes, a "normal day" in the German Occupation, if the constant Nazi foot patrols and armored vehicles scooting about the narrow streets and alleyways of the Old Town could ever be considered "normal." Certainly, the local population possessed a resigned drabness that said more than mere words could express.

A sharp turn here, another one, a hairpin, there. The accelerating convoy swiftly approached its destination, the State Institute of Forensic Medicine and Criminalistics, ably assisted by *Feldgendarmerie* personnel, who theatrically stopped all traffic at strategic city intersections with huge red traffic paddles to enable the caravan to pass through.

Since the turn of the century, the elegant baroque building housing the Institute had been located in a refined neighborhood close to the slopes of Wawel castle. Etched in impenetrable granite, its motto "Justitia et Scientia" dominated a gabled facade. A sprawling staircase leading up to the main portico only seemed to accent the importance of its scholarly enterprise.

Its outward appearances were deceiving for, by 1943, no justice and precious little science functioned within its austere confines. The Institute conducted thousands of autopsies on the remains of persons who died of unknown causes within the boundaries of the General Government. Ironically, in what was the ultimate perversion of Teutonic efficiency, the Nazi overlords had coupled the highly organized mass killings of innocents with a macabre preoccupation with minutely codifying every cause of death, within the government's ambit, however benign the reason.

The Nazi administrator of the facility, Doctor Werner Beck, had initiated and supervised the recording and categorization of documents and cadavers using terminology that was shockingly candid. Voluminous reports recorded the icily somber prose of life and death under the Nazi occupation in all its dystopian guises. The accounts outlined the casualties in the initial days of the German invasion—the innocent targets of hundreds of random Gestapo street roundups, arrested and deported to Auschwitz-Birkenau, a concentration camp located only 60 kilometers from the medieval grandeur of Kraków Castle.

Arbitrary killings were also carried out to further the perverse interests of Nazi "medical science," using captured British and Soviet spies and even lifers brought in from Kraków's notorious Montelupich prison. And, as with all others, such deaths were dispassionately itemized in a veritable "Doomsday" Book of soon-to-be-forgotten souls.

Meticulously written chronicles spanning half a decade were expanded to include victims of a typhus epidemic in the ghetto, those who sadly starved to death in the grinding ballet of war, humdrum deaths of elders, and even the commonplace casualties of traffic accidents. All in all, the end-of-life sagas recorded as autopsies of more than 5,000 people were stored in bankers' boxes that lined the serpentine halls of the Institute.

The armed caravan came to a halt in the circular driveway of their destination. The SS troopers hopped out of the lorries and, boots clattering at double time on cobblestones, formed a protective cordon around the vehicles.

Two middle-aged men emerged from the varnished main doors of the Institute, one in the black uniform of the Gestapo, the other wearing an oversized lab coat. They both wore the insincere smiles that tended to accompany meetings like this one, forced encounters that invariably intruded on their daily regimen. Henschell bounded up the steps to greet his hosts. The introductions were brief and functionally polite. Beck introduced the man in the lab coat as Doctor Jan Robel, one of the top forensic scientists in Poland and a person who had taken a personal interest in finding out who murdered his countrymen.

After dismissing Robel, Beck invited Henschell and Matuszek into his first-floor office. It was furnished in heavy oak furniture with the walls covered in blood-red damask, standard form for Prussian *grafs* and those similarly ordained to rule in Adolf Hitler's ever-expanding Third Reich. A large black-and-white photo hung in solitary splendor immediately behind the director's desk featuring a beaming Beck shaking hands with an equally beaming Führer. The desk itself was almost bare. If the doctor had any paperwork to complete, it was either already finished or hidden somewhere secure, away from prying eyes.

There were a few items on the desk. One was a miniature flag with its red field, centered white disk, and black swastika tangibly reinforcing the owner's loyalty to the Reich and its leader. The other was a framed photograph of a middle-aged man and woman. He, dressed in a Lutheran clergyman's collar and bland business suit, and she in a sturdy flower-print dress. Kneeling at their feet was a young boy, perhaps eight or ten, dressed in a classic white and blue sailor's suit. And kneeling adoringly beside him, his face wrinkled like a dried prune, a shar-pei puppy.

"My parents Oskar and Maria and me, and, of course, Ludwig, my pet dog," Beck proudly exclaimed. "Taken in 1908. At the time, Father was the pastor of a Lutheran mission post in Lüchow. I was eight. Then, just after China officially declared war on the Kaiser in 1917, we were repatriated to an embattled Germany.

"Father was assigned to a parish in Heidelberg, where I continued my schooling. I did so well at gymnasium, I was accepted to the university. I never forgot how Germany was treated at Versailles—the rioting in the streets verging on insurrection, the real possibility of a Communist takeover of my country, and the utter shame it all brought to my heritage and our collective sense of self as a nation. I was a committed Nazi by then—even organized the first book burnings in the University Square. I'm proud to say I hold one of the first membership cards in the Nazi Party.

"As an interesting aside, in the center of the photo it's hard to miss the huge blue and white porcelain flower vase. It is my parents' pride and joy, and must stand at least two meters in height. I used it as a secret hiding place for my valuables and memories." He chuckled to himself. "My mother thinks I still do."

"Father is retired. They live in Radebuel, a pleasant town north of Dresden and well out of harm's way. A small house near his last posting at the local church. I visit them as often as my office permits. It is, and always will be, my safe haven."

"You are close, then?" Henschell offered by way of polite comment.

"As close as a son can be to his elders," Beck beamed. "But enough of my story," he smiled politely and gestured his guests to be seated.

"It's been a while since I saw you last, Henschell." Beck's smile became more fixed. Artificial. "May 1940, near Le Paradis in the Pas-de-Calais during our race to the Dunkirk beaches. Some British soldiers conducting a futile last stand against *SS Division Totenkopf*, was it not?"

"Yes, Doctor," Henschell nodded warily. "On that occasion, we truly valued your timely professional opinion, and that of your investigative team, as to the causes of death."

"Opinion and, more importantly, support, no?" The smile on the doctor's face had lost its luster.

"Yes." Henschell admitted with no small degree of reluctance. "And support."

The room was still for an uncomfortable period of time.

Beck adroitly broke the silence, his point made. "May I offer you another drink? Schnapps?" He motioned for them to sit in a huge leather chesterfield without waiting for their response and strode over to a generous assortment of liquor bottles located on a heavily lacquered table behind his desk.

He poured two glasses of schnapps and brought them over to his guests. He then turned back to the table and poured a drink for himself. Matuszek noted it contained twice the amount of liquor as theirs.

Beck sat down across from them, twirled his drinking glass for a moment and then, standing as erectly as if he were on parade, he raised it. "A toast. To the Führer and to the success of our mission."

Henschell robotically did likewise, enthusiastically clicking his heels as he raised his glass and downed it in a hearty swallow. The Pole remained seated and silent. The toast over, he pointedly swallowed his schnapps in a single gulp.

Beck began the ensuing conversation by way of explanation. "As you can see the place has had a name change. We are now called *Das Staatliche Institut für Gerichtliche Medizin und Kriminalistik*—the State Institute of Forensic and Criminal Medicine. We function under the authority of *SS Obergruppenführer* Krüger, commander of the SS in the General Governement. Krüger in turn reports directly to Governor

General Hans Frank. I can tell you with utmost confidence that it is Frank's express wish that the Institute and its highly trained and motivated staff are to be at your complete disposal."

He stopped to take a sip from his glass and gestured to his guests to do likewise. Then, suitably quenched, he continued.

"Given the length of time the corpses may have been interred, any documents we examine will be covered by the adipocere wax created in the decomposition process, which is usually formed in a moist, cold environment. The kind I strongly suspect that the Katyn forest provides."

Henschell nodded his agreement.

"In layman's terms," Beck went on, "you might call it 'corpse wax.' One of my departments—Medical Chemistry—will begin treatments to remove the wax. This should make any handwriting we uncover legible, enabling such items to be photo-stated. My Polish subordinate, Robel, has gathered an excellent team of Polish forensic specialists to conduct the full restoration process."

Henschell interrupted with a cautionary raised hand. "May I speak with you in private for a moment?

"But of course."

When they were out of hearing distance of the Pole, Henschell asked what was for him the obvious question. "Can we trust your associate Robel?"

"I believe so," Beck responded with a mischievous gleam in his eye. "He is a recent inhabitant of *Sachsenhausen*, released specifically for this project. I don't think he wishes to be sent back to the camp where he might just disappear in a puff of smoke." He snapped his fingers and chuckled dismissively.

Henschell chanced a sideways glance to Matuszek. The Pole's eyes narrowed just a fraction, but he said nothing. The German shrewdly changed the topic. "Excellent to know, *Herr* Doctor. I am curious. What will your tests ultimately provide us with?"

Beck understood the new direction he was to follow. "The results will allow us to issue formal death certificates to Polish next of kin, who will reinforce the reality of the Soviet horrors at Katyn to the world's media. In a more humanitarian vein, once our analysis is complete, the victims' personal possessions may be claimed by their families."

"And when will this process commence?" Henschell asked.

Beck responded as if on cue. "Tomorrow morning. It will take some weeks to complete. During that time frame, the Katyn boxes will be safely stored in the cellar of this building. Situated as we are immediately next to a large SS barracks, they will be very secure."

Beck brushed some lint from a pant leg. He glanced at his watch. Then, seemingly satisfied that there was nothing pressing happening in his world, he returned to form.

"There is one more thing," Henschell whispered with great urgency.

"And it is?" Beck was growing impatient.

"A specific item of evidence we have delivered from Katyn that I wish you to pay special attention to." From his tunic, he removed a large envelope and handed it to the doctor. "You may find the remnants of an officer's greatcoat among the evidence in exhibit 865. I would examine the coat carefully. Who knows what you might discover? It may be the talisman that saves your life if the war takes an unwelcome turn."

Opening it, Beck found a slip of paper and written on it: "Body 865. Ryszard Franciczek Manel (Captain)."

Henschell smiled grimly. "Consider it repayment for your thorough investigation of the incident at Le Paradis."

Beck wordlessly put the slip into his tunic pocket. He nodded slightly in appreciation.

"Gentlemen?" The same false smile. "Are you certain I cannot interest you in a top-up? Good. There is nothing more satisfying than some good strong schnapps to make one relax after a long day serving the Fatherland. And this war has certainly made one dearly need strength from all sources, even the most unexpected, don't you think?"

The armed escort spent the night in the adjoining SS barracks, departing for their Katyn base as a vermillion-tinged dawn broke over Kraków. After a light breakfast, Henschell and his Polish guest left an hour later. They took a more northerly route edging the outskirts of Warsaw and slashing decisively into the city core so that Henschell could drop Matuszek at his apartment before he continued to Katyn.

In mid-afternoon, the Phaeton glided to a stop in front of a tidy low-rise complex located in a quiet suburb of the Polish capital. As he fumbled in his pocket for the key, Matuszek tersely thanked Henschell for enabling him to be present for the movement of the evidence. Then, when he was certain the Phaeton had gone, he stopped fumbling and set off eastwards at a brisk pace toward the old town, every so often looking over his shoulder to see that he wasn't being followed.

His final destination was several kilometers away in a working-class district. The makeshift loft was in the rafters of an industrial building that also housed a body shop and tool-and-die operation, as well as storage space for period costumes rescued from Poland's artistic show-case, the Grand Theatre, which had been largely destroyed in the 1939 Nazi bombing campaign.

That evening, he had a simple supper and later sat in a cozy corner of a dimly lit room losing himself in a travel novel, *Man and Mystery in Asia,* by Ferdynand Ossendowski, an acclaimed Polish writer. Sometime close to midnight, he paused and went to his bedroom and emerged with a Catholic breviary, given to him as a parting gift by a Franciscan monk. He found a bookmark and placed it at Ezekiel 41:8. With a pencil, he faintly underlined a phrase in the scripture text: "I saw also that the house had a raised basement round about it . . ." Then he returned to reading about a journey to Asia. Before sleep overcame him, he set the alarm and then drifted off to a dream-less night's rest.

The next morning, Matuszek went to the early Mass at St. Benedict's, an artless neighborhood church. The nave was nearly empty and pun-gent with the overwhelmingly Catholic scents of incense, candle wax, and linseed oil. In the gray pre-dawn, a faint ruby glow came from the sanctuary lamp beside the tabernacle, a votive candle to remind all of the presence of Christ, even here in the heart of Nazi-occupied Warsaw.

Five elderly women knelt on wooden *prie dieus* near the altar as they loudly clinked rosary beads. At the rear, near the baptismal font, a smattering of laborers lingered, drawn there by force of habit, if not contrition. Their heads were bowed by exhaustion as much as reverence. One of the workmen coughed loudly, a deep hacking sound that echoed to the rafters of the church. Outside, the clatter of a horse on pavement. A bicycle bell trilled.

Matuszek had brought the breviary, turned the pages intently as he read it and, ever the good Catholic, had taken communion.

At the end of the service, he stayed behind to pray, remaining on his knees long after the other faithful had departed to the dismal world out-side the confines of St. Benedict's. Now, no one and nothing remained but Matuszek and an eternal mystery defined by a votive candle. He glanced at his watch. Near the appointed time, the door to the nave creaked. The hollow echo of footsteps on tile. He rose, genuflected, and departed without looking at the approaching stranger. They wordlessly passed each other.

Outside the church, Matuszek casually lit a cigarette. He took a deep drag, then slowly exhaled. Out of the corner of his eye, he saw the stranger leaving St. Benedict's—average height, nondescript brown on gray clothing, a black patch over his left eye, and carrying Matuszek's breviary. He took another puff of the cigarette and then moved to one side to allow a cyclist to pass. When he looked back to where he last saw him, the stranger was gone.

CHAPTER 8

Extermination camp at Treblinka,
German-Occupied Poland
June 1943

In the beginning of June 1943, the Germans finally terminated the Jewish quarter of Lwów and all of its inhabitants. As Nazis entered the ghetto, they were met with desperate acts of armed resistance, including grenades and Molotov cocktails. However, most Jews tried to hide in prepared dugouts and buildings. Many of these buildings were saturated with gasoline and burned to "flush out" the Juden. Some managed to escape or to conceal themselves in the sewer system. Almost all of these were either killed on the spot or captured to be killed later. Those few still living were taken to the nearby Janowska camp to be shot on the nearby "Sands."

Simon Goldkind was not among them. Courtesy of his German protector, *Oberführer* Altmann, he would receive very special treatment.

The camp was located some distance from Lwów and run by the *SS-Totenkopfverbände*, an SS Death's Head Unit run by an old friend of Altmann's, who invited him to pay a call.

Altmann readily assented, provided he could add but one name to the list. This proved to be no problem, inasmuch as three crowded freight cars from Lwów were to arrive for disposal at Treblinka on the day of Altmann's visit.

It was an overcast day as Simon Goldkind stood in a line of naked men grimly awaiting his turn. They inched slowly toward the brick building. Some of the men began to whimper. For his part, Simon Goldkind would not give the phalanx of armed SS guards shepherding them to certain death the pleasure of seeing such weakness.

Unbeknownst to the pitiful procession, a number of onlookers watched from a nearby wooden viewing platform. They wore garish Nazi regalia and black leather overcoats as they looked on, laughing at each other's jokes as if they were on an outing at the *Deutsches* Derby.

Altmann stood there among them, laughing, always the bon vivant. He'd arranged for one of his underlings to search through Goldkind's personal effects before they left Lwów. The underling found the item in question and discreetly handed it to his superior. He glanced down at a list of the condemned men provided by the camp authorities until he found the name "Goldkind. S." He circled it with a grand flourish of green ink.

"A wonderful creation, this fountain pen," Altmann said to no one in particular on the viewing platform. "They surely don't make them like this anymore."

"It is very nice," the camp commandant responded politely. "Where did you get it?"

"A friend left it for me," Altmann lied effortlessly, for it had become such a natural thing for him to do. "He once said something that I have taken to heart. 'We must always possess something unique that marks our time on this earth. After all, life is too short.'"

"A truly wise man, your friend," the commandant agreed.

"Yes, he was," said Altmann. "Yes, he was."

After a few moments delay, Simon Goldkind entered the chamber, where he was packed against a wall of human flesh. Sweat. Fear. Urine and excrement. He found himself savoring the odors, for they were the scent of everyday life.

The gas pumped into the space was extremely effective. Simon quickly found himself becoming drowsy. And what would he do—could he do—in these last few moments to mark his time on earth?

He hastily looked around and found a piece of charcoal wedged in a gap between a floorboard and a brick. Simon scratched the names of his wife and two children on the wall in front of him.

Then, quite precisely, he added a mathematical equation and its solution in honor of their names. The solution to his greatest riddle would die with him.

US Army Corps of Engineers,
109 East Palace Avenue,
Santa Fe, New Mexico
27 June 1943

Situated amid a row of patched adobe storefronts and located a hundred yards from the grand Cathedral Park was a rectangular plywood sign, angled like a tacky barber's shingle: US ARMY CORPS OF ENGINEERS–NEW MEXICO. Beneath the sign, a screen door, badly in need of repair, suggested you had arrived at the wrong place.

A dilapidated orange school bus, with the words US ARMY gamely stenciled onto its sides, idled in front. The bus was loaded to the brim with brooms, mirrors, potted plants, and children's toys. A woody station wagon screeched to a halt beside the bus. The driver, an army corporal, led Stanley Ulam and the three other passengers into the building.

A plump, middle-aged woman in a blue tweed suit greeted the latest newcomers with a cheery smile. Behind her, four men in business suits waited nervously and uncomfortably on rickety kitchen chairs.

Ulam glanced around the room; to call it an office would have been overly generous. It was more like a country general store, and a poor imitation of one at that. The conflicting odors of linseed oil and camphor were pervasive. Mops, pails, brooms, canned goods, an assortment of light fixtures, kitchen furniture, and living room sofas—the place itself looked to be in transit. Now Ulam knew where the flotsam and jetsam blown about by the twister in *The Wizard of Oz* had eventually landed.

Still smiling, the matron in the tweed suit calmly counted heads and seated herself behind a creaky office clerk's desk situated amid the organized clutter. A phone call was made. The newcomers were asked to line up and identify themselves with proper documentation against a master list the woman kept on the desk. Once satisfied, the woman produced sheets of paper for each in turn. These were to be their passes into the Los Alamos Project.

Suitably vetted, the eight newcomers hopped on the school bus. In the next few minutes, it grudgingly groaned up the Taos Highway and then switch-backed onto a washboard dirt road.

The actual site proved to be 40 miles northwest of Santa Fe, but the drive was far from tiresome. Red earth, pink rocks, dark shrubbery on ochre cliffs. In the distance, they could see the lavender vistas of the Sangre de Cristo Mountain range. Everywhere along the roadside stood squat adobe houses, many with strings of scarlet chili peppers hung out to dry along their frontages like forgotten Christmas ornaments. And on practically every flat rooftop, lay regimented rows of yellow, blue, white and red ears of corn drying in the blazing sun.

In due course, the bus arrived at a narrow gate set into a high barbed-wire fence that stretched both ways, seemingly to forever. A twelve-member squad of military police in neatly pressed khakis, shimmering white helmets, and blancoed puttees stood at parade ease behind the sealed gate, eyeing them suspiciously. Behind the soldiers, and within firing distance of the bus, were two cement pillboxes and a queue of randomly staggered tank traps. Sinister objects protruded adder-like from the shadowy apertures of each pillbox.

The bus stopped. The gate creaked open. Upon a barked command, an MP squad broke ranks. A trio of military police boarded the vehicle and carefully checked each pass against a master list. Once satisfied, the bus and its occupants were permitted to continue the remaining three miles into the security area proper. They debarked at a stone pump-house where they were confronted, fingerprinted, and photographed by a team of no-nonsense WACs. They were then issued passes, to be kept on their persons at all times.

His security procedure complete, Ulam stepped out onto the patio and critically studied the panorama that stretched before him like a patchy Navajo rug. The "Manhattan Project" was housed on a solitary mesa high up in the Jemez Mountains in an abandoned boys' ranch. Its buildings were an eclectic mix of ranch-style cottages, log cabins, ancient adobe structures, army prefab huts, and dormitories. Under strict military oversight, the United States Army literally owned the minds and hearts of all its occupants. Drab khaki jeeps and deuce-and-a-half trucks roared about, creating angry dust storms in their wake. An ant-like legion of individuals, some in uniform, but most in casual summer attire, filed continuously through a maze of what passed for streets with a determination that only a singularly steely purpose could bring. As if to ensure their continued focus, teams of white-helmeted MPs were everywhere.

As they departed the pump-house, the newcomers were herded

sheep-like into prearranged groups and sent off on foot and with guards to their respective lodgings. Ulam's party was assigned a small cottage by a pond tucked away behind a long, low line of wood and gypsum-board duplexes. The walk, with suitcases in hand, was long. Stands of Ponderosa pine provided some shade, but the New Mexico sun was viciously unrelenting, and Ulam could feel sweat trickling freely down his back and drenching his shirt.

After unpacking and refreshing themselves with a quick shower and, in most cases, a change into more casual clothes, the newcomers were escorted by a pair of MPs to a drab Quonset hut next to an old shingled water tower in what seemed to be at the middle of the project.

The group entered a large modular space. It was already crammed full of civilians, all presumably scientists, physicists, or mathematicians. Ulam took a chair at the back of the room.

A man of middle age and stature, with arched eyebrows and an intense expression, stood on a makeshift podium. Identifying himself in German-accented English as Edward Teller, he proved to be the official greeter for the project and the head of its theoretical division. Teller limped slightly as he paced back and forth in front of a blackboard that listed the usual "welcome wagon" contacts. His opening remarks were short and matter of fact. He brought greetings from the overall head of the project—Doctor Robert Oppenheimer—and then abruptly walked out of the hut.

A trio of speakers came next. A schoolmarmish administrator with an exaggerated Georgia Peach accent spoke about the need to have all their records in order, including their wills. She went over the list on the blackboard. Until they had passed a period of probation—what it was and for how long was left unsaid—they were not allowed off the site. But not to worry—a nervous smile—they were being paid a premium salary. Generous food supplies were available at the nearby Commissary. Run by the Army with the help of civilian employees, it included two butchers, a vegetable counter, and a teller's window where checks could be cashed.

There was a PX, a post exchange, with a drugstore where cigarettes, chocolates, and souvenirs were sold. The PX also boasted a soda fountain, juke box, and dance floor. And, of course, there were first-run movies direct from Hollywood three nights a week. The entry fee? A dime. With this last tidbit of information, she was met with resounding applause.

140

The Georgia Peach was followed by an Army surgeon who dryly explained that Manhattan had a fully functioning, if somewhat small, hospital and a team of highly qualified doctors at its disposal.

That facility, he went on, was more than a place to remedy sunburn or the occasional ankle sprain. In its short lifetime, it had already overcome two crises.

Because everyone on the project site seemed to have brought a dog with them, the first scare had been rabies. A little beagle had become rabid and, for a time, all dogs and children disappeared from sight and certainly from the PX. An ironic chuckle rippled through the room.

The second scare was more serious. Polio. The project was home to many young families. When a teacher at the base school was stricken with polio and subsequently died when moved to the hospital in Santa Fe, the project went semi-comatose for several weeks until the scare had passed.

In closing, the surgeon ominously intimated that the project itself faced enormous challenges and health risks, some yet totally unknown to human experience. These risks would test the abilities of the most skilled physicians to the utmost. They were collectively embarking on a journey far beyond the boundaries of traditional medicine. He hoped that his medical team would be up to the challenge.

With that sobering thought lingering in their minds, the last and most obvious speaker bounded up to the podium. The MP captain was refreshingly blunt as he began by quoting the relevant provisions of the Espionage Act of 1918. He seemed to particularly enjoy the section about the death penalty.

The captain made no bones about the new reality that, although this might be their home away from home, their mail would be routinely vetted, outgoing telephone calls were not allowed, and visitors from the outside world were strictly forbidden.

As to the issue of being confined to barracks and the period of probation alluded to earlier? In a week's time, once they were settled in, they were free to leave the Mesa with a signed pass, but only to travel within very rigid boundaries. Overnight stays required ultra-special consent. Moreover, they were forbidden to talk to friends and strangers on any trip. To ensure this was happening, they would be actively monitored by Army (G2) Intelligence and the FBI. The captain ended his sober speech with the inevitable anecdote.

As his captive audience would soon discover, the driver's licenses for all scientists at the Manhattan Project had numbers instead of names and were not signed. All occupations were listed as "engineer" and their addresses as PO Box 1663. With gas rationing in effect everywhere but at Manhattan, most traffic between Lamy, Santa Fe, and Taos was "project driven." One day on the Taos Road, a caravan of army sedans carrying a group of Nobel Prize winners and deans of science, all traveling under false names, was flagged down for speeding. When the state trooper asked for the names of the occupants, each refused as politely as possible to provide it.

"Tell it to the judge," retorted the trooper, as he wrote out a series of summonses determined to teach the Army a lesson it would not forget.

"I'm sorry, officer," ventured one of the scientists. "We can't appear either."

Finally, an Army driver calmed the state trooper before he arrested the entire ensemble with a promise to take the entire batch of summonses to his commanding officer who would promptly look after them.

A pointed personal phone call from the White House Oval Office to the Governor of New Mexico quickly straightened things out.

The state trooper was judiciously reassigned to another zone, and all military sedans in the Project Manhattan motor pool had speed governors placed on them to ensure they were driven within New Mexico's speed limits.

"Of course," the captain confided with a conspiratorial wink, "We don't have the authority to tamper with the engines of those of you who have, or will shortly purchase, your own motor vehicle."

The room burst into laughter.

Ulam left the hut with mixed emotions. He recalled the words of Charles Dickens: "It was the best of times. It was the worst of times . . ." It was Project Manhattan, which seemed to be a little of both. But there was one thing Ulam knew for certain—it certainly wasn't Occupied Poland.

* * *

In the next few days, Ulam, who thrived in the abstract dance of pure numbers, was assigned to work with Teller in a select group—the theoretical division—dealing with nuclear fusion. While the division was instructed to focus on implosion, it soon became apparent to Ulam that Teller was far more interested in the future possibility of a thermonuclear explosion—of a hydrogen or "S"-Super Bomb—than in the atomic bomb that Los Alamos was developing using strictly nuclear fission.

As he became more involved in Teller's "S-bomb," Ulam began to painstakingly reconstruct a complex theoretical challenge he had once seen, written in green ink in a book kept at a café in Lwów. He recalled it was the work of a young professor named Goldkind. He began to speculate on the impossible—that what was contained in the book could be the answer to the project's final puzzle. Yet would Teller even listen? If they somehow gained access to the book and Goldkind's probing question, he believed they might be able to complete the equation and resolve the current conundrum he and Teller faced. But the book still lingered on a hidden shelf in the rear of a café in Occupied Poland—and only if the café still existed.

The following day, at 0600 hours, Ulam and Teller convened in the offices of the head of the Manhattan Project, a gruff army general named Leslie Groves. A professional engineer and career soldier, Groves's previous assignment had been overseeing the construction of the largest office building in the world—The Pentagon in Washington. After a brief exchange of insincere pleasantries, they got down to business. Over piping hot coffee and hot buttered corn bread, Ulam wrote the parts of the formulas he could recall. The formulations were complex, but General Groves had a sharp mind and readily grasped the concepts and their ultimate thrust. He then asked two questions: "Where is the book now?" and "Have you discussed this with anyone else?"

Hearing their unambiguous replies, the general dismissed the two scientists with his trademark comment, "Leave it with me."

Mayfair, City of Westminster,
London, United Kingdom
5 July 1943

The meeting had been requested by a no-nonsense Irishman from New York named Flaherty, who operated from an address in upscale

Mayfair, a slender five-story Georgian that housed the European headquarters of the Office of Strategic Services, America's newly formed intelligence agency. Until that fateful Sunday at Pearl Harbor in December 1941, Patrick Aiden Flaherty had been a lieutenant in the New York Police Department. His specialty? The Mob. As a decorated veteran of the First World War, and as someone accustomed to dealing with bureaucracy, his current wartime posting was a natural. The Pentagon. His army rank was captain. His area of responsibility? Military Intelligence.

The instructions of his London superiors had been abundantly clear: to discreetly determine the existence and exact whereabouts of this Scottish Book and use whatever means necessary to obtain it.

The place Flaherty was bound for, a tastefully understated West End club, had been selected by his British counterpart. Among the oldest gentlemen's establishments in London, the Palladian-influenced edifice had been named Gordon's in honor of General Charles George Gordon—the legendary "China" Gordon—who'd been slain by Muslim zealots in 1885 near the culmination of their year-long siege of Khartoum.

Charles George Gordon had sacrificed himself in a bygone era that enshrined glory, honor, God, and Empire. As such, there was no address plate on either of the Portland stone pillars that flanked the entrance to the club, but merely a slight gilded statue depicting Montu, the ancient Egyptian falcon-god of war, now barely visible behind the heavily sandbagged facade. For those who mattered, the name Gordon's was enough.

Flaherty arrived at the same time as another individual who nodded pleasantly in his direction. The American instinctively sized him up. Tall, with a distinct military bearing, the stranger wore a double-breasted gray suit, well worn but pressed, and a tie of conservative blue with the dated motif of a griffon. Shirt clean, though with cuffs slightly frayed. Brogues polished.

The stranger's appearance seemed generally unremarkable until he turned to face Flaherty. What seemed to be a dueling scar ran faintly down his right cheek. Flaherty made a studied calculation. Certainly not British, Dutch, or Norwegian. Perhaps French or Central European? Given the state of his clothing and his air of confidence? In all probability, a Pole.

Early in his police career, Flaherty had worked with Polacks at a precinct in Queens. Good guys. Great cops. Loved their drink and always covered your back in a jam. More importantly, their sports heroes were also his—Bronco Nagurski, the bruising Chicago Bears fullback, and Stan Musial, the twenty-two-year-old St. Louis Cardinal who made the All-Star team in only his second year in pro baseball.

Surprisingly, Flaherty had never met a real homegrown Pole. He had read of their aerial exploits during the Battle of Britain. How their infantry had fought on in France, even after the French capitulated, and the British were evacuating Dunkirk. And how a Polish rifle brigade had held out with the Aussies during the land-siege of Tobruk.

Impatiently, he rapped several times with the brass knocker that graced the front door. The two men were met by a solemn-faced butler who acknowledged them with a slight nod. "The colonel is expecting you."

They mounted a massive staircase overlooked by a corniced ceiling. On the wall were vivid renderings of the Empire's martial grandeur. On the ceiling, and indeed throughout the club's hallowed halls, Britannia still ruled the waves and fully one-quarter of the globe's land mass.

Their destination was a room on the upper floor in a secluded portion of the building. It was tastefully furnished with walls covered in royal-blue velour and trimmed with a regimental flourish of claret and autumn gold.

A trio of high-backed chairs faced a darkened fireplace. Looming above the hearth was an ominous reproduction of Paul Nash's painting "The Menin Road." It depicted a brutal Great War landscape of flooded shell craters, shattered tree stumps, and a smoke-singed sky. Flaherty's eye was drawn to two struggling soldiers trapped in the hellish eternity of their surroundings.

The Englishman rose from the middle chair to greet his visitors, then made the requisite introductions. Flaherty learned that his companion was Colonel Fabian Lis, the Polish liaison with MI6 who had just returned from a stint in Warsaw with the Polish Underground.

Flaherty glanced around the room. There were no refreshments for Vickery's two guests, not even a pot of tea on the side table. This was clearly going to be a business meeting and on terms set by his host.

Commander Charles Vickery, titular head of MI6 until recently transferred to a similarly high echelon within the SOE—Churchill's Special Operations Executive—opened the discussion by leaning forward toward the American.

"Patrick." A forced smile. "You indicated you wished our assistance involving something in Poland."

"Yes, Commander," Flaherty answered modestly. "I've been asked by my bosses to inquire about something called the Scottish Book?" With a slight smile he turned to the Pole. "It's supposed to be in a place in Poland called *L-wów.*"

"Lwów," the Polish colonel politely corrected him. "It is pronounced *Lvooff.*"

"Right." Flaherty's freckled face turned faintly red.

Vickery pressed on. "Is there any specific reason they want to know, Patrick?"

"No," Flaherty had been given a set-piece response by his superiors to this obvious question. He paused. "It came up on our radar when we were speaking to one of our sources about another matter."

Vickery was not fooled by the prevarication. "But what makes it so crucial to call us to a meeting?"

"That's all I was told," the Irishman shrugged. Flaherty sensed a bit of a chess game. He chose diplomacy. "Look, we're all in this together. We need your help."

Vickery appeared appeased. "You can tell your superior, Mr. Donovan at Grosvenor Street, that we are making very real progress in determining the whereabouts of the Scottish Book, and more importantly, in ensuring its recovery."

"Where is it?" Flaherty asked, hopeful for something, anything at this stage to somehow satisfy his bosses. And, after a respectful pause, "What is it? I haven't been told."

"Where? At this stage, we believe we know. All I can say is that our efforts are targeted at Lwów." Gazing deferentially to the Pole seated to his left, Vickery made a point of pronouncing the word correctly.

"As to the second question, we think the Scottish Book is a complex series of numbers and formulas. Something neither you nor I, nor even Fabian here, who fancies himself the second coming of Copernicus, would be able to understand." The Polish intelligence officer tried to hide a bemused smile. "Isn't that right, Colonel?" A slight nod.

"We, as well as your masters, are keen to know its contents."

"And if you are able to retrieve it, you would let us know immediately?"

"Of course, dear boy," Vickery responded glibly. "A united team defeating the Hun. Just as we did in the Great War. And, as you so rightly said, we certainly would not withhold information from each other now, would we?" He paused for a moment. "And before you inquire, I will respond to the last question your superiors would assuredly want to know the answer to, which is: 'Who currently has this book in their possession?'"

"We don't actually know."

Flaherty was sufficiently experienced to recognize that the formal meeting ended with that succinct comment. It bothered him to play second fiddle. However, there was little he could do about it, at least not yet. Like policing, the intelligence game was all about territory and respect. And both had to be earned.

The three shared innocuous small talk about the progress of the war against the Nazis. Vickery quite generously congratulated the American on the successful OSS intelligence effort in largely neutralizing the Vichy French officer corps in North Africa so that it could not resist the Allied invasion. Flaherty returned the compliment, lauding Vickery's people for their work in providing the Allies—and more particularly Stalin—with partial plans of *Operation Edelweiss*, the unsuccessful Nazi thrust to capture the important oil fields of Azerbaijan.

Lis, in turn, spoke soberly of the recent tragedy that had befallen the Warsaw Jewish ghetto, the lives lost, and the sheer heart-breaking hopelessness of it all. He then outlined the continuing Polish sabotage of Nazi infrastructure and, in closing, remarked that while in Poland, he had used the Home Army grapevine to pass on the generous thanks of MI6 to two elderly Polish janitors who had been sent to Peenemünde as forced labor. He now took this occasion to relay the janitors' pointedly anxious response—that the RAF had put their critical information to good use, but only when they themselves were off the island.

And that was that.

Flaherty had sufficient staying power for the obligatory round-table sharing of ideas, and an empty few minutes of chit-chat that began with a collective commentary about the dry weather that had enveloped the British capital and ended with a far more somber discussion about the recent death of the actor Leslie Howard. Howard had been on a scheduled passenger flight over the Bay of Biscay when the Douglas DC-3 was tragically intercepted by a pack of German JU 88s. Then Flaherty rose, offered the requisite courtesies, and departed.

On his way back to Mayfair, Flaherty collected his thoughts. Concerning the Scottish Book, he had discovered little information of any use that he strongly suspected wasn't already known "Upstairs" before he was sent out on this foray.

Conversely, Patrick Flaherty did have a curious gem to send up the intelligence ladder for some bespectacled analyst to mull over, glamorize with flowery terms, and call his own. Beyond the vague promises from Vickery, which were obviously generalizations, and would be dismissed as such at Number 70, the information from the Polish colonel was certainly worth a report.

And yet, he had unanswered questions. Where was Peenemünde? What were Polish janitors doing there? And finally, why were those janitors so concerned that the Royal Air Force might act while they were still working on site?

He cursed himself inwardly for not having the nerve to ask. But many of the essential facts for his report were staring him in the face.

With what he could surmise, he was certainly experienced enough to cobble together a plausible report from jagged puzzle pieces. He would commit to paper that the Polish Home Army had provided MI6 with critical on-site information to make this place called Peenemünde a serious target for Royal Air Force bombing raids. Case closed. Perhaps it wasn't the exact information that he had been sent to uncover, but it was something. A completely unexpected strategic piece of information of great value to the US Army Air Force. Accomplished with little effort on his part.

Vickery seemed to relax after the American had departed. He rang for the butler and, upon his arrival, ordered a Booth's Gin served two fingers, neat, for himself, and a vodka for "my good Polish friend."

When the drinks came, Vickery toasted his ally, took a sip of his drink, savored it, then spoke. "That American is a damn fool cowboy, trust me. He doesn't understand Europe. I suspect Patrick Flaherty must learn the game of life as we have played it for centuries before he can strut into Gordon's and demand something for nothing. Yanks, Fabian. Bumbling newcomers to our blood sport."

He took a bigger sip and chuckling to himself continued, evidently pleased with his observations. "They can't even time their entrance into a world war with any credibility. Three years late getting into the Great War. Two years late into this one. Johnny-come-latelies. That is all they are. Waltzing in with infinite bags of money but no *savoir faire* in how to properly spend it."

"And yet . . ." He twirled the glass in his outstretched hand, admiring the crystal. "I believe the Americans are up to something, and I suspect it is something big. They need that book, Fabian. As do we. I trust your continued silence in this matter implicitly."

"As you are well aware, the British intelligence community, in concert with our trusted Polish allies, has been aligned for some time with a prized agent they call Tadeusz—an undercover Polish military intelligence officer—and they have been aggressively seeking him since the brutal occupation of your nation. Rest assured we will find this person. And with him, the book. Once we have in our possession what is essential to our mutual cause, we will determine our next course of action."

Lis nodded soberly in seeming agreement. He had not touched a drop of the vodka. He gazed again at the depressing starkness of the painting above the fireplace. It reminded him of the homeland he had just left, and of its total isolation and destruction. The Englishman had no idea of how the world was changing. No idea at all. Or perhaps Vickery did recognize the change and it was, he—Fabian Lis—who was deluding himself as to the world and Poland's future place in it.

Lis had heard two disturbing reports in his short time back in London: firstly, that the London Poles were being accused by Whitehall of a willful blindness bordering on hatred toward their Soviet "allies," and secondly, and more troubling, that there were unconfirmed rumors of a possible Soviet infiltration of MI6—a high-level access that would not bode well for the government-in-exile and for Poland.

It was as if Vickery was reading his mind. "I offer you a lesson learned from my own life experiences, Fabian," he confided. "Don't always trust your allies. They will disappoint you, like these Americans, and in ways you can't begin to imagine."

Lis turned to his companion. "What is it that the Chinese military strategist Sun Tzu wrote in the *Art of War*? 'Keep your friends close, and your enemies closer'?"

He downed his vodka in one gulp. "I truly hope you British don't adhere to that philosophy, because if you do, we Poles will be isolated long after your other Allies are victorious against our shared enemy."

Vickery's gaze strayed to the far wall, his features suddenly blank. "What was that you said, dear boy?"

Lis sighed knowingly. He had his answer. "It was nothing, Vickery. Nothing."

Gibraltar
5–6 July 1943

The flight from Cairo as the only passenger aboard an RAF Sunderland had been exhausting. The final leg of his journey had been equally disquieting, as the dumpy flying boat had been forced to land in utter darkness to avoid marauding *Messerschmitts*. After a gut-wrenching cork-screw, the plane descended onto the black surface of the Mediterranean.

Antony Eskenzi was ferried ashore in a naval cutter. In the distance, looming like the Berber fortress of Jabal Tariq, as it was once known, was the brooding magnificence of the British bastion of Gibraltar.

A nondescript Humber, and equally nondescript driver were waiting at the pier. From the darkened bay beyond came the distinct sounds of metal on metal as navy divers continued their ceaseless inspection of the hulls of ships at anchor, groping their way, yard by yard, along the underside of each vessel, gingerly feeling for limpet mines the enemy might have placed there.

Some 700 meters from the newly constructed eastern runway and corralled by a series of booms, buoys, and focused high-beam lighting, a glum mooring vessel and a flurry of lesser craft bobbed about in the choppy waters. Frantic activity punctuated their presence. The obvious signs of controlled panic were everywhere, while in the distance, a Leander-class cruiser gracefully knifed into the Mediterranean murk followed by a pair of destroyers.

The driver placed his duffel bag in the trunk. Eskenzi calmly took his place in the burlap-covered back seat and gathered his thoughts as the vehicle inched across the tarmac toward the principal encampment. Out of simple curiosity, he finally broke the silence. "Corporal? That activity off the runway? Did they catch an *Itie* mini-submarine?"

The driver quickly glanced at Eskenzi in his rearview mirror. "No sir. One of ours, sir. An aircraft." He broke eye contact and stolidly continued driving.

On this clammy summer night, Eskenzi was attired in the open-necked desert khakis of a captain in the Royal Army Service Corps. By the dearth of campaign medals on his tunic, Eskenzi's war had been outwardly quite unremarkable. And that erroneous perception certainly suited him. Scant few things he had done while in the service of His Majesty could, or should, bear public scrutiny.

After the fall of Poland, Eskenzi resolutely soldiered through the ignominious collapse of France and the Low Countries, handling dozens of raw agents and even more raw data, venturing out himself on one occasion behind German lines to a village near Arras to unsuccessfully search for what had proved to be a double agent.

He glanced off into the darkness. Agents? The first ones he had dealt with had been so ill-prepared, so naively gullible. Yet, he had dutifully sent each to an early grave with a hypocritical wave and disingenuous small talk about imminent victory and comprehensive Allied support, neither of which truly existed. Eskenzi would dispassionately monitor their movements until they died—one by one, like heat-frenzied moths before a raging flame.

Those initial intelligence fiascos on the Western Front were inexorably followed by equally humiliating debacles in Norway, Greece, and Crete. And now, after three pitiless years, with a dance card nearly filled with the names of individuals he had sent to their deaths, he was well past being fatigued and disillusioned by the war and his venal part in it.

He had spent the past year in Cairo at General Headquarters, Middle East. Hidden away inside a shambling block of commandeered flats surrounded by barbed wire in the Garden City district of the seething metropolis, he stolidly upheld the well-crafted cover provided for him by V, an inconsequential role in the machinery of war with no real operational impact.

A virtual bystander to the Allied victories beginning at El Alamein and ending in Tunisia, Eskenzi spent his days signing off on pink requisition slips and canary-yellow invoices by the cartonful, all the while patiently awaiting a package that he knew was out there somewhere on the Occupied Continent—a package he was determined to find and deliver to his superiors.

His posting to Cairo had afforded him the opportunity to travel to British-controlled Iraq to visit the training camps of thousands of Poles who'd been freed from Stalin's Gulags to form a nascent army under Major General Wladislaw Anders. Once there, he had debriefed countless men in passable Polish—men with hollow eyes and hollow souls—none of them bringing him closer to the one he sought. Yet still he kept digging away at shadows. He had failed so many others. Now he had but one remaining individual to fail—himself.

The journey to the officers' quarters at Devil's Town Camp was short, less than ten minutes. It was well past midnight, and the encampment deathly quiet. Even the Barbary apes on Gibraltar's craggy slopes seemed to be slumbering. His footsteps echoed on the cut-stone walkway. The lone night sentry at the mess entrance came to brisk attention; the spiked bayonet tip of the Lee-Enfield glistening evilly in the moonlight. As he entered the darkened guest room, he was greeted by sultry silence. He crawled into bed and slept without dreams.

The moist Mediterranean dawn came all too soon. A token shave and hasty ablutions followed. Eskenzi dressed in rumpled khakis and, after a rushed breakfast of watery eggs, toast, and tepid Earl Grey tea in the deserted mess, he made his way to the entrance where the Humber and driver awaited. A quick journey to Casement Square brought him to his destination—Gibraltar Police HQ.

The main report room was just inside the lobby. The antechamber was cooled by a breeze from oval-shaped windows that let in a honey-gold light. A stocky station sergeant sat toad-like behind a massive oak pulpit, scratching entries into a duty roster. He glanced up, like an overworked accountant interrupted at his ledgers. "Room 106," he grumbled as he jabbed a pen in the general direction of the staircase.

The door to Room 106 was closed. Eskenzi knocked. Once. Twice. No answer.

He entered a small chamber that contained chairs of questionable vintage and a rectangular table. A faded King George V stared down from one wall. A twenty-four-hour clock on the other. A half-open window framed in Belgian lace overlooked a small bricked-in courtyard below.

Eskenzi sat on one of the chairs. After what seemed an interminable time, a trim, studious man of indeterminate age walked through the door holding a manila folder in one hand. He seated himself in the other chair and wordlessly opened the folder. He glanced at it, then

152

looked off into the distance as if in thought. Dressed in an immaculate white cotton suit, button-down shirt, and requisite striped school tie, he looked and acted like an imperious academic. The newcomer cleared his throat and shrewdly scrutinized his guest as he would an errant undergraduate.

Eskenzi broke the silence. "Might I ask why I'm here?"

A soft breeze wafted into the room, rustling the drapes. The piercing "tring" of bicycle bells in a nearby street. A stray dog howling balefully. A soccer ball thumping off a concrete wall.

"Your name, sir?" Eskenzi demanded.

His host brushed a speck of lint from a shirt cuff. His cufflinks were square and gold, and they bore a heraldic symbol. Given the man's imperious demeanor, dress bordering on the effete, and fashionably long hair, Eskenzi concluded he was an Oxbridge type. Ministry of Silly Widgets. Boffin. Snoop. Eskenzi knew their kind all too well. The missing part of every operational equation he had ever encountered. The sort of individual who coldly sent men to their dutiful deaths. Without hesitation. Stroke of the pen. Turn of the page. Pip, pip, old chap. The Show must go on, you know. For King and Country. And certainly, all before the late afternoon gin break and perhaps a friendly frame of snooker with "C."

"My name is unimportant." In the context of the individual facing him, Eskenzi dolefully accepted the implied condescension. It could not have been otherwise.

"As to the reason for your attendance? You were specifically directed to be here at ten. And it is"—he glanced at the wall clock—"seventeen minutes after. An order from GHQ Middle East should be sufficient for an officer of your rank and operational experience to be present in this office without question and on time, don't you think?"

Without allowing Eskenzi time to muster a response, the man opened the file. "Let's get to the business at hand, shall we? You worked for Special Branch in Shanghai, correct?"

Eskenzi nodded.

"I assume you were involved with the Russian expatriate community in that city."

"I was."

"White Russians?

"Largely so."

"Any problems with the Bolshies?"

"The Soviets? No. Never."

"And the Chinese Communists?"

Eskenzi momentarily relaxed his guard and lapsed into the vaguely comforting doublespeak of the intelligence officer he was.

"By 1928, Chiang Kai-shek had pretty much eradicated the Chinese Communists. But the Russians?" He nodded his awareness. "Totally different species."

Eskenzi unconsciously leaned forward in the chair, suddenly keen to continue. He was now in a comfort zone, and he was being asked to provide a briefing.

"In the fall of '37, Stalin sent hundreds of pilots and planes to help the Nationalists in their struggle with the Japs. Called them the Soviet Volunteer group. They set up shop at a makeshift airbase outside Shanghai."

"So, I take it that you liaised with the Russkies?"

"Liaised?" The sharp sortie from this unexpected direction snapped Eskenzi back to reality.

"Come, come," the man sniffed, exasperated. "I wasn't born yesterday. And neither were you. Every Russian military formation, particularly a volunteer one, has a political commissar. He's the chap who monitors thought, keeps his charges in line, the usual Bolshie stuff. I assume you weren't *that* naive when you carried out your Shanghai duties. You did liaise with *those* Russians, correct?"

Eskenzi chose his next words with extreme care. "Let's just say, we were mutually appreciative. They dug around Shanghai a bit, but they never caused me grief. We rather complemented each other."

"I take that to mean a 'yes.' You worked with the Soviets."

Eskenzi allowed himself a slight nod.

"Your file also indicates that just before the war broke out you worked extensively with the Poles."

Eskenzi hesitated, then, "I had a card in that deck."

The hint of a sardonic smile. "Let us hope it wasn't the seven of spades."

Eskenzi did not respond.

"How good is your Russian?"

"Passable."

"And Polish?"

"Better."

"Captain Eskenzi, we think that we have your man. The one you were to have met at the Romanian border in '39. The London Poles tell us he's dead, that he was murdered at Katyn. We're not so sure."

"Still alive? How do you know?"

"Three days ago, one of our monitoring stations in Damascus received a communication originating from Poland. A curious musical cryptogram repeated several times, a piece I've been told is called the *Hejnał*. Each time it ended with the missing note from that same musical piece. The failsafe mechanism for your man, was it not?"

"Yes, it was. When there'd been a long period of radio silence, sending it was his way of confirming that he was still alive."

"Good to know." A slight nod. "We're sending you in to find him and return him to England for a full debrief. If you can."

Eskenzi was thoughtful, contemplating the enormity of his task. "Under whose authority am I doing this?"

"Vickery." He had no need to say more.

"Now to the nitty-gritty. Maisky, the Soviet ambassador to London, is staying on the Rock tonight as a guest of the governor. He and his party will take off at daybreak for Moscow. You will leave with them, landing in the Soviet capital. From there, we've asked the Russians to smuggle you into Occupied Poland where you will work with the Polish Underground. They've been briefed to assist you with whatever you may require, though they obviously don't know the true nature of your mission."

Eskenzi's expression was incredulous. "Getting an Englishman into Poland? The Russkies won't allow it."

"Not to worry. We've told them that because of your extensive history with the Poles, you will be able to successfully meet with the Polish Underground—the Home Army—to smooth the westward movement of Soviet armies in that nation. We've also told them that, to accomplish this task, you have the full blessing of both our prime minister and the London Poles."

"But the London Poles hate the Russians with a passion bordering on fanaticism."

The man shrugged; utter contempt evident when next he spoke. "We don't care a fig how those Poles feel. My mission is to get you into Poland. And as to the Polish Underground, you'll eventually come

155

across leaders within the Home Army. Humor them if you must. That is all. In any event, anything more than bland politeness is a sheer waste of time. Frankly, the Warsaw Poles don't much matter anymore in the greater scheme of things."

He handed Eskenzi a plain manila envelope. The codename of your man is the same as when you attempted to meet him at the Polish-Romanian border in 1939. Tadeusz. Your transmission frequencies are straightforward. You know the drill: read, memorize, and destroy. You will use Home Army transmitters. Communicate in the code you find in your instructions—but only when necessary. Whatever you send will reach me personally. This assignment came directly from V, and I alone will be your conduit to him."

A disarming collegial smile. "Have you read Kipling?"

"Of course."

"Quite," the man instantly slammed the door on any bonhomie Eskenzi might have felt toward him.

"Your codename is Mandalay. And in your case," he continued solemnly, "let us hope that the dawn does not come up like thunder on this enterprise."

His host leaned forward, his voice a precise whisper. "Find our man, Captain. Find him and bring him out. His return to London, with pertinent formation only he knows of, is crucial to the entire war effort in ways that I can't explain at this time. In the end, if all else fails, it is the information we need. The man himself is superfluous."

Eskenzi stood up to leave, then stopped. "An aircraft bought it last night off Gibraltar? Is that usual?"

His host's eyes narrowed ever so slightly.

"Just curious," Eskenzi pressed on, as he correctly sensed an ever-so-subtle change.

After a telling silence, his host responded. "That one? A Liberator. Apparently, a misjudged take-off. The runway is frightfully short. Moreover, it's so close to the Rock that wind shear can easily cause a pilot to lose control and the aircraft to tumble into the sea like a bad penny. Fortunes of war. Oh, and while I've got you here . . . when you first came in, I believe that you asked for my name?"

"I did."

The man feigned a smile, but soon lost his way on the attempt. "I suspect with the daunting task I've given you that it's the least I can provide you by way of reciprocity. My name is Harold Philby, Captain. But I also go by the nickname of 'Kim.' Just like the orphaned vagabond who singlehandledly saves the Empire. Though I daresay that unlike Kipling's memorable creation, I'm not particularly fond of engaging in the Great Game."

CHAPTER 9

Gibraltar
6 July 1943

Philby left the police station a respectable two hours after Eskenzi had departed. He got into a whale-gray Vauxhall with the obligatory CD disk on its front bumper and drove casually back to the border crossing.

Before formally entering Spain, he pulled in to the Guardia Civil checkpoint, where he was greeted by two uniformed officers wearing uncharacteristically pleasant smiles. Perhaps it was the diplomatic plate on the Vauxhall or his ready facility with Spanish—unusual for a British diplomat—but Philby sensed there was more. The mood at the border had perceptibly changed since his last foray into Gibraltar a few months before, fed in no small part by the latest Axis setbacks and the copious quantities of oil doled out by the Allies to Franco's government to sustain its very survival.

Clearing the frontier after only the most perfunctory of checks, Philby traveled westward along a dirt coastal road for no more than twenty minutes until he arrived at a tapas stand located on the high ground opposite an ancient cemetery.

The proprietor of the stand had been an engine room officer on board the Republican dreadnought *Espana* during Spain's bloody civil war. He had been invalided out with a bad hip wound shortly after the ancient battleship had struck a mine and sank to the bottom of the Bay of Biscay.

After that, and even with the ascension of the Franco regime, he had been largely left alone by Franco's secret police. Vengeance, after all, only had a purpose if it could be radiated to others as a stern warning. A battle-scarred navy veteran living in relative isolation was not on Madrid's radar.

Philby stopped at the stand whenever he was in the area, and it wasn't only for the tapas. Over the years, he and the owner had become good friends. It had begun in the most innocuous of ways. Before his diplomatic posting, Philby had been *The Times of London* correspondent covering the Spanish Civil War. He had met the survivors of the dreadnought sinking and chanced upon a wounded man who, upon hearing of Philby's nationality, wished to speak of the war and to practice his English.

Alphonso Cordoba had studied English literature at the University of Barcelona. His interests were diverse—Kipling, Hardy, Stephenson and, of course, Shakespeare and Dickens. Philby shared the man's appreciation of literature. After their initial meeting, they continued to correspond. Occasionally he had sent Cordoba books.

When war broke out, Philby left Spain and continued his work with *The Times*, reporting on the retreat of the British Expeditionary Force and the subsequent debacle in France. He then joined MI6, subsequently being posted to Madrid with responsibility for Spain and Portugal. It was a good time to meet up again with Alphonso Cordoba.

Philby always kept a ready supply of classics in the boot of his car. In the curious spirit of literary ecumenism, he soon found several persons throughout Spain who shared this unique passion for English literature. It was surely a mere coincidence that they were, each and every one of them, good friends of Alphonso—military veterans of the defeated Second Spanish Republic. It was even more curious that each listened avidly on a clandestine shortwave to Radio Moscow and a weekly cultural program celebrating the life and times of Charles Dickens and other British literary giants.

Philby spent the better part of an hour luxuriating over the carafe of red wine and the platters of food he was served—a series of *banderillas*, small food items skewered together and pickled in vinegar, deep-fried white anchovies, rings of *calamares*, and *chorizo* sausage cooked in red wine, and his favorite—prawns sautéed in peppercorn sauce.

As he did so, he thumbed through the pages of *Hard Times*, Charles Dickens's fictional indictment of the industrial revolution in the British

Midlands, halting occasionally to mark specific letters within the words on certain pages against a prepared sheet he had taken out of his valise.

Completing his indexing, he neatly folded the sheet and placed it back into his valise. He finished his meal and waved a pleasant goodbye to Alphonso as he went out into the searing sun and got into his car. On the tiny table where he had dined, he had left a respectable tip and, alongside it, the book. The text had been curiously marked in a manner that Alphonso would understand, translate, and forward promptly to a location some 3,000 kilometers to the north.

There, in the secured basement of an imposing building complex off Dzerzhinsky Square, someone would copy the random numbers, thumb through an English edition of *Hard Times*, and convert them to an equally illegible alphanumeric sequence. Transcription completed, a single sheet would be spirited to a third-floor office where the final code-breaking was done by one individual and one individual only.

* * *

She was at her desk as she always seemed to be. A guardian of the masses had no other life. The envelope was marked самый секретный—MOST SECRET. She cut the wax seal with a letter opener and scanned the contents. An alphanumeric sequence.

Fedin turned to a lower wall safe situated immediately behind her, twirled the tumblers in the required order and took out an English copy of the Charles Dickens novel and the current edition of the Moscow Center Code Book that had been specifically set for her use in such matters. And hers alone.

She began to efficiently decipher the encoded page. The message was not long, a few critical words capturing the essentials she required to move forward. She put her pencil down.

The who, what, when, where, and why were now plainly there on the page for her to see.

It was indeed useful to know that British MI6 was sending someone to Moscow and from there to Poland. And better still, to know the reason why they would do so—for the retrieval of a mysterious book of calculations secreted in a café in the center of Lwów. This could dovetail hand in glove with what she already knew.

Fedin smiled inwardly for a moment. Charles Dickens. The formidable chronicler of a bygone era and timeless icon of the decadent British bourgeois. Who would ever believe that, after being dead and buried for nearly three-quarters of a century, he would become such a useful aid to the Proletariat?

Number 2 Ulitsa Bolshaya Lubyanka, Meshchansky District, Moscow 10 July 1943

Nadia Fedin's intercom buzzed. Reception. Her guest was being escorted up. Fedin rose from her desk and glanced one final time at her briefing notes. The commissar had given her explicit instructions as to the meeting she was about to have and its desired outcome.

The reception suite, located on the floor below, was as bleakly anonymous as the rest of the building. An armed guard was stolidly planted outside her oak door. He would remain there until she had finished her meeting and would then escort the visitor back to the main floor entrance.

She entered the room. Its only occupant stood erect and confident as only one accustomed to a military lifestyle could be. He wore the tailored dress of a Russian staff officer, but unlike his Soviet army counterparts who had no collar badges, the pair he wore displayed the Polish white eagle without the traditional crown adorning it.

"I am only too happy to serve, Comrade Fedin." A gold-toothed, shark-grin.

"Comrade Berling. So glad you could come on such short notice." She held out her hand and he shook it, clicking his heels and bowing gallantly in the traditional manner of the pre-war Polish officer cadre. Nadia resisted the frown that began to form. Old habits were hard to break.

"Your Russian is excellent," Nadia remarked congenially. "I must apologize if we speak in Russian . . ."

"No need to apologize. It is as it should be at this time and place." The Pole gallantly gestured to the worn leather chesterfield. As they made themselves comfortable, Nadia shrewdly considered her guest.

Zygmunt Henryk Berling was tall and broad-shouldered, with a peasant's nose, a jutting jaw, and jug ears greatly accentuated by a shaved skull. There was a subtly coiled tension about his movements. If he had not been an officer and gentleman, he could well have been a bouncer in a seedy Murmansk nightclub.

A career army type who had fought the Russians in the 1920s, Berling had left the Polish army in early 1939 under acrimonious terms to work as a civil servant in Wilno—the direct consequence of a sloppy divorce allegedly involving the theft of his wife's property.

When the Soviets occupied Lithuania that September, he had been arrested as a potential subversive. But if Zygmunt Berling was anything, he was first and foremost a survivor, a trait that Lavrentiy Beria readily understood and could just as readily manipulate. As indeed he had.

While his fellow officers died at Katyn, Berling acquired Russian citizenship and moved into an NKVD villa in Małachowka, where he cynically identified Poles susceptible to Communist entreaty. After the German invasion, the commander of the Polish Armed Forces in the USSR, General Wladyslaw Anders, woefully unaware of Berling's active NKVD connection, appointed him as chief of staff of the yet-to-be-formed 5th Infantry—the "Wilno" Division.

Soon, the rapidly escalating tension between the London Poles and the Kremlin *Presidium*—a mood exacerbated by the massacre at Katyn—led most Polish soldiers and civilians in Russian territory to leave the Soviet Union and form the 2nd Polish Corps under Anders in the Middle East.

But not all Poles loyally fled east to fight alongside the Allies. During their evacuation to Iran, Berling, with two other officers, deserted the embryonic Polish Army being formed by General Anders. With him, Berling also took highly sensitive personnel files that he willingly surrendered to Beria and the NKVD.

Nadia Fedin had been his handler for the past year—personally selected by Beria for that role. They had verbally fenced over a number of issues, from staffing, to equipment, to the mandate of the emergent Polish 5th Infantry Division that would allegedly serve shoulder to shoulder in solidarity with Soviet armies on the Eastern Front. The Polish colonel was as multi-layered and complex as a *matryoshka*, a Russian nesting doll, but of one thing Nadia was certain—at the end of the day, Zygmunt Berling was most definitely a self-serving piece of work.

"You've heard of the tragedy that has befallen the London Poles?" Nadia asked.

"The plane crash at Gibraltar?" Berling responded tonelessly.

"A Liberator bomber carrying General Sikorski," Nadia blithely offered, dangling the reality in the space between them.

"Pity," was the only word that escaped the Pole's lips, and even it was uttered grudgingly.

Nadia tilted her head. "I take it you and the general were not on the best of terms?"

"An understatement," Berling replied tersely. "It is common knowledge that he wished to court-martial me."

"Does that trouble you, even now?"

"Nothing that comes out of London troubles me, comrade," the Pole archly replied. "Sikorski and his crowd are bourgeois rabble, rudderless, and without a future. They are completely irrelevant. The London Poles have no concept of reality. The Russian nation has bled and continues to bleed on the battlefield, and has earned the right to determine the destiny of Eastern Europe. Including that of Poland."

Nadia smiled politely. "Then what I ask you now might be somewhat unusual . . ."

Berling slowly raised his eyebrows as Nadia continued.

"We've been advised that an English agent is traveling to Moscow. If the British are to be believed, his mission is to secure the assistance of the Polish Home Army in support of our mutual effort to capture Berlin. You've been detailed by Comrade Beria to help this person to get into Poland and to aid him thereafter in any way you can."

She relished the words she uttered next if only to see the response they would evince. "It appears that he has the support of the London Poles . . ."

Berling's face was expressionless. "Who is this man?"

"Newly assigned to Churchill's pet project, the Special Operations Executive. That's all I know," she answered obliquely. "Our people say it would be advantageous for us to assist."

"Our people?"

"General," Nadia's manner turned steely. She had lost her patience and it showed. "There are certain things you need not know about—things you must leave to me. That is our agreement, is it not?"

"There is a working ratline through Ukraine. We can get him into Poland that way."

"You have friends in the Ukraine, Comrade Berling?

"There are loyal comrades in the field. Always."

"See to it then. Keep an invisible leash on the Englishman from the moment he leaves Moscow until the time he departs for England. We do not trust our British allies to be honorable."

A compliant nod of the head. "Comrade."

She stood up, trite niceties at an end. "Through me, Commissar Beria is to be kept fully informed of the Englishman's movements until he enters German-occupied Poland."

"Of course." The Pole rose slowly until he loomed over her. "How unlike him not to be."

"I beg your pardon?' Fedin flashed.

"Nothing," the Pole replied, pursing his lips. "I was just complimenting Comrade Beria on his thoroughness. And yours." His voice trailed off, as if he were wandering away looking for a place to hide.

"Of course," she responded crisply and was gone. In the hallway, she stopped and turned to the armed guard. "Escort him downstairs," she commanded tersely. "Don't let him out of your sight for an instant. Not one single second."

She next placed two calls. The first, to a nondescript shipping desk located in the sub-basement of the GUM department store. "Follow that fool wherever he goes," she directed with flinty precision. "Keep the tap alive on his phone. I want a daily report of everything the Polack colonel does and everyone he meets. And I do mean everyone. We wouldn't want Comrade Berling to suddenly develop a conscience—certainly not without our knowing about it, now would we?"

The second call was much warmer and circumspect. It went through a highly classified trunk line via neutral Sweden to a Persian art shop overlooking the *Spiegelgracht* canal, two hundred meters from the *Rijksmuseum* in Amsterdam.

The proprietor was a well-traveled Farsi. The shop was frequented by the highest-ranking Nazi elite, for the owner had access to some of the finest works in all of Europe and was the personal buyer of many remarkable pieces of art for *ReichsMarshal* Göring.

A long-time client, Nadia wanted to know if the four canvasses she had recently purchased had been sent to their destinations. The

164

Farsi reviewed the list, confirming their movement and receipt. Each item had been sent to someone specifically selected by Fedin, and each recipient had much more than works of art on their mind. A maritime shipper in Cairo. A pro-German architect in Stockholm. A Franco-supporting neurosurgeon in Lisbon.

Fedin also inquired if one creation in particular, a miniature by an obscure seventeenth-century Dutch painter named Jan van der Leeuw, was available. She then advised the proprietor that there was a refined gentleman serving in the German occupation forces in Warsaw who was extremely interested in the piece, and she wished to purchase it for him using the usual arrangement.

As a personal favor, she asked if the dealer could make the gentleman aware of an inscription on the painting that she knew would validate its relevance, if not authenticity. She repeated the elements that were to be found at the base of the work as the dealer assiduously made note of them in a tattered leather-bound journal.

It would be done exactly as she wished. She sighed, quite pleased with herself. Her business was making tiny items of potential intelligence fit into something real and palpable. If her ruse worked, it would prove a suitable trap for a traitor. And if not, it would be a welcome addition to the man's art collection.

* * *

Early the next morning, following the specific instructions he had been provided, the dealer himself took the painting, well secured in paper and twine, to Amsterdam *Centraal* train station and personally handed it over to a trusted contact to commence the seventeen-hour journey to Warsaw, a trip punctuated only by the mandatory stopover in Berlin.

It was understood that the journey might be sporadically delayed, subject as it was to the challenges of a temperamental *Kriegslokomotive* assigned the task of pulling fourteen war-battered coaches to their destination in broad daylight while fully exposed to the strafing whims of predatory American Eighth Army Air Force fighters.

The Amsterdam-Berlin-Warsaw dayliner endured a harrowing voyage, during which it was constantly shunted to lay-bys to enable heavily laden troop trains to roar eastwards to add fresh blood to the hemorrhaging Eastern Front. On one occasion, just outside Duisburg, the train was nearly blown sky-high by errant stick of bombs discharged by an American B-25 bomber.

It could be called a miracle that the train arrived at all, huffing and puffing, at the bomb-battered *Warszawa Główna* railway station, only a few hours behind schedule.

Railway station? "Adequate" would be a transparently deceitful compliment to describe what was once showcased as the most modern train depot in Europe and was now battle-degraded to a quasi-functioning shambles. Still, though the *Warszawa Główna* had been badly damaged during the initial months of the German occupation, it had managed to stubbornly struggle on with Ruritanian solemnity, if not efficiency.

The Amsterdam courier alighted from his coach and briskly walked to the rendezvous, careful not to appear too suspicious to the ever-watchful Blue Police. Any form of running, even a moderate jog, not only drew immediate attention. In these uneasy times, one also risked a bullet in the back. Or the head.

It was nearing midnight, but the building was still a hub of frenzied activity. The platforms were overflowing with German infantry dressed in either *feldgrau* or mottled camo—furiously smoking and backslapping, coiled-spring tense. Mingling uneasily among them were the obligatory clergy and stoop-backed peasants with their cheap cardboard suitcases tightly wrapped in rough-cut twine.

On the main tracks, locomotives muscled past in a steady stream, all heading east, pulling every imaginable type of rail stock; each wagon loaded to the brim with dispirited *Wehrmacht* troops. An occasional Red Cross train passed through, bound the other way. For *Der Vader land*. It always moved much more sedately, at an almost funereal pace. Considering the fragile, shattered living things carried on board, it was mainly out of kindness, he supposed.

At the station entrance, he was met by a pleasant-looking, middle-aged man in a black leather trench coat and matching homburg, whose erect posture could only have come from years spent bashing on a parade square. The man spoke German with a slight Eastern European accent. They exchanged discreet, coded pleasantries. The man in the trench coat partially undid the twine and appeared satisfied that the painting was the one he required. He gave the courier a slight smile and subtle nod.

Financial reconciliation would come later. As it always did. With a sharp heel click of his cavalry boots, the courier turned away and marched over to a sporty Mercedes Benz 320 Cabriolet driven by a uniformed *Wehrmacht* orderly, which quickly vanished from sight.

East Grinstead,
County of Sussex, United Kingdom
12 July 1943

East Grinstead was a placid town in the Sussex Downs, some 30 miles south of London. Laid out by one of the French nobles who crossed the Channel in 1066 with William, Duke of Normandy, its principal claim to fame was being the birthplace of Blessed John Story, a sixteenth-century martyr according to one authority, and a bloody butcher and traitorous rebel according to another. The town originally prospered from its strategic location on the main road between the seaside resort of Brighton and the English capital. It was also known for the quality timber hewn in the nearby Ashdown forest, universally known to children as the mythic abode of Christopher Robin's beloved honeypot teddy—Winnie-the-Pooh.

The nationwide period of depression between the world wars was mitigated in East Grinstead by two government construction projects: the Radio Centre, an Art Deco building that could accommodate 1,200 persons in its main theater, and a new hospital on the Holtye Road named in honor of Queen Victoria.

East Grinstead was too often an inviting secondary target for German bombers that had failed to hit their primary target elsewhere in the south of England. On the afternoon of Friday, July 9, 1943, that perverse familiarity turned deadly. A *Luftwaffe* Dornier returning from a failed bombing mission over London's West End became separated from its formation. Following the main line, it spotted a passenger train entering the railway station. Sensing easy prey, the bomber circled the town twice before dropping seven bombs. Two fell on the Whitehall Theatre, a cinema on the London Road, where 184 people were watching a Hopalong Cassidy short in advance of the main feature, Veronica Lake in *I Married a Witch*.

The other five projectiles struck an adjacent row of small businesses,

167

among them an ironmonger's shop that had 500 gallons of paraffin in the basement. The fuel exploded violently. The resulting blast swept through the cinema and a nearby row of shops. A total of 108 people were killed inside the Whitehall, including children, many of whom were themselves evacuees from the London Blitz.

Callison had arrived at the Victoria Hospital on Holtye Road mere days after the tragedy. He had been shipped to the Victoria as a "faint-hope" case. Initially treated at an RAF Burns Unit in Hertfordshire, his injuries had been deemed severe, almost irreparable.

His ward held five other occupants, all RAF types in varying stages of bodily reconstruction. He was assigned a bed by the window overlooking golden fields of barley—a timeless scene with farm hands tossing sheaves of grain onto rickety carts pulled by plodding horses, laboring in an ages-old rhythm. The transoms were open, and a soft breeze tickled the sheer draperies that framed the bucolic tableau. Occasionally, Callison could make out the faint drone of twin-engine Oxfords engaged in navigation exercises somewhere out there in the flax-blue Sussex skies. Other than that, there was nothing but blissful silence, broken only by a dog barking or farm hands shouting to each other.

For most of that first day, he lay in the bed, silent, full of unrelenting self-pity and resentment, as the realization of the dismal future he now faced as a deformed parody of his former self, sank in. Yet, peering bleakly around the room and beyond it into the hallway, he had been shocked to see others in far worse condition than himself. Men without noses or chins. Men with one good eye and a seared gaping hole where the other one used to be. Men with stumps for hands and lumps of curdled flesh for fingers. And all wearing combinations of flying kit and various items of civilian attire, oh-so-casually mixed, as if they were seated on lawn chairs watching a cricket match in the village green instead of what they had become in his eyes— nightmarishly grotesque caricatures of human beings.

For the next two days, Callison made no attempt at friendship. The nursing sisters assigned to him were pleasant and undemanding. The other occupants in the room occasionally made polite attempts at conversation, but he would have none of it. He was alone in his world and that was the way he wanted it to be.

Mid-morning of the fourth day, a creature wearing the rank

markings of a squadron leader approached the bed. His face was a mass of purple scars, the skin stretched and shiny, his lips bulbous. His eyes—one angled slightly lower than the other—seemed to travel in different directions under the scarred forehead. He placed a fingerless hand on the bed railing. "Listen, old boy. You are getting rather tedious lying there doing bugger-all, you know. This place offers every kind of support, but pity isn't support and, moreover, this isn't a hotel that welcomes pity. So, don't just lie there feeling sorry for yourself, you silly f——ing git. Are you coming over to join us for a grogging party in the mess, or not?"

Callison's response was hesitant at first, but he forced himself to go and found that he was not alone. Where he thought he was grotesque in appearance, there were others who were far more so. No matter how bad he looked or felt, there was always someone closer to the precipice. Someone who could benefit from his friendship.

The specialist surgeons noticed the subtle change in him and did their part to reconstruct Johnny Callison. In the next weeks, large areas of skin loss were repaired by tubes of skin taken from his abdomen and chest. In addition, scar tissue that had developed over his wounds was cut away and replaced with healthy new skin from another part of his body.

Victoria Hospital was unlike any other. Regular entertainments were arranged with visiting celebrities who came from London to perform. Books, squash, tennis, swimming classes, typing, accounting, bookkeeping, and even dances with the prettiest local girls—all these greatly helped to maintain high morale. But the hospital staff didn't only mend Callison's body; they gradually reconstructed his mind to an intensity he never thought he would ever reach again.

After two months, Callison was well on his way to membership in a unique band of brothers, the Guinea Pig Club. It was a painful and humbling experience, yet necessary, for that was the way Johnny Callison came to find himself among the living again.

**Somewhere in the Muranów neighborhood of Warsaw,
Generalgouvernement für die besetzten polnischen Gebiete
9 September 1943**

The warehouse was located on the west bank of the Vistula, down a jumbled laneway amid a lacework of shadows that lingered within weeping distance of the former Jewish Ghetto. It had no windows and reeked of fermented cabbage oozing from 60-gallon casks stacked, thimble-like, along its chalked interior walls. Foot-long rats brazenly slithered about the damp floor space, oblivious to a battle-scarred cat sleeping contently underneath a vacant watchman's desk.

Antony Eskenzi rested warily on a wooden stool in a corner of the office. A pair of light bulbs dangling awkwardly from overhead rafters provided a nebulous creamy halo.

He wore the rough-hewn farmer's clothing and scuffed work boots that had been provided by a kindly peasant woman somewhere along the journey. His anonymous escorts had wordlessly departed an hour before. Four strangers now loomed before him—three men and a not-unattractive brunette, all intensely young and armed with captured German pistols that they seemed determined to use if he made a false move.

Eskenzi had been smuggled to this final rendezvous after a serpentine trek from Moscow through the Russian forward lines and into the dank, mysterious Pripet marshes, past the ghostly German defense perimeter bristling with machine-gun nests. Guided initially by Berling's people—a ragtag bunch of Ukrainian misfits and rabidly socialist intellectuals—before being awkwardly handed over to hostile Polish partisans at the tiny border village of Samary, his perilous passage to Warsaw had taken the better part of a month.

Once he had crossed into the dense twilight of Occupied Poland, Eskenzi had spent a week in a variety of safe houses—barns, church halls, farm dwellings. Daily, he confronted an ever-changing cavalcade of dour faces, their features uniformly hardened by the harsh demands of their calling. For members of the Armia Krajowa, the organized resistance in the Occupied Poland of 1943, there was no future. As guerrillas, they lived, fought, and died with persistent regularity. If they were lucky when their time came, as it inevitably did, they might be afforded a wooden cross and a shallow grave. More often than not, they were left by their callous Nazi adversaries to rot in the solemn forests and shabby farm fields of the vast Polish plain.

Eskenzi cautiously peered around the dimness. He knew his hosts were members of the AK. Like all the others who had handled him, they remained nameless. One of the strangers approached him. He was tall, well-dressed in beige jodhpurs and a herring-bone tweed hunting jacket. His blond hair was fashionably long and wavy. He moved with the easy confidence and demeanor of someone to the manor born. Eskenzi guessed him to be no more than thirty years of age.

"*Parlez-vous français?*" the man demanded in perfectly accented French.

"*Oui. Mais je parle aussi Polonaise,*" Eskenzi responded.

"It is your choice, then."

Eskenzi nodded.

"Very good," the stranger continued. "London has verified your mission. But we don't trust you, Englishman. You were brought here by the Russkies. And for us, they are little better than the Nazis."

"Why do you say that?"

"Berling was your Moscow contact, correct?"

"Yes." Eskenzi recalled meeting Zygmunt Berling, a tall patrician colonel, in the Moscow hotel where he had stayed for three days in disquieting solitude upon his arrival in the Soviet capital. Their one and only encounter, punctuated by Berling's probing questions, had been on the twilight of the first day and had lasted for less than an hour.

"Berling." The well-dressed stranger repeated with ill-disguised revulsion. "You are aware he has been discredited and disowned by London?"

"He is working with the Allies," Eskenzi said lamely. "The Russians are our Allies."

"Perhaps to you they may appear as such, Englishman. To Poles, the Russians are historic and hostile occupiers of our land. And Berling and his kind are traitors to the Polish nation."

"But will you work with them, and with us, to expel the Nazis?" Eskenzi chanced.

"I would work with the devil to do that. Perhaps I already do." He sighed. "I understand from my associates that you are looking for someone?"

"Yes. In September of '39 I was ordered to get an individual I knew out of Poland."

"By whom?"

"My superiors"

"Why?"

Eskenzi's eyes narrowed. "Like you, I am rarely told the reason for such things."

The man seemed to accept the response. "Go on."

"I was unsuccessful. With the collapse of the Polish defense positions, our target moved toward the Romanian border. I was to meet him there."

"And before that?" the Pole probed. "Did you know the individual before the war?"

"Yes. I knew him here. In Poland. I considered him a friend . . ."

"So?" the Pole mulled over the answer. "That was another time. It doesn't explain why you are here now, four years later."

Eskenzi chose his words carefully. "My superiors believe that this person might still be alive . . ."

The Pole seemed perplexed and increasingly wary. "They have proof?"

Eskenzi nodded.

"His name?"

"I was never given his real name." Eskenzi responded. "He always communicated using a codename."

"Which was . . ."

"Pan Tadeusz."

"Pan Tadeusz." The stranger became contemplative. "The famous epic by Poland's revered poet. It speaks about a revolution to expel the foreign occupiers of Polish soil. Your superiors have a curious sense of humor."

Eskenzi shared the irony. "It's a British trait."

The Home Army soldier's manner suddenly shifted. "Many of my compatriots are not pleased with your government."

"May I ask why?"

"We feel the British are unwilling to admit what actually happened at Katyn, and now they won't blame the Soviets for the recent loss of our leader."

"Sikorski."

"Yes. General Sikorski. On the night of his death, the Soviet foreign minister's plane was parked on the apron at Gibraltar next to the Polish Liberator. That act alone afforded the Russians a golden opportunity for sabotage. Sikorski's public denunciation of the Katyn cover-up is an obvious motive."

"I can't speak for what happened at Gibraltar," Eskenzi countered awkwardly. "I want to accomplish what I've been tasked to do. We share a common cause. Destroying a mutual enemy. Let us focus on that."

"Our enemy?" The young Pole snorted. "You truly believe there is only one?" A long pause. "There are many enemies you will shortly encounter. Even some very highly situated within your own ranks. No matter. I've received instructions from our government in London. We will assist you."

"Then why so many questions to get to this point?"

"One can never be too sure," the Pole shrugged. "If the shoe were on the other foot, would you not undertake similar precautions regarding a complete stranger mysteriously arriving from Moscow?"

"Yes," Eskenzi admitted. "Yes, I would."

"Good." A thin, sullen smile. "I'm glad we understand each other. Since we are looking for Pan Tadeusz, it is a sign of our good fortune that my operating pseudonym is Adam and I will be what you English call your handler. Come. Tomorrow we begin to seek 'Tadeusz' in earnest. But tonight? You will depart with my friends."

The man who called himself Adam gestured to the waiting trio of armed guards. "We have a safe place for you to rest. Be aware that we must be extremely cautious. The wolves are on the prowl, and Warsaw is under curfew."

Hampstead Heath,
London, United Kingdom
13 September 1943

Caen Wood Towers was a Victorian mansion dominating the north edge of Hampstead Heath and situated a mere ten-minute stroll from Highgate Cemetery. Until 1942, when it was purchased by the British Air Ministry and reborn as Royal Air Force Station Highgate, it had been the principal residence of the managing director of the Shell Oil Company.

The Station immediately became home to the RAF Intelligence School and included accommodation, a messing, equipment stores, and a medical center. Shrewdly, the true reason for the site was not made fully public, and it operated under the guise of an Air Force convalescence hospital.

Johnny Callison's arrival at Caen Wood as one of its first students raised few eyebrows, beyond the involuntary gasps from members of the public whenever he ventured forth into the surrounding Borough on an infrequent day pass.

The intelligence course took the better part of five weeks and prepared Callison for the rigors of strategic planning, as well as the stressors of aircrew debriefings at the completion of a combat mission. It was a bittersweet feeling to know that he was beginning to contribute to a war he had almost forgotten existed, and so he attempted to block the memory of his own suffering from his mind. But he could not fully accomplish that task. The full-length mirror behind the door of his quarters remained, so that he might present an officer-like appearance while in uniform. But the compact facial mirror in his clothing locker was covered at all times.

He needed no reminder of what remained of John Paul Callison, the once-proud China Marine. For it was now but a faint memory, best forgotten. He realized he had become something grotesquely foreign to much of the outside world. But inside, in some small part of his soul, he also knew he was still the fresh-faced farm boy from Elkhart Kansas. And so he would always remain.

CHAPTER 10

Somewhere west of Algiers,
French Colonial Algeria (Algérie française)
19 October 1943

After passing his Highgate course and receiving a promotion to Squadron Leader, Johnny Callison was immediately posted to Number 148 "Special Duties" Squadron. Situated at a secret location near a seaside village 15 miles west of Algiers, the squadron was officially known as Interservice Signals Unit 6 and code-named "Massingham."

At Massingham, Number 148 Squadron initially operated a fleet of ungainly Westland Lysanders, which were ideal for covert ops—landing on tiny, unimproved airstrips behind enemy lines to drop off SOE operatives and equipment for the underground while picking up those few fortunate enough to get out. Their drops covered France, Italy, and the Balkans.

Callison's role in the scheme of things was straightforward—to debrief each pilot as to any variances during his mission that caused him to divert from the original flight plan. Simple distractions like German anti-aircraft fire, roving ME 110 twin-engine Zerstörers, or a compromised drop zone.

What went on in the SOE debriefs in a blacked-out hut in a distant portion of the airfield was none of his concern. In his own universe, he had become able to emotionally distance himself from the "no shows." Ultimately, it was just another shot-down Lysander, like a dead crow.

In the early fall of 1943, the Allies had occupied Brindisi, a tranquil harbor port on the Adriatic. A grass flying field named Campo

Cassale was located among its suburbs and designed before the First World War as a base for military dirigibles. After the Treaty of Versailles, it became a service facility for seaplanes of the Royal Italian Navy. Then, during Mussolini's reign, the flying field reverted to a drab backwater, a failsafe site for distressed aircraft and a jumping-off point for the daily Ala Littoria postal transport to Belgrade.

Immediately after the Allies seized the territory, Campo Cassale was evaluated for use by the US Army Air Force. It was described as "Dangerous for heavy aircraft Nov-May, surface damp and unserviceable in winter"—which made it a perfect site for the RAF 148 Special Duties Squadron.

After their arrival, 148 Squadron had gradually added several warweary Halifax and Liberator bombers to its inventory, expanding its flying complement to include a veritable United Nations of pilots and aircrew. Their zone of operations moved eastward and now encompassed Poland as well as Yugoslavia. Most of the bombers were nothing more than metallic patchwork quilts—spent victims of the constant operational tension and abuse they had faced, as were many of the aircrew who flew in them.

Johnny Callison could truly relate to both.

Inside the Kremlin compound, Moscow, Soyuz Sovetskikh Sotsialisticheskikh Respublik 19 December1943

Josef Vissarionovich Stalin, the General Secretary of the Central Committee of the Communist Party of the Soviet Union and Supreme Leader of the Soviet People, loved Hollywood movies—so much so that in each of his residences a state-of-the-art home cinema was installed. The Kremlin housed the largest of these in the former winter garden connected to the main palace by underground passages.

Every night, even when the Nazis threatened the very gates of the Soviet capital, the Supreme Leader would gather his inner circle—Beria, Khrushchev, Malenkov, and Molotov—in the Kremlin cinema to view his screenings. The films would start no earlier than nine in the evening and finish about three in the morning, with Stalin always sitting in the first row. He adored Hollywood westerns, and in particular, *Stagecoach*, with John Wayne as the Ringo Kid, the misunderstood bandit with a heart of gold. As he shyly confided to Beria as they viewed the film for the fourth time in as many months, Stalin saw his role in combating Hitler's hordes as that of Ringo, a solitary cowboy riding shotgun on a New Mexico stagecoach to successfully fend off Geronimo and his marauding band of Apaches.

During the evening's intermission, as the projectionist changed the reels, and the invited guests adjourned to a lavish vodka bar, a jovial Stalin beckoned Beria to a plush red chair next to him. There was a mischievous sparkle in the Supreme Leader's eyes as he filled his pipe with Herzegovina Flor blend.

"Comrade Beria," he whispered, "do you recall the hero of Borodino, the great Russian patriot—Pyotr Bagration?"

The chief of the NKVD sagely nodded his head in agreement. Who had not heard of the great Tsarist general?

"I have studied his tactics carefully and have asked the Stavka to plan a major spring offensive, one which will strike at the very center of the German line. We shall call it Operation *Bagration*, in tribute to that great general's resolve, determination, and enterprise. I have directed that *Bagration* not be a single battle, but rather a series of carefully orchestrated operations. The strikes will be differentiated both along the front and in depth—a new offensive beginning elsewhere, while the previous one is either in full swing or nearing its end. I am confident that with proper planning, *Bagration* will succeed, and we will finally sweep the Hitlerites back to their lair in Berlin and totally destroy them!"

Beria wisely agreed. It was one of the reasons he had survived for so long in Stalin's inner circle and others had not.

Stalin sighed with contentment and sat back in his chair.

"How is your young Captain Fedin doing?" His eyes darted to confront Beria.

"Very well, Comrade Leader," the head of the secret police replied, uncertain of the reason for the question.

Stalin's eyes gleamed impishly. "I am certain you are providing her with your usual personal guidance . . ."

"Of course."

Stalin nodded as he again packed tobacco into the pipe bowl. "And I can assume that she is handling the Katyn affair with suitable discretion?"

"Of course."

"Good." A reptilian smile. "I want you to promote her to Major of State Security."

"It will be done, Comrade," Beria answered with relief, for he had come to expect bewildering "death delivered with a grin" demands from Stalin.

The Supreme Leader, satisfied by the response, craned his neck tortoise-like to the throng lingering behind him at the bar. "Come, come everyone!" he clapped his hands with childlike enthusiasm. "The next film is starting soon! What is it, Dimitry?" he shouted over his shoulder to the projectionist.

A bald gnome of a man lurked next to the Super Simplex Projector, a personal gift to Stalin from the new American ambassador to the USSR. "*Tarzan's New York Adventure*, Supreme Leader," the man said, somewhat nervously.

"Do you know how many times I have seen this film, Beria?"

"No," the NKVD head lied strategically, for he had learned long ago to do so.

"Nine," the Supreme Leader asserted with obvious pride. "And this will be number ten!"

Beria sighed. He too had seen this film while seated at Stalin's side. Nine times.

The Supreme Leader energetically tapped the armrest of Beria's chair. "You know of course," he confided, "that the Tarzan movie is about a man who escapes the horrors of the capitalist world by fleeing to the jungle where he finds freedom and happiness."

And for what would now be the tenth time, the head of the Soviet Secret Police simply answered, "Yes."

The theater darkened.

Outside, beyond the vast red-bricked labyrinth of the Kremlin walls, a humid night ensnarled the Soviet capital in its spell. Yet here, in the womb-like private cinema, Josef Stalin sat, eyes transfixed on the screen, as Johnny Weissmuller arced through a canopy of trees boldly screaming his signature jungle call. A smile formed on Stalin's lips. He sighed contently. All was well in the world of the Supreme Leader. And for those trusted confidants in this hallowed chamber, and the legions of ordinary Russians who would never enter it, that was all that mattered.

Vesuvio Playground,
Manhattan, New York
1600 hours, 5 February 1944

Just before 4 p.m. on a bleak mid-winter afternoon, two men converged on a vacant lot near a playground on Manhattan's lower east side. One was thin and prim, wearing conservative tweeds and horn-rimmed glasses. He carried a green book, and despite the bitter winter chill, a tennis ball. Seeing the ball and book, a short, tubby man—wearing one suede glove and clutching the other—sidled up and asked for directions to Chinatown.

"Chinatown closes at five o'clock," the tweed-jacketed man responded blandly, completing the recognition signal. And with that, Klaus Fuchs, a young German exile newly arrived in the United States and Harry Gold, a traveling suitcase in the employ of the Pennsylvania Sugar Company, began walking together and into the pages of infamy.

Gold introduced himself as "Raymond," and after a short time hailed a Checker cab.

Before it had traveled four blocks, he stopped the vehicle and hustled Fuchs into a nearby subway entrance. This intentional deviation eventually landed the duo at an expensive steakhouse on 3rd Avenue. Over a T-bone steak, Gold boasted of the evasion tactic he'd used to thwart possible tails, but Fuchs openly dismissed it as juvenile. He also scolded Gold for the annoying habit of constantly swiveling his head as they walked looking, for suspicious persons who might be following them. "That only attracts attention," Fuchs remarked dismissively.

Klaus Emile Julius Fuchs was not an ordinary refugee from Hitler's Germany. Born in Russelsheim am Main, an ancient city near Frankfurt and the birthplace of Reisling wine, he'd been forced out of the Reich for his Communist activities. He subsequently fled to England to engage in the study of nuclear physics. He'd recently arrived in New York City as a respected member of the British scientific delegation to work on the Manhattan Project which, as he discreetly explained to Gold over his sirloin, medium rare, was inching toward the manufacture of a mega-bomb—an atomic weapon of unprecedented power.

After their first meetings, several others followed in rapid succession—in Brooklyn, the Bronx, Queens, and, in all instances, at publicly frequented places—bars, movie theaters, and museums. Occasionally,

Fuchs handed Gold an envelope; inside, there would be pages filled in a tidy script with diagrams and mathematical formulas—all top-secret research.

Afterwards, they often discussed chess and classical music. Fuchs spoke about his family, including a sister in Massachusetts. For his part, Gold told Fuchs about his twin children and his wife, a statuesque red-head who modeled for a department store. This, however, was just the wretched fantasy of a lonely man, for Gold was unmarried.

Belvedere District of Warsaw,
Generalgouvernement für die besetzten
polnischen Gebiete
4 March 1944

Eskenzi and Adam, his Polish underground handler, sat silently in the *Nur fur Deutsche* (For Germans Only) Number 35 tram as it trundled crab-like through what remained of the venerable central district of the Old Town. The morning was depressingly gray and wintry, even by the harsh standards of the Nazi occupation. Wearing the uniform of an SS officer, Eskenzi felt understandably anxious. Expertly tailored to his exact measurements by members of the Underground, as was Adam's. what remained of their original owners, killed in a midnight ambush, burbled about in a vat of acid at the Ursus heavy machinery plant on Wolska Street. Perhaps their mutated organisms would one day meld into one of the *Wesps*, the self-propelled howitzers manufactured at the facility for *Wehrmacht* service on the Eastern Front.

Eskenzi forced his mind to wander from these gruesome thoughts until it focused once more on his mission and the man he was determined to find.

For several months, he and his Polish handlers had sought out the mysterious Pan Tadeusz. AK units they approached had either never heard of the man or feigned total ignorance, for the Underground Army was fraught with dreadful unease, caught as it was between a brutal Nazi regime and a seething horde of historically hostile Soviet armies rapidly advancing from the east.

Eskenzi had dutifully forwarded this information to his handler in Gibraltar, or wherever Philby might be, knowing as he did so that it would be met with mounting frustration, approaching an anger that would be tastefully disguised as indifference. Like so many agents who had ventured forth into Nazi-occupied territories before him, he was creeping ever closer to organizational anonymity—a lost soul with no purgatory to claim as a safe abode.

The closest they had come to a positive identification was a senior AK cadre commander known only by the codename *Niedźwiadeka* (Bear Cub), whom they had met at a rendezvous in dense woodlands beneath the shadows of the red-brick Teutonic castle of Malbork. Bear Cub had arrived furtively with a support team from far-off Lida to take receipt of a large arms cache concealed in the forest.

The weapons—fifty much-valued Mark II Sten guns—had been parachuted in by a Liberator bomber operating out of Brindisi on a clandestine supply mission. Bear Cub and his followers desperately needed the weapons for a large-scale uprising they were initiating, designed to cause maximum distress to German forces already retreating in the face of the Soviet armies thundering across the Belarus–Lithuanian borderlands.

Bear Cub recalled that some months before, a mysterious traveler had been concealed in a parish church in the town of Grodno. For three days, Cub's AK team had successfully kept the man hidden from the fervently pro-Nazi Lithuanian security police teams that roamed the borderlands like rabid dogs and gleefully killed any Pole who dared to admit to their heritage. The AK team had even eliminated a probing security police patrol that had chanced upon them on the church grounds.

According to the AK commander, the word was that the priest and his wounded charge had somehow continued their clandestine journey, moving through the underbelly of the ravaged Polish nation using a succession of safe houses to reach their final destination, Warsaw.

True to form, no questions were asked about their journey. It was better not to know. Better that, when captured—as most AK members assumed they would be—they could remain loyal to their comrades, their cause, and to strangers who to them remained just that. For loyalty to such ideals was all that remained of the Polish nation as it once was.

"*Hauptsturmführer?*" a shrill voice interrupted Eskenzi's musings. He started. A mealy-faced woman leaned over to him from her seat across the aisle.

"*Ja?*" he responded warily.

"Good sir," the woman began, obviously pleased with herself. "It is wonderful to see you here in Warsaw and in that uniform. It makes us all very proud."

Eskenzi tensed, unsure of what to say. Leaning forward, Adam adroitly intervened. "*Danke, mein frau.* Like you, we remember our sacred duty to the Führer and to the Reich, even here." The German matron plopped back into her seat smiling smugly to those seated around her.

Alighting at their destination, Adam glanced at the windows of an unpretentious chemist's shop across the way. The bottles of colored water in the window were positioned at "safe." With this discreet affirmation that the Underground in the Mokotow district was not anticipating enhanced German patrols today, he hailed a *dorozka* for the remainder of their journey.

A short canter over cobbled streets bereft of life. Within six minutes of the appointed time, they arrived at Number 48 Belvedere Street, a well-kept apartment block located in an upper-class enclave in the Polish capital. They nimbly mounted the staircase to the third floor, their polished riding boots echoing forcefully on the harsh concrete.

Flat 32. The bell chimed in the apartment.

"Name, *bitte?*" A disembodied eye shrewdly scrutinized them through the peephole.

"We have an appointment with Colonel Kolchak," Adam responded, a suitably imperious Prussian growl in his voice.

An inner door opened. A sturdy middle-aged man, dressed in a well-cut business suit advanced to greet them, hand outstretched in a warm welcome. Nothing in his jovial manner hinted at any cause for alarm. The hand-shaking seemed to carry on interminably. He seemed to know Adam well and, by association, accepted Eskenzi as an equally trustworthy acquaintance.

Their host guided them into an elegantly furnished lounge. They seated themselves in plush emerald-green wing chairs that would not be out of place in London's best gentleman's clubs. Several paintings graced the walls; they appeared to be the work of Old Dutch masters. For a time, their host exchanged innocuous pleasantries with Adam, explaining the origins of the paintings.

He then turned to Eskenzi.

"You speak German?" A nod.

"Polish also?" Again, a slight affirmative.

"Russian?" A negative.

"French?"

"*Un petit peu.*"

A clap of hands and a uniformed orderly appeared from another room. A bottle of expensive Macallan whiskey and three crystal glasses on a silver tray were deftly placed on a side table between them. Their host smiled like a Cheshire cat. "Courtesy of the British Army in France, 1940. Dunkirk."

A perfunctory toast.

"I see you are interested in my paintings." He gestured to a rich cityscape, all canals and gabled houses, church steeples, and beefy Dutch burghers in broad hats and brocaded clothing. "I particularly like that one. An item I acquired—without *Reichsmarschall* Göring's intervention I might add—from his personal dealer in Amsterdam.

"It's by an eighteenth-century Dutch artist, Jan van der Leeuw. He liked to paint towns, their topography and architecture, and how the citizenry formed these into a singular unity. I particularly admire his rendition of the Church of St. Servatius and its surrounding plaza in Maastricht. I like such things, particularly in van der Leeuw's attempt to meld man, religious architecture, and their places within creation.

"Van der Leeuw was quite religious, a Catholic who lived in a strict Reform-mandated religious enclave located in the town of Delft. He liked to place discreet authenticators in all his works. His signature was always followed by a biblical citation." Kolchak pointed to the bottom right-hand corner of the work. "You see, 'J van der L John 14.22.'

"And that simple biblical quotation, as plain as day, is our clue. For you see, in the Bible, John was known as Judas Lebbaeus. He was also known as Jude the Apostle, the author of the epistle that bears his name. In that very epistle, he is said to be 'not Iscariot,' to distinguish him from the Betrayer. His surname was actually 'Thaddaeus.'

"The question put by Thaddaeus to Christ in the Gospel of John the Apostle in 14.22 is simple: 'Lord, why are you going to reveal yourself only to us and not the world at large?' That anonymity was used to perfection for your agent's particular circumstance and Polish codename—'Tadeusz.'"

Kolchak made his guests comfortable. He had a willing audience.

"Indulge me for a few minutes," he said, gesturing with his left hand to the painting, "for I would like witnesses to my own place in creation." He began to speak about his past.

As a young man, Vitaly Kolchak had been a captain in the *Preobrazhensky* Lifeguard Regiment, the most elite cavalry formation in the Russian Empire, charged with protecting the Tsar himself. At the end of the Great War, he and his family had fled the Bolshevik Revolution to seek refuge in Germany. Reaching safety, he had changed the family name of Smirdlovsky to Kolchak, in homage to the star-crossed Russian admiral who'd led the forces of the White Russian Provisional Government against the Bolsheviks from 1918 to 1920. The admiral was betrayed and executed by the Bolsheviks when the White Army tragically fell apart.

Because of his anti-Bolshevik background, Smirdlovsky-Kolchak had moved smoothly into the officer cadre of the resurgent *Wehrmacht*. Being a direct descendant of a Prussian Junker grandmother who'd also been a close relative of the great chancellor Bismarck certainly didn't hurt his rapid climb through the ranks.

The newly minted Kolchak would become the driving force behind *Plan Otto*, the bloodless 1938 *Anschluss* of Austria—the union of Germany and Austria. Then, in July 1940, he and his team had devised a plan to successfully invade the Soviet Union. They christened it *Barbarossa* after the fabled Holy Roman Emperor who, legend claimed, slept soundly with his knights in a Thuringian mountain cave, guarded by an unkindness of circling ravens, waking only to restore Germany to its ancient greatness. According to that same myth, when the ravens ceased circling the mountain, Barbarossa would arise to fulfill his destiny.

That first year, as Nazi legions swept eastwards encircling armies of ill-prepared Soviet troops, isolating Leningrad and surging toward the very western suburbs of the Russian capital, the ravens had indeed returned to their perches as Hitler began to vigorously reclaim Germany's vast eastern realm.

However, 1942 brought with it a deleterious shift in Nazi fortunes. The Soviet front line miraculously stabilized. Then, all too quickly came Stalingrad, the bloodiest land battle in history, immediately followed by Kursk, the largest tank battle the world had ever seen. In both, the proletarian armies of Comrade Josef Vissarionovich Stalin had emerged victorious.

The Reich's resources in men and materials were being severely drained in the face of Russia's sheer vastness and extreme climate. At the same time, war materiel from the Western Allies was pouring into Murmansk and Archangel through northern convoy routes in increasingly impressive quantities and quality.

On the home front, German strength of will and production capacity were being sapped by round-the-clock Allied bombing, compounded by the necessity of manning the Atlantic Wall against an anticipated invasion from Great Britain. More tellingly, North Africa was lost. The Allies swiftly conquered Sicily and successfully advanced onto the jagged Italian toe of Continental Europe at Calabria, as well as at the critical harbor ports of Salerno and Taranto. In summation, Hitler's much-vaunted "Thousand-Year Reich" was in grave danger of crumbling to ashes after a mere eleven years.

Kolchak ended his narrative. "The Führer's nascent Russian Liberation Army is commanded by Andry Vlassov, a captured Soviet general. Out of the millions of Soviet troops taken prisoner on the expanding Eastern Front, it has been largely formed by press-ganged Russians, principally Ukrainians. For propaganda purposes, Vlassov is head of that army, and I am seconded to it as chief of staff. In reality," he confided with a wry smile, "I am the true power behind the throne." The smile disappeared.

"Yet the job has required me to spend far too much time herding a bunch of sheep and goats who pitifully masquerade as soldiers of fighting caliber. The only reliable people I have are a small team of seconded *Wehrmacht* officers who have experience with the Russians, having fought them on the Eastern Front. Unfortunately, I lost my best officer soon after he started here in Warsaw. Transferred to the Katyn project. Name of Schneider. Iron Cross recipient. Fought at Stalingrad."

Kolchak downed his whiskey and nimbly poured himself another as he abruptly changed the topic. "You know," he continued with smug assurance, "the Führer trusts me implicitly. That is why I spend so much time at the Wolf's Lair. In fact, I will be leaving for Rastenberg again tomorrow."

He offered the bottle to his guests. Both declined.

"The press reports of a million-member Liberation Army?" Kolchak sniffed derisively. "A blatantly manufactured fiction. The numbers are much lower. Moreover, the recent Soviet advance into Europe has acutely affected even that inflated figure. Desertions have mounted dramatically. There have even been some successful mutinies."

Kolchak continued. "Himmler visited me here recently to discuss this staffing crisis. The *Reichsführer's* solution is to transfer borderline Liberation Army divisions to Italy and Yugoslavia to suppress the partisan menace in those regions. Formations deemed untrustworthy for front-line deployment in the east are to be sent to France to assist with fortification of the Atlantic Wall and to resist the Allied invasion across the English Channel, which we all know is coming."

"And has this happened?" Eskenzi probed.

Kolchak frowned. "Our most unreliable units are currently deployed at the Pas-de-Calais, monitoring seagulls and drinking cheap Bordeaux with French whores. And the rest? They are dying for *Herr* Hitler on the furthermost fringes of our Eastern Front, albeit with a Luger pressed to their backs to ensure their continued loyalty."

A sudden gust of wind rattled a set of French doors that led to a balcony overlooking Belvedere Street. Outside, a horse's hooves beat a steady tattoo on battle-blasted roadbeds. A truck horn bleated. A man's shout, hesitant, half-hearted, meekly summoning a distant friend. The labored symphony of a city inching toward abject despair.

After what seemed an eternity, Kolchak raised his glass in mock toast. "So, don't you wonder why you are in this apartment, Englishman?"

He viewed Eskenzi's shocked face with unmistakable bemusement. "Rest easy. The Polack briefed me before your arrival."

Adam deftly interceded. "Vitaly is a friend. He controls a dozen agents in German-occupied Russia. Some operate within the Soviet Union; perhaps even within Number 2—eh, Vitaly?" A roguish wink as he alluded to the ominous address on Dzerzhinsky Square. "Here in Poland, the colonel has been extremely useful to the Underground, and continues to be."

Carefully placing his glass on a side table, Kolchak shrugged in mock humility. "I try to do my best."

His gaze was piercing, his demeanor abruptly sober. "I maintain close relationships with the department heads of German intelligence. I know their true thoughts about this continuing farce. A number of high-ranking military commanders have become gravely disillusioned with the Führer and his lackeys. Gentlemen. Both they and I believe that this war is well and truly lost. It is sheer madness for Germany to continue to fight on one front, let alone two."

He hesitated and then spoke in the calculated manner of the survivor he was. "I must therefore make suitable and immediate plans to provide for myself and for my wife. After all, even the Führer cannot conquer time."

The air tasted of stale tobacco and the jasmine and lavender of expensive cologne.

"I have a proposition for you to consider. I know where you may find this Pan Tadeusz. But . . ." He raised an index finger in seeming caution. "Before I provide you with this information, I will require safe passage to Sweden for myself and my darling Helga."

"That may be difficult," Eskenzi hesitated at the unexpected demand. "I have no authority for this."

The Russian sighed. "The choice is yours, Englishman. If you want your man, it can be done. If you don't . . ." A tell-tale shrug as he scanned his guests for their reaction.

"Realize that this is a true gem that I have not shared with either of my current or previous masters, Nazi or Soviet. Let us just say it was something you English would say will allow me to walk away 'scot-free.'"

Eskenzi wavered, then finally nodded.

"Good. Then it is agreed. Now, in the manner of all successful negotiations, such critical exchanges require distinct trade-offs. I will provide you with all you require on Pan Tadeusz. And you, in turn, will provide me with safe transport to Sweden."

"Oh, and one more thing, Adam," he added, with the pallid smile of a man who made a career out of personal survival. "As a show of good faith and, more pragmatically, to ensure you promptly deal with your end of the bargain, I will provide one more gem."

Kolchak gestured to the nearby wall, where an ornate timepiece overpowered the space it occupied. "A cuckoo clock."

He stood and took the gaudy ornament from its mooring, holding it proudly, as one would a hunting trophy. "An innocuous item at the best of times, don't you agree? I purchased this in Bavaria last year. It set me back far too many *Reichsmarks*, I must tell you," he muttered to no one in particular.

He scanned his guests, sensing their confusion. "Patience," he declared confidently. "It will be over in a few minutes."

Precisely at 2 p.m., the chamber doors of the clock opened and a feathered cuckoo emerged to announce the hour. Kolchak grasped the wooden bird in mid-motion. With a free hand, he deftly removed what appeared to be a tiny speck from its beak before allowing the thing to retreat into its dwelling. He then took a white silk square from his breast pocket, placed the speck onto the handkerchief, and handed it to Adam.

"That speck is a microdot," he noted. "Contained on it is Hitler's plan to destroy Warsaw."

The room was jarringly still. The Pole's face turned ashen. "Bloody lunacy," Eskenzi remonstrated in disbelief. "The Soviets are at Warsaw's doorstep. Only an insane man would consider such folly."

"Insane?" Kolchak shrugged. "That may well be. Something diabolical contemplated by a madman? Most probably. But it will happen. It is the Führer's wish."

"Go on." Eskenzi responded warily, at once both curious and appalled.

The Russian began in a disarmingly unruffled manner, as if he were critiquing the Van der Leeuw on the wall and not the destruction of an ancient city. "In 1939, Uncle Adolf approved a detailed proposal to completely level Warsaw before turning it into the perfect provincial capital, but with an exclusively German population. It was to be named *Die Neue Deutsche Stadt-Warschau*—the New German City of Warsaw. The complete plans for it are on the microdot that you now possess. I managed to obtain a copy some time ago from a reliable source."

He paused then went on. "The scheme was to utilize Polish slave labor for the demolition. With Ivan knocking at the door, that fantastical new town will never be built, but with these plans, it can still be effectively destroyed by systematic demolition. *Herr* Hitler may never have his 'Utopia' on the Vistula, but neither will Stalin."

"The date this devilish plan is to commence?" Eskenzi pressed.

"Not so fast," the Russian tut-tutted. "Not so fast. I will provide you with Pan Tadeusz. And also with the date my so-called associates plan to begin the complete destruction of the Polish capital. But only when my wife and I are safely on our way to Sweden. And only then."

Kolchak clasped his hands together in exaggerated triumph. "So? Do we have an understanding?"

Dead leaves scratched furiously at the French doors of the

apartment. The world beyond them was bathed in a stern northern light that caused Eskenzi's eyes to ache. He looked at the Russian and sensed an almost palpable feral cunning.

Reluctantly, Eskenzi nodded approval.

Yet somehow it didn't seem to count for much anymore. For he knew from that moment onward, that he was well and truly in the belly of the Beast and what he would do next required absolution only God could provide.

70 Grosvenor Square, Mayfair
City of Westminster, London
7 April 1944

The five-story Georgian was situated just east of Grosvenor Square Garden and within sight of the American embassy. To describe the building as bland, gray, and nondescript was to flatter it. But, as with many things in wartime London, outward appearances could be—and, in this case, were—very deceptive.

For who would ever have believed that the epicenter of American intelligence activity in Europe was hiding in plain sight. The newly formed OSS was located directly across the street from two eminent British ladies' clothing shops—Ann Taylor and Jacqmar—and a mere block away from one of the most prestigious department stores in the Empire, Selfridges on Oxford Street. But such was the art of covert operations.

Wild Bill Donovan, personally selected by Roosevelt to head the OSS, had, at its inception, specifically asked for Pat Flaherty to be seconded from the Army Intelligence Corps to his top-secret unit. It was a natural choice for Donovan to make, and as natural for the burly Irishman as a plate of corned beef and cabbage washed down with a pint of Guinness. And now, holding the Army rank of brigadier-general and, with the implicit blessing of the President of the United States, Donovan was given whatever he asked for.

Donovan knew Flaherty from 1918 at the Argonne where, as a young infantryman at the battle of Landres-et-St. Georges, the lad had loyally followed Donovan, then commanding the Fighting 69th Regiment—the Irish Brigade—to attack a German position that was well entrenched on a steep ravine. Donovan had been wounded three times in the doomed attack, but refused to leave the field until his troops were seen to. It was an eighteen-year-old private, Patrick Aiden Flaherty, who ultimately carried his commanding officer to safety under heavy fire and at great risk to himself. For his singular feat of bravery, steadfastness, and leadership, Bill Donovan was awarded the Medal of Honor, and young Flaherty, the Distinguished Service Cross.

Reporting directly to Donovan, Pat Flaherty had become a highly innovative manager of the diverse case files he'd been given responsibility for—from accumulating accurate field intelligence that culminated in the successful Allied landings in Morocco and Tunisia, to a "most secret" deal he'd co-brokered with US Navy intelligence.

That deal, aided in no small measure by Flaherty's time in the NYPD, enlisted the support of one of the most powerful Mafia dons in America, Charles "Lucky" Luciano, born Salvatore C. Lucania. Convicted of operating a prostitution ring, Luciano was serving a thirty- to fifty-year sentence in maximum security in a New York State prison.

Luciano proved to have critical Mafia contacts who provided the Americans with key information and logistical support in the form of detailed drawings and pictures of Sicily's coastline and its harbors, which proved vital for the successful July 1943 invasion. After a mere thirty-eight days and due in no small part to the active intervention of the Mob, the rugged island that was the native home of the Cosa Nostra was conquered.

There were, however, certain tolerance levels for a seasoned NYPD cop like Flaherty, even working for Donovan, whom he greatly respected. Flaherty knew he had massively overshot those levels in his dealings with Wild Bill and some of his closest contemporaries at the OSS.

During his tenure there, Flaherty had become increasingly concerned about his boss's ambivalence to the presence of actively pro-Soviet members within the higher ranks of the organization. It wasn't just their philosophical allegiance to the radical tenets preached by Stalin. What was more troubling was their open and rabidly unilateral support of pro-Soviet partisan rather than democratic movements in Occupied Europe. One day in casual conversation, Flaherty brought his reservations to Donovan's attention.

The major brigadier-general's cool response? "I'd put Stalin on the

OSS payroll if I thought it would help defeat Hitler."

It was not long after that telling comment that Captain Flaherty requested to be sent back to Washington.

CHAPTER 11

Somewhere on the Baltic Sea,
North-northwest of Leba, Poland
Latitude: 55°, 21' minutes, 37.73"
Longitude: 12°, 19', 22.7922"
9 April 1944–15 April 1944

The Baltic night was wickedly malevolent, a dejected half-moon thankfully hidden by cloud cover. A cotton-wool mist inched outward from the shoreline and hung heavy about the rowboat, shielding its four occupants from view. A pencil-beamed searchlight arced randomly over the waters, operated by indifferent German garrison troops stationed at the nearby *Kriegsmarine* base.

The small flotilla of R-boats that daily roamed this portion of the Polish coastline lay at anchor, but for a solitary craft. An hour earlier, it had been sent scurrying eastwards into Gdansk Bay and away from their route in response to a carefully staged decoy—a random series of flares intentionally ignited by parties unknown.

The anonymous man in the rowboat's bow peered patiently into the gloom. His companion, a burly fisherman, tackled the unwieldy oars with mule-like resolve. The two passengers they ferried, a middle-aged man and woman, were huddled in the center of the boat, a coarse gray army blanket covering them.

Earlier in the day, another anonymous man had bribed the *Kriegsmarine* guards, a trio of guileless Flemish conscripts patrolling the impoverished fishing anchorage at Leba, to look the other way as the rowboat cast off from the pier. His inducement? The oldest one of all, the offer of sexual favors from older, more experienced women.

As a result of such shrewd actions, the tiny craft's progress beyond the huge closed area safeguarding the Hel Peninsula and its defense garrisons along the northern Polish coast had been remarkably easy. Still, a growing sea swell made the rowing difficult.

But for the wind and the waves, the night enveloping them was as ominously silent and forbidding as the deepest dungeons of the Teutonic castle at Malbork. The man and woman seated in the boat sat motionless. The rough blanket provided only slight warmth, but some warmth was better than none. The two spoke infrequently, a staccato mixture of Russian and German, but not a word of Polish. It was irrelevant, for the two men with them understood every word, even when they pretended not to.

The man in the bow squinted seaward until he spotted it on the horizon. He gestured to the passengers and stilled their expectant whispers with an abrupt brush of an outstretched hand.

What seemed like a mirage took shape as they inched closer—a dilapidated steam drifter drunkenly wallowing, its mizzen sail swinging madly about. A tattered Swedish flag flapped erratically from the stern in the face of a brisk southwest wind. A tall, flute-like funnel punched skyward, emitting hesitant puffs of smoke. A faint light illuminated a matchbox-like wheelhouse. Inside the cabin, an oil-skinned figure at the helm calmly kept the vessel aligned with the prevailing gusts.

Shadowy figures moved about the main deck of the stubby wooden ship as they readied for the morning's herring haul. The figures were speaking in a foreign language—throaty Nordo-Germanic with a sing-song lilt.

The man in the rowboat stopped rowing.

The man in the bow hissed at his passengers, his Polish heavily accented as if it were not his native tongue. "We are now at the maritime boundary between Poland and Sweden. You were to give us some information?"

"Not so fast," The male passenger responded arrogantly as he clutched an envelope close to his chest. "Not so fast. A bird in the hand, my friend, is worth two in the bush. And I still hold the bird you need right here in my hand."

The man glowered. "Which means?"

"I will hold onto these documents until I am safely on Swedish soil."

The two men glared wordlessly at each other. Finally, the man in the bow spoke. "Suit yourself. We aren't a taxi service. Wojtek can row us back to the Polish coast as easily as we rowed away from it."

"If you row back, you bastards will face certain death," Kolchak blurted, his face turning red.

The man in the bow shrugged. "As will you. We've made certain that your counterparts in the Gestapo are very much aware of your desertion."

The passenger glanced apprehensively at his wife. Then, slowly, he handed over the envelope.

"Now, that wasn't so hard, was it?" The man in the bow remarked soothingly. He tucked the envelope into the pocket of his vest and took out a jet-black object. Two shots rang out from a Walther pistol. Two bodies slumped over and were soon roughly pushed into the inky Baltic waters. The man in the bow dropped the pistol into the sea.

Suddenly, a wraithlike voice stabbing into the night from the general direction of the fishing smack. "*Vem går där?*"

And then, when there was no reply in Swedish, the same question repeated in poorly accented German, "*Was passiert?*"

"*Nichts,*" the boatman replied in a composed voice.

"*Brauchst du Hilfe?*" A second query from the ship.

"*Nein.*"

With a few words of direction to orient the men toward the Polish coast, the rowboat turned back and made its way slowly, ploddingly, toward Occupied Poland.

When Kolchak and his wife did not show up for three days, there was concern in Warsaw for their whereabouts, but it was not unusual for the colonel to go off on some mysterious errand for the higher-ups in Berlin. Perhaps this time he had taken his wife with him.

The uniformed orderly assigned to the Kolchaks had been given a week's leave and been advised by the colonel that he and his wife were touring along the Baltic coast with a break at Zopot and its famous spa.

A check of the hotel confirmed that the Kolchaks had checked in on Monday and driven off with a prepared picnic basket for a day's outing at Malbork Castle on Wednesday. It was now Friday, and they had not returned to their hotel lodgings, though their suitcases were still in the room, and it all had the lived-in appearance that one might expect of casual vacationers. As an added precaution, the colonel's workplace and flat on Belvedere Street were thoroughly searched. Nothing was amiss. All his papers and files seemed in order.

194

On Saturday morning, what remained of the colonel's Cabriolet was located by a roving patrol on a seldom-used road some 20 kilometers from the Castle grounds. It had been destroyed by what appeared to be a high-intensity roadside bomb; only cindered and grotesquely shrunken figures remained of its two occupants.

Kolchak was mourned by all who knew him as a hero of the Reich. His photo, framed in funereal black trim, appeared in the official Party tabloid *Der Stürmer* and in all mainstream German print media. When the Führer was informed of his death, he was visibly moved by the passing of an individual who he deemed to be "one of those who was always loyal to me and who has paid for it with his life." When word of his demise became public in the Nazi-controlled press in Poland, the Home Army claimed full responsibility for the deed, judiciously avoiding any commentary as to the method it had used in the killing.

Planty Park,
Beneath Wawel Castle, Old Kraków,
Generalgouvernement für die
besetzten polnischen Gebiete
13 June 1944

Jan Robel liked to take his lunch in Planty Park, a cool and shady green belt that had for more than a century girdled Wawel Castle with benign acres of towering pines and lush flower beds. Lunch for him had become a hugely exaggerated term. A single egg obtained from a farmer for two times its worth, a stale piece of kielbasa, three slices of hard-as-rock black bread—all wrapped in an old newspaper—and a thermos filled with bitter chicory coffee. But his ritual at lunch allowed Robel to escape, at least figuratively, from the harsh regimen of the Institute, and it was assuredly a world away from the starvation rations he'd received while a political prisoner of the SS at nearby *Sachsenhausen*.

Robel knew full well that his release from *Sachsenhausen* had been driven solely by necessity and not to right any injustice, for he possessed a particular scientific skill that the Nazis desperately needed, which was to positively identify the Katyn evidence to their satisfaction. This meant that after each item had been defatted and cleaned, he and his team could attach actual names and human identities to the putrid lumps resting within the Institute—the photos, decorations, banknotes, billfolds, cigarette holders, combs, and personal correspondence stuck together with body wax and contaminated with Belorussian soil.

Nothing more. Nothing less.

The park around him was filling with its daily clientele—elderly office workers and thin-as-a-rail shop clerks having a lunch break, harried mothers pushing rickety prams, packs of stray dogs foraging for food, the occasional *Wehrmacht* officer strutting to barracks—passed for normalcy in a time of hostile occupation.

A dungareed park employee shuffled past Robel's bench pushing a wheelbarrow partially filled with refuse. The worker stopped for a moment and wiped his brow with a grimy handkerchief. He glanced at Robel. "Mind if I sit here, boss?" he asked timidly.

Robel, munching on the kielbasa, gestured vaguely to a spot on the bench beside him.

The worker noisily blew his nose on a soiled handkerchief as he accepted the offer to sit down, stretching his legs as he did so.

"Hot day today, isn't it, sir?" he offered politely.

"Yes," Robel muttered with faintly disguised annoyance.

A Gestapo major walked hurriedly past them toward the castle entrance, seemingly late for an appointment with his Aryan destiny. The two men sat staring vaguely into the distance, lost in their own solitudes, until the German had safely passed.

After a time, the worker rummaged in his pants pocket until a shriveled apple emerged. He took a bite and began chewing. "How is it going?" he whispered without looking at Robel.

Robel poured coffee from the thermos into a cup. "We've identified about one thousand victims so far," he offered under his breath.

The worker sighed and took another bite from the apple. "Then we have time . . ."

Robel sipped the coffee and grimaced as he did so. The chicory-flavored distillation, which seemed to accompany Nazi occupation, was brutally tart. That alone, he thought ruefully, was a good enough reason to do what he was continuing to do. "Not really," he said finally. "The Germans wanted it completed a month go."

"And?"

"We told them it was an impossible task. Luckily, Beck agreed with us—so we are safe for now."

Whispering breezes rustled the pines above. A red squirrel darted past them, heading for a nearby copse of trees. Moments later, a dog followed, bounding in pursuit. A sliver of cloud momentarily hid the sun.

"The storage area is the same?" The worker continued in hushed tones.

"Yes. The basement."

Then, a lengthy silence, broken only when the laborer awkwardly stood and stretched, his apple eaten, his rest-break complete. He haphazardly tossed the core into the wastebasket and missed. The red squirrel reappeared and ran off with its trophy.

Robel finished his meager meal and tossed the used newspaper wrapping into the wastebasket. He turned to the laborer. "Take care, friend."

"And you too, sir," the man politely doffed his cap. He then continued with his assigned chores diligently emptying the contents of the wastebasket into the wheelbarrow before stepping off at a leisurely pace in a direction leading away from the castle.

Robel waited a few minutes, glanced at his wristwatch, and then stood up, brushing a few breadcrumbs from his pants. He could never get used to seeing that eye patch on his younger brother, Amadeusz. Beaten to within an inch of his life by the Gestapo six months ago during one of their routine roundups, Amadeusz was simply in the wrong place at the wrong time. He had gravitated into the Movement without any coaxing. Now he toiled in a seemingly harmless job—a parks laborer—which conveniently placed him in daily contact with Robel and the critical work being conducted at Number 7 Kopernick Street.

That night, Amadeusz sat on his cot in the tiny garret. He carefully unwrapped the newspaper he'd collected from the wastebasket. Carbon-copied sheets of paper were tucked neatly inside the folds of the newspaper. As usual, his brother—the good doctor—was as good as his word.

At the Institute, Robel followed a standing operating procedure set in place to deal with the Katyn evidence. Once what remained of a human buried in that Belorussian forest was positively identified and somehow connected to a name, a document attesting to their verified identity was signed off by Robel and a member of his staff and forwarded to the director of the Institute.

Amadeusz now held carbon copies of those confirmation sheets that verified the true identities of Polish officers and members of the intelligentsia murdered by the NKVD. By morning, this information would wend its serpentine way to London. Within twenty-four hours, the Polish government-in-exile would have a more current and comprehensive list of the Polish casualties at Katyn than either Adolf Hitler or Josef Stalin—if they even cared to know.

Mabel's Breakfast,
857a Washington Avenue,
Brooklyn, New York
6 July 1944

On a sweltering afternoon in early July 1944, Klaus Fuchs and Harry Gold had scheduled their eighth meeting at a working-class greasy spoon located near the Brooklyn Museum. The German physicist didn't show. Given how precise Fuchs always was, this worried Gold. But they had a backup meeting scheduled a few days later in a coffee shop near Central Park.

Fuchs missed that meeting, too. A troubled Gold returned to Philadelphia. An invaluable spy—and a man he considered a good friend—had gone missing.

For a time, neither Gold nor his Soviet higher-ups knew where Fuchs was. But after months of searching, Gold finally tracked his friend down through Fuchs's sister in Massachusetts.

Incredibly, through a combination of luck and lax government security, the Soviet spy had received a personal invitation to the very inner sanctum of the Manhattan Project—the weapons lab at Los Alamos.

Number 2, Ulitsa Bolshaya Lubyanka,
Meshchansky District, Moscow,
Soyuz Sovetskikh Sotsialisticheskikh Respublik
10 July 1944

Nadia Fedin was furious. And understandably so.

The NKVD had been meticulous in securing their core work

against hostile outside threats, and particularly within Number 2 Ulitsa Bolshaya Lubyanka, the crown jewel of their intelligence empire. To that end, the NKVD had unearthed Kolchak's agent with the time-honored ruse of feeding him false information and watching it being traitorously redirected to Warsaw using a medium they also controlled at the Polish end.

The turncoat who had done the deed had operated as a senior watch commander within the NKVD central communications center for some time. In the past, there had certainly been rumors of a leak within the organization. There had even been the beginning of an evidentiary trail starting mere weeks after an NKVD agent was arrested in Estonia while building an operating cell of like-minded comrades, and another was shot by the Gestapo within days of her arrival in Latvia, before she even had time to find secure lodgings. But it was mere speculation at best and never critically connected to the Lubjanka. Until now.

Inevitably, the spy was tortured and a connection to Kolchak's Russian past was soon established. Whatever influence or hold Kolchak had over the agent—blackmail, money, a promise of freedom—it was hard to believe anyone would take such a risk. Fedin didn't have the time to find out more. She watched the execution and took a degree of pleasure from seeing the man's blood flowing rich and darkly red onto the earthen cell floor. As she stood there in the dank cell while the limp body was removed to be dumped into the building furnace, she clinically reviewed the operation in her mind.

The original message from Schneider that concerned the possible identity of the Polish Red Cross official never reached Kolchak. It had been intercepted at the Lubyanka and, after swift analysis, was moved on to Warsaw, becoming cheese in the trap Fedin had set. And Kolchak had fallen for it.

His phone had been tapped—a leak in the Polish resistance, the Armia Krajowa, had advised them of the meeting the Polish underground leader and Eskenzi would be holding with Kolchak. In addition, all the rooms in his flat were bugged.

For some time, Fedin and Kolchak had surreptitiously communicated with each other. For his part, the White Russian fancied himself a master in the game of espionage, a wheeler-dealer who skillfully played both ends for his own designs. Fedin sensed this and believed Kolchak did it specifically to feather his own nest and escape to a neutral nation as the war ground to a thoroughly unsatisfying halt.

The time was ripe. Fedin had been feeding Kolchak selectively plausible misinformation for the better part of a year and, accordingly, had been able to link smoothly into his networks. The artwork was real. Its pretense for shipment was easily arranged. It was the second teaser of her bait.

Now, all she had to do was to ensure that Kolchak was foolish enough to use it. And he did.

The anonymous duo who'd bribed the *Kriegsmarine* guards and then rowed the Kolchaks to their doom in the Baltic were Soviet operatives, not Polish patriots. The contents of the letter they received from Kolchak before murdering him and his wife were invaluable tools for Fedin in her Katyn investigation and, as a bonus, she now also had a new quarry—someone with the codename "Pan Tadeusz."

And then, somehow, something had gone terribly wrong. For the two operatives were nowhere to be found. She strongly suspected they were the burned remnants found inside the Cabriolet on the dirt road near Malbork.

Fedin sensed a Polish Underground Army double-cross and that made her extremely angry. For the Poles now also possessed the contents of Kolchak's letter. She was not accustomed to losing. Nor would she allow it to continue.

**фронтов советской армии (Soviet Army groups/fronts),
Advance westward to Belarus,
Aiming at the very heart of the German Reich
June–July 1944**

After months of careful planning by the *Stavka*, on June 22, 1944, Operation *Bagration*, the seminal brainchild of the Supreme Leader, had been launched on four broad fronts. As Soviet forces advanced relentlessly forward, they trapped 100,000 German troops in Minsk, clearing the Pripet Marshes, then ranging northward to take Vilnius, most of Latvia, and the ancient textile center of Białystok. They triumphantly arrived at the Polish border in a mere twenty-four days, capturing 158,000 German soldiers, 2,000 tanks, 10,000 guns, and 57,000 motor vehicles while also claiming to have killed 381,000 German troops.

On July 17, 1944, Soviet Army generals convened talks at the Byelorussian Front Headquarters with the Wilno Branch of the Polish *Armiya Krajowa* under the pretense of planning a joint attack against the retreating Nazis. The meeting was attended by leaders of all the Polish partisan units, including *Niedźwiadek*a—Bear Cub. The discussion was short and sweet. After it ended, the Polish officers were all disarmed and arrested by the NKVD.

Bear Cub was of particular interest to a young NKVD investigator named Tretiak. When they first met the advancing Russian troops, Bear Cub and his team had in their possession a number of new British Sten guns. Tretiak was as cunning and ruthless as a Siberian fox; the source of such weapons was always relevant to an occupying power. In a candid, albeit manipulative, discussion between Slavic brothers-in-arms, Tretiak pounced on his unsuspecting prey. And Bear Cub fell into the trap.

The NKVD investigator was an avid chess player and knew Petrov's classic offense, which he now executed. As life would imitate art in such matters,] it was all too easy for him to lure the naive Pole into inadvertently telling him everything he needed to know. Bear Cub bragged that his Home Army Unit had been remarkably effective and, among other things, had certainly proved their worth one hundred percent in an ambush that had decimated an overly curious Lithuanian security police patrol. It had happened in a place called Grodno, when his team was charged with guarding a priest and his mysterious injured friend on church grounds during the duo's trek toward Warsaw.

Ivan Tretiak was both thorough and ambitious. He knew that each piece of field intelligence he gathered—however insignificant it might seem—was important to someone somewhere within the ultra-paranoid NKVD world, where he was a trusted member. He also knew that Moscow was constantly seeking pertinent information on Polish clergy, viewing them as a serious threat to Soviet control in the occupied Polish territories. Accordingly, Tretiak ensured that Moscow Central was immediately informed of the curious incident with the priest and his mysterious companion traveling through Grodno.

Within the hour, Nadia Fedin had another useful piece to fit into the slowly forming jigsaw puzzle.

At the same time, Ivan Tretiak was personally test-firing a new

British Sten gun. He found it to be sufficient for his immediate require-
ments. A pity he could no longer converse with his Slavic brother, Bear
Cub, about it, but then a dead man isn't the best conversationalist—certainly not after confronting a fully loaded Sten.

Arlington Hall,
901 South Randolph Street,
Arlington, Virginia
12 July 1944

Arlington Hall was a Doric-columned monstrosity located on a
pleasantly treed 100-acre campus a short distance west of Arlington
National Cemetery. Founded in 1927 as a junior college for women,
the building, if not the college, had somehow survived the Depression
until it was taken over in 1942 by the US Army Signal Intelligence
Service under the authority of the American War Powers Act.

The Signal units located there were originally involved in decoding
Japanese systems, including PURPLE, the code used by the Empire of
Japan's diplomatic corps. And they became quite good at it.

But in early 1943, a secret group began what would become a
lengthy project code-named *Venona*—its mission to intercept all the
diplomatic messages—not of an enemy, but of an ally, Soviet Russia.
Venona came into being as the direct consequence of information
received that a possible German-Soviet peace deal was in the works.
The information proved faulty, but a treasure trove of other important
data had been collected and the project continued.

The methodology the teams at Arlington used was straightforward.
Soviet message traffic was generally encrypted using a singularly unique
code to convert words into random strings of numbers or letters from
one-time note pads, effectively encrypting the document.

It was simplicity, both in theory and execution. Since each additive
key was unique, the encrypted wording was virtually unbreakable.

However, because of the intense pressures brought to bear during
the initial Nazi advances, which challenged Moscow itself, the Soviet
firm manufacturing the one-time pads inadvertently produced 35,000
pages of duplicate keys. This replication was detected by the cryptolo-
gists at Arlington Hall and laid a logical baseline for their subsequent

code-breaking work.

Thus, it was to Arlington Hall on a smoldering July afternoon that Captain Patrick Flaherty was ordered to report.

Peenemünde, Germany, heading due east
Latitude: 54.13591° N Longitude: 13.773348° E,
Air speed: 196 mph (315 km/h) at Angels 22
1102 hours, 18 July 1944

Shortly after eleven o'clock on a bright July morning, with nearly 100 percent visibility, 377 US Army Air Force B-17 Flying Fortresses, flying in a polished cobalt-blue sky and escorted by Lightning and Mustang fighters, bombed the Peenemünde V2-rocket experimental establishment where Hitler's super weapon was being developed. Three B-17s were lost and sixty-four damaged. Two more American successful daylight raids of Peenemünde followed in rapid succession.

The USAAF had been latecomers to *Operation Crossbow*, the RAF bombing campaign designed to cripple the Nazi V2 rocket program. But Patrick Flaherty's intuition in his short meeting with Vickery at Gordon's men's club had kick-started the Yank Army Air Force brass to more actively participate in what had, until then, been a singularly British operation.

As a reward befitting his initiative, Patrick Flaherty was promoted to major.

There would be three equally extensive B-17 raids on Peenemünde in August.

Planty Park,
Beneath Wawel Castle, Old Kraków,
Generalgouvernement für die besetzten polnischen Gebiete
22 July 1944

The team was larger than Eskenzi had expected. Adam had brought six armed men from Warsaw, and the Kraków AK had provided a similar number of young Poles who, over the course of two hours, brought with them fourteen boxes shaped like miniature caskets smuggled into the rendezvous from a nearby goods lorry. They soon met their guide—a mysterious-looking man with an eye patch—in the darkest recesses of Planty Park.

It was after midnight when the assault team cautiously entered the Institute through a basement transom left open by a sympathetic lab technician. The plan was audacious. Replicas of the Katyn evidence boxes had been made and would be smuggled into the basement of the Institute. Each box had been lined with tin and fitted with a lid that could be hermetically sealed. The team would transfer the documents from the German boxes to the airtight Home Army ones. Those boxes would then be taken to Kryspinow Lake, located just outside of Kraków, and sunk for safekeeping in its waters until such time as their contents could be revealed to Poland's trustworthy Western allies—if they still existed. The plan had originated in the fertile mind of a member of the AK known only as Pan Tadeusz, supposedly a senior and trusted representative of the Polish Red Cross.

The ensuing firefight was surprisingly swift and savage. The nearby SS garrison had been tipped off beforehand and had placed MG 42 machine guns in strategic firing lines within the basement of the Institute to deal with the intruders.

When it was over, twelve AK members lay either dead or dying on the musty concrete floor. Only two escaped. The mortally wounded were summarily dispatched by indifferent pistol shots to the head. Eskenzi and his guide, the man with the eye patch, survived. In a moment of relief and candor often afforded to those who have confronted the Angel of Death and yet lived to tell the tale, he provided his name—Amadeusz.

The Scottish Café,
Akademichna Street,
Lwów, Poland
26 July 1944

On July 23, 1944, the Polish Underground in Lwów rose up against Nazi occupation forces at the same time as the 4th Soviet Tank Army approached its eastern outskirts. Allied for a time, the Russians and Poles united to engage in vicious street battles with the German defenders.

On the morning of the third day, the city core had been largely cleared. A strike team of heavily armed NKVD officers, led by Nadia Fedin, was accompanied by a custodial duet of T34 tanks and a platoon of seasoned infantry as they made their way to the roundabout by Akademichna Street and their destination: the Scottish Café.

The five-story edifice with its twin faux turrets had stood there since 1909. The building was peppered with stray bullet holes and peeled white paint, exposing its more pedestrian red brick like an ice cream cone wilting in the summer heat. But it was there.

Fedin entered the foyer and immediately located the bar to her right. Despite the ongoing fighting a mere block away, an old man sat in a darkened corner nursing a glass of vodka. Perhaps he was the watchman, perhaps the bartender. Perhaps, Fedin thought to herself, he was just plain mad.

Through an interpreter, she began asking questions, gently cunning ones that did not arouse immediate suspicion. The fellow's name was Jacek Federkowicz, a retired professor in the pure sciences faculty at the nearby university. He was often here in the café. It was home to many of the faculty and had been long before war broke out. In fact, it had been owned by some of the professors before *this* . . . He nodded contemptuously at the wholesale destruction visible at the very doorstep of the café.

Yes, there had been a special book kept by the pure mathematicians—persons like Stanley Ulam and "his kind"—a book where they kept their computations. The book was stored behind the counter in a safe when it wasn't used. The bartender, a pleasant fellow named Manel—Ryszard Manel—was its keeper. He hadn't heard of Ryszard's whereabouts since just before war broke out. He had learned from his colleagues at the university that Manel had entered the Polish Army during an early call-out of reservists and that he might have been posted to the eastern part of Poland—the Kresny.

Fedin thanked the old man who diligently continued sipping his vodka. Ryszard Manel. She now had a real person's name. It frustrated her to no end, for even as she was inching ever closer to her goal, she was still so far from achieving it.

The retired professor nursed his vodka for some time after the Russian intruders left, then poured himself another drink. Later that night he welcomed a man with a scar, a man known to him only as Pan *Dzik*. He carefully related the details of his afternoon meeting with the Ivans.

Dzik—wild boar—it was an apt pseudonym for the world the man confronting him inhabited—facing both Soviet and Nazi adversaries. A headlong rush toward almost certain anonymity and death. The old professor smiled wryly to himself. What did it matter anyway? There were just too many names and aliases for him to keep track of in this never-ending war. What mattered were results.

Warsaw,
Generalgouvernement für die besetzten
polnischen Gebiete
1 August 1944–5 August 1944

Initiated in 1943, a detailed plan for a full-blown national uprising called "Burza"—or "Tempest"—had been developed by the London Poles. Its realization had been accelerated by the fear that the Soviet armies would occupy Warsaw before the Polish Underground could gain control of the city, legitimately claim it, and thus invite the Soviet armies into a Polish-held capital. This urgency was compounded by the discovery of Hitler's macabre scheme to completely level Warsaw in the none-too-distant future.

Caught in such a draconian vise, the Poles knew it was indeed time to act. On Tuesday, August 1, 1944, after 1,769 days of hated Nazi occupation, Warsaw exploded. At 1700 hours—Zero Hour—fighting between the German occupiers and Polish insurgents wearing red and white armbands broke out in all districts of the capital.

The Underground's attacks on most of the key installations—Warsaw's two airports, its German SD, SS, and Gestapo barracks—a formidable Tsarist-built, red-brick citadel commanding the west bank of the Vistula, and the four critical bridges traversing it—proved to be suicide missions. A smattering of captured howitzers and anti-tank guns, hand grenades, rifles and pistols in the hands of civilians, however motivated, were no match for fortresses, tanks, and highly trained troops.

And yet there were real successes. The central post office, the city's massive power plant—which would ultimately supply the insurgents with electricity for the duration of the Uprising—and the *Waffen SS* supply depots (which provided enormous quantities of food and a huge cache of SS uniforms including camouflage smocks, trousers, helmets, and rucksacks) fell to the insurgents.

Spontaneous barricades soon criss-crossed the city. Although they were decidedly amateurish, such obstacles were as effective as the trenches in the First World War.

Countless civilians soon became adept at manufacturing weaponry for the Home Army: items such as *filipinki* grenades, made by hammering an old meat tin, pushing in tiny pieces of iron garnished with explosives, enabled an expert to complete the process with a simple detonator; the *Polski Sten,* a copycat Mk. II British Sten engraved in English to fool the Nazis into thinking it came from distant Allied factories; the *Błyskawica* or Lightning submachine gun, conceived, designed, and manufactured based on a template of a captured German MP-40; the Sidolowka—named for Sidol, a German-made household cleaner popular in pre-war Poland—resembled a bottle of the ubiquitous disinfectant, each filled with 250 grams of homemade explosives and shrapnel.

The Home Army had also created its own flamethrower, the *Wzor K* or K-pattern, which included a double-cylinder backpack, a length of rubber hose, and a gun assembly housing a nozzle and trigger. There was even an armored fighting vehicle—the *Kubus* or Little Jacob. Built in a Warsaw garage mere days before the launch of the uprising, the Kubus was a steel-plated Chevy truck outfitted to carry up to a dozen resistance fighters into combat.

Still, after the confused mayhem of the opening day's forays, the Warsaw battlefield somehow achieved a semblance of surreal stability. On August 2, the AK managed to get the city's loudspeaker system to work and, for the first time since 1939, Warsaw's population publicly heard the Polish anthem. Throughout the capital, German paraphernalia and swastikas were unceremoniously ripped from buildings, while pictures of Hitler, obligatory in every German office, were placed on barricades so that the occupying troops would have to shoot at an image of their Führer.

By the fourth day, most of the Old Town was in Polish hands, and numerous Nazi attempts to overrun it were successfully met by sustained barrages of Molotov cocktails. By the morning of the fifth day of the insurrection, the Underground Army controlled 125 square kilometers of the Polish capital.

The two sides soon found themselves locked in a frenzied stalemate. While the insurgent Poles may have lacked sophisticated arms and the formal training of the German occupation forces, they possessed one unalterable advantage—they were fighting in their own city amid endless apartment blocks and office buildings, meandering alleys, and richly forested parkland that they knew intimately.

For the Nazis, the newly combative Warsaw was rapidly turning into another Stalingrad—an urban nightmare the German High Command greatly feared—with an openly hostile population operating in a maze-like topography, replete with daunting concrete form and structure, a surging incubus with a brutish Soviet adversary on the eastern banks of the Vistula just waiting to pounce on what remained.

It was in this crazed universe that Antony Eskenzi suddenly found himself. Secreted by Amadeusz to a safe house in an apartment complex located somewhere in center of the Wola district of Warsaw, he anxiously awaited a promised meeting with Pan Tadeusz.

Wola District of Warsaw,
Generalgouvernement für die besetzten
polnischen Gebiete
9 August 1944

The mid-afternoon Polish sun was hidden by smoke, dust, and flames. Everywhere it seemed the hollow echoes of explosives permeated the air. Entire Warsaw streets were afire; the skies above them tinged a devilish red.

In the midst of this chaos, *Obersturmführer* Oskar Dirlewanger stood on a street corner inside the Wola district, cheerfully humming his favorite tune, "*Alle Tage ist kein Sonntag.*" He luxuriated in the pandemonium around him. It was wickedly sublime in its perversity: to be given carte blanche to defeat a civilian insurrection by destroying their homes, neighborhoods, and city. To rob, rape, and ransack; to trample on the bones and rotting flesh of the dead without retribution. He loved every blood-soaked minute of it as did his brigade of murderers and misfits.

The *SS-Regiment Dirlewanger* had arrived in Warsaw on the fifth of August as part of an unorthodox gang of reinforcements to stiffen the spine of the beleaguered *Wehrmacht* occupation troops facing a stubborn and motivated Polish underground on the capital's rubble-filled streets. They were joined by a peculiar horde of non-Aryan campaigners spawned by the relentless bloodletting on the Eastern Front—among them Azerbaijanis, White Russian Cossacks, and ultra-nationalist Ukrainians.

By now, the German army garrison in Warsaw was severely understaffed, morale was generally low in light of massive German defeats on two fronts and—in the end it came down to something quite rudimentary—no *soldat* wanted to lose his life to a sniper's bullet for a lost cause.

Just prior to this deployment, Dirlewanger's unit had been enhanced by 2,500 troops, among of them undesirables who came from an obscure punishment facility under the control of the *Waffen SS*. Located at Matzkau near Danzig, it was a stockaded camp where SS members of all ranks found guilty of offenses as varied as theft, desertion, or failing to obey an order were stripped of their ranks, insignia, and decorations. They were thus expelled from the SS to undergo brutal discipline and "re-education" as civilian inmates. Once that deed was accomplished and they were suitably broken, they could rejoin the *Schutzstaffel*.

On their first operational day in the Wola district, Dirlewanger's barbarians had advanced a thousand yards. Street by street, inhabitants, induced by false promises of evacuation, were ordered to leave their homes to be taken to fixed points. As soon as large groups were assembled, they were herded together into cemeteries, factory forecourts, and community squares, where SS soldiers fired machine-gun bursts into the human mass until there were no signs of movement. The SS then piled the limp corpses into large heaps, poured petrol over them, and set them ablaze.

Built at the turn of the century by a Polish philanthropist and bearing his name, the red-brick Wawelberg blocks were located on Gorczewska Street in the heart of Wola. They were among the first co-op buildings in the Polish capital. All too soon, they would become a tragic episode in the greatest outrage ever perpetrated on a national capital in the Second World War.

At dawn on Day Four of their macabre operation, troopers of the

SS-Regiment Dirlewanger surrounded the blocks and sealed the perimeter gates. At the shrill sound of a solitary whistle, the operation began. They merrily lobbed hand grenades into basement apartments. Those who tried to escape were burned to death by flamethrowers. Those trapped upstairs who tried to jump for safety became flaming torches as Dirlewanger's men gleefully targeted them with satchels containing a white incendiary powder that ignited on contact with living flesh.

A *Wehrmacht* captain from the Warsaw Garrison, leading a general patrol into the area, chanced upon the horrific scene as it descended rapidly into pure insanity. This was not something he had been trained for nor would tolerate.

"Halt," he shouted coldly at an SS sergeant. "I command you to stop at once!"

A half dozen SS soldiers turned to face this unwelcome stranger in their midst. They lurched drunkenly forward, waving their weapons menacingly. "You what? Command us?" their NCO chortled. "And who the fuck are you?" A dismissive pause. "Sir."

The *Wehrmacht* captain tensely drew his pistol, and his men, their firearms.

The SS sergeant stiffened. A hand from behind brushed him roughly aside.

"You don't appear to have learned from our last encounter, *Hauptmann* Schneider." Oskar Dirlewanger confronted Schneider, his submachine pistol at the ready, its safety-catch off. He fired the full clip. And Schneider fell to the ground, dead.

"Has anyone one of you seen this?" The colonel demanded staring at the shocked *Wehrmacht* platoon. "Of course not. I didn't expect any of you would be man enough to admit it even if you had."

The SS troopers broke into robust laughter. The colonel casually stepped over the body of the German officer and gestured for his men to follow.

The *Wehrmacht* patrol backed away from the scene—all but one, a young corporal deployed in a punishment battalion shipped in from Montenegro to assist in quelling the Uprising and recently added to general patrol duties to buttress the Garrison's rapidly diminishing strength. He glanced down at the murdered German, then carefully bent down to remove the Iron Cross from the body of his friend.

"You deserve better than this, Captain Schneider. We all do."

210

The corporal slowly turned about to rejoin the platoon.

Before their return to base, he and his comrades would fabricate a tale about how their young captain had been killed by a sniper's bullet. It was not a falsehood relished by Wolfgang Weber, but it was a simpler path out of this man-made Hades than to relate the harsh and dirty truth.

For the reality was that Dirk Schneider was dead, and they were now all surviving as best as they could, led by madmen who wore German military uniforms. Later that day, his comrade's body would be removed from where it had fallen and placed in a makeshift army morgue by a heavily armed section led by Weber.

The Wawelberg blocks were connected by an underground passage to an adjacent apartment complex. Two men struggled through the passage, coughing heavily in the smoke-filled corridors, their faces wrapped in cloth soaked in water. The taller of the two, dressed in a scruffy Polish army greatcoat, ran awkwardly with a pronounced limp, but he knew the way. A sharp turn to the left, then 50 meters to the right, then just ahead of them, a door. Then up twelve stairs, as he led his bewildered charge out into a deserted courtyard. Pan Tadeusz silently handed his English friend a single piece of paper. And then, as staccato gunfire from the advancing SS troopers inched ever closer, they parted and were never seen together again.

Number 148 Special Duties Squadron,
RAF Station Brindisi
Apulia region of southern Italy,
14 August 1944

The steamy wind outside the Nissen hut had grown abruptly stronger and more persistent, as claps of thunder rumbled over the water toward the airbase. Morning storms were not unusual over the Adriatic, and Brindisi had certainly endured its share of them. Today would be no exception.

The rain briskly thrummed on the hut windows as Johnny Callison sat behind a desk in a quiet corner of the debriefing area, engrossed in a paperback that he had found in the officers' mess several days ago. The novel, *Winged Victory*, was extremely popular with airmen. Written by a British pilot who'd survived the Great War, it gave an unvarnished account of the horrors of aerial combat through the eyes of its tragic hero, Tommy Cundall of the Royal Flying Corps.

Outside the hut, the brief deluge ended abruptly, leaving behind a blanket of moist air. He put the book down and reflected on the crews he'd dispatched to beleaguered Warsaw late yesterday evening.

It had been the unit's first-ever mission to supply the Polish underground. Fourteen Halifax bombers on an eleven-hour, 2,000-mile round trip, beginning over the Adriatic and reaching Croatia near sunset to enable them to reach the Hungarian Danube under cover of darkness. And then, a steep climb over the Carpathians into Soviet-held territory to make the final approach to Warsaw from the southeast.

Each bomber carried twelve waterproof metal containers filled with Sten submachine guns, PIAT anti-tank launchers, 9mm ammunition, and medical supplies. The cylinders used drogue parachutes to slow their descent and required a low, slow, near-suicidal approach close to their target to ensure delivery.

The return leg was routed over eastern Germany and Austria, with the bombers scheduled to arrive back at Brindisi by mid-morning. The fourteen planes were traveling without fighter escort and had to rely on their on-board armaments to ward off marauding German fighters. A *Luftwaffe* night-fighter training school at Kraków posed a threat, as did ground-based anti-aircraft artillery located along the entire route. He wondered how many of the crews would make it back.

Through the hut's window shone gilded spiderwebs of light. He went back to his book.

Then he heard the awful rasp of a shot-up engine. He knew the first plane had landed. When it was on the ground, another landed. This one smoother. Callison put the book down once more.

Silence. Then, after a time, a third, this one hitting the runway hard. Twenty minutes passed by before the next Halifax landed. It was met by the hysterical clanging bells of the base ambulances and fire brigade. Ten minutes later—the steady hum of engines—a perfect touchdown. Then silence. Another landed ten minutes later. Then, for a seeming eternity, nothing. Absolutely nothing. Callison forced himself to keep reading:

> The light of his lamp showed dimly the three empty beds, the three ownerless washbowls and chairs, the shaving tackle, and other personal items.
>
> The social table stood in the middle, covered with the

green tablecloth that had been their joint property. The dull light peopled the hut with shadows, grotesque caricatures that bore scarcely any resemblance to the objects that cast them. They were a society of ghosts, immobilized by his human presence, waiting to crowd into deep penumbra for some damnable purpose.

As long as he watched, they were harmless. But he couldn't watch them all. Some behind his back flitted . . . what the devil was he thinking? But there seemed to be a congregation of shadows in Seddon's corner. God! He sprang to his feet. He had seen Seddon sitting on his bed. He was going mad. But no, he had known all the time it was pure illusion. He was sane enough. Overwrought.

But it had seemed real. Had Seddon really gone down in flames? Was there no possibility of a mistake? It might have been another Hun plane. Forster might have made a mistake. Impossible. Seddon was dead. Yet there was just a chance in a million . . .

"Oh, Seddon, for God's sake come back," he said aloud. The door opened. His flesh crept. Someone came in. The door slammed. It was Williamson.

A firm knock on the door of the hut. The Duty NCO. Stiff-limbed and somber-faced. A Yorkshireman.

"How many, Sergeant?" Callison asked.

"Six, sir. There are six aircraft back. With several serious casualties on board them too, I'm afraid."

Callison was stone-faced. "Very well. We'll commence the debriefings in fifteen minutes. Crews will attend the hut in their order of landing"—he corrected himself—"those that physically can."

"Sir." A crisp salute and the sergeant was gone.

Callison tossed the novel to one side and opened the logbook on the desk. The debriefing journal mandated that all notations be made in ink to ensure clarity, accountability, and disciplined thought. That was just the way things were done.

He casually picked out a pencil from several relegated to an old beer tankard on the desk. It needed sharpening. As he awaited the inevitable knock on the door and arrival of the first aircrew, he began to fill in the date. As far as the remainder of the journal entry was concerned, he was growing weary of dancing with the devil. The pencil in his hand would do fine.

CHAPTER 12

Room 17, dormitory T 102,
Los Alamos, New Mexico
14 August 1944

Klaus Fuchs, newly seconded, settled easily into the drab bachelor quarters at Los Alamos. Intellectually, a middle-of-the-road member of the British scientific delegation, Fuchs was assigned to a group working on the hydrodynamics of implosion. His section head was Edward Teller, and his specific role was to develop mathematical calculations for the yields and efficiency of an atomic bomb, one with either a uranium core or an implosion-type plutonium device. Both were theoretically deadly beyond human comprehension.

Everyone in the close-knit Los Alamos community soon knew of Klaus, with his hoot-owl specs and country-fresh face, but few knew much about him. A confirmed bachelor, he quickly gained a reputation as a good dancer and willing babysitter. A reasonable, predicable sort. As ordinary and predictable as white-sugared apple strudel and black Viennese coffee.

Edward Teller had a bad habit of not following up on his nominal responsibilities in the theoretical section. Yet he was, for all intents and purposes, singularly brilliant. It was for those precise-as-lightning flashes of brilliance that Oppenheimer allowed him to remain with Manhattan. And so, as Teller focused on his peculiar pet projects involving plutonium, he delegated much of the more pedantic work he'd been assigned at Los Alamos involving uranium, to Fuchs. But, unbeknownst to Teller, it was the future destructive application of plutonium that truly interested the bespectacled Fuchs.

For the British MI5 team that had conducted background checks, Fuchs's anti-fascist credentials had been impeccable, and that was enough to satisfy their American FBI counterparts.

For his part, Stanley Ulam was certainly affable enough toward this newest addition to Teller's team, although he did find Fuchs an odd duck—a soft-spoken socialist, yet one who seemed dedicated to science and a form of universal justice so chaste that it was almost fanatically Christian.

In all of this there was something amiss, something about the young German that Ulam couldn't quite put his finger on. A sense that he was just too perfect, not genuine. Ulam sensed the same self-righteous zealotry he had confronted when Nazi Brownshirts had strutted around the Free City of Danzig, strong-arming and humiliating Jews. Only that could not be happening here—not now. Or could it?

Dolphin Square, Pimlico
City of Westminster, London
11 September 1944

The bedside phone rang shortly after three that morning. In the pitch-black room, he fumbled about for the receiver. Just beyond the elegant confines of his Dolphin Square flat, a raging thunderstorm had buffeted Pimlico before sweeping past Gravesend and outwards toward the Channel.

But for the occasional bursts of receding lightning, London now slumbered placidly in an ill-defined murkiness. The blackout was still in effect over the great city, and for good reason. The Allied raids on Peenemünde, including the most recent ones in August by US Army Air Force Flying Fortresses, may have set the Nazi's V2 program back, but on the morning prior, a V2 rocket had struck the assembly shop of the Chrysler works in the London suburb of Kew, killing eight and injuring four. Two hours later, a V2 had descended on Dagenham, another London suburb, devastating the Bentry School grounds and a pre-school day center, seriously injuring twelve children and passersby while narrowly missing the massive Ford Motor plant located in the town.

During the V2's early trials, one of the rockets had veered wildly off course and exploded above Sweden. In a top-secret project named

Big Ben, the valuable wreckage had been shrewdly exchanged by the Swedes for new Mark IX Spitfires. The Royal Aircraft Establishment located at Farnborough was now busily completing a workup of the salvaged items under the frenzied edict of the War Cabinet and the Prime Minister himself.

He fully expected this call to come from senior staff at the Cabinet War Room in Westminster. Or better still from a gruff, cigar-smoking Buddha of a man at 10 Downing Street sipping Johnny Walker Red and impatient that the boffins at Farnborough had not yet found the means to save his Sceptered Isle from the scourge of *Herr* Hitler's missiles. It would not have been the first phone call he had taken in middle of the night from that individual code-named "Hallam." It would certainly not be the last.

"Hello." His voice was hoarse with sleep. He carelessly brushed a hand through tousled hair.

The high-pitched voice speaking through the static on the other end of the secure line was not that of the PM, but was still very familiar to him. The words he heard, however, proved to be totally unexpected and equally disturbing. "Philby here. I'm afraid there has been no word from our man in Poland, sir. We must consider him lost to us."

"You are certain?"

"Quite."

A long pause. "When was the last time we made actual contact?"

"July." The unvarnished answer. "He went on a raid with the Home Army in Kraków in search of our target and was captured. We believe that he was subsequently tortured and may have died as a consequence. I've been in contact with the London Poles. They have all but confirmed his capture and disappearance."

Through rain-spattered windows, the man glanced out over Pimlico and beyond. He thanked his caller and placed the receiver back in the cradle. He clicked on a reading lamp and sat for the longest time in silence. All too often, SOE Operatives were dispatched behind enemy lines and, in short order, disappeared. It was their lot in life. Flickering candles in a raging storm; they were easily extinguished.

But this one was different, and the stakes were greater—much greater.

An errant sheet of lightning illuminated the bedroom. And for the briefest moment, he was there again. 1916. Eastern Sinai. The four

217

2.7-inch mountain guns of the Hong Kong and Singapore Battery ranging in supporting fire for what proved to be a successful cavalry assault on the Ottoman garrison holding Magdhaba village. He thought of his friend, the young subaltern who had shared their imminent victory with boyish enthusiasm and crazy war-whoops as he galloped past a bemused Vickery and into the fray on a chestnut brown stallion. A man now like him in late middle age, who had just sacrificed his only son somewhere in Occupied Poland for the continued glory of "the Empire." And then the moment was gone. Duty would not allow for it.

As ever, the British Empire ruled supreme and without emotion.

**Warsaw, the Old Town,
Generalgouvernement für die
besetzten polnischen Gebiete
2 October 1944–4 October 1944**

While the Soviet armies halted on September 14 on the east bank of the Vistula River in the working-class suburb of Praga, a skillful attack by Nazi *Generalfeldmarschall* Otto Moritz Model had prevented them from crossing into central Warsaw to support the beleaguered Polish Underground fighters. But tellingly, the Vistula was only 600 meters wide at its crossing points. In 1942, Stalin's armies, with far less equipment and little or no training, had been able to ferry troops across the 1,000-meter wide Volga at Stalingrad, even as they confronted constant bombardment from German gun batteries and screeching attacks from *Stuka* dive-bombers.

Still, that was Stalingrad—and this was Warsaw. The Polish capital was being contested by two dueling forces—Nazis and London Poles—both of which the Soviet High command considered extremely hostile to Comrade Stalin's long-term plans for Central Europe. So, it was deemed best that the two historic adversaries battle it out until one reigned supreme. In the end, the inevitable—and exhausted—Nazi victor would find itself confronting the mysteriously recouped might of the Workers' and Peasants' Red Army in all its vengeful glory.

By the ninth week, the insurgency had all but petered out, even as it still controlled vast swathes of the decimated city. For its part, the German command had wisely replaced Dirlewanger's thugs with what were assuredly more disciplined *Wehrmacht* troops and, although the random killings of resistance fighters and those caught in the wrong place at the wrong time continued, they proved to be more isolated and selective in nature. Incongruously, the Germans hoped that, in spite of all the brutality they'd been subject to, the Poles might somehow see the light and join their Nazi tormentors as fraternal combatants.

On the autumnally cool Monday evening of October 2, 1944, after sixty-three days of bitter fighting, the Polish Underground Army surrendered, bringing to an end the Warsaw Uprising.

That Wednesday, as German film crews, reporters, and photographers looked respectfully on, some 15,000 Polish Underground fighters were allowed to march out of their last stronghold in the Old Town—four abreast, weapons in hand, their red and white armbands and Polish eagles in full display.

The citizen soldiers defiantly trooped past a *Wehrmacht* honor guard, dropped pistols into woven baskets held by German soldiers and deposited larger weapons onto long tables before marching to freight trains that would take them to POW camps and, for some, the death camps.

During the Uprising, almost 200,000 Warsawians had been incinerated into humble dust or lay buried and forever stilled in the mountainous ruin of their beloved city. The remaining 500,000 who yet lived there were forced to leave the city, never to return. Among those proud and wretched souls, neither Pan Tadeusz nor Antony Eskenzi, nor any trace of them, could be found.

The vibrant Polish capital, once considered the Paris of the East, had become a ghost town. Two weeks later, to complete its destruction, the Germans used high explosives and flamethrowers to erase Warsaw completely from the map.

CHAPTER 13

Broadway Building,
54 Broadway,
City of Westminster, London
5 October 1944

It was a grim eight-story edifice with a prominent mansard roof, located only a short stroll from Buckingham Palace. A brass entrance plaque identified its principal occupant as the Minimax Fire Extinguisher Company. However, since 1926, it had held various departments of the British Security Intelligence Service. Its most recent inhabitants were part of the reconstituted Section MI9, Investigation of Communists. MI9's newly promoted head was Harold "Kim" Philby.

Broadway House, as it was then known, proved to be a decrepit multi-storied warren of wooden partitions and frosted-glass windows. The eighth floor housed MI9, a pinstriped brigade composed of mainly effete intellectuals who, through connections and perceived value, astutely avoided active military service on the various forward firing lines of the Empire.

For some time, Philby had brooded over Eskenzi's apparent disappearance and the tremendous burden it placed on his future plans. But all that changed when he returned to his private office after morning prayers with his section heads, for he'd been the recipient of an unexpected gift of extreme importance—a remarkably detailed message from the middle of a war-ravaged continent from the agent officially known to him as "Mandalay."

Philby accomplished its decoding within the hour and then personally forwarded the critical information via a secure link to someone temporarily residing in a modest motel just outside of Albuquerque, New Mexico—someone purportedly in the employ of the Philadelphia Sugar Company.

The coded reply that he received from Fuchs's handler three days later was extremely troubling. It appeared that whatever Mandalay had sent from Poland was useless. The calculations that Philby had been led to believe came from the Scottish Book did not even begin to complete the missing elements in the scientific puzzle Fuchs was surreptitiously trying to unravel at Los Alamos. On the contrary, the equations appeared to have been intentionally misleading.

Hoping against hope that he was merely misinformed, he pressed Mandalay for accurate information. There was—and would be—no reply. Mandalay had completely disappeared from the radar. For Kim Philby, a seasoned professional used to operating on the dark side, there was only one conclusion to be drawn and one outcome that would inevitably follow.

Philby returned to his Belgravia flat early that afternoon and immediately went to his private study. There he found the Dickens where he'd last placed it—on the shelf resting comfortably between Hemingway's *For Whom the Bell Tolls* and Graham Greene's *The Ministry of Fear*.

Philby opened the book and began the drill, compiling a short list of random words and letters from selected pages that he then efficiently transcribed onto a blank sheet of paper. He next went to his favorite novel, H.G. Wells's *War of the Worlds*, and opened it. Inside the flyleaf, he found the mini-code book that he used to rework the random alphanumerics into a final missive. Using a micro device specifically designed by Moscow Center for his use, he then communicated the finished code to the catacombs of Number 2 Dzerzhinsky Square, where it was descrambled and forwarded to one person in a third-floor office.

The message Nadia Fedin decoded was short and to the point: "Mandalay. If located, interrogate as extremely hostile. If necessary, erase."

And that was all that Nadia Fedin needed to know.

* * *

Philby's gift was a Trojan horse—or in this case, a Polish horse.

The message Philby secretly relayed to Los Alamos was not sent by Mandalay and did not originate from within Occupied Poland. Its origin was Station Eight. Its author was a skilled Polish military intelligence officer, one well versed in higher mathematics and physics.

The physical danger to Mandalay had now become very real, but when measured against the magnitude of the information he possessed, which might end up in the wrong hands, it was deemed by the Poles a risk well worth taking.

Critically, the Poles did not relay what they suspected about Kim Philby to their British counterparts. Those days of mutual trust were swiftly receding, but the Poles did have discreet conversations about their suspicions with a particular American army officer, a Major Patrick Flaherty who was working on a top-secret project named *Venona*.

Polish Institute of Forensic and Criminal Medicine,

Kraków,
Generalgouvernement für die besetzten
polnischen Gebiete
18 January 1945–19 January 1945

In the latter days of the third week of January 1945, the 60th Soviet Army of Marshal Ivan Konev's First Ukrainian Front freed Kraków from Nazi occupation. The German military appeared to have had little interest in defending the ancient city and fled it, without wanton destruction. The Germans now focused on slowing down the Red Army's advance to gain precious time and allow German forces to marshal in Upper Silesia and along the natural defensive line of the Oder River.

Kraków was also in Nadia Fedin's sights. She was nothing if not determined. She had traced the movements of the Katyn boxes to the Kraków Institute. She was reliably informed that the boxes were housed in the Institute's basement.

By midday on January 19, Fedin arrived at the Institute with her trusted support team only to find the building closed. A thorough search of its offices and basement for the boxes went unrewarded. But somewhere, tucked in the rear of a desk drawer located in a main floor room, there was an item of written correspondence dated July 22, 1944.

It was a directive from the head of the Gestapo in Kraków to "destroy the items immediately." Attached to it by a paperclip was the carbon copy of a terse response indicating it was done and signed by a Doctor Werner Beck, Director. Scribbled in pencil at the bottom of the page were fourteen Kraków addresses.

Acting on a hunch, Fedin dispatched personnel to the fourteen locations to ask a simple question: "Why?"

The answer to her question came by nightfall. The numbered boxes with critical evidence from Katyn and removed to the Kraków Institute had been sent to private homes to prevent their seizure and destruction by the NKVD. When the occupants of the residences in question were asked why their addresses were on a recent Institute document signed by its director, Fedin's minions were informed that the residents had no knowledge of the contents of the boxes and were doing a favor for Doctor Beck. But the stench seeping from each box had made any explanation unnecessary. Meanwhile, the name Werner Beck found its way to the top of Fedin's list as an individual of extreme interest.

Unbeknownst to Fedin, the boxes had been swiftly removed and were in a secure and secret space in an abandoned warehouse near the train station.

The next morning, Fedin and her team again returned to the Institute to continue their investigation.

It was when she walked through Beck's ransacked office that Fedin spotted it on the mantlepiece, a photograph of a middle-aged man and woman. The man was dressed in a Lutheran clergyman's collar and bland business suit, the woman in a sturdy flowered print dress. They were seated on a park bench situated in the bend of a large river with the vague outlines of barges and canal boats on the snaking waterway behind them. On the horizon, arching high into the summer sky, was a massive church dome, with four lesser domes surrounding it, like cardinal points on a compass.

The photo spoke of family Sundays languid July afternoons by the river, with Viennese coffee served in demi-tasse cups and Neapolitan ice cream spooned onto delicate Meissen china.

It also provided Nadia Fedin with a very solid lead for Doctor Werner Beck within the culturally vibrant capitol of Saxony—a place called Dresden. A Polish doctor on the institute's staff, a man named Jan Robel, was quite reasonable, even providing her with the address of

Beck's parents living in one of Dresden's suburbs. Fedin wasn't certain if it was shrewd servitude on Robel's part in the face of Poland's new masters, or a desire for revenge against the hated Nazi occupiers. Either way, he was surely what Lenin would have termed a useful idiot.

And, as with all useful idiots who inhabited the ever-expanding captive realm that Stalin now called his own, after providing the information that Fedin wanted, Jan Robel was arrested and held in custody for several months until his interrogators were satisfied that he had told at least a reasonable facsimile of the truth. Then he was released to return to the Institute. As with so many others, he would be kept under surveillance for a lengthy period thereafter.

But Robel was far from an idiot, for he was eminently useful to his associates in the Polish Underground, providing them with comprehensive details concerning Beck's parents several months before the Russians had come crashing into Robel's world.

Supreme Headquarters Allied Expeditionary Force (SHAEF),
Le College Modern et Technique, rue Henri Jolicoeur,
Aka the Little Red School House,
Ville de Reims, Marne, Grand Est Region, France
0241 hours (Central European Time), 7 May 1945

On Monday, May 7, 1945, the German Armed Forces High Command in the person of *Generaloberst* Alfred Jodl signed the unconditional surrender of all German forces—East and West—at the Supreme Headquarters Allied Expeditionary Force (SHAEF), located in the cathedral city of Reims, the traditional coronation site of the French kings.

Jodl had initially hoped to limit the terms of German surrender to only those formations still fighting the Western Allies, but General Dwight Eisenhower, commanding Allied Forces in the West, demanded complete capitulation of all German forces, which meant those fighting in the East as well. If this demand was not met, Eisenhower was prepared to seal off the Western Front, thereby preventing Germans from fleeing west from the surging Soviet forces. Jodl radioed Grand Admiral Karl Donitz, Hitler's successor, who ordered him to sign. Fighting would continue in the East for most of the next day. By then, all fighting in the West had ceased.

Still, the definitive text that would end the Second World War was signed not there but in Karlshorst, Berlin, by representatives of the armed services of the *Oberkommando der Wehrmacht* (OKW) and the Allied Expeditionary Force, together with the Supreme High Command of the Red Army, on Tuesday, May 8, 1945, at 2120 hours local time.

And somewhere out there in the rapidly dissipating fog of war, a mystery man known only by the codename of Pan Tadeusz patiently waited—not for a moment of power or glory or redemption—but rather for the completion of a mission he had been charged with since September 1939.

* * *

The Second World War was over. For Johnny Callison, awaiting demobilization at Brindisi, the war's conclusion would not be as profound or as far-reaching as it would be for others. He was no longer a very small cog in the gears of a Great Game. For Callison, war's end meant the grim realization that there was no future for him on "Civvy Street." Battle-damaged goods—that's what he was. And that was that.

Callison had recently been asked if he would take command of a new unit. There was no one else of suitable rank and operational experience left in the postwar Commonwealth air forces who had wanted it. So, in the end, he had stoically accepted the offer of a renewed commission and patiently awaited orders for his new posting.

Approaching Osnabruck, Germany, heading due west
Latitude: 52°27'25" N Longitude: 8°04'77" E
Air speed: 173 knots (322 km/h to 200 mph) at Angels 9
2331 hours, 21 May 1945

She was alone in the sky over Germany and absolutely nothing was happening. And that took her crew a lot of getting used to. A Mark III Lancaster, serial number R5918 "L for Lucy" had been built by A.V.

Roe at Newton Heath, a suburb of Manchester, in late 1942. She had 55,000 moving parts and was powered by four Packard-built Merlin 28 (Mark XX) engines that guzzled over 2,000 gallons of high-octane fuel, enough energy to transport her slightly over 2,500 miles in ideal conditions. Her present mission was easily within that range.

On this warm May night in the Year of Our Lord, 1945, she carried eight persons crammed inside sixteen and a half tons of ponderous technology—seven crew and one mysterious guest, lying on the rest-bed amidships.

Painted a dreary black matte, with an olive and brown mottled upper surface, Lucy was plain bullfrog ugly, and it showed on every inch of her battered frame. She rattled and creaked and groaned mightily like the elderly lady she was. But after a legion of combat missions, and a seemingly charmed life that had enabled her to survive flack and Jerry fighters alike, her appreciative crew essentially tolerated such unappetizing quirks.

Under the cockpit window, Lucy displayed laurels that were both peculiar and profuse for such a cranky dowager. Four bombs for forty-plus missions over Nazi-occupied territory. Five pictograms for enemy aircraft destroyed; a number of wound stripes for body damage suffered as a consequence of her stubbornly combative nature. A few etched flour sacks for Project Manna, when she had air-dropped foodstuffs to starving Dutch civilians. A stick man for Project Exodus when, a few days back, she'd ferried newly freed Allied POWs from the Continent back to the United Kingdom.

L for Lucy crested a harsh west wind and was tossed about like driftwood on an inky ocean. Like some mythic flying dragon, she grudgingly managed a cruising speed of 320 kilometers per hour. They had been airborne just under three hours and, according to the penciled notations on the chart nestled in the cramped navigator's cubicle, they were approaching the Dutch–German border near Enschede.

That innocuous landlocked position signaled more than an hour's flight time before touchdown at their base in the windswept Yorkshire moors. From lift-off at a bomb-splattered airfield in the newly occupied Russian zone just outside the ruins of Potsdam, to their current plotting in the hemisphere, it had been an utterly uneventful flight.

At 9,000 feet, they were admittedly traveling perilously low by wartime standards. But in the relative quiet following the unconditional

Nazi surrender, her pilot, Flight Lieutenant Liam Foster RAF, was unconcerned. After years of playing hide and seek with searchlights and flak, he rather enjoyed this journey.

The immense sky over Europe was now a space where safety depended on visual acuity. Only a smattering of military flight controllers monitored the airspace over the continent, and most of these were jealously intent on shepherding their own brood home to safety and indifferent to any other aerial wanderers.

Foster peered through the cockpit Perspex into the vast and vacant heavens. High above them, floated wispy cirrus clouds. It had been an eerie feeling flying the round trip over Germany without fear. Still, even though the lands below were at peace for the first time in six years, his craft carried over 17,000 rounds of .303 ammunition to supply the eight machine guns that girded her. The weapons had been prudently cocked and switched from "safe" to "fire," and the sight-lights adjusted for brightness since their departure from Potsdam.

The war in Europe had been over for less than three months. Old habits were hard to break.

Foster started, then glanced over his shoulder into the tight companionway abutting the navigator's table. A figure loomed, an oxygen mask dangling to one side of its face. Foster wrinkled his brow and shrugged. "I don't understand Ziggy," he remarked affably. "You know I don't speak your language."

The man nodded. He shifted to heavily accented English. "There is no-tink out dare to wary about. No-tink but, how you say, sea gills?"

"Gulls," Foster corrected him.

"*Tak.*" An enthusiastic nod. "Yes. Sea gills."

Bemused, Foster turned his attention back to the skies. Ziggy Nowak was the flight engineer on L for Lucy, on secondment from a Polish heavy bomber unit based in Lincolnshire. Having supposedly learned the King's English as an undergraduate at the ancient Jagiellonian University in Kraków, Nowak had been chosen for assignment with the British squadron because of his linguistic prowess. But Foster soon realized this was at best a dubious claim. Nowak had been with the crew for nine months, and his English was as lacking in sophistication as that of a Form One school boy.

No matter. It was technical abilities, not his fluency with Shakespeare, that kept the Pole secure on Lucy. Nowak knew the inner workings of the Lancaster with a passion reserved for its creator. He was, simply put, the best. And Foster had become adept enough in such matters to pass judgement.

At twenty-six years of age and close to being too old for an operational pilot, Liam Foster was an experienced skipper. Lucy had flown thirty-four missions since entering service in January 1943, and he had occupied the cockpit for every one. His crew was original but for two killed: the tail gunner, a taciturn Australian who bought it on their fifth mission over St. Nazaire, and the mid-upper, a career RAF sergeant who'd been decapitated only two weeks ago in a flurry of Heinkel cannon fire somewhere over Aachen.

Remarkably, the rest of the lads had survived the usual bomb runs. Among them Hamburg for five trips. The Phillips electronics plant at Eindhoven. Bremerhaven. The Krupp armament complex at Essen. The Renault plant outside Paris. And the "Big City"—Berlin—on seven nail-biting occasions.

Nowak leaned forward until he nearly touched the controls. He delicately offered a tin cup. "Herbata, sir?"

Foster nodded. He grasped the battered tumbler offered to him to one side and away from his line of vision. The Pole unscrewed a large silver thermos and filled the cup to its brim.

Foster took a sip. The tea was very bitter and smelled as pungent as burned turnips. Nowak had furtively obtained it in a barter from a Russian field kitchen cook for three sticks of Yank chewing gum just before take-off on the return leg of their mission. Not only was the tea abysmal, so were the buns that accompanied it. They remained untouched.

Nowak caught Foster's ill-disguised grimace. "I also managed to get farmer's honey from the Russian cook," Nowak offered optimistically. The Pole removed a spoon from his shirt tunic and from another pocket he took out a glass jar. He unscrewed the lid and spooned a golden dollop into Foster's waiting cup.

"Is better?" the Pole asked in a plaintive tone as Foster began to sip the tea once more.

Foster nodded agreement.

"Good." The Pole was happy once more. "Now I'll go to the crew."

Nowak was adept at scrounging for the men wherever they went. Granted the entire German stopover had been just under two hours, leaving them barely enough opportunity to top-up fuel, check the motors, and take a stretch about the tarmac. It would have been even shorter if their mysterious passenger had been on time.

The Russians hadn't laid out a proper meal for their British guests. They hadn't even volunteered a light snack. To add to the insult, as the crew ambled out from beneath the Lancaster's sheltering wing, they were confronted by machine-gun-toting sentries and surly stares that confined them to the immediate tarmac.

Above the roar of the Merlin engines, Foster heard Nowak bragging to Mellor about a Wren officer he'd dated on his last London furlough. He missed the punchline, but the sudden ribald laughter left little to the imagination.

He glanced over to the rest-bed where their mystery passenger sat staring into space. The man was sharp-featured with the exacting manner of someone who spared no movement needlessly. Wearing an oversized battle tunic, rumpled Royal Air Force shirt, and stained tank-crew trousers, he appeared at best haphazardly kitted. His mix-and-match had been hurriedly finalized by a Coldstream major newly appointed to act as something of a liaison to the Soviet land forces occupying Berlin. However, the stranger's boots were Russian-made, cavalry cut with a high gleam, and his tie was expertly knotted.

The name he offered up for the flight manifest was probably not real, but it matched the one provided at the operational briefing. Foster was able to surmise from a terse conversation that the stranger had been one of the cloak-and-dagger sorts smuggled into Occupied Europe to wreak havoc in the Nazis' lair. And now, dirty deeds done, he was returning home. SOE he was. Special Operations Executive. Well, now that the war was finally over, it didn't really matter what alphabet soup initials he possessed.

All that Foster knew for certain was that this day had commenced innocuously enough at Little Crofton, their home base. A casual midday flight to keep them spry and ready, an undemanding training hop that had turned edgy when they heard the unnerving rumor that they were being considered for Tiger Force, an elite RAF bomber group forming up to help the Yanks deal the knockout blow to Japan.

And as they sat there gloomily mulling over their fate, Foster was abruptly summoned to the base commander's office, handed a top-secret envelope and some weather charts, and sent traipsing across much of

Europe to bring back "a package from Potsdam."

They had landed at a gutted *Luftwaffe* airfield on the southern out-skirts of the revered Prussian city as a flaming sunset settled in the west amid cascading layers of tangerine- and maroon-tinged clouds. The Guards-type scrupulously brought the mysterious officer to the crew hatch of the Lancaster, where it became readily apparent that he was the "package." And Lord only knew why.

Approaching the Dutch–German border,
Heading west-northwest, passing near Apeldoorn,
Province of Gelderland, Netherlands
Latitude: 52°21'12" N Longitude: 5°96'99" E
Air speed: 181.4 knots (336 km/h to 208 mph) at Angels 8
0023 hours, 22 May 1945

For what must have been the hundredth time, Foster's eyes glanced at the strip of paper fluttering from the direction finder. It was a most peculiar thing to be dangling from the instrument panel of a heavy bomber of His Majesty's Royal Air Force—a Bank of England £10 note, torn in half.

As the stolid Lancaster droned on thunderously, he calmly recalled how he had acquired the currency. It had been on a hazy afternoon in the early spring of '45. He and Clarke had squared off over darts at the local village pub. A silly match really, entered into after too much ale and far too much ego. Just one of many such sophomoric tests Allied airmen throughout England entertained that day to mask their dread as clearing skies seemed to suggest a Bomber's Moon that night over the Continent.

So, they had bought tankards of ale and bragged about their respective crews. Derek Clarke had become his closest friend in the squadron. He was a burly Londoner from the dockyards whom Foster had befriended three years before when they had traversed the Atlantic for flight training in Canada. They had done Basic together in the grim Prairie winter. Then they had moved eastwards to the humid flatlands of western Ontario in Canada and more demanding aircraft, before finally completing the bomber-conversion course on twin-engine Hampdens in Yorkshire. On qualification, they had been posted to the same unit and survived an equal number of missions relatively unscathed. They were now the two most senior pilots remaining in the outfit.

The dart match had ended in a draw. The two friends were too weary to arm wrestle for boozy supremacy of the waning day, yet too apprehensive to return to an officers' mess where there were so many lingering ghosts.

It was Foster who brought up the topic of precision, blearily equating the accurate bombing of their next target with the categorical supremacy of one of two crews—either his or Clarke's. To solidify the wager, he had taken a £10 note and cut it in half with scissors proffered by the barmaid. Double or nothing he had challenged. Winner gets twenty quid.

As night fell, they had muddled back to quarters, where they had heard the welcome news. According to the Met Officer, skies were becoming overcast over the British Midlands. That, coupled with strong westerlies and the report of choppy weather over the Irish Sea, made bombing of Occupied Europe impossible for the foreseeable future. The Gods of War had granted them all at least a few more days of life.

The fateful sortie had happened four days later. It turned out to be a twenty-seven-bomber affair intended to pulverize the V2 rocket storage area that lay along the boundaries of the North Sea in a forest near the Dutch resort of Wassenaar. The assignment would also mark Derek Clarke's last few hours on earth—his aircraft, Q for Queen, did not return. Neither did five other Lancs. Seventeen men lost their lives over Holland that night. A further eighteen were noted as fate unknown.

Liam Foster had seen Clarke's bomber go down.

Q for Queen was to be the lead ship. Their designated landmark was a massive whitewashed windmill known to the local population as the Deacon's Pulpit. It was visible for miles amid the flat landscape of the polder lands and therefore recommended by the Dutch Underground as the most suitable homing-marker.

Just as Q for Queen made the turn into target, she was picked up by searchlight beams.

To break contact, Queen had unsuccessfully tried to side-slip down the beam. Suddenly, the Lanc was hit amidships and exploded. The flak came from a German anti-aircraft gun cunningly positioned in the very peak of the windmill. In rapid succession, more strikes, as the Lancaster shuddered in mid-air, badly burning, but gamely kept on flying.

Then, a direct hit on the rear turret. A billowing burst of filthy black smoke. When it dissipated, the rear gunnery position had disappeared. What was left of the turret dangled in space by feeble wires. The crewman who had sat there moments ago was reduced to vapor.

The stricken Lancaster dipped sharply and began to tumble. A figure lunged desperately outward from its doomed hull. A parachute began to open. Fire chased, then caught the silk—and soon the canopy blazed like a rolled-up newspaper as the figure plummeted to the ground like a lead weight.

What remained of Q for Queen forced itself west. A ruddy halo now encircled the cockpit. Foster imagined Clarke in the pilot's seat, struggling to maintain control as acrid smoke and searing heat and the unearthly screams of melting crewmen rapidly reduced him to madness.

The bomber crashed mercifully into the North Sea. And it was over.

Liam Foster had nightmares about his friend's last moments for some time thereafter.

He reverently touched the severed bank note. The other portion was out there in the gloom—a quarter of a mile below their aircraft, somewhere under the choppy surface of the North Sea, floating inside the ghoulish coffin of an aircraft filled with the rotting dead.

Ten minutes passed.

He peered down at a map taped to the right thigh of his flying suit. Their ops plan had been a clear-cut, scarlet-crayoned line, running true as a hunter's arrow from Yorkshire into the vast abyss of Greater Berlin airspace, ripping into the very heart of their former nemesis with precision and invigorating audacity, before returning to their base.

Somewhere over Apeldoorn, he made up his mind, banked the Lanc slightly to the left, then nosed down. L for Lucy began a long graceful descending arc toward the darkened earth below. At 2,000 feet, Foster leveled off.

Tree copses and checkered farmers' fields surged past beneath the cabin, as orderly and precise as a Mennonite's quilt. A stone cottage. Barns. Another dwelling. Then a small Dutch village with gabled rooftops, a delineated road grid, homes, a village church, a railway line.

"Sir?" It was Tomlinson his navigator on the intercom gingerly expressing the obvious. "You've changed course."

"I know." Foster's voice was crisp. Pragmatic.

Dead air. Then a click. "Sir? Our passenger is on a deadline."

"I'm well aware of that," Foster snapped in a tone he instantly regretted. Then kinder. "We're dropping down to see something that has intrigued me for a while, okay Charlie? I figure it'll be all of an extra ten minutes . . ."

A rustle in the cockpit. Their mysterious passenger inched forward. The hint of cheap black-market cologne. "Captain, your navigator tells me that we've changed course. Is there something wrong that I should know about?"

Foster shook his head. "No, sir. Just attending to some unfinished business for an old friend. It won't take long."

Then Foster was alone once more in the blackened solitude of the cockpit. Ahead, through the Perspex, was a vast and wondrous landscape. The homes became more numerous, the buildings more substantial. Infinite blocks of apartments stacked like castles of dominoes. Church steeples and parks. Factory chimneys. Streetlights twinkling like candles on an immense birthday cake. Spread beneath him was a festive garland, the pulsating ethereal glow of an immense living thing. The Lancaster was closing rapidly on the stately capital of the Dutch Royal Court and its seat of government.

"The Hague," he called out tonelessly as if he were a streetcar conductor and this was the next stop on his daily route.

The languid cushion of air bobbing along under the Lancaster caused Foster to prudently raise the nose of the aircraft several hundred feet. Licorice tracings of tram tracks on broad boulevards. A solitary human wandering the streets, a few others on bicycles, looking like tiny yet determined ants at a picnic. Then a broad plaza with a café patio. Lots of people now no longer under curfew.

Barely visible under a forest tapestry below, a barge canal running arrow-straight to a penciled horizon. Another neatly bisecting it, moonlight making the water shimmer like glazed mercury. A profusion of trees lacing an open common. Slate-tiled rooftops peeking through openings in the foliage. Widely spaced. Regal. The apartment blocks of the city dwellers and bourgeoisie were now far behind, and the metropolis became sedately more affluent along its periphery as the Lancaster coursed across the last minutes of night leading to dawn.

Looming ahead, a host of cream-colored dwellings. Grecian design. Massive, orderly, and serene in their solitude. The villas and elite pensions of the resort town of Scheveningen. Then, firmly ensconced like

Hadrian's Wall, an undulating wasteland of sand dunes, which stoically guarded the lowlands from a North Sea that seemed like a solid muck of ponderous grease.

A spindly wood-braced pier jutted, crab-like, out over the water. At its furthest point, a glass copula loomed imperiously atop a palatial structure that reminded Foster of St. Paul's Cathedral. He recalled from briefings that it was a famous pre-war casino.

He guided the bomber straight out over the sea for a mile, then jagged north-northeast and sharply back to the shore so that he was heading due east and back toward land, cruising just above the water at a height of 900 feet. The North Sea raced by beneath them. Foster watched the bomber's shadow playing impishly on the moon-flecked surface. Occasional whitecaps frothed the calm.

Pillowed dunes ahead glowed in the predawn light like colossal mounds of sugar. Cleverly plopped among them were the now-dormant pillboxes of Hitler's once-vaunted Atlantic Wall. Occasionally, larger concrete structures lay atop the high ground—the bigger-caliber gun emplacements shrewdly situated for an optimum field of fire.

And there, less than a mile back from the mountainous sands, primly nestled in a man-made clearing in the forest and surrounded by barbed wire and elevated sentry posts, was the object of their mission—a precise array of hangers, concrete pads, and a runway that marked the V2 rocket storage area near the Hague Forest. Foster took small consolation from the fact that the entire installation was pock-marked with bomb craters, and that some of them were surely from his recent bombing raid.

Rocket fragments lay inert on abandoned Meillerwagen flatbeds or were stacked haphazardly about the tarmac. When daylight came, Allied military engineering units would continue their task, scavenging the site for an army of lab-jacketed boffins waiting somewhere in southern England who would eventually dissect every diode and cathode until they were little more than meaningless spaghetti wiring.

So, this is what they had died for that fiery night—this blasted piece of camouflaged cement. He recalled their faces. Clarke and . . . who was it? Ferguson, his navigator? And that fellow from Leeds—Pollitt? And from the other crews? Lochhead and Ryan, and Birgeneau, the somber French Canadian. He let his hand drift to the pound note and closed his eyes. He whispered a silent prayer.

An abrupt gust of wind. L for Lucy impishly waggled her wings in response. Foster started. Then, alert again, he began a slow and stately arc that would bring the lumbering bomber westward once more to face the North Sea. England. And home.

Just ahead of their trajectory, a diminutive necklace of streetlights twinkled in the receding gloom—a village divided in orderly segments like a checkerboard. Foster vaguely recalled the pattern. There was an ungainly thing rising out of the center of this town that he also recalled—a structure as solemn and solid as a tombstone.

Suddenly, the base of his neck began to throb. Shrill droning engulfed his head, and his vision blurred. He felt tremendous weakness, and the world began to turn and turn and turn. Foster felt his hands drop onto his lap and felt himself sinking forward until he abruptly hit the control column. At almost the same instant, the muscles in his chest cramped and he began to spasm. Then Liam Foster passed out.

Lieutenant Nowak felt the plane lurch, then dip into a drunken dive. He rushed forward to the cockpit and pushed Foster away from the control column. Then he too experienced cramping and nausea. The words "Emergency! Pilot down!" formed in his mind and even reached his lips. But he was unable to say them before he collapsed on the floor, insensible.

The Pole's urgent shouts would not have mattered, for within seconds, much of the crew was comatose.

The huge Lancaster began to drop earthwards with resigned grace, commencing a long leisurely descending spiral that was the opening movement in its dance of death.

* * *

Nollie De Groot inhabited the third-floor flat above a dressmaker's shop run by her eldest daughter Tessa. And she sensed she would die there. She had lost Wilhelm, her husband of thirty-four years, to the war in a Tommy air raid in 1942, and her sister and two cousins to the recent tragic peace that followed the Hunger Winter of 1944–45—a hideous time when Dutch folk, still captive in the Nazi-occupied western portion of the Netherlands, had roasted tulip bulbs like chestnuts and subsisted on a pitiful diet of "roof rabbit"—cats and

235

dogs—to fend off starvation.

But for a short period during the mid-1920s, when she had worked in a confectionery in Den Haag, De Groot had spent all her adult years in Oude Wassenaar, a typically Dutch village, unremarkably bland, with orderly streets and orderly lives.

Her flat on Laamermarkt Laan overlooked the windmill, which, along with *speculaas* cookies from its bakery, was the hamlet's claim to national prominence. Built in 1810 during the Napoleonic occupation of the Netherlands, the mill was deemed a historic monument. And that was sufficient.

So, the structure stood stolid, as it had for more than a century. Its four blades functioned only spasmodically, cutting the air like dreary bamboo fronds as its patched girth cast a long and dismal shadow on the nearby canal. For the little good the mill accomplished, it was no wonder the rickety old thing was cynically known to the town's population as the Deacon's Pulpit.

Vrouw De Groot slept with windows open in summer. The North Sea was less than two kilometers away, and the pleasant ocean breezes acted as a tonic to her insomnia. Tonight, the sounds of raucous chanting down in the street. Timmerman the greengrocer was entertaining again, having a few Heinekens with the local policeman and the others. Laughter. The cascading "clink" of glass breaking. Then more raucous laughter and singing. The black market must be prospering, she mused.

Then she heard it coming. Somewhere above her building, high in the sky. A long, low moaning sound like a steam engine emerging from a deep tunnel.

Outside her apartment, the massive windmill blades creaked morosely on, as the strange sound grew louder, ever more insistent. Her shutters began to shake. The noise was overpowering.

She leaned out the window. She knew it to be a British bomber by the distinctive RAF roundels on its torso, motors spinning as it careened toward her. She stood transfixed, almost exhilarated, by the sheer delirium of the moment.

Vrouw De Groot thought she saw a face in the cockpit where she imagined a pilot would sit. The young man was lurched forward and appeared to be peacefully asleep at the controls.

A giant crack rent the air as the plane clipped the windmill top and sent it tumbling into the air like the head of a condemned prisoner at the guillotine. The force of the impact caused the bomber to veer abruptly away. It began to cantilever and spin like a giant boomerang over the gabled rooftops, then dropped from view above the Nazi-enforced forbidden zones] abutting the North Sea, which made up Hitler's vaunted West Wall.

Vrouw De Groot's little apartment was again politely tranquil. Yet she heard her own heart beating an anxious tattoo and felt it pulsing along her throat. Abruptly, the shouts of neighbors from other windows and out on the street below. Anxious. Terrified. Hysterical.

After what seemed an eternity, the inevitable meeting of machine with the unforgiving North Sea.

CHAPTER 14

Officers' Quarters, RAF Breda–St. Willebrord,
North Brabant, Netherlands
0311 hours, 22 May 1945

A knock on the door. Pause. Again. Then a series of raps, persistent as a woodpecker tapping hardwood, only this time accompanied by a deferential voice. "Sir? Mr. Callison, sir? It's urgent!"

The inert figure roused grudgingly out of the creaking cot and stumbled to the window tearing open the blackout curtain. Milky moon-glow flooded the shadowy chamber. The slumbering airbase lay like a Gothic painting daubed a deep Prussian blue. A tiny figure inched out from underneath the bed, a furry white thing with coal-black eyes. A guarded growl.

"Quiet, Jessie," Callison shushed the dog. The terrier sleepily wagged its tail a few times and obeyed.

He switched on the light. A bare bulb dangled harshly from a cracked ceiling. It illuminated a Service bed surrounded by functional austerity: a plank side table, a utilitarian oak desk and hard-backed chair, and a gunmetal-gray locker for uniforms. The walls were stained an institutional pea-soup green; the hardwood floor worn to the tone of dried bacon rind. All in all, the lodgings were austere even for a Trappist hermit.

But then again, he hadn't expected five-star accommodation.

A battered duffel bag sloped against the locker. His identity was stenciled onto it—Squadron Leader J.P. Callison RCAF—the recently bumped-up rank a transparent panacea to retain him in a new and generally distasteful task that most ops personnel abhorred. The bag contained his worldly possessions, most of which he hadn't bothered to unpack: assorted short-sleeved shirts and turtlenecks, desert boots, underwear, knee socks, and several pairs of patched corduroy pants—an affectation he'd acquired in the desert and was loath to give up. A pair of dress Oxfords, spit-shone; muddied galoshes; and high-laced flying boots stood at parade rest under the bed. A powder-blue issue overcoat hung from a hook on the door.

The top of the desk was as austere as his wardrobe. A green-shaded lamp, some stationery, an ink-bottle and fountain pen, and an ashtray filled with cigarette butts—Macdonald's. There were two framed photos. One of himself taken in 1937 on a busy Shanghai intersection somewhere just outside the International Settlement near the entrance to Nanking Road. He looked aggressively young, dressed in starched khaki and campaign cover over a Marine Corps regulation cropped head as he posed next to a towering, ramrod-straight Sikh sergeant of the Shanghai Municipal Police.

The second, a snapshot taken a few weeks after he'd arrived in the North African desert. Callison, already sunbaked and broadly smiling at some long-forgotten joke or rapidly fading memory of better times, crouched on the fawn and chocolate wingtip of his Kittyhawk. Beside him cheerful as ever, his newfound mate and, by his own humble admission, a salesman extraordinaire, Jubal Crampton.

While in the POW camp, he found out from a British pilot officer that Crampton had bought it a few weeks after Callison had been taken prisoner. His rendering of Jubal's last minutes on earth was like so many cold obituaries of other unfortunates. Caught behind enemy lines. Shot down in an out-of-the-sun ambush. No parachute spotted. A fully blazing wreck jack-knifed into the broiling desert sands like a discarded Swiss Army knife. There was nothing that remained of his robust friend from London who vowed that he could sell ice boxes to Eskimos. And now never would.

Callison opened the door to his quarters. The corporal stood there stiffly, holding a tattered white towel neatly folded and an enamel washbasin brimful of tepid water. A ruddy-faced fellow with perpetually shiny shoes and brilliantined black hair that roguishly covered a bald spot at the very crown of his head, Rufus Napes looked and acted like the perfect butler. Career RAF he was. Squadron Leader Callison's personal batman.

"Duty Officer wants you in five minutes, sir," Napes brushed into the room. "Lanc in the drink off The Hague. Don't appear to be any survivors." He soundlessly closed the door, but not before he'd discreetly tossed a stale dinner biscuit onto the floor for the terrier.

As the dog chewed on her prize, Callison completed his ablutions, then donned his working kit: tie, shirt, battle-dress pants, and Oxfords. He leashed the dog and exited the building through a door that squeaked as it swung open and slammed shut with a resonance that cannonaded down the darkened corridors.

The mess was a stolid brick and mortar structure completed in April 1940 for officers of a Royal Dutch Air Force squadron piloting outmoded Fokker fighters, which they barely used before they were confiscated as spoils of war by their victorious Teutonic enemy. It had served as a *Luftwaffe* fighter base for five years until they too had met their match in the skies over Western Europe. Now it was crammed with thirty-one Brit fighter pilots and sundry support types impatiently waiting for repatriation to Blighty.

Callison moved carefully along a tidy path edged by whitewashed stones, the terrier waddling at his side. A faint mist seeped out of flowerbeds crammed with blood-red tulips. The buildings to either side of the footpath were darkened. Admin block. Motor Pool. Military Police. Inflexible trappings of martial order fittingly arranged. A loud drunk had shut down the officers' mess three hours before, and the "Other Ranks" canteen had officially run out of its beer ration at eleven. RAF Breda-St. Willebrord now slumbered tranquilly.

Callison walked with a pronounced limp; it would remain with him forever. He coughed. A plume of damp air wafted from his mouth. The Westie panted alongside him, straining at her leash. In the imprecise gloom, Callison made out the contours of a jackrabbit bounding for its warren. He bent and patted the dog's head. "There, there girl." The dog calmed at the sound of his voice.

The firmament above was awash with mountain ranges of stars; the moon bold and hard. Callison easily identified the far-off stars and constellations. Arcturus. Sagittarius. Ursa Minor. A warm glow fringed the northern horizon. He supposed it was the port of Rotterdam. But it could have been any one of a dozen Dutch towns in the dense suburban sprawl that straddled the Maas River. After half a decade of near-universal blackout on the European continent, the gentle radiance of thousands upon thousands of streetlights, joyously arching into the night, seemed strange to behold.

A row of Tempests roosted on the nearby runway at parade rest, their spiky beaks thrust arrogantly upward. Further afield were other Allied aircraft, a flock of elegant Spitfires in combat plumage. A score of dour Dakotas from Transport Command. A trio of American P-51 Mustangs, their pilots visiting overnight from a Yank station in northern France. A Beechcraft Expeditor belonging to some Very Important Personage, or pretender to the title. Nestled under a stand of beech trees were a gaggle of Juno-engined Folke Wulf 190D-9s and a lone Storch observer plane, resignedly awaiting the wreckers' torches.

The main gate to the camp was faintly visible in the distance, a massive affair pompously constructed by its last tenants—*Jagstaffel* 56. A balsa-wood archway painted Viennese cream and turquoise, it had been surmounted by a Nazi swastika and an eagle rampant on a lustily stuccoed globe. The vulgar icons had been instantly removed by a well-placed salvo from the gun of a camouflaged Daimler scout car belonging to the British Fourth Hussars. After the round had left its robust impression, all that remained of the monstrosity was a concrete pedestal and, rising out of it, a shattered globe. The eagle and swastika had vanished into thin air.

The place was officially rechristened RAF Station Breda-St. Willebrord. In the very first week, the local *burgomeister* confronted the station's commanding officer with a vigorous complaint that a large quantity of pigs had been stolen from area farms. The CO, an ex-Tempest pilot named Scarborough, had summarily confined the entire unit to barracks in a fruitless attempt to find the culprits. He suspected, and was right, that the Canadians had liberated the pigs, and the confinement to barracks was treated as a bit of a lark.

As Callison approached the sandbagged entrance to the Duty Office, the night picket challenged him. He responded with the correct password and was waved past. The routine was redundant. He knew the corporal by name and the corporal knew him. The disciplined dance of discovery was enacted for formality's sake. After six years of warfare, they knew no other way.

The duty office was a grim little affair of frosted glass and heavy furniture that lay next to the coalshed in the very bowels of HQ block.

It still reeked of dirty socks and cabbage and over-boiled sausages—the residue of its former Teutonic occupation. Damp, dark, and depressingly dirty, with walls covered with dog-eared memo notices, and a huge board marking the status of sub-units on the base. The room boasted one occupant—the duty officer—a young, buck-toothed pilot officer named Moulton who slumped behind a desk besieged by banks of black phones and unruly stacks of paper.

Moulton bleakly raised a carrot-topped head as Callison approached. He'd never fired a shot in anger or even optimism, arriving mere days before the war officially ended in Europe. He had drawn the midnight shift as duty officer ever since, and seemed destined to complete his military service in the nether regions of RAF Breda-St. Willebrord without viewing "friendly" daylight hours on the continent.

The youngster handed Callison the Telex. "A Lancaster, sir. She bought it up by The Hague. Your Dakota is ready to take you and the lads to the nearest airport. Schiphol." He added, earnestly, "It's a short hop, I'm told. The army has secured the crash scene, pending your arrival. Your fellow Roberts has already been up to see me and been briefed, sir," he continued, his voice rising in pitch. "He's rousing the others."

Callison thanked the boy who seemed to appreciate any attention. He genuinely liked Alfie Roberts, a cynical, street-smart flight sergeant who, before the war, was an undertaker's assistant in Birmingham. He would need him on this downing. He had come to need him on every one.

Moulton caught his superior's somber expression. "I'm sorry, sir."

The last while had been an altogether bad time for Callison's nine-member unit. They had moved onto base a week ago from their previous billet—a slapdash muddle of tents and lean-tos near Maastricht on the Belgian border with Holland. The rationale for their relocation was straightforward. Their current posting was a proper working facility rather than an afterthought—as the tent city had been—and their work was deemed extremely important to "the war effort," although that phrase was already redundant. For Breda-St. Willebrord had several now-superfluous hangers, each spacious enough to deposit body parts for sorting and tagging.

Although the telling slash of combat ribbons on his faded battle serge swiftly stilled derision, Callison and his people were accepted only grudgingly into their respective messes. "Nothing personal, old chap. But you know . . ." And then the sidelong glances that followed him everywhere. It was as if he and his team were pariahs, for they dealt with the inescapable consequences of aerial combat—that no matter how skillful they might believe themselves to be, pilots were not invincible. Yet who could blame them for their standoffishness? In their minds, they were forever young and forever competent. They had to have blind faith in this delusion to keep on flying. It was often the only thing that kept them sane.

It wouldn't have mattered if Callison could turn back the hands of time to the Kansas farm where he grew up inhaling the pungent the scents of loamy earth. Or to North Africa, his Kittyhawk spitting dust as it waggled up from ochre-tinged *wadis* to strafe Axis tramp steamers foolish enough to traverse the Med to North Africa without escort. Or even to the *Luft Stalag*, where he'd struggled to pace the crumbling hardstand behind the barbed wire, his unyielding pride preserved in every trudging step of his captivity.

No. Stationed here at a captured *Luftwaffe* aerodrome just off the main road joining Tilburg and Breda, some 30 miles southeast of Rotterdam, where farms were verdant with life, and the very air he breathed was heady with the optimism, Johnny Callison found that he hated the earth he trod on and all that it represented with a passion he had formerly reserved only for the Nazi enemy.

Until the war, fields like these had engendered relatively common-place expectations. They were places where people planted things and foodstuffs grew; where people erected their homesteads and started families. And lived.

But not for him. The soil beneath his feet now had only one sobering function. It was the final repository for too many comrades to be viewed any other way. After all, it wasn't as if he were the Base Education Officer or a mealy-mouthed RAF padre from Dorset. His task was more sinister and finite. There was no getting around it.

For very recently, Squadron Leader John Callison had been made officer in command of an RAF Air Ministry Casualty Unit. He was officially the Chief Gravedigger. The Reaper of Death.

243

Approaching Schiphol Airport, Netherlands,
Heading north-northwest, passing over Woerden,
Province of Utrecht
Latitude: 52°4' 47.3844" N Longitude: 4°51'45.9064"
Air speed: 170 knots (315 km/h) at Angels 6
0848 hours, 22 May 1945

Callison sat buckled up in the spartan cabin of the Dakota and glanced over at his team fitfully asleep in the transport's raw interior. The aircraft was full to the ceiling with equipment they would need for a recovery operation—a jumbled variety of shovels, crowbars, hammers, heavy-duty rope, flashlights. He always had a loaded plane on standby for just this eventuality. This morning, his people were cramped inside wherever there was space, shifting and jostling uncomfortably as the transport pitched and yawed in an angry wind roaring in from the North Sea. Such discomfort was something a nerve-grinding war had made them accustomed to.

He reached into the breast pocket of his bomber jacket and once more glanced at the communiqué he'd been given. The initial portion of the document reflected the jargon of military life—dry, dull, and direct.

Paragraph One provided the flight plan—Sparenberg airfield, just south of Berlin in what was now Soviet-occupied Germany to RAF Little Crofton, and with it the crew manifest for L for Lucy, listing names, ranks, and serial numbers. The deceased were all Allied Air Force types, but for one. Added at the bottom was what had obviously been the sole passenger—Antony Eskenzi, captain, Royal Army Service Corps.

Paragraph Two outlined the Lancaster's current whereabouts in the waters just off Scheveningen by longitude and latitude. It also provided radio frequencies for the Canadian infantry unit whose personnel had secured the wreckage and casualties. There was a contact for an RAF liaison type attached to the crash site, followed by a layman's description of the location.

The next two paragraphs were more layered:

Paragraph 3: Responsibility of RAF casualty unit #14 RAF Station Breda-St Willebrord will be to extract all bodies, and all parts thereof from Lancaster serial number R5918-L for Lucy and to secure all valuables.

Said human remains and valuables are to remain in military custody pursuant to the conclusion of this investigation, and immediately after release of crash report they are to be forwarded under armed military police escort to RAF Brize Norton, where they are to be secured, pending final determination as to their disposition.

Paragraph 4: The determination of cause of death and relevant findings shall be forwarded under guard to the Air Ministry in a sealed Final Crash Report, attention W/CO Wilfred Bowes, Royal Air Force Police Special Investigation Branch, within 14 days of closure of said investigation. Repeat within Three Hundred and Thirty-Six Hours, said hours commencing upon Unit's first arrival at crash site.

If plan requires amendment or operational actions not noted herein, communicate same IMMEDIATELY via secure channel to Wg/Cmdr Wilfred Bowes, Royal Air Force Special Investigation Branch.<EXT>

One month? Why the hurry? Full autopsies had yet to be commenced, let alone conclusions drawn from their results. Moreover, all relevant evidence had to be extracted from the aircraft and removed from its watery grave and all plausive theories tested before Callison could even begin to put pen to paper to draft his findings. Even in the best of circumstances, it might take months before any definitive conclusions could be made.

Callison prided himself on completing his assigned tasks with thoroughness and the requisite dignity. But one month? And a sealed crash report. That was the clincher! Who among the dead had been that important? And who among the brass at the Air Ministry and beyond was in that "need-to-know/sealed-report" category?"

He methodically folded the communiqué and placed it back in his tunic pocket. He was suddenly aware of a questioning look from Alfie Roberts. Finally, his flight sergeant could hold back his curiosity no longer.

"It's the passenger that they're interested in—not one of the aircrew isn't it, sir?" he half whispered. "That mysterious captain who hitched a ride with us out of Berlin." The wiry Brummie drew out the syllables of the dead man's name is if they were strands of Birmingham-made Blue Bird toffee.

"This one's different, sir," he sniffed. "It's got establishment written all over it," he asserted enthusiastically with naive conviction. "I know."

"Well, *you* may know," Callison snapped with more fervor than he intended. "But I certainly don't."

"And then there's always the Polack officer on the manifest . . ." the sergeant continued, undeterred. "Never know about them Slavs— always fighting each other. Could well be the Bolshies are in on this one, guv'nor." A conspiratorial wink.

"I shouldn't think so," Callison responded impatiently. "And even if they were, we'd still have to prove it, wouldn't we?"

Heads turned within the confined cabin. Callison's cold stare silenced any further discussion.

Inside closed area, the former German Atlantic Wall,
25 meters beyond waterline, low tide
Katwijk, Netherlands
0919 hours, 22 May 1945

The journey aboard the Dakota had been short—just over twenty-five minutes from take-off at Breda-St. Willebrord to a bumpy landing at Schiphol. Callison peered out of the tiny window. As low clouds scudded in from the North Sea, it began to drizzle lightly. What had been a thriving international airport before the war was now just a series of bomb-cratered runways with makeshift barracks modified for passenger and cargo use and a wooden two-story building serving as a makeshift control tower. War. Bugger it all. It had spared nothing and no one.

A column of Allied army lorries waited as the C-47 taxied to a stop. After transferring their equipment, gear, and then themselves from the aircraft to the vehicles, the convoy sluggishly moved off. The rain grew heavier.

They parked their transport adjacent to the closed area. Leaving his team to have a smoke break, Callison and his sergeant went on in the direction of the sea, cautiously using a flagged walking path swept clear of mines by military engineers.

L for Lucy loomed beyond the crest of the highest dune, stately in repose as an Aztec emperor's tomb. The Lanc had left a deep furrow in the pebbled shoreline as it knifed its way toward land, its Plexiglas snout collapsed as if punched by an angry giant. Two of its propellers and reduction gears lay about 25 meters behind the aircraft's resting point. The propeller blades of the remaining engines were broken and twisted like flimsy metal toothpicks. An infantry section stood sentry, guarding the wreckage.

Callison and his sergeant immediately conducted a cursory inspection of the plane's exterior. It revealed no other signs of distress. He was then briefed by the liaison officer. The Canadians had removed eight bodies to a nearby government building where they were under guard, and witness statements were being obtained by the Dutch police.

Sergeant Roberts arranged to have the team and vehicles brought forward by a secure route. For the remainder of the day, and for the better part of the week that followed, the personnel in RAF Casualty Unit #14 feverishly scurried about the wreck like scavenger ants on a crow's carcass. The bodies of the aircrew were to be taken to a prison hospital where a local coroner would perform basic autopsies. A nearby school gymnasium was commandeered to store evidence. The team would sleep in a nearby grammar school.

Polizeigefängnis (Police Prison, known to the ordinary citizen as Oranje Hotel), Van Alkmadelaan 1258, Scheveningen/Den Haag 1432 hours, 27 May 1945

Callison arrived at his destination before three on a dusky summer afternoon. The regional prison was in the nearby resort community of Scheveningen, a kilometer or so from the crash site. Constructed in 1919, with 500 single cells in a ground-floor configuration, before the war, it had been a custodial remand center for petty thieves.

After the 1940 German invasion and capitulation of the Netherlands, the Nazis took over the place using it as a *Polizeigefängnis*, a lockup for those arrested by the *Sicherheitsdienst*—the SS. Upwards of 25,000 individuals were subsequently held captive within its red-brick walls. Many were in transit to concentration camps or worse—to be shot in batches, execution-style, in the nearby dunes. Among the Dutch population, the prison had become a symbol of resistance to Nazi rule, earning it the nickname *Oranje Hotel* in tribute to the exiled Dutch royal family—the House of Orange.

The prison had a small morgue and refrigerator room for cadavers awaiting removal for burial or further investigation. The bodies extracted from L for Lucy had been there for the better part of six days, guarded day and night by military redcaps.

As he waited in an anteroom to speak to the coroner, Callison mentally went over what he knew. The local authorities had been quite helpful but could only deal with what was available to them.

L for Lucy's initial impact on the beach had not been witnessed; moreover, it had occurred within a heavily mined closed area. However, the earlier event at the hamlet of Oude Wassanaar was another story. There had been several witnesses to the Lancaster's fateful journey above that town. Three stood out in the summary notes that the Dutch police had provided Callison.

A man named Adrianus Timmerman who ran a grocer's shop had heard a hellish roar and spotted a British bomber heading toward the village windmill. The aircraft had clipped the structure's top and veered away toward the North Sea.

Those observations were confirmed by a Dutch police officer named Nienhuis, who added the following pertinent information—the four motors were running full tilt, the plane had no apparent surface damage, and there was no sign of smoke or a fluid leak.

And finally, a woman named De Groot corroborated the other accounts, but added a crucial element. The pilot appeared to have collapsed as if he had been sleeping.

Callison and his team had gone over the Lanc with a fine-tooth comb. Nothing suggested failure of the airframe or the ever-dependable Merlin engines. The aircraft appeared to have been mechanically sound. It might have been pilot error. But Flight Lieutenant Foster had been a flyer with extensive experience, and his CO at Little Crofton had considered him very capable. He had, however, veered off his official flight path. And an eyewitness indicated he'd been unconscious at the controls.

The door opened and the town coroner entered, wearing a worse-for-wear suit that matched his haggard facial expression. The good doctor had a slight eye twitch, and his breathing was labored. The war had obviously not been kind to Jacob Flink, and it appeared the coming peace offered little room for improvement. Pince-nezed, with a small goatee fringing a forced smile, the man was tightly wound. The deadly winter famine in occupied Holland would do that to anyone.

Doctor Flink introduced himself in passable English and got directly to business.

"I've done rudimentary workups on the deceased. They all appear to have been relatively sober. Their stomachs held foodstuffs digested in a time frame consistent with having an evening meal within five hours of the crash. They have assorted broken bones consistent with a forceful landing. The pilot has crushed vertebrae and the severe internal injuries that one would expect from his position in the front of the aircraft. No one was ejected."

"Your preliminary conclusions, Doctor?"

The doctor nodded. "According to the reports that you provided, the crew were buckled up in their positions when they were discovered. It appears they were dead before the crash. Perhaps . . ." he hesitated. "Perhaps they died in other ways."

"Yes," Callison replied soberly. "I was thinking exactly the same thing . . ."

"Unfortunately, I'm not equipped to do a proper analysis." The Dutchman paused. "You see, my old friend Isaac Stein specialized in such toxicology, and he is no longer with us. Taken away by the Nazis with his family a year ago. As were most of the Jews in Scheveningen."

"I understand," Callison responded gently as the unspoken truth of what had befallen the town's Jewish population passed between them. "Thank you for what you have been able to do. In the circumstances, I could not ask for more."

The Dutchman tactfully changed the subject. "You are a Canadian, Squadron Leader?"

Callison politely smiled. "American. But I've been in the RCAF for most of the war."

"I commend you for your service in freeing Holland."

Callison gave a slight nod of his head as he accepted the compliment. "And I commend you for your dedication in helping us, Doctor. Where did you learn English if I may ask? You speak with remarkable fluency."

The doctor responded with simple modesty. "I worked in the Dutch East Indies before the war. A hospital in Indonesia. I was single then and traveled the Orient extensively. Rangoon. Kuala Lumpur. Singapore, where I particularly loved Raffles and its Long Bar." He gazed into the distance. "That's where I met my wife Evelyn. She is . . ." he paused "*was* originally from Coventry. She died just before the liberation."

After a respectable time, Callison broke the silence. "I'm going to make arrangements to have the bodies removed to England for detailed analysis. Scotland Yard has excellent labs. I've seized everything inside the aircraft that might provide our forensic people with a lead. I'll certainly ensure you are sent the final report for your files. But it may take a while."

"So I've been told."

"I'll also need copies of your notes as a benchmark for the Yard to begin their work."

"Certainly."

"Oh? And doctor?"

"Yes?"

"Thank you again for all you've been able to do. I know it has been hard."

"Yes," the elfin Dutchman replied. "Yes, it has. But I somehow sense that, for you and your team, this investigation is only the beginning of something equally hard . . . and far more profound."

* * *

Callison crouched inside a Signal Corps van and waited for the connection to London to be made. Crackling sounds at first, and then, finally, a voice at the other end. A Geordie accent. Imperious, verging on impatient. He tried to imagine the owner of that voice, a male, sitting in some discreet office overlooking Hyde Park, sipping a brandy neat as he absently shuffled through files.

The chatter between them began, and the basics were quickly reviewed. All the required boxes tick-marked complete, as they would be in a conventional aircraft crash. As if the suspicious death of eight men in the circumstances that now confronted Callison could be deemed "conventional." But then, Callison mused as he pondered the facts he knew—what, after all, in wartime, was a "conventional" death?

Callison refocused his attention on the voice on the line. "I'm going to confide in you, Callison." The clearing of a throat. "Do you recall the mass breakout of Allied officers from a German POW camp—*Stalag Luft* III—located in a place called Sagan in Poland?"

"It happened last year, in '44."

"Seventy-six escaped; sadly only three made it to freedom. Fifty of those recaptured were subsequently murdered in cold blood by the SS acting on the direct orders of Hitler."

"Yes. The murders caused quite an uproar, if I recall. It was even brought up by the foreign secretary in the House of Commons."

"Quite." Stillness, then crackling in the line.

More silence. "Well, Special Investigations is shortly to be assigned the file. My unit is to capture the killers and bring them up on war crimes charges. Which brings me to your crash."

Crackle. Crackle. The voice pondered what it would say next. Then it began once more.

"Most of my resources will be focused on the murderers of those fifty Allied officers. The chaps at the Air Ministry have dictated that you are to continue with your investigation. I can offer you informed guidance should you require it, but I have nothing to provide in either materials or personnel."

"Nothing?"

"Nothing."

Callison responded. Abruptly, impatient for support. "I'm not an investigator. My team locates bodies and ensures they are properly processed. That's all. I'm not Sam Spade and neither are any of my men."

"But you and your lot can conduct a basic crash analysis, can you not?"

"The basic elements? Yes. Though we normally do uncomplicated recoveries, some of my team are reasonably well versed in such things. Sergeant MacAteer, for one, was an experienced technician in that area long before I came into the unit."

"Good. Then it will have to do."

"Repeat, please."

"I said that it will have to do."

Callison felt a sudden pressure behind his eyes. "And the deadline I've been given to do this?"

"A week has passed. That leaves you with three. And, Callison?
"Yes."

"Tomorrow morning you've been detailed to fly to a Soviet airfield south of Berlin to determine what transpired while L for Lucy was there. A place called Sperenberg."

"I'm sorry?"

The voice continued as if it hadn't heard. "Whitehall has made all the arrangements. It's something that must be done to tie up loose ends. I'm sure it will all be fine. Now, as to L for Lucy. Your team is competent enough to do the necessary work—whatever needs to be done there until you return.

"The Kremlin has assured us that they will provide all the assistance you may require. To that end, when you land, you'll be escorted to a major of Soviet State Security, who will be your intermediary. Work with them Callison, as best you can. We don't expect miracles. A word to the wise. Potsdam is in the Russian-occupied zone, so I would tread lightly if I were you. I've been told the Russkies on the ground can be quite trigger-happy."

More crackling and growing interference over the airways. The voice at the other end growing fainter, then barely discernible.

"I'm setting up a command post at RAF Station Celle, an old *Luftwaffe* base outside of Hanover. It should be up and running shortly. If you require additional support or if anything important crops up, do contact me through them. Don't hesitate."

The connection abruptly went dead.

Wing Commander Freddie Bowes, newly promoted head of RAF Special Investigations Branch in the British Air Forces of Occupation, was obviously an extremely busy man.

CHAPTER 15

Boarding Bristol Buckingham KV311,
Schiphol Airport, runway 04-22,
50 kilometers south of Scheveningen
0753 hours, 28 May 1945

The next morning, just before eight, Callison boarded a dowdy Bristol Buckingham as its only passenger. The flight from Schiphol was quick, albeit rough. The twin-engine bomber-turned-courier transport gasping for air until it touched down at Sperenberg, a captured *Luftwaffe* airbase located south of Berlin.

Several Yak fighters and a quartet of lend-lease King Cobras sat on the patchwork landing apron. The Buckingham taxied past the battle-tested aircraft to a spot near an ancient gull-winged biplane. Sperenberg was a beehive of activity with countless press gangs of German POWs filling in potholes in runways and hammering clapboard siding onto crumpled airplane hangars.

The Soviet Army captain who met Callison as he exited the aircraft was overweight, dour, and intentionally obtuse. He stank of vodka, and his uniform was unkempt and spotted with food stains, but he had a row of combat ribbons on his chest and a badly stitched wound that zigzagged from the tip of his mouth to the lobe of his left ear. It definitely had not come from shaving too closely. He gestured to Callison to follow him to a waiting Jeep.

The American-made vehicle had seen better days—and more probably—years, as it rashly jackrabbited out of the base and onto a straightaway sentinelled by charred tree stumps and the rusting hulks of tanks, half-tracks, and lorries. The driver drove the Jeep as he would a farm tractor, plowing belligerently through stubborn road furrows and deep depressions with unbridled enthusiasm. The Russian officer sat hunched alone in the back seat, furiously puffing on a hand-rolled cigarette, occasionally grimacing as its hot ashes flew back, stinging his eyes.

The journey proved to be as sobering as it was bumpy. The sky overhead was a brownish-gray monochrome; the air smelled of dank concrete mixed with smoke. Countless olive-drab T-34 tanks clatter-rumbled down the street heading west, followed by shaggy little horses pulling carts for Russian infantry soldiers stiff with dirt. Thin cows trotted behind the carts and chickens cackled in wicker cages wedged between rugs, chairs, clocks, paintings, and commandeered items of expensive clothing. The rising morning heat carried with it the pervasive odor of rotting flesh. Bloated torsos floated half submerged in bomb craters filled with fetid water. Carcasses of farm animals dotted the way, their rib cages starkly exposed where scavengers, both human and otherwise, had foraged for sheer survival. Abandoned clothes, furniture, and body parts were strewn everywhere, mingling with mounds of rubble, glass, and fine mahogany. "The Thousand-Year Reich," Callison muttered under his breath. "Heil Hitler!"

The Jeep arrived at Wünsdorf. A once-genteel town with elegant ruins now cascading into decay, it was nestled in the heart of what remained of a forest only 25 kilometers from the total devastation of what was now Berlin. Wünsdorf had already served the military ambitions of two German Kaisers by the time the First World War began. The facility, covering an area of 60,000 acres, was once the biggest military base in Europe. Used by the German Olympic team to train ahead of the 1936 Games, it then became the home of the German Supreme Command of the Armed Forces—the *Oberkommando der Wehrmacht*—representing the apex of Nazi military decision-making throughout the Second World War.

The Jeep came to a jolting halt before what appeared to be a row of abandoned Bavarian chalets. Callison noted each held decorative flower boxes placed in front of fake window frames painted on rock-solid concrete walls. The Russian captain proudly pointed to the damaged buildings. "Maybach. *Ein kaput.*" He merrily beamed in broken German, clasping his hands triumphantly, "Hitler und Alles ist *kaput.*"

They entered the third chalet through an open doorway, passing a duet of totem-pole-erect uniformed sentinels. The guards' uniforms were spotless, their deportment as precise and purposeful as if they were protecting a member of Stalin's inner circle.

The cracked entrance walls of the chalet were dank with moisture. Strips of plaster dangled from the ceiling. Naked bulbs hung here and there, powered by diesel generators, providing what passed for light in the long winding corridors the captain led him down. They met an occasional sentry, each as anonymously correct as the previous one.

Down a flight of stairs, then a second, until there were no more, and they were in the very depths of the place.

A double sentry posted at a solid iron door. The Russian captain pressed a red wall buzzer. The door opened, and they entered a high-ceilinged chamber. A wizened sergeant escorted them to the back where Callison came face to face with the NKVD major he was to meet. He was struck by her blonde hair tied tightly in a knot, classic Nordic features, and haunting green eyes. Seated confidently behind a massive desk as overpowering as an anti-tank obstacle, she greeted him with a steady gaze and then rose with a polished smile. Callison saw that she was supremely fit and shapely in a crisply ironed uniform. With well-polished high boots and riding jodhpurs, her appearance was immaculate, and her spoken English was equally impeccable.

He introduced himself, and the major did likewise. "Fedin. Nadia Fedin." Callison rightly sensed that the medals on her blouse were not decorative.

After dismissing the captain with a curt nod, she offered Callison a seat, which he accepted, and a cognac, which he gracefully declined.

Fedin poured herself the liquor from a crystal decanter resting on a cargo crate that had until recently been used to ship *Wehrmacht* stick grenades, or so the Gothic stencil on its facing indicated. As she returned to her chair, she gracefully gestured around the chamber. "Maybach. At one time this was a truly impressive complex, Squadron Leader. The very heartbeat of the German military command—from day one of our Great Patriotic War until the bitter end. With walls a meter-thick these buildings are so solidly constructed they prove extremely difficult to damage, let alone destroy. And so, we came up with a solution Comrade Stalin would be proud of. We have made this complex our temporary headquarters for Berlin."

She placed her drinking glass on the desk. "The Nazis' entire Second World War campaign was guided from the Zeppelin communications bunker located less than a kilometer from here. The site was constructed of alternate layers of earth and concrete, dug 60 feet deep into the earth, making it extremely difficult to destroy. Zeppelin provided the *Oberkommando der Wehrmacht* with direct telex contact to all the fronts—Stalingrad, France, Holland, and even Africa. Fascinating is it not?"

"Yes, it is." Callison responded politely.

Fedin set her glass on her desk. "Now. You are here to investigate a British Lancaster bomber that took off from an airfield in Soviet-occupied territory and subsequently crashed?"

"Yes."

"It is my duty to help you in any way I can." Glancing occasionally at a large buff-colored folio resting on the desk before her, Fedin began to provide background details: "Lancaster serial number R5918 arrived at Sperenberg airfield, which is actually a ten-minute drive directly west of here, at 2023 hours on the evening of Monday, the twenty-first of May, and departed at 2141 hours on the same date."

She handed Callison a typewritten piece of foolscap. "Here is the list of the seven Soviet Air Force ground crew who attended to the aircraft. They are all loyal workers with pristine records. No fascist POW was allowed near the airplane."

Callison politely accepted the page, skimming over the names as he did so. "Did your ground personnel provide the bomber crew with any food or refreshment?"

Glancing downward, her index finger flitted across a page. Fedin looked up. "No, no they did not."

"Did the crew ever leave the immediate area of the bomber?"

"No," Fedin asserted once more. "According to this report, the Lancaster pilot advised us that his personnel had no desire to leave the tarmac. Since there are still active Nazi werewolf packs in the area, we naturally provided an armed security perimeter to safeguard our Allies."

"Can you tell me anything that you might know about the passenger," Callison asked, changing tack.

She flipped over several pages and stopped. A moment later, she looked up from the folio.

"On May eighteenth, at about eleven in the morning, an unarmed person dressed in what appeared to be a random mixture of military and civilian clothing, was found by one of our roving patrols wandering in the Berlin suburb of Pankow. He identified himself to us as Captain Roland Blasingham." She stopped and carefully spelled the surname.

She looked up. "All indications were that Blasingham had recently been in a German POW camp. Once we established that he wasn't a spy . . ." She met Callison's puzzled look nonplussed. "We must be ever vigilant, Squadron Leader. The Nazis are quite devious."

Fedin adroitly changed tack. "We soon satisfied ourselves as to Blasingham's identity, then promptly advised the British military authority who immediately sent over your permanent liaison—a Major Trevor Simmonds—who took him away for a few days of well-earned rest among his fellow officers in the British zone. When the Lancaster arrived at Sperenberg on the evening of the twenty-first of May, it was Simmonds who accompanied Blasingham to the aircraft. "

"And where is the major now?"

"He's stationed at British HQ in the Grünewald district of Berlin. If you wish, we can arrange transport for you to get there and return."

"Thank you. That would be most helpful."

After ensuring the vehicle was ready for Callison, Fedin escorted him to the entrance of the bunker. Callison could not but help sense the discreet wafting of perfume in the air—subtle lilac, expensive. What a man would naively term—Parisienne. Nadia Fedin was certainly not your average intelligence officer, but then, Johnny Callison had never dealt with the NKVD.

Elster Platz,
Grünewald District, Berlin,
British-Occupied Zone,
1526 hours, 28 May 1945

Situated at *Elster Platz* amid Berlin's leafy upper middle-class parklands, the British occupation headquarters proved to be within the newly coined Mackenzie King Barracks. Originally built as a Jewish seniors' home, the Germans used it as a dreaded Gestapo staging facility. Mere days after the Allied victory, it became home to the Third Battalion, Canadian Army Occupation Force, and was renamed after the Canadian prime minister. In short order, the First Battalion Coldstream Guards had sent an advance team to take over from the

Canucks, and it was readily apparent that they wanted to make a determined and distinctive mark of their own from the very outset. The Canadians might have provided stolid foot soldiers to patrol Berlin's stinking rubble for the short duration that they were there, but the zone they operated in was decidedly British, as was the spit and polish command structure preparing to run it.

Callison's meeting with the Coldstream major was brief but eventful. The office he was directed to was as austere as Fedin's was relatively opulent. A wooden desk that looked worm-eaten, a stick-pin-infested wall map, and a half dozen functional folding chairs more suited for a church bingo than for Trevor Simmonds's position as the Chief Liaison Officer, British Army of Occupation (Berlin).

With his tidy twin rows of campaign medals, and a swagger stick resting on the desk, the Guards major was initially as imperious as he was to the point. After gesturing for Callison to take a seat opposite his, the Guardsman outlined what he knew, with the cool precision of a Sandhurst instructor.

A British officer had been found wandering in the Soviet occupation zone of Berlin. That same day, he'd been handed over to the major at the Soviet Berlin headquarters at Wünsdorf. "Captain Blasingham . . ." he glanced down at the black notebook he used for such matters. "Actually, that was not his name."

"According to what the man related to me once we were clear of Wünsdorf, he'd landed in Poland on a hush-hush mission, which he quite correctly would not tell me about. He worked with the Polish Underground to further that mission, was in Warsaw during the recent uprising, and was subsequently captured by the Nazis somewhere near the Polish–German border. He shrewdly masqueraded as a downed RAF bomber pilot and was immediately imprisoned in *Stalag Luft* IV. When the German defenses in that region collapsed in the face of Soviet advances, the guards took all the POWs westwards with them. What began as a disciplined forced march soon broke down into a struggle for survival. Antony Eskenzi, for that was his real name, was able to escape from the horde somewhere near Seelow and made his way westward through Nazi Germany, hiding in barns and foraging from the land."

"It appears he was captured by a solitary *Wehrmacht* officer named Dorfmann, who, instead of killing him outright, safely shepherded our man westwards until they were inside what remained of Greater Berlin.

There they somehow parted. Eskenzi was obviously the *Kraut's* insurance policy to the West and away from the Soviets."

"Do we know where this fellow Dorfmann is currently?"

"I thought you might ask. We actually do." The Guards officer smiled showing perfect teeth. "Major Heinz Dorfmann, allegedly of the 562 Volksgrenadier Regiment, was captured by our troops near Wismar. He is currently being held for interrogation at Number 74 in Bad Nenndorf."

"Interrogation?" Callison was curious.

The smile left the Englishman's face as abruptly as it had appeared. "You don't think we believe every Fritz that stumbles across our path do you, Squadron Leader?"

Callison mulled over the unspoken implication. "And where might that interrogation be?"

"Number 74 in Bad Nenndorf."

"Pardon?"

"Number 74. The Combined Services Detailed Interrogation Center, run by a select group of intelligence officers. Their job is to break hard-case Nazis and get what passes for the truth out of them. Their commandant, Robin Stephens, is an old friend of mine." A slight chuckle. "'Old Tin Eye' used to be in the Ghurkas. He fought on the northwest frontier—Khyber Pass, Wuziristan—that sort of thing."

The Guards officer glanced at his wristwatch and stood, gesturing to the door. "Well, enough of the boring stuff, Squadron Leader. Let's adjourn to the mess for afternoon tea and drinks. I'll introduce you to the lads, and we'll set you up for the night in the officers' quarters. Tomorrow morning, bright and early, I'll take you to Number 74."

CHAPTER 16

Bad Nenndorf, District of Schaumburg,
Lower Saxony, British-Occupied Zone
1102 hours, 29 May 1945

Bad Nenndorf was a compact, battle-ravaged town located less than an hour west of Hanover. In years past, the pungent odor emanating from its many sulfur springs had been disparaged by the locals as being Satan's excrement. But in the late 1700s, those same waters were found to possess the most powerful arthritic healing agents in Europe, so much so that the place became a spa and was quickly acknowledged as being "Royal"—suitable for and favored by Prussian royalty. Shortly after the Allied armies occupied the town in 1945, the spa's mudbath chambers were used as prison cells to house suspected Nazi leaders.

When they arrived at "Number 74"—the interrogation complex—shortly before eleven o'clock, Callison and his Guards companion were taken to the commandant's office where they met Lieutenant Colonel Robin Stephens. "Old Tin Eye" did indeed wear a monocle in his right eye. Callison was later to discover it was not an affectation but the result of exposure to Italian mustard gas encountered when Stephens worked with a British Red Cross team in Abyssinia in the mid-1930s.

After perfunctory introductions, Callison got straight to the point. They were looking to interview a man named Heinz Dorfmann.

Stephens nodded knowingly. "Yes. Now *there* is a prisoner. He had serious issues with us from the moment he first arrived. Attitude you know. Still has. The man's an inveterate liar. He tries my patience and that of my team. Mind you, I've seen more than my share of them, both here and at Number 20."

"Number 20, sir?" Callison asked, puzzled by the cryptic address.

"Latchmere House just outside London," Stephens replied with measured calm. "I ran it during the war as an interrogation center for MI5. It held high-ranking Nazis we'd captured. You can pretty well guess what went on within those walls.."

"Lots of body and fender work, I assume," Simmonds interjected with a tight-lipped smile.

"No," the colonel responded firmly. "Violence is always taboo under my watch. Never strike a man. In the first place, it is an act of cowardice. And secondly, it is not intelligent. A prisoner will lie to avoid further punishment. More importantly, everything he says thereafter will be based on false information.

"Come," Stephens gestured. "Let us take you to your chap's current abode."

The three men briskly made their way out of the office and down a dim corridor, before traversing several flights of stairs as they passed through a series of cast-iron doors, each guarded by an alert British MP, each requiring a new and seemingly distinct set of keys to open it.

The last door was the most daunting of all for they faced a trio of grim-faced MPs who tensed visibly on their arrival. A sign-in log rested on a plain office desk to one side of the door. In it, Stephens made a short notation as to the time and date, their names, and the prisoner they were to visit. The colonel signed his name with a flourish; the document was co-signed and verified by the senior MP present.

The youngest of the MPs strode over to a buzzer. A look-see in the door slid open and a pair of vigilant eyes stared out at them. Satisfied as to their identities in the presence of his unit commander, the man slid the opening shut. Moments passed, punctuated by a series of keys being efficiently turned.

Finally, the door creaked open slowly, and they were met by a burly redcap sergeant.

After a brisk salute and an equally sharp about-turn, they followed the MP down an ill-lit, narrow hallway. The MP's boots clattered loudly as he strutted ahead of them.

A series of stark iron doors—ten in total—loomed on both sides. The MP stopped at the third door on his right. He peered into the peephole then nodded, satisfied the man was still in the world of the living. "Stand up prisoner! You have visitors!"

The MP selected a key from a loop dangling from his blancoed Sam Browne and carefully opened the door.

Cavern-like, the cell stank of resignation. The creature inside rustled quickly to attention. The man was of indeterminate age and of average height, with hair cropped short to the skull.

Dressed in formless gray prison garb, he stood parade-square rigid beside a prison-issue cot. The bed coverings were hospital-cornered as befitting someone who practiced military discipline, even in defeat. A rudimentary metal desk and hardback chair were the only other furnishings. The chamber was austere, verging on vindictive.

Callison intentionally stood to one side, enabling the dim shadowed hallway to keep him from the prisoner's view.

"Heinz here speaks the King's English," the sergeant offered to no one in particular, not bothering to mask the utter disdain in his voice. "Claims he learned it at the University of Heidelberg."

A nod from the captive German. Callison felt it verged on obsequiousness. But then he'd never been a prisoner of war with a Nazi past.

"You stated to our investigators that your name is Heinz Dorfmann." Stephens began the discussion in the same calm and measured tone he used for all investigations.

"My rank is major. 562 Volksgrenadier Regiment. Or what was left of it. We fought the Soviets at Seelow heights," he added without prompting. "We were totally crushed."

"Shortly after your arrival here, you told our interview team that just before you were captured you were traveling through what was then Nazi-occupied Germany in the company of a British officer."

"Yes. Our defenses were collapsing against Ivan. I spotted this fellow in ragged bits of military clothing, which identified him as either a German deserter or an escaped Allied POW. He was wandering aimlessly in a small village a few kilometers west of Seelow, doing so much of nothing. When I approached him to speak, he avoided my gaze. Jumpy, like a deer in the headlights. And after that, it was easy to confront him and confirm my initial suspicions as to his identity. An escaped *kriegie* in hostile territory. And, as you English say, 'Bob's your uncle.' From that moment onward, this Britisher was destined to become my insurance policy."

"Quite," Stephens remarked dryly. "Why did you not take him to the nearest Gestapo unit for questioning?"

The German allowed a frown of disbelief to flit across his face. "Colonel Stephens, by late April, even I could see the war was well and truly over. What would it gain for me to surrender a wandering Tommy to the Gestapo? A medal from Uncle Adolf?" He paused as if considering the benefit of what he would say next. "Moreover, this particular Englishman was quite valuable."

"How so?"

"As I have told you, I quickly assumed he was more than a Britisher somehow freed from a POW camp, wandering westwards toward the Allied lines. Over time, he admitted to me that he had something of great significance on his person, something the Russians would not have been pleased about."

"Did he say what it was?"

"No. Nor would I blame him. But he did mention it involved a place I knew of. A place called Katyn . . ."

"Katyn," Stephens slowly mulled over the word. "I have recently heard disturbing rumors about what happened there . . ."

"They are not rumors, Colonel Stephens," the German whispered.

Stephens let the comment pass. "How many days was the English officer under your control?"

"I wouldn't use the word 'control,'" the German subtly corrected. "I prefer to say we had a gentleman's agreement. I would help him navigate what was left of the Führer's empire and then . . ."

"Yes?"

"And then, I hoped that he might reward me with a kind word when I surrendered in his custody to your people."

"Let me ask you again," Stephens pressed. "For how many days did this mutually advantageous trade-off exist?"

The German paused to consider the question before he answered. "Several. Perhaps six or seven. But as we neared Berlin, it became apparent that I was at even greater risk for a bullet in the head than my British companion."

"I beg your pardon?"

"Oh, come now," the German allowed himself to display a glimmer of genuine emotion. "In the last days of the Reich, surely you saw the bodies hanging from light standards throughout the zones you had liberated, hanging compliments of the fanatical few still loyal to the Führer. I for one had no intention of being a Hitler ornament on a streetlamp."

"So? You parted ways?"

The German nodded. "In this instance, it was best for both of us. The Russkies were on the verge of taking Berlin, and I was suddenly a fugitive in my own country."

"Where did this leave-taking happen?"

"Somewhere near Rudersdorf on the Kalksee," the German answered methodically. "From there, I continued west then headed toward the Baltic. I was captured by Tommies near Jutland."

Stephens had what he wanted. He abruptly changed tack.

"One of the reasons you are here in these luxurious lodgings is that we discovered that you have a scar under one arm . . ."

The German blinked nervously. "A village doctor's abysmal effort to remove a birthmark."

Stephens lost his patience. "Funny how you Jerries all claim it's something innocuous like a birthmark. Damn it all! It is nothing more than a shabby attempt to hide a blood-type tattoo—a means of field identification on their troops that only the SS use."

The German remained silent.

A voice in the shadowed hallway behind Stephens. "I know you, *Obersturmführer* Henschell. I know you very well."

The German's face turned ashen. "No. No, you are mistaken."

Callison brushed past Stephens and moved into the glare of the single cell bulb, his aviator glasses hiding any hint of emotion, the paisley Ascot pushed high about his face. "Look at me. You remember Katyn? I certainly do."

The German captive seemed to shrink in stature.

"Henschell?" Stephens interjected. "I know that name from somewhere." He gestured to the redcap. "Stand by sergeant. I'll be back in a moment."

When the colonel returned, he had a folio in his hand. Opening it at a tabbed spot, he glanced down the page then spoke.

"Paulus Henschell?" Stephens stared hard at the German, affirming the obvious. "It states here that you are wanted in a serious war crimes investigation. Something that happened in 1940. In May of that year to be exact. A village called Paradis in the Pas-de-Calais Prefecture . . ."

"No," the German's face twitched ever so slightly. "I had nothing to do with it."

"But you do know who did, don't you?" Stephens pressed. "Your life is hanging by the thinnest of threads as it is. And only you can change its trajectory. Who ordered the killings?"

Silence.

"Answer me!" Stephens thundered.

The German finally spoke, his voice a plaintive whisper. "I am aware of the man who ordered it."

Stephens turned to the military policeman. "Sergeant Selby. Process this prisoner under his real name. Section Four Regulations for the Trial of War Criminals. Inform the relevant investigators in Berlin. They will certainly want to interview him."

The German interjected, abject terror in his face, "But I, myself, did not take part in these killings. I was vehemently opposed to them. In fact, I reported the matter to my superiors . . ."

Stephens abruptly dismissed the comment. "As a good German officer always does. But at the time, you did nothing. Spare me the dogma. I've heard that one before. And all too often."

The prisoner stared blankly at the British officers confronting him.

"There *is* an option." Stephens's tone abruptly changed. "You could help us convict the perpetrators by becoming a witness for the prosecution. Or conversely, you could allow our investigation of your own involvement in those murders to continue."

"So, you have captured him?" The German asked cautiously. "You have Knöchlein?"

Stephens did not answer the question. "That is not your concern, Henschell. Such matters have a way of resolving themselves." He adroitly moved on. "Let us be brutally frank, shall we? If you don't help us, you will face a showcase trial operating at breakneck speed at which you will be the star defendant. A trial with judges who are your sworn enemies and who will preside over your dubious future with a preordained end as the only conclusion you can ever contemplate."

"Or you can become a witness for the prosecution with a chance at freedom and life-long anonymity. I will let you ponder your options and will expect your answer tomorrow."

Before the German could respond, Stephens ordered the door to the cell closed. The three Allied officers calmly departed the prisoner block, the MP sergeant leading the way.

When they had returned to the commandant's office, an "urgent" message from Scotland Yard was waiting for Callison. He immediately returned the call to London on the secure military communication net. After the usual protocol, satisfying himself as to Callison's identity, a dryly methodical forensic scientist outlined the test results. The Yard's labs confirmed what Callison had strongly suspected. The crew of L for Lucy and their sole passenger had been murdered by ingestion of a unique poison. The act had been quick and thoroughly professional. Callison took copious notes, for he knew he would need them in short order to confront both what might be dubious allies and would certainly be formidable adversaries.

His next call was to RAF Celle, a recently captured *Luftwaffe* airfield located northeast of Hanover. The connection was good, and he was soon speaking directly to the individual he sought, Wing Commander Bowes, head of RAF Special Investigations Branch in the British Air Forces of Occupation.

After exchanging passing pleasantries, Callison coolly honed in on the essentials.

"It's as I strongly suspected—a multiple murder." He went on to crisply outline his theory, that persons unknown had intentionally poisoned the crew of L for Lucy for a motive he was unable to divulge at this early stage.

"And where was this act committed?"

"Berlin."

"Precisely which zone, Callison?"

"The Soviet one."

"There is nothing we can do. Absolutely nothing. Politics, you know."

"So, you let the killers of eight men go free?"

A patronizing sigh. "Mr. Callison. I am currently investigating the deaths of fifty Allied officers executed by the Gestapo for escaping from *Stalag Luft* III in what is now Soviet-controlled Polish territory. If you can find the authority from the Soviets to get us to Sagan for the investigation of those murders, we will certainly assist you in your own inquiries. But I must warn you that the odds of getting an agreement to allow either us or you into Communist-controlled lands is as rare as snow in the Sahara. In any event, do keep me apprised."

Click.

It was after the calls were made that Callison sat down with his two British compatriots and outlined his rapidly emerging plan. He would need the prompt and unquestioning assistance of both to make it happen, and before he left with Simmonds on the journey back to Berlin, he had received just that.

Arnsberg, Nordrhein-Westfalen,
British-Occupied Zone
1015 hours, 30 May 1945

The last Wednesday in May was overcast over much of the north Rhine and Westphalia. It was like the land was in mourning. Defeat had set in like a funeral pall.

Trudy Bach woke early and had a cup of coffee substitute and black bread. With some difficulty, she was just growing accustomed to her second widowhood. In early January, her husband had been impressed into the *Volkssturm*, the ragtag militia made up of pseudo-pensioners, teens, and cripples created by Hitler in a manic bid to save what little was left of his *Reich*. He was killed less than a month before war's end on an anonymous country road of no military importance less than ten minutes from his home, his battered *Panzerfaust* no match for a Sherman tank.

She walked three kilometers in the drab morning, crossing the bridge to the cemetery in nearby Halden. Trudy Bach had never learned how her son Dirk had died, only that he had been a German casualty during the Warsaw Uprising. She had made the trek to the cemetery without pause since the day of the funeral and interment. His was not the only military burial, but she could be thankful that, unlike most German parents in mourning, her son's body was recovered and returned to her.

A young man had arrived at her home in the first weeks following the war wearing the tattered uniform of an infantry NCO. He had lost an arm, a makeshift cloth patch covered his left eye, and a shabby Iron Cross dangled from what was left of his dreary tunic. The man identified himself simply as Wolfgang. He said he had sought her out as a promise he made to her son when they were last together in Warsaw. He told her how brave Dirk had been in combat and how he had cared so much for the well-being of every one of his charges, as well as for many anonymous civilians until the moment he died. Then, just before he left, the young man handed her an Iron Cross. It was her son's.

She thought of the corporal's words as she stood at the graveside. Comfort was a word with no meaning, suitable only for cheap novels. But Trudy Bach now appreciated its pitiable successor—resignation.

There was no rank or any mention of military medals earned on the plain black cross confronting her. In a Germany thoroughly defeated in war and supplicant to the victors in peace, anything other than a simple memorial would be out of place. It started to rain.

**Brandenburg Gate,
Pariser Platz, Berlin
1025 hours, 30 May 1945**

The Brandenburg Gate, erected in the late seventeenth century and featuring the Quadriga, a chariot carrying a triumphant Victoria, the Roman goddess of Victory, had become for a time synonymous with Germany's aspirations.

On this tin-pot gray morning, even the low clouds threatening rain scudding in from the northeast seemed ironic, as a Soviet flag fluttered in the breeze above the Gate. Brilliant crimson standards draped the Quadriga, which had been forced off its pedestal to lurch eerily in space by an errant artillery shell. Gaudy posters of Lenin and hammer-and-sickle red pennants cascaded down its colonnades.

A British Austin staff car noisily geared down before stopping at a spot close to the Gate. It held two occupants—an RAF officer and driver. As he alighted from the bug-like vehicle to await his counterpart, Johnny Callison was frustrated and angry. He did not like being manipulated, yet he sensed this was exactly where he now found himself.

He glanced over to where the remains of the Reichstag stood. Once the glorious heart of the Third Reich, it was now a ravaged skeletal shell. Beyond it, Berlin had become a pancake-flat city with iceberg-like ruins jutting angrily into a grim sky in all directions as far as the eye could see. The pungent stench of sour wet masonry and death filled the air.

Everywhere he looked, Callison saw brigades of "rubble women" wearing patched trench coats, wandering Sherpa-like over fallen beams and indifferent debris as they stubbornly reclaimed bricks from giant mountains of utter devastation, their heads wrapped in kerchiefs against the dust and base stench of human decomposition. Callison felt he had landed on an alien and inhospitable planet with no way to escape.

A mud-splattered Soviet GAZ sedan emerged from the Russian-occupied zone and braked to a halt next to the Austin. A creaky US Lend-Lease Jeep, with a gaggle of heavily armed soldiers astride it, pulled up behind the sedan.

Major Fedin emerged from the back seat of the GAZ. Even in a drab NKVD uniform, she had a distinct presence. A quartet of flat-faced soldiers armed with burp guns bounded out of the jeep and assumed an at-the-ready position around the vehicles.

Callison greeted her with a slight nod of his head. Unsmiling, he swiftly dismissed her half-hearted attempt at pleasantries.

"Let me get to the point, Major Fedin," he began. "This morning I received the results of lab tests conducted by Scotland Yard on the contents of a Stanley brand thermos—the kind originally made for the US Army Air Force. Only this one had the words '240th Fighter Aviation Division' engraved on its base in Cyrillic writing. It was found in the cockpit of the Lancaster next to the pilot.

"Traces of a poison were found in the stomachs of all occupants of the aircraft, including the passenger who boarded at Sperenberg airfield. I believe the entire crew of L for Lucy was murdered."

Fedin offered a mere shrug. "They were thirsty. It was probably bad vodka."

"Don't be trite. The contents were tea."

"Then, as you wish. Bad tea leaves."

"Major. The tea contained Batrachotoxin, a nerve agent that will cause death by paralysis within hours of ingestion."

"You had a Pole on the crew. Perhaps it was his doing."

Callison was taken aback at the unexpected retort. "How did you know who was on the aircraft, major? I never told you their nationalities."

What little patience Fedin was prepared to grant to Callison wore thin. "Please don't play games with me," she commented frostily. "What is your point, Squadron Leader?"

"The evidence implicates Soviet agents."

"That is an unwelcome theory. Have you considered that the man you claim was a British officer, this curious 'passenger' you sent an aircraft across half a continent to pick up, had previously worked with the Polish Underground? And in all probability with the Fascists? He provided us with a false identity. His real name was Eskenzi. He may well have been a spy. A spy!" She spat out the word.

"We are an ally, Squadron Leader. I will take your accusation no further. Be thankful."

It began to rain, a few droplets at first, then more steadily. No one moved. The shower had a coppery tinge and carried with it the stink of rotting corpses. A curious steamy mist filtered up from the rubbled city. It was as if the dead were trickling upwards into the world of the living.

"I would like permission to continue my investigation in your zone."

"Denied." With one word, Fedin abruptly shut the door to co-operation. "We have completed our inquiries and provided you with all you need. My superiors consider the matter closed."

"All well and good," Callison countered. "Then my superiors will launch an official protest to the Russian commander in Berlin."

"This is getting tiresome. I've briefed Field Marshal Zhukov on the entire file. He agrees with my findings. This matter is but another instance of mischief by the Poles, as was Sikorski's demise at Gibraltar."

The rain had become an unrelenting downpour. Fedin stood stolid, while Callison raised the collar of his bomber jacket. "So, you will not assist me in your zone?" he asked.

"*Nyet*. The matter is closed."

"And if I enter the Russian zone without your assistance?"

Fedin sighed. "Some of your countrymen wander into the Soviet zone without authority. They are either arrested as black marketers, pimps, or drug dealers, or . . ."

"Or?"

Fedin's face went abruptly serious. "Or they are shot outright as spies."

"Are you threatening me, Major Fedin?"

"No. Squadron Leader. Just stating facts. Look behind me. My security detail is from the Tajik People's Republic, a place more famous for breeding dull-witted shepherds who munch on cheese curd than for intellectuals who spend a lifetime contemplating Marx's dialectical materialism or those who put on the uniform and actually protect the proletariat from fascism. These men are unquestioning herdsmen. Comrade Stalin feeds and clothes them and provides for their families while they are here serving Mother Russia. These men will do as they are told and be grateful to be allowed to obey."

"Including an act of cold-blooded murder?"

Fedin laughed outright, a grim, calculating gesture as hard and unfeeling as cold steel. "Twenty million Russians have been slaughtered by the Fascists in the last six years. One more death means less than nothing to them and certainly nothing to me. Always remember this, Squadron Leader Callison. It was our war, our victory, and now it is our Berlin. We tolerate your presence in this city. . . if that. If there is nothing more?" An impatient pause. "Good day."

Fedin returned to her sedan. Within moments, the Soviet staff car and its armed escort had scuttled down the Unter der Linden. Callison stood alone in the shadow of the Brandenburg Gate and watched the vehicles until they were but receding specks on a chalkboard horizon.

Without warning, the rain stopped, leaving only a dank mist. A pack of surly dogs emerged from nowhere chasing a scabrous cat. Their mad scramble swiftly headed into the shabby relics of nearby buildings. The dogs appeared to be gaining.

It was clammy. John Callison was miserable. Berlin was the capital city of a vanquished nation. And he was one of its conquerors. Yet strangely, he felt supreme melancholy at that thought, for victories were meant to be enjoyed and not endured.

He jumped into his Jeep and ordered the driver to head west to Bad Nenndorf as quickly as the vehicle could take them, stopping only to pick up an essential passenger. He had urgent business to attend to. Callison had not expected much from the Soviet major. Her threats no longer held any meaning for him, for he had nothing left to lose.

**No. 74 Combined Services Detailed Interrogation Centre,
Bad Nenndorf, District of Schaumburg.
Lower Saxony, British-Occupied Zone
1548 hours, 30 May 1945**

The army sergeant opened the cell door and stood watchfully in the background, his holster cover open to reveal the blue-steel butt of a Colt pistol, as the three officers passed him and entered the room—Callison first, then his newfound confederates—Robin Stephens, Commandant of Number 74, and Coldstream Guards Major Trevor Simmonds.

Callison had stopped en route at the British Occupation Headquarters at Elster Place to pick up Simmonds. Then, as they raced westward to the holding facility on a bomb-cratered road, he briefed the British major on his meeting with Fedin. The two men agreed it was time to activate their plan. There was no alternative.

"Oh, you're back," the German in the cell commented dryly as he unhurriedly rose to his feet. Whether he was resigned to his final fate or simply insolent, he did not appear at all nervous.

"You have had time to consider yesterday's offer?" Stephens asked.

"I have."

"And?"

A pregnant silence.

It was Callison who spoke next. "We have something you can assist us with—something that you might find more palatable than confronting a former comrade in an open court."

Henschell's eyes narrowed. "Go on."

Simmonds methodically completed the proposal. "In return for your help in a very particular matter, we have the authority to place you in South America, Canada, or even Australia with an ironclad alias. You can start a new life and no one will know anything. We will even provide you with a generous annual stipend."

"In perpetuity?"

A pause. "Yes."

"To what do I owe your sudden generosity?" the German responded with no small tinge of arrogance.

"I wouldn't be so bold," Stephens raised his voice. "Always remember, Henschell, history is written by the victors. And so is justice. It may be blind, but the scales can be easily fixed to whichever outcome we determine is appropriate."

"Meaning?"

The German was still too sure of himself, so Stephens pressed on. "Meaning that either you help us or you will be charged as an active participant in the cold-blooded murders in 1940 of ninety-seven British soldiers in the Pas-de-Calais."

Henschell's silence spoke volumes.

"The prosecution's case is ironclad. Two British soldiers survived the massacre. They will identify German officers who were present and did nothing to stop the killings, especially those in the SS."

The German sighed, his shoulders slumping ever so slightly. "Go ahead then. What are you proposing?"

"Right," Callison stated matter-of-factly. "Let's go over this one more time. Do you have any idea as to what the English officer you were traveling with carried that was so valuable?"

Henschell responded in the same business-like tone. "He said he had something in his possession . . . something very important from an impeccable source. As I told you before, he also mentioned Katyn."

"And you didn't ask what he meant by mentioning Katyn?"

"Squadron Leader Callison, sometimes it is better not to ask." He paused as he contemplated the import of his next words. "But I do know of one person who might possess such evidence. And I believe I know where he and the evidence might be."

"Go on."

"I can lead you to this place, and perhaps even the person, but I must be freed of this," he glanced contemptuously about the tiny cell.

"Agreed," Simmonds responded seamlessly. "We will develop a working plan and Squadron Leader Callison will accompany you to this place.

"And, Henschell, another thing. This morning your parents living in Spandau district were placed in protective custody, in a residence in a very secluded area guarded at all hours by an excellent detachment of Royal Marines. That safety net can be withdrawn as quickly as it was put into place."

"Your ongoing assistance would be much appreciated," Major Simmonds continued, relishing the moment. "However, should you lie to us or your co-operation ever cease, we will publicly let it be known that you are fully co-operating in the Pas-de-Calais investigation. Who knows where that might leave you and your loved ones?"

Henschell was many things, but he was no fool. "Then the deal is done, gentlemen. Let us proceed. But first. Perhaps I might get a civilized meal. A *crêpe* would be fine. Even a German-made one."

CHAPTER 17

Dresden, State of Saxony,
Soviet-Occupied Zone
31 May 1945

A quintet of Studebaker 2.5-ton trucks, shepherded by a posse of jeeps
and Greyhound armored cars belonging to the 76th Calvary Recon
troop, neared Dresden. Task Force 76, as it was prosaically called, had
recently transported a number of high-ranking Allied generals held
captive during the war in the huge fortress at Königstein, located
nearby on the Elbe, to freedom. The Task Force was now returning to
the Fortress to collect the generals' belongings. Each vehicle carried
pass cards in English, German, French, and Russian, granting them
safe passage for that purpose.

Traveling at dawn from Bad Nenndorf to their drop-off at an
American camp outside Halle had taken Callison, his armed escort,
and their reluctant German guest the better part of the morning. At
Halle, they made a brief stop at the American "pony soldier" barracks
for coffee and a sandwich, and to change their identities.

Embedded in Task Force 76, Callison and Henschell were now
shabbily dressed as freed German POWs returning to what was left of
their homes, stowed away in the back of a truck, centrally positioned
in a military caravan.

At edge of the Elbe River, the convoy slowed down abruptly as
the two men hopped off the truck. The Task Force then picked up
speed, rapidly heading south toward Königstein, while the pair ventured north toward their destination, a suburb of Dresden.

As they gingerly walked along the riverbank, Callison found

himself gagging on the fetid air, even as he avoided Henschell's accusatory stare. He'd heard of the Allied bombing of Dresden. He carried a Webley, for a part of him still didn't trust his companion.

After a brisk half-hour's hike, they came to an inverted S bend in the path, then turned to the right down a steep incline. The rowboat was exactly where Simmonds had said it would be, hidden from sight in a thick stand of long-stemmed cattails.

The river was calm, and the journey to the north bank relatively short. They hid the rowboat amid the water flora in a place where it could be readily located on their return.

The area they entered was once a tranquil suburb of Dresden. Until recently, it might have been deemed quite affluent; a leafy sanctuary of wealthy burghers and Party members and their families, and all those mindless sycophants who dutifully followed them. But now the streets and laneways stank of mildew, and human waste oozed out of countless broken watermains. There were cars to be sure, too many Volkswagens to count and even some very expensive ones—Opels, Mercedes, Daimlers—but no fuel to propel any of them. Instead, the citizens of greater Dresden used simple wooden carts for transport, occasionally drawn by a horse or oxen, and everyone appeared to possess a jealously guarded bicycle. Those buildings still standing on the main street had their windows blown out and were surrounded by piles of rubble.

Plaintive messages were posted on makeshift bulletin boards. The entreaties of a vanquished people. "Uncle Erich is dead." "Rudy, the Wismer family has moved from here. We will find you, somehow." "To friends, relatives, and associations of any resident of 43 Harmoniestrasse, there is no one alive or who has been positively identified in the physical remains of that location. If you have any inquiries, please contact the local police authority at Birkenstraße 15."

Rubble women in headscarves and threadbare *Wehrmacht*-issue pants moved pails in a robot-like assembly line from bombed-out structures to street level, where others separated the detritus, cleaned the redeemable bricks they found, and stacked them in orderly piles amid the organized anarchy that surrounded them.

Suddenly, one of the women atop the mound shouted down to the street, where another woman waved a grim acknowledgment. A hand-chosen group of women picked up a stretcher from a nearby cart and went up to the top of the mound. There they picked up a rag doll from among the debris, turning their faces away from the rank stench as they carried the small body to the cart.

The sun lingered until just past nine. As the dusk purpled, they found the parkette they were looking for. The open ground in its center was stacked with bloated human corpses.

Callison found a spot to one side atop a shattered park bench and out of street view of the roving Soviet patrols and he waited. After what seemed an eternity, but could not have been more than ten minutes, out of the darkness he heard someone whistling from a nearby copse of trees. It was short, a tune of some sort. Then it abruptly ended, as if in mid-note.

Callison responded, with the note and pitch he had been instructed to use by Simmonds.

The eerie harmony was repeated once more in the anonymous night, followed by Callison's one-note response.

A tall man emerged from the copse, dressed in a scruffy greatcoat and worn homburg. He walked with a pronounced limp. He carried a Sten gun with the casual aplomb of an experienced fighter.

The man spoke first in heavily accented English. "And you are?"

"Johnny." He answered with the agreed-to password. "And you?"

"And I am Tadeusz."

The stranger named Tadeusz shrewdly sized up Callison's companion. "Your choice of friends is very suspect, Johnny," he mused. "If I do say so."

He nodded toward Henschell with an ill-disguised sneer. "Why is he here?" Then he answered his own question. "I presume it is to help you find what I am also seeking at a home here in Radebeul."

"Yes."

"Before we begin this dance, a word of warning," Tadeusz gazed dismissively at Henschell. "If your German friend knows me as someone else, then he would be wise to remain silent. Now. And in the future."

"I agree," Henschell answered wisely.

Tadeusz motioned to a spot on the bench next to Callison. "May I sit, Johnny? You can truly rest your legs and stop worrying about the effectiveness of the pistol you carry."

"And you?" He motioned to Henschell. "At all times you will

remain standing in front of me, where I can see you."

He turned slightly toward Callison. "Now Johnny, I understand the agent I met in Poland died recently in mysterious circumstances in a Lancaster over Holland."

"Yes," Callison nodded. "I was involved in the body recovery of the crew and the agent in question."

Tadeusz's demeanor softened. "He seemed a nice enough chap. I'm terribly sorry it happened. I admit to a serious error in providing your man with the only version of the formula's equation I possessed at the time." He sighed." I never believed he would meet such a tragic end.

"And so," the Pole continued matter-of-factly, "that is why you are here. Because you, Johnny, and I believe the original item we seek exists in Radebuel, and that is why we are going on this little jaunt, am I correct?"

"Yes."

The place Henschell led them to was located at the other end of Radebuel. A Lutheran church dominated the night sky. Standing adjacent to it were a pair of Opel Blitz trucks captured from the Nazis and now sporting sloppily painted red stars on their doors. They belched puffs of foul smoke from their exhausts as their drivers ratcheted their way into gear.

As the tiny convoy passed them heading eastwards, Tadeusz motioned for Callison and Henschell to hide within the shadows of nearby homes. As the last Opel rumbled by, Callison noted the silhouettes of armed men crowded uncomfortably in the rear of the vehicle. Their tell-tale uniforms marked them as members of the NKVD.

After their departure, an olive-drab GAZ sedan remained on site, parked in front of an austere dwelling immediately adjacent to the church. Two uniformed NKVD leaned against the side of the sedan, casually puffing on cigarettes. One, a woman who directed the conversation with aggressive hand gesturing toward the home, and the other, a burly Asian, in all probability her bodyguard-driver. After a time, the two Russians butted out their cigarettes and cautiously entered the residence.

Minutes passed. Then Tadeusz gestured for the other two to follow him.

Callison entered last. His vision slowly grew accustomed to the dimness. It appeared to be a modest dwelling for modest inhabitants. What Callison beheld when he could see more clearly reminded him of the worst twisters to hit his native Kansas. The floor was littered with broken objects and furniture, wall hangings teetered on shattered frames, a chesterfield and several high-back chairs were gutted to their springs, crockery crushed to dust. The NKVD search teams had done a thorough job of ransacking the clergy house of Pastor Oskar Beck and his wife, Maria.

The three men stood stock-still, careful not to make a sound. Items upstairs were crashing to the floor. Loud cursing. Boot-heels grinding into the floor. Whatever the first NKVD team had sought, their subordinates had not found either. Then the noise became more subdued, down to a murmur.

If ever there was a moment he knew he was nearing something he had sought, it was here in the parsonage at Radebuel.

Tadeusz peered about the darkened living room until he seemed to spot something. He made his way toward it, careful to make only the faintest of sounds. Then he paused. The floor in front of him was littered with everything imaginable, but in that debris were numerous fragments of blue and white porcelain china. He looked up and over to a nearby wall.

An intact sandalwood base and remnants of porcelain held all that remained of a shattered Chinese vase.

Inching slowly and quietly toward it, he thrust his hand inside the remains of the vase. Then, turning back to Callison, he smiled triumphantly as he withdrew an envelope bearing the words "Exhibit 865." He opened the envelope and found a sheet of paper, read it, then resealed it. A knowing smile crossed his face.

Henschell suddenly stumbled as he shifted his weight in the darkness. Bootsteps crashing down the staircase. A woman shouted in German, "*Wer ist das?*"

Tadeusz rapid-fired his Sten at the soldiers on the staircase. Fedin ducked as bullets hit the plaster walls. She had instinctively unholstered her Nagent and fired into the room below.

The Sten gunner responded with staccato efficiency. The blast hit Fedin's gun-hand and she screamed in pain. She lay flat on the staircase, expecting another round. But the enemy had departed.

With her free hand, Fedin fumbled into her tunic pocket and

withdrew a walkie-talkie. Composing herself, she called for assistance. The two Opel trucks could not be far from here. Her orders? They were to return to the church parking lot and commence their search there. The intruders, whoever they were, fleeing on foot, could not have gone very far.

Tadeusz guided them along a circuitous route through back alleys and abandoned homes, careful to stay away from the riverbank and to avoid the roving Soviet patrols in the town proper. After a time, they reached some high ground. They gazed down at the river. From their vantage point, they spotted the two Opel trucks, their headlight beams bouncing wildly as the vehicles careened over the bomb-pitted river road, racing back toward the church and away from where Tadeusz was leading them.

They soon found the rowboat. After handing Callison the envelope, Tadeusz said a quick and unceremonious farewell. Henschell was pulling away from shore when Callison ordered him to wait.

"Tadeusz. A last question. Why are you here? After all, it's quite a long way from home."

"Why? Because I swore an oath as a soldier. Let it never be said my friend that honor is merely a word in my nation's vocabulary.

"After your Lancaster crashed and my British contacts reached out to me, I had no choice. The agent who died on the plane was a good man, and it was my duty to fulfill the task he began."

Callison nodded silently. He understood.

"Now be off, Johnny," the Pole commanded with the smallest hint of emotion. "Or whoever you really are. Remember, we both have much work yet to accomplish. As we Poles would say, 'For our freedom, and yours.'"

Making himself comfortable as Henschell rowed westward across the Elbe in furious strokes, Callison sat with his back turned to the north shore. When he turned around to wave a parting goodbye, the man he knew as Tadeusz was gone.

As Dresden's church bells tolled midnight, an American Army truck, accompanied by a 76th Cavalry Greyhound armored car, awaited them at their rendezvous point. They quickly climbed onto the rear of the truck, where two MPs greeted them. They efficiently took charge of Henschell. The taller of the two politely asked if Callison might want some sleep. Before he could reply, the man withdrew a silver flask from his Eisenhower jacket and handed it to Callison. "A nightcap? They say it's good for the soul as well as whatever else ails the body. Sir." Within minutes, he was sound asleep.

En route to the safety of the American zone, armed personnel at Soviet checkpoints were blithely indifferent, waving them through with a mere glance at their paperwork. It was apparent that the Russian soldiers they encountered were as war-weary as their Allies and one-time enemies. And no amount of vodka could conceal their melancholy.

When Callison awoke in the middle of the moonless night, they were just entering the American camp at Halle. Their vehicles halted before a small convoy of trucks and armored cars. A bevy of British redcaps and white-helmeted MPs waited beside the convoy.

Henschell's security detail stretched cramped muscles.

Their German prisoner had not slept. He turned to Callison. "We have a deal, if you recall."

Callison nodded.

"As you can plainly see, I have done my part."

"And?" Callison rose to the challenge.

"I expect our deal will be honored." There was unusual authority in their prisoner's voice, which momentarily startled the two MPs.

Callison could not resist a final volley. "*Herr* Henschell, you wish our understanding to be honored in the same manner as Hitler did in the agreement with Chamberlain, which provided for peace for our time?"

He paused, then sighed. "Yes, Henschell, we are not liars and murderers. We will honor it."

A ruddy-cheeked British redcap appeared at the truck's rear gate. He asked first for Squadron Leader Callison and, after saluting, helped him out of the vehicle to a waiting Humber staff car.

"And you, *Kraut*," he gestured menacingly to the German. "We have a VIP escort arranged just for you. Back to Bad Nenndorf it is. Who knows? You might even get to enjoy your time in the Royal Spa."

"Gentlemen"—the redcap smiled graciously at the American MPs—"thank you most kindly for your assistance. My lads will take over now." Two Glaswegian redcaps hopped onto the vehicle and personally escorted Henschell to a British military panel truck. Henschell was being returned to the once-famous Prussian spa, aka Number 74.

Ninth US Army Air Force at Hesse,
10.4 kilometers southwest of Frankfurt
1300 hours, 6 June 1945

An Army Air Force Hudson awaited them at a series of runways newly constructed by an engineer aviation battalion. Callison clambered on board, hunching over in the narrow cabin of the transport before taking the first seat he could find. He carried a small leather valise under his arm that contained the items he'd been asked to bring. Flaherty followed him in. No one else. The plane stank of the detritus of war, kerosene, gun grease, vomit, and the feral scent of fear.

Callison worried about his appearance. He'd wanted to bring enough uniforms with him to look respectable, but Flaherty had stilled him with a ready smile. Clothes, both uniform and civilian, were already packed and sitting in cargo. And toiletries? The same.

It proved to be a short and chilly flight to the west coast of Scotland. After landing at Prestwick, he and Flaherty were swiftly escorted across the tarmac to a gleaming four-engine C54 Skymaster. Inside the darkened cabin, they were met by an immaculately attired flight crew. Callison quickly realized they were the only two passengers on board.

La Guardia Field, USAAF Base,
East Elmhurst, Queens, New York City
1910 hours, 8 June 1945

The Skymaster landed at La Guardia airfield on a foggy June evening. The two officers were swiftly hustled away by an Army sedan to their lodging, a five-star hotel situated directly across from Central Park. After a hearty full-course meal in the main dining room, they made their way to their rooms.

When Callison awoke early the next morning, he found a complementary *New York Times* hanging from his door. It was the only newspaper on any of the doors along the entire hall. There were two room-service trays with semi-finished meals on either side of his room, and nowhere else on the floor. His night's sleep had assuredly been secure, as was the leather valise by his bedside.

The next leg of the flight took a little over seven hours with a stop-over at Malden Army Airfield in Missouri for refueling. Once again in the air, Callison began to view the vastness of America for what seemed like the first time. It dawned on him that, for all his combat flight time in Europe and North Africa, he had never flown over the land of his birth. He felt suddenly humbled by its immensity and beauty. But in ways that he was now only beginning to comprehend, while sitting in the cabin seat of the luxurious military transport, he felt very much a foreigner.

Walker US Army Air Force Field, Roswell, New Mexico 1517 hours, 9 June 1945

The military transport descended into Walker Army Airfield as a golden sun shone overhead in the bright western sky. Walker Army Airfield was located a few kilometers from the New Mexico desert town of the same name and 5 kilometers south of its central business district. From aircraft to staff car, his surroundings made him think of why he had left Elkhart. Roswell reminded him of a one-horse town where the horse had fled long ago.

The El Rancho Roswell—an almond and pistachio-swathed layer cake of whipped stucco walls edged by cheap rosewood trim—was nestled near the junction of highways 70 and 285, a single-story mock-pueblo-style, with a neon sign at its entrance blaring NO VACANCIES in full flamingo-flushed glory. Several government-issue Dodge sedans were parked strategically about the lot.

Absurdly fit young men stood randomly along the length and breadth of the motel's courtyard and perimeter. They wore tailor-made seersucker suits, accented by expensive ties and the sort of snappy fedoras favored by detectives in the B-grade Saturday matinees that featured George Raft playing himself. To Callison, they all looked alike—extras at an Atlantic City gangsters' convention. After a cursory search of their vehicle and an equally short verbal exchange, they were directed to room 106. There were no other vehicles nearby.

Flaherty knocked. A gruff voice bid them enter. A quick glance around the room convinced Flaherty that the motel's exterior flattered the interior, a crass mixture of Tijuana brothel, aided and abetted by broad strokes of US government surplus.

Drapes, threadbare as fishnet stockings, were drawn across the window and the room was dimly lit by the one table lamp that worked. The bed was poorly made, the twin pillows under-stuffed beyond redemption, the taupe-tinged blankets filthy and rumpled. A lopsided dresser with one too many coats of paint slathered onto it slumped along one wall. A Sonora radio sat atop the dresser, unplugged. The entire place stank of cheap cologne and lousy tobacco. A few hard-backed chairs and a round table completed what passed for décor.

Two persons sat at the table—an Army general who reminded Flaherty of Orson Welles, and another man, middle-aged, a little florid, and dressed in an off-white suit with matching beige tie. Flaherty divined he was European.

A government-issue security team was assembled in the background.

There were two unoccupied seats next to the general, who motioned the newcomers to sit down. He spoke to Flaherty. "You are?"

"Major Flaherty, sir. And you?"

"Ask me no secrets and I'll tell you no lies." The general cracked a mirthless smile.

He turned his gaze to the officer seated next to Flaherty. The air-force type wore dark aviator sunglasses and carried a slim folio. Much of his face was covered with a buff-colored ascot. In the areas that were exposed, the general noted surgically latticed skin.

"And this man is?'

"Squadron Leader John Callison, RCAF," Flaherty replied evenly.

"A Canadian?" The general raised a doubtful eyebrow. "I hear you flew in North Africa, Callison, and spent time in a Nazi POW camp. Well, you're in New Mexico now, son. Not the Sahara." His tone eased up, softened. "You can unravel the ascot and take off the glasses. I like to see the face of the man I'm speaking with. A preference of mine, if you will."

"I'm actually not Canadian," Callison said, after removing the aviators and ascot. "I'm a Jayhawker, born and bred in Elkhart, Kansas. A China Marine in Shanghai in '37 before I went up to Canada to join a real war effort. Respectfully, General, I suspect I started my fight with the Axis four years before you came on board."

The American seemed grudgingly satisfied with this answer and, if he wasn't, Callison was too indifferent to care.

"Gentlemen," the general grunted, without introducing the civilian seated at the table next to him. "I believe you have something for us?" He inclined his head toward the civilian.

Callison opened the folio and handed the civilian a single page filled with a combination of numbers, characters, and symbols. He quickly reviewed it and passed it to the general with a nod. The civilian then turned to Callison and caught something in that war-scarred face. "It has been a long journey hasn't it, Squadron Leader?" he commented softly.

"Yes, sir. It has," Callison allowed a sigh. "This part"—he motioned to the paper in the general's hand. "Well, it began at Katyn."

"You were there?" The civilian's voice sounded incredulous.

"Briefly."

"And so, you saw it for yourself. It is true?"

"Yes."

The general gruffly interrupted, indifferent to what had passed between the two men. He asked Callison, "Who gave these items to you?"

"Someone I knew only briefly. He called himself Tadeusz."

"But that was not his real name . . . ?"

"No, sir. It was not. He had a very pronounced limp and spoke quite good English. Tough as nails he was—he had a real presence about him."

Callison reached into his tunic pocket and handed the European a torn photo. "He also gave me this to give to you."

Faded with the abuses of time, the partial photo featured a pre-war Polish army officer in full dress uniform—the four-peaked garrison cap, tawny brown tunic with two combat ribbons, classic riding jodhpurs, and shining cavalry boots. And a fine-featured face with a pencil-thin mustache.

The European whispered but one word. "Manel."

"Sorry?" Callison asked.

The general tersely intervened, verging on the razor's edge of out-right rudeness. He gave Flaherty a fleeting, and not very pleasant, glance. "Nothing. It appears that my associate has all that we need, Major. You may escort the Squadron Leader out.'

"And thank you, Mr. Callison," he added. With a nod to the security team, he brought the meeting to a close.

CHAPTER 18

On board a USAAF C54,
Flying east-northeast from Roswell, New Mexico,
toward the Great Lakes
10 June 1945

The next morning, after a restful sleep and a cholesterol-packed breakfast, punctuated with endless cups of coffee, the two men returned to
Walker Airfield and boarded the C54 for their return journey.

Later that day, the aircraft landed on a runway just outside of
Detroit. As the plane cut its engines and came primly to parade rest,
Callison spotted a drab-colored sedan bouncing across the field toward
their aircraft, laboriously followed by a lumbering aviation fuel bowser.

A short time later, an army second lieutenant in ill-fitting khakis,
and barely entering the second decade of his life, nimbly climbed up the
ladder-ramp into the C54. He paused as his eyes grew accustomed to the
muted interior, then advanced to the front of the cabin where Flaherty
sat waiting. He saluted with an exaggerated flourish and handed the
major a sealed envelope. As the youngster passed by Callison to exit the
aircraft, he didn't even acknowledge Callison's presence.

Flaherty glanced at the file for a few moments while the Skymaster's
engines grudgingly accelerated to a steady whine. Then seemingly
pleased with what he read, he moved back to where Callison was seated
and handed him the folder.

It was a thin document, only a few pages in length.

"Mission accomplished," the Irishman beamed. "You may not know
it, but officially you've spent the last few days dealing with technical
experts at the Packard facility here in Michigan. The plant has been

building a Packard variant of the Merlin engines used by Lancaster bombers under license since 1942."

Flaherty took a seat opposite Callison and made himself comfortable.

"I'll read the summary for you to save you the eyestrain."

"As you're probably aware," Flaherty began, "the updraft carburetor throat on each of L for Lucy's four engines was controlled by an automatic boost control within the throttle linkage. Working properly, whatever changes in the Lanc's altitude that occur, it will maintain the right manifold pressure to prevent the over-boosting of the engine. As the Lancaster increases altitude, air density naturally decreases, and the throttle valves progressively open to accommodate the reduced atmospheric pressure surrounding the aircraft."

Flaherty paused and leaned closer to Callison as if sharing a secret with a friend.

"And now it gets interesting," he added. "In low-level operations, the valves open only partially. But it's the considered opinion of Packard engineers that, as L for Lucy descended in those final moments, the valves somehow opened fully, causing the engines to surge to a hell-for-leather speed. This action should not have occurred. But it did and caused a dramatic loss of altitude and the inevitable crash you and your team were called in to investigate."

Flaherty triumphantly clasped his hands together.

"If you're ever asked, you worked extensively with three engineers who reached these conclusions. Their signatures, professional credentials, and findings are all over this document."

"But I've never met them," Callison challenged. "And they've never even seen the aircraft."

"No," Flaherty shrugged. "But they are experts. The closest you have is an RAF sergeant with rudimentary training in crash-site reconstruction. You also have statements from eyewitnesses that speak about the Lancaster rapidly dropping."

"But that's not what happened, is it."

"It doesn't really matter what happened." Flaherty replied abruptly as if he were a tenured professor chiding a freshman who had dared to question his authority. "This version of the crash will satisfy both Whitehall and the Russkies."

"Look," Flaherty went on, as if he were cutting a deal with a reluctant defense counsel. "This is from a purely strategic standpoint. The Allies lost ten thousand heavy bombers to enemy action during this war. The chance of surviving thirty missions without being shot down, killed, or captured was less than 30 percent. But, more tellingly, the second stiffest loss of life was in non-combat accidents."

"Johnny. There's no shame if L for Lucy's crew have officially died in an aircraft malfunction. They were professional and knew the price they might be asked to pay, as did all aircrew who crashed in take-offs and landings, routine training flights, or mid-air collisions through equipment failure or mechanical wear and tear. Let's face it. The craft they were sent up in were often bags of bolts, held together by chewing gum and chicken wire. In the end, it's a numbers game and the brass in Whitehall and the Pentagon are not interested in mere 'accidents.'"

Callison was incredulous at what he was being asked to consider. "So, is that what you would call the deaths of the nine military personnel on L for Lucy? An accident?"

Flaherty was becoming impatient, and it showed. "The war in Europe cost us one hundred thousand Allied airmen, dead and buried or lost forever in the North Sea. I prefer to say the loss of one Lancaster bomber is a reasonable price to pay as we move forward."

Callison let the comment pass, unanswered.

"In any event, it's too late to change. Wing Commander Bowes, Head of RAF Special Investigation Branch, and who I believe has overall charge of your investigation, has approved the crash designation as mechanical malfunction. Based on the information we have here, he has signed off. And closed the file. It's all a formality now, you see."

"And what of the poisoned tea?" Callison ventured. "The Scotland Yard lab was quite certain . . ."

"You must have misunderstood the fellow you spoke to on the phone. We have the final forensic report. Be happy to share it with you. Seems the tea was tainted all right, but it was natural poisoning. Honey drawn from something called the Andromeda plant native to Russia. They found deposits in the stomachs of all the aircrew. No Soviet conspiracy there, Squadron Leader. It was a tragic fluke."

"I can't agree," Callison challenged.

"Whatever you personally think, the matter is officially closed. Period." And then he returned to his seat at the front of the cabin.

Callison gazed out of the portal at the cotton-wool clouds and azure-blue sky. Then, suddenly totally drained by it all, he let his mind drift as he slipped slowly into himself.

He was stirred from his musings by a nudge. Then another. When he opened his eyes to protest, he faced an overtly a jovial Flaherty. Tie askew and ruddy-faced, the Irishman had been drinking.

"We're stopping next at Gander to top up," Flaherty informed him, raising a glass filled with an amber fluid in his bear paw of a hand. "And then we head over the Pond."

He turned to walk back to his seat then stopped, turning to Callison as he raised his glass in a mock toast. "Thought you'd like to know that your team has begun a recovery operation for a downed Wellington that the tides exposed near the Dutch island of Texel. It appears the crew bought it homebound from a mission over Hamburg. We'll drop you off at Prestwick. An air transport will take you to the landing field nearest to the Texel crash site."

Flaherty turned momentarily somber. "If it is any consolation, the crew of L for Lucy didn't die in vain. They more than did their part. The Second World War might be over, but you will soon discover that another, far more intense, conflict is well underway."

He shambled over to his seat and plonked himself down with a loud thud. In a few minutes, the uneven rasp of the Irishman's snoring echoed through the cabin.

The C54 swept gracefully over the north shore of Lake Erie, aided by a strong west wind. In the afternoon haze, Callison could just make out the American shoreline to the south. Below the aircraft, a checkerboard landscape of emerald and tan dappled fields spanned the horizon. Liberally sprinkled here and there were ancient farmhouses, red-box barns, placid herds of cows, a manic plume of dust where an old truck skittered down a county road. The land below seemed almost normal. For Johnny Callison, it evoked sone kind of distant emotion. One he had not felt for years.

Yet he didn't feel homesick. After being at war for most of a decade, Callison had no sense of what the word "home" meant anymore. Pensively, he touched the campaign ribbons on his tunic and thought of his father. The thought passed as fleetingly as the wispy clouds skimming past outside the aircraft.

A copy of the *Chicago Daily Tribune* had been provided by a smiling flight attendant just before take-off. He glanced down at it.

In a detailed interview at Supreme Headquarters Allied Expeditionary Force, or SHAEF, General Eisenhower commented that the Germans knew the jig was up three days after their Ardennes offensive began but held out in hopes of splitting the Allies. However, the general saw perfect harmony continuing, with Soviet State Radiot describing the Russians as peace-loving. He also believed that Germany was unrepentant, with the majority of her population denying any war guilt.

A second story caught Callison's eye. US Army ordnance experts had completed a month-long study of a huge rocket assembly plant built 800 feet deep into the heart of the Kohnstein Mountains, near the Thuringian city of Nordhausen, Germany. They discovered that improved V2 rocket bombs—nicknamed "flying telegraph poles"— were capable of pinpoint accuracy at a range of 3,000 miles. Captured German scientists attested that in next two years, they could have developed rockets capable of traveling 15,000 miles.

In the Pacific theater, American forces were engaged in the final stages of a bloody battle with the Japanese for Okinawa. In the air, B-29 Superforts were pounding Osaka, blasting the ancient Japanese city in massive air raids four times in fifteen days and destroying one-third of its core.

And in sports, Brooklyn Dodgers General Manager Leo (Lippy) Durocher and a security guard at Ebbets Field were dealing with charges for felonious assault brought on by a medically discharged soldier who told police that they had fractured his jaw and inflicted other wounds on him during a night game because he had heckled Dodgers players.

After enduring heavy front-line censorship for much of the war, Callison was overwhelmed by the barrage of information that seemed to bracket his consciousness. He attempted the *Trib*'s crossword, but found he had difficulty concentrating, so he gradually dozed off into a fitful sleep.

His feeble attempt at rest was interrupted all too soon by the same brunette flight attendant who'd handed him the newspaper. Callison noticed her eyes were a deep hazel and her smile was fixed.

"Coffee sir?" she asked in a practiced southern drawl. He gratefully accepted the beverage. Served in bone chinaware and monogrammed with the initials SHAEF in rich claret lettering, it none too subtly reminded Callison whose aircraft he was on. And why.

Somewhere over Lake Ontario, the C54 hit an air pocket. Coffee spilled from the cup and over the rim of the saucer. It left a spreading stain on the Lancaster crash report resting on Callison's lap, a stain that neither he nor time could erase.

Alamogordo, New Mexico
05:29:45 hours, Mountain War Time
16 July 1945

The 30-meter-tall tower on which the "device" rested was located in an area of the mammoth Alamogordo Bombing and Gunnery Range known to early Spanish settlers as *Jornada del Muerto*—the Route of the Dead Man.

The Jornada was a shortcut on the Camino Real, the historic "Royal Road" that connected Old Mexico City to Santa Fe, the capital of New Mexico. The Camino meandered north from Mexico City until it met the Rio Grande near El Paso, Texas. The trail then followed the river valley to where the waters curved westwards and the valley narrowed, quickly becoming impassable for wagon trains. To avoid this natural obstacle, travelers took a dubious detour across the Jordana, where they faced 60 miles of desert, precious little water, and hostile Apaches determined to safeguard their ancestral homelands at all costs.

The device had been hoisted onto the firing tower at precisely 1700 hours Mountain War Time. Three observation bunkers had been constructed 10,000 yards north, west, and south of the tower to gauge the symmetry of the implosion and the amount of energy released. Additional measurements would be taken to determine damage estimates, and sophisticated equipment would record the behavior of the fireball. The biggest concern was the radioactivity the test device could generate and, for that reason, the army stood ready to evacuate every living soul in the surrounding areas.

The scientists involved in the Manhattan Project arrived at one of three assigned bunkers in the early evening hours and waited with mixed feelings of anticipation and fear for zero hour. Klaus Fuchs been allocated to the central control bunker—S-10,000—and stood at the edge of the gathering, ever attentive to the anxious small talk that permeated the site. One never knew what inadvertent comment might be worthy of follow-up.

For the ultra-disciplined Lieutenant General Leslie Groves, this was his legacy, even exceeding his instrumental role in the building of the Pentagon.

For Robert Oppenheimer, the project code-named "Trinity" was a much more complex puzzle. Though intensely vain, ambitious, and driven to push others to their limits without mercy, he was troubled by inner musings as to the potential of the 54-kilogram device to alter civilization in ways that humanity could never imagine.

In 1933, while a young physics professor at Berkeley, Oppenheimer had studied Hindu Sanskrit under Arthur Ryder, a renowned Orientalist who was both chairman and sole member of the university's Sanskrit department. Ryder had introduced him to the *Bhagavad Gita*, which they read together in the original language.

After a few minutes, Fuchs inched back to where Ulam lurked, smoking endless cigarettes. The Pole offered one to his younger protégé. Fuchs, ever the Puritan, politely refused. They had become good, if not close, friends during their time at Los Alamos. Fuchs casually joked about the FM radios they had been provided with to monitor the test-code named "Trinity." The radios supplied to the perimeter guard stations, the base camp, and its vehicles had been assigned the same frequency as the main railway freight yard in San Antonio, Texas. They could hear individuals ordering the shifting of freight cars and presumed that they, likewise, could hear the preparations at Ground Zero. Tiny Socorro Municipal Airport, located more than 100 kilometers away, appeared to be listening in to Ground Zero too.

As he stood peering into the stormy desert darkness on this rainswept night, Oppenheimer tenuously held to the lessons of the *Gita* that although war was evil, it could sometimes not be avoided. Moreover, when justly waged in a noble cause, such a battle was in accordance with divine will.

In Oppenheimer's mind, the current bloody hostilities being conducted against the Imperial Japanese Empire were surely that—a just conflict. And, accordingly, Trinity was a morally justifiable weapon.

Naked light bulbs dangled overhead, buffeted by strong gusts of wind. Thunder boomed, and rainfall beat an incessant tattoo on the desert landscape. outside. Even the heavens appeared uneasy with what was transpiring in the Jornada del Muerto desert. As the minutes ticked by, there was a very real likelihood that the test would be delayed or even canceled. To break the palpable tension, one of the senior scientists in the bunker began offering anyone who would listen a wager as to whether or not the bomb would ignite the atmosphere, and if so, whether it would merely destroy New Mexico or obliterate the entire world. Ironically, "Oppie" himself had wagered ten dollars against another scientist's entire month's pay that the bomb would not work at all.

During the evening hours of July 15, a tremendous thundershower had rolled across the desert. Now the weather threatened the timing of the experiment. General Groves and Robert Oppenheimer peered out of the slit opening of theS-10,000 bunker and discussed what to do if the weather did not break in time for the scheduled 0400 hours test.

Just before 0445 hours, the Met officer provided Groves with a comprehensive weather report and a reasoned prediction that at 0530 hours the weather at Ground Zero would be acceptable, if not ideal, for detonation.

At precisely 05:29:45 hours, Mountain War Time, the device exploded over the New Mexico desert, vaporizing the tower and turning the asphalt around its base to dark, jade-tinged sand. Seconds later, a huge blast wave and consecutive waves of hellish heat seared out across the desert. The fireball stretched up and spread. A second column, narrower than the first, rose and flattened into a mushroom shape. The shape grew to about 7.5 miles, generating the destructive power of 20,000 tons of TNT and a shock wave felt a hundred miles away from Ground Zero. The test created a flash of light brighter than a dozen suns and 10,000 times hotter than the actual surface of the fiery globe that warms the earth. The nuclear age had begun.

The Trinity explosion could be seen over the entire state of New Mexico and over vast stretches of Arizona, Texas, and northern Mexico. Shimmering gold and violet, amethyst, indigo and gray, it lit every crevice and ridge of the nearby mountain ranges with unearthly clarity as it incinerated the Buffalo grass and yucca spears that had survived natural challenges on the desert floor for millennia.

Fuchs stood next to Ulam. He seemed bereft of human emotion. Then he did something he had never done before. He quietly asked Ulam for a cigarette.

Inside the crowded S-10,000 bunker, its occupants were hushed into mute submission by the apocalyptic blast enveloping the distant horizon. Suddenly a chastened voice could be clearly heard among them: "Now I am become Death, the destroyer of worlds." It was Robert Oppenheimer, quoting from the *Gita.*

Cecilienhof Palace, Potsdam, East Berlin, Russian-Occupied Zone, 24 July 1945

Code-named "Terminal," the final Allied conference of the Second World War began on Tuesday, July 17, 1945, at Cecilienhof, a mock-Tudor estate in Berlin's suburbs that Kaiser Wilhelm had built for his son Prince Wilhelm, the last crown prince of Prussia, and his wife, Cecilia of Mecklenburg–Schwerin.

Hosted by the Soviets, the estate's thirty-six rooms and Great Hall were fully renovated and palatially furnished for the daily meetings of the Big Three.

The leaders and their delegations were housed in the nearby leafy district of Babelsberg, which had suffered minimal damage in the Allied bombing raids and offered the added advantage that the streets leading to the conference venue were easy to defend against any attack by Nazi zealots.

From the first day onward, Winston Churchill, Josef Stalin, and Harry Truman—who'd replaced Roosevelt—held a series of highly charged sessions to deal with the reparations and administration of a defeated Germany and the demarcation of Poland's future borders, among other items of importance and contention.

At 9:20 a.m., Andrew Stimson, the American Secretary of War, made his way upstairs to President Truman's office in the Little White House, a Babelsburg villa overlooking Lake Greibnitz that the American leader called home while he was at the Conference. He delivered a top-secret message:

Operation may be possible any time from August 1, depending on state of preparation of patient and condition of atmosphere. From point of view of patient only, some chance

293

August 1 to 3, good chance August 4 to 5, and barring unexpected relapse, almost certain before August 10.

A month earlier Truman had agreed to plans to invade Japan in November. Tens of thousands of Allied soldiers, sailors, and aircrew who had just returned from the battlefields of Europe were being readied to go to war with the Japanese on their own soil. The President asked General George Marshall, Chairman of the Joint Chiefs of Staff, what it would cost in lives to land on the Tokyo plain and other sites in Japan. His calculated response? Such an invasion would cost a minimum of a quarter of a million casualties. And those losses were just during the initial phases of the Allied incursion.

That afternoon, at 5:10 p.m., Truman called the eighth plenary session of the conference to order. On its agenda was the composition of future governments of Eastern Europe and, once again, Poland. At the end of the second hour, the American President called for a short break in proceedings. He casually strolled over to the Soviet leader without taking along his State Department translator.

It was Pavlov, the Russian interpreter, who translated Truman's words to Stalin: "The United States has a new weapon of unusual destructive force."

Surprisingly the Soviet leader merely nodded, responding that he was glad to hear this and hoped it would be put to good use in the pending invasion of Japan.

And "The Man of Steel" had every reason to be dispassionately calm. For he had already pulled tens of thousands of Russian physicists from their respective military services to work on a revolutionary nuclear device. That very night, Stalin sent a secret telegram to Lavrentiy Beria, head of the project, ordering him to greatly accelerate his efforts.

As NKVD teams aggressively combed the smoking ruins of the Third Reich in their quest for scientists who'd been involved in *das Uranprojekt*—the failed Nazi attempt to develop atomic weapons—Beria anxiously waited. His mission was for the USSR to move beyond uranium to plutonium-based weaponry. From fission to fusion. For that to occur, both the German experts and the formulas that Fedin was tasked to find were essential to enable Stalin and the Union of Soviet Socialist Republics to achieve their ultimate aim—global supremacy.

All the while, as other subordinates labored through lists of German prisoners of war held in Soviet camps to locate the missing director of the Kraków Institute, Nadia Fedin was tracking down the Scottish Book, the secrets it might hold, and how they might relate to Katlyn, with renewed vigor.

Fedin's strenuous efforts to find these critical items on behalf of Beria did not go unnoticed. As a consequence, she was promoted to the rank of colonel. Beria advised Nadia that her mentor, Georgy Zhukov, Marshal of the Soviet Union, was instrumental in making this recommendation with which Beria, as People's Commissar of Internal Affairs and head of the NKVD, fully concurred. Both the marshal and the commissar were delighted with her advancement, and Fedin returned the favor to each one—individually—in mutually satisfying, if highly unorthodox, ways.

CHAPTER 19

Commandant's Office-Headquarters,
Группа советских оккупационных
войск в Германии
(GSOFG—Group of Soviet Occupation
Forces in Germany),
Wunsberg, Occupied East Germany
1107 hours, 10 April 1946

On the morning of Tuesday, April 10, 1946, while indulging in a black-market Chesterfield cigarette, Marshal of the Soviet Union, Georgy Zhukov, received written notice that effective immediately he was demoted in rank and directed to report to Odessa in the Southern Military District to eradicate criminal organizations operating there.

During, the Second World War, Zhukov had been the most prominent Soviet military commander, winning critical battles including the Siege of Leningrad, the Battle of Stalingrad, and the crowning jewel of all, the Battle of Berlin. Well respected by many, feared by some, he was at the peak of his prowess and power.

A horribly brutal war against Hitler's Fascists had ended triumphantly, and in the newly brokered European peace, Zhukov's continuing postwar approval with the Soviet military and Russian masses began to cause him serious personal complications. The unspoken truth was that his popularity was deemed to be a direct challenge to The Leader.

After holding the exalted position of Commander of All Land Forces in the Russian zone for only 205 days, Zhukov was suddenly accused of counter-revolutionary behavior and selfish "Bonapartism." Not long after such transparent humiliation, Zhukov had his first heart attack.

For the next while, Georgy Zhukov spent his time in the USSR's idyllic seaport of Odessa, battling major criminal gangs like Black Cat and Dodge 3/4. In late 1947, local authorities proudly announced that the organized criminal syndicates that had thrived in Odessa immediately after the war had been thoroughly crushed.

Still, Stalin felt greatly challenged by his absentee general. In 1948, he sent Zhukov even further from the Kremlin's seat of power, appointing him commander of the Ural Military District in Sverdlovsk, 1,700 kilometers east of Moscow. Those in the know snickered that the once great Marshal Zhukov had been effectively moved from a second-rate posting to a fifth-rate one. To compound the insult, that same year Zhukov was also falsely accused of selective looting during the wartime Soviet capture of Berlin. He remained in Sverdlovsk in virtual exile until 1953, when Stalin ordered the great general to return to Moscow.

But it was not an act of kindness or reconciliation that influenced this gesture by the Man of Steel. Stalin had become increasingly paranoid and needed Zhukov's military experience to prepare for what Stalin believed would be an imminent war against the West.

University of Southern California, Los Angeles Fall 1945–46

Stanislaus Ulam left Los Alamos to become an associate professor at the University of Southern California in Los Angeles, arriving for the start of the 1945 fall term on September 12. In addition to his teaching load, he continued to work at integrating the formulas from the Scottish Book into his own theses. By late April 1946, he had developed enough relevant data to attend a secret conference at Los Alamos chaired by Edward Teller.

During his time on the Manhattan Project, Teller had directed all his team's efforts toward the development of a "super" weapon based on nuclear fusion rather than a fission bomb. Now, in a private admission at the conference, Teller grudgingly acknowledged to Ulam that what he truly required to realize his dream was the Scottish Book formulas, which Ulam now possessed, and the scientific conclusions he was drawing from them.

Oxfordshire, England
April 1946

On a glorious spring day in April 1946, Klaus Fuchs returned to Britain to work at the Harwell Atomic Research facility in Oxfordshire. He continued providing his Russian contacts with valuable data on the fission-based atomic bomb, stolen from his colleagues on the Manhattan Project.

On August 29, 1949, the Soviet Union successfully tested its first fission bomb, the RDS-1. Created under the overall supervision of Lavrentiy Beria, the weapon was identical to the "Fat Man" device dropped on Nagasaki in 1945 by a specially adapted American B-29 bomber called "Bock's car," after its commander, Frederick Bock. Much of RDS-1's fission design was based on detailed information surreptitiously provided by Klaus Fuchs.

On the basis of incontrovertible evidence provided by the American *Venona* project and rubberstamped by British MI9, on December 21, 1949, Klaus Fuchs was confronted at the security gate entering the Harwell facility and arrested as a spy. Tried and found guilty at the Old Bailey, he was sentenced to fourteen years. The only reason he did not receive the death penalty was because the USSR had been an ally and not an enemy of Great Britain when the crimes for which Fuchs had been charged were committed.

Fuchs would never know that he had been betrayed by Philby who knew it was far better to sacrifice a German scientist who had outlived his usefulness to the cause than to leave himself vulnerable.

Enewetak Atoll,
Pacific Ocean
1951–52

In January 1951, Ulam advanced an idea to channel the mechanical shock of a nuclear explosion to compress the fusion fuel. Almost immediately Teller saw its merit but noted that soft X-rays attendant in the fission bomb would compress the thermonuclear fuel more strongly than mechanical shock and suggested ways to enhance this fission-driven effect.

On March 9, 1951, Teller and Ulam submitted a joint report describing their innovation. A few weeks later, Teller suggested placing a fissible fuel rod or cylinder at the center of the fusion fuel. The accelerated detonation caused by this "spark plug" would help to initiate and then enhance the resultant fusionable reaction. The report was instantly accepted. With the basic fusion reactions now confirmed, and with a feasible design in hand, there was nothing to prevent Los Alamos from testing a fusion-driven thermonuclear device.

On November 1, 1952, the first true H-Bomb—code-named "Ivy Mike" and with a yield of 10.4 megatons—exploded on Enewetak Atoll within the US Pacific Proving Grounds. It was also the first thermonuclear device based on the Teller–Ulam principles of staged radiation implosion. Three stories tall and 82 tons in total weight, the projectile proved to be so immense as to be unusable as a weapon of war. But it did provide the United States with a threat so profound and surreal in its implications that it dwarfed all challengers in the macabre American race with the USSR for primacy in developing weapons of mass destruction.

The existence of the H-Bomb was certainly noted in the Kremlin, where the Man of Steel was troublingly morose. It was also felt within the NKVD, particularly in those dark and dangerous places inhabited by both Beria's defenders and the contenders for his throne. Neither faction treated the merest hint of failure lightly, and both sensed the blood of a wounded animal within their midst.

For Nadia Fedin, those wounds were beginning to tell. The deepest of those cuts would come soon enough and from an unexpected source.

Convening of the Madden Committee, Washington, DC 1951

In late 1951, the American House of Representatives established the Select Committee to Conduct an Investigation and Study of the Facts, Evidence, and Circumstances of the Katyn Forest Massacre. It became known as the Madden Committee after its chairman, Representative Ray Madden of Indiana.

One of the last and most critical witnesses before the Madden Committee was one John Paul Callison, a serving Squadron Leader, RCAF, and an American who had been present at Katyn in 1943, who related in rich detail his experiences and professional observations.

With the walls closing in on her on all sides, Nadia Fedin astutely realized that she could not keep her friends close because she had so few. And her enemies? They were much closer, almost at her throat, and gleefully beginning to sharpen their knives for the final kill. It was only the fraying connection between her and Beria that kept them at bay. And even that tenuous linkage would, one day, dissolve.

The Kremlin, Moscow
12 February 1953

In the dismal pre-dawn of an unusually harsh Russian winter, Josef Stalin left the Kremlin in a heavily guarded motorcade for the twenty-minute drive to his *dacha* in the nearby town of Kuntsevo. Located in a densely wooded birch forest, it was secured by 30mm anti-aircraft guns, a double perimeter fence, and 300 Special Forces troops. The two-story, avocado-green compound had been his home for much of the Great Patriotic War. He was inexplicably drawn to it now in this strangely unfamiliar thing the unwashed and hopelessly naive masses called "Peace."

Terribly depressed when left on his own, the Man of Steel began to summon members of his inner circle to join him there for a nightly movie and a marathon meal topped off with copious quantities of vodka and Khvanchkara, a Georgian ruby-red wine that was the Leader's favorite.

As was their habit after dinner, they would adjourn to the study for movies. For a reason known only to him, Stalin kept watching the same film night after night—Charlie Chaplin's *The Great Dictator*. And, more curiously, he asked that one segment—the Great Dictator's last speech—be repeated over and over: "Greed has poisoned men's souls, has barricaded the world with hate, has goose-stepped us into misery and bloodshed. We have developed speed, but we have shut ourselves in. Machinery that gives abundance has left us in want. Our knowledge has made us cynical. Our cleverness, hard and unkind. We think too much and feel too little. More than machinery, we need humanity. More than cleverness, we need kindness and gentleness. Without these qualities, life will be violent and all will be lost . . ."

In the morning hours of March 1, Stalin's guards became alarmed when there had been silence for some time from their master's quarters. They broke into his chambers to find Stalin on the floor in his pajamas, and the hardwood floor surrounding his prone body covered with urine. It appeared that the Great Leader had suffered a stroke. Members of the *dacha* staff carried Stalin out and onto the dining room sofa, where they covered him with a blanket.

The consensus among the civilian staff was to immediately call for a doctor, but the military guards stalled until they received instructions from the Communist Party leadership. Eventually, a staff member reached Beria by telephone. He directed that they tell no one of Stalin's illness. Beria then began making calls to medical and political confidants.

On March 2, 1953, at 7 a.m., the Soviet minister of health summoned personally selected physicians to the *dacha*. The doctors found Stalin unresponsive, his right arm and leg paralyzed, and his blood pressure alarmingly high. They ordered total rest, placed a cold compress on his head, and recommended he not eat.

Two days after the specialists saw him, Radio Moscow made the fateful announcement revealing that Comrade Josef Stalin, "Father of Nations, Builder of Socialism, and Leader of Progressive Humanity," had suffered a stroke and was receiving medical treatment under the watchful eye of Party leaders.

On the evening of March 5, 1953, his daughter Svetlana was at his bedside when Stalin's eyes opened with "a terrible look—either mad or angry—and full of the fear of death." Simultaneously, the "faithful servant of Lenin" raised his left hand, pointing upwards, perhaps threateningly, perhaps in abject resignation, and then, abruptly, he expired.

The news broke to the outside world that evening and well into the night. But in the dystopian world that the USSR had become, the long-suffering Russian people themselves were the very last to find out their leader was no more.

At five minutes past three in the morning on March 6, 1953, Yuri Levitan, the chief announcer of Radio Moscow, pronounced the fateful words:

> The Central Committee of the Communist party, the Council of Ministers and the Presidium of the Supreme Soviet of the USSR announce with deep grief to the party and all workers that on March 5 at 9.50 p.m., Josef Vissarionovich Stalin, Secretary of the Central Committee of the Communist Party and Chairman of the Council of Ministers, died after a serious illness. The heart of the collaborator and follower of the genius of Lenin's work, the wise leader and teacher of the Communist party and of the Soviet people, has stopped beating.

Stalin's body lay in state for three days in the House of the Unions, following which the coffin was delivered to Red Square for placement in Lenin's Mausoleum. As it was being interred at precisely noon Moscow time, a minute of silence was observed nationwide. The bells of the Kremlin tower chimed, sirens and horns wailed, and a twenty-one-gun salute boomed out from within the ancient fortress. Immediately after, a military band played the *Internationale*, and a massive military parade of the Moscow Garrison was held in Stalin's honor.

As first deputy chairman of the Council of Ministers and an influential Politburo member, Lavrentiy Beria saw himself as Stalin's natural successor. Yet on June 26, 1953, Nikita Khrushchev convened a meeting of the Presidium of the Supreme Soviet, where he accused Beria of being a traitor and spy in the pay of British intelligence. Beria was taken completely by surprise. Others quickly spoke against the First Deputy Chairman, followed by a motion by Khrushchev for his instant dismissal, a motion which passed unanimously.

When Beria finally realized what was happening, he appealed to Georgy Malenkov, an old friend, to speak up for him. Malenkov hung his head and pressed a button on his desk. This was the prearranged signal for Georgy Zhukov and a select group of armed officers in a nearby room. Beria was arrested.

Lavrentiy Beria was initially taken to the Moscow guardhouse and then to the headquarters bunker of the Moscow Military District. The

Kantemirovskaya Tank Division and *Tamanskaya* Motor Rifle Division were ordered to Moscow to prevent Beria's loyal security forces from rescuing him. Many of his subordinates, protégés, and associates were also arrested.

On December 23, 1953, Beria and his closest followers were tried by a "special session" of the Supreme Court of the Soviet Union, with neither defense counsel nor right of appeal. He was quickly found guilty of treason, terrorism, and counter-revolutionary activity in 1919 during the Russian Civil War.

Beria and his allies were sentenced to death that very day. The other six defendants were shot immediately after the trial ended. Beria was executed separately, pleading for his life and collapsing to the floor before being shot through the forehead. His body was cremated and the remains buried in Communal Grave No. 3 at Donskoi Monastery Cemetery in Moscow.

It did not help his cause that Beria had not been able to effectively still the ghosts of Katyn, specters that now haunted the hearings of the United States House Select Committee. Or that he was unable to acquire the necessary data for Soviet scientists to win the race in developing the hydrogen bomb.

Number 2 Ulitsa Bolshaya Lubyanka,
Meshchansky District of Moscow,
Soyuz Sovetskikh Sotsialisticheskikh Respublik
15 April 1954

On an uneventful April morning in 1954, a little over a month after the second successful American H-bomb detonation at Bikini Atoll, Nadia Fedin stood up from her desk in the Lubyanka and gazed into a full-length mirror—her first purchase upon being given an office in the KGB citadel. After all this time, it had become her lone companion. She quietly smiled. Now in her thirty-seventh year, she was still attractive with a trim figure, finely sculpted face, and those fascinating green eyes.

For the same reason she had held her age so well, she had also held true to several simple virtues, and chief among them was loyalty. But the world around Nadia had changed dramatically and forever. Beria, one of her two patrons, had been recently erased from the Soviet version of history. The other, Georgy Zhukov no longer returned her calls, seemingly because he was busy with affairs of state in his role as advisor to newly created Kremlin potentates. Also, she thought wryly, he probably had younger, more venal, female affairs on his mind.

Even the venerable institution she had served since she was a young woman had changed its name and its focus. Unlike the NKVD, which handled public order and secret police activities, in addition to the more unsavory aspects of the Soviet totalitarian state such as the Gulag system and extra-judicial executions of untold numbers of citizens, the agency she worked for was now called the KGB. Its focus now encompassed a vaguer, and more lofty function, that of "state security."

She glanced at the wall clock and at the pile of reports resting atop the in-tray. None was pressing. Her correspondence had become largely pedestrian. Signing off on transfers, reviewing and, if necessary, correcting arcane procedures, endlessly evaluating minute irrelevancies to see where they would situate themselves in relentless, yet pedantic work, more befitting a team of monkeys than someone of her rank. It had not escaped her that she—Nadia Fedin—had become what she had most feared—her father's daughter—a disposable bureaucrat in the worst bureaucratic system in the world—the totalitarian state.

At noon she left her office to walk to the Hotel Metropol for her customary lunch of *borscht* followed by a healthy main course of breaded cutlets and boiled potatoes, topped off with a decadent desert of vanilla ice cream and apple pie.

Nadia Fedin crossed the street as she approached the hotel. She never looked to see if cars were approaching. There was no vehicular traffic in this area; it was too close to the epicenter of the Soviet universe for ordinary Russians and, besides, none but the party elite owned a car in the Communist people's paradise. And even most of those anointed few were wary to be seen on hallowed ground inside an item as bourgeois as a motor vehicle without official dispensation from the greater powers.

The Ziz 101 had been tailing the KGB colonel at a snail's pace for some time, keeping its distance. Midway across the road, she had no chance. The force of the collision propelled her into a concrete barrier. The passenger in the car checked for a pulse. Satisfied, he returned to the car, which unhurriedly left the scene, and left a once-faithful—but failed—servant of the State, stone dead.

Passersby who had observed the incident stood there, mute, unquestioning. No one called for an ambulance. No one rushed to the aid of the fallen KGB officer. No one. For they knew all too well of such black-lacquered vehicles and their anonymous occupants. And all too often, it was just not healthy to know too much. This was one such occasion.

The suspect Zis was soon returned to the guarded underground parking compound of 2 Lubyanski Prospect, one of several pool vehicles assigned to VIP escort and select members of the KGB. The blood splatter on its front fender was polished away. It had served its masters well for twenty years and continued to do so. For it was both the limousine of record to the Red Star and, in this particular instance, the perfect weapon of choice.

Fedin's funeral was held in the cavernous Great Hall of the Lubyanka, a paramilitary affair with the usual cast of suspects in attendance—peers, peacocks, and pretenders—outwardly resplendent in gleaming gold braid but lacking any real human emotion. The appropriate words were spoken about duty and allegiance to the nation.

At the end, they all rose for the singing of the *Internationale* and finally, the powerful national anthem of the Union of Soviet Socialist Republics. Then, en masse, they vacated the room to an adjoining salon to swill vodka and devour blinis and caviar until they were raucously red-faced.

They left the cherrywood coffin with the cold body of Nadia Fedin inside for an army of anonymous minions to dispose of. Like her departed father, she had failed the State. And for that, there was no remedy or salvation.

Fedin would be buried without further ceremony in a plot reserved for officers of the various institutions of omnipotent state control that had run the Russian silent state since its inception—NKVD, SMERSH, and now KGB—resting alone with row upon row of equally forgotten superiors, contemporaries, and subordinates. As with so many interred there, no one would mourn her loss. No one would immortalize her accomplishments, nor even remember her name. And, like her father, she would be deleted from the consciousness of the enlightened proletariat.

She had become the first victim of the newly minted KGB. And into powdery dust she did return.

305

POSTSCRIPT

THOSE WHO LIVED AND THOSE WHO LIVED IN THIS BOOK

Robert Jacquinot de Besange S.J.
(March 15, 1878 to September 10, 1946)

Robert Jaquinot was a French Jesuit who created a successful model of safety zones that saved over half a million Chinese people during the Second Sino-Japanese War. His family originated from aristocratic lineages in Lorraine, northeastern France. He arrived in China in 1913 as a missionary serving in Hongkou and as chaplain to the Shanghai Volunteer Corps. He lost his right arm in an explosion while conducting chemistry experiments for a class of Chinese students and became known as the "one-armed priest."

The Jacquinot model began with the Shanghai Safety Zone in 1937 during the Second Sino-Japanese War. It was a demilitarized area for Chinese civilians located in the Old City of Shanghai adjacent to the French Concession. The zone was respected both by the warring sides and Concession authorities. It was administered by an international committee of representatives from American, British, and French communities and policed by the Chinese. Between 1937 and 1940, the zone saved thousands of Chinese residents until it was abolished after Jaquinot left Shanghai.

Following the example in Shanghai, foreigners in Nanking created their own safety zone. The model also inspired those in Hankou, Zhangzhou, and Shenzhen to do likewise.

His works are acknowledged in the Commentaries to the 1949

Geneva Convention and in a 1977 Protocol as a fine example of "neu-
tralized zones" created to protect civilian populations caught in the
winds of war.

Oberführer Oskar Dirlewanger

On April 17, 1945, while commanding the 36th *Waffen* Grenadier
Division and fighting the Soviet armies along the Oder-Neisse line, Oskar
Dirlewanger was seriously injured in combat for the twelfth time. He was
promptly evacuated to a hospital in Althausen, Bavaria, to recover from
his wounds. In the interim, the French First Army had crossed the Rhine,
traversed the Black Forest, and spread south and east toward the town.

Released from care three weeks later and confronting the inevitable, Dirlewanger fled to a remote hunting lodge located on an isolated
switchback trail 7 kilometers from Althausen, where he was hidden by
sympathetic Nazi Party members who provided him with false documentation and civilian clothing.

Acting on credible information, on June 1, 1945, Moroccan
Goumier infantry of the French First Army smashed down the doors
of a wine cellar in the lodge. There, they located a hollow-eyed skeleton
of a man cowering in the shadows. He provided false papers and initially identified himself in broken French as a runaway Slovak conscript
hiding from marauding Nazi sympathizers.

But in the end, Oskar Dirlewanger couldn't help himself. The mere
thought of being held by the bearded unwashed Arabs he now confronted was too much for him. And so, he blurted out his true identity
and brashly demanded in flawless Parisienne French to surrender to
someone of the equal rank and culture as he possessed.

A rifle butt to the face quickly disabused him of his Arian fantasy
of racial supremacy.

Dirlewanger was forcibly taken to the local jail in Althausen. The
town was now governed by the Free French and, as fate would have it,
the guard detail when the Goumiers arrived with their prisoner happened to be a small section of Polish soldiers who'd been serving in an
active liaison capacity with the Free French units since Falaise. Their
senior NCO was a former teacher and a native of Warsaw. He had lost
a wife and a young child during the Uprising.

Oskar Dirlewanger died mysteriously in his cell during the night of June 4–5, 1945. No questions were ever asked as to the cause of his death and no one ever requested his remains. There certainly wasn't an autopsy. It seemed altogether fitting to end such a brutal life in such a shabby manner.

Colonel Fabian Lis, aka *Dzik*
(Wild Boar)

Fabian Lis survived the Second World War as an active and highly respected member of the Polish Underground. He lived quietly thereafter in a small town outside Torun teaching geography at the local gymnasium to indifferent adolescents. But in the new Socialist People's Republic of Poland, times had drastically changed.

In 1947, Lis was arrested by officials of the Ministry of Internal Security and charged with political subversion and membership in an outlawed organization—the wartime pro-Western Armia Krajowa. After a brief in-camera trial, he was convicted of all charges. Returned to his cell, Fabian Lis was never seen again. His body was never found. He became one of the faceless, nameless thousands of Poles who fought both the Nazis and Communists who had savaged his country. Like many of his brothers and sisters, death may have claimed his life, but never his soul.

Major Patrick Aiden Flaherty, Ret.
(US Army Counterintelligence; NYPD)

Because of his previous investigative background in the NYPD, and firmly buttressed by supportive words from his military bosses at Project *Venona*, in September 1945 Major Patrick Flaherty was seconded to the US Army Counterintelligence Corps and given the task of rounding up important Nazis in Occupied Germany and newly liberated Western Europe. To accomplish this mission, he used skilled rank and file teams who spread out like eager bloodhounds in search of their prey.

Over the course of the next year, Flaherty's people arrested an impressive number of relatively minor Nazi functionaries who had neither the intelligence nor fiscal wherewithal to flee from the scenes of their crimes.

In early 1947, Flaherty's unit had an unexpected major breakthrough. Ex-SS *Obersturbannführer* Fritz Knöchlein was discovered lingering in relative anonymity inside a prisoner-of-war camp in Sheffield, England. He'd been picked up in Aachen by an American infantry unit acting on a tip, then transferred and interned in a US military holding facility in Yorkshire until his identity could be verified. The long search for the author of the 1940 massacre of ninety-seven members of the Royal Norfolk Regiment had ended.

Major Patrick Flaherty resigned his commission shortly after the conviction and hanging of Knöchlein. It seemed only fitting that he ended his military service on a high note. After a short vacation in Maine, he returned to New York City only to find the place had moved on. The war was over, the veterans were back, and a hell-bent economic recovery was well underway.

Undeterred, Pat Flaherty spent the next years back in the job he loved, rising to the rank of an NYPD precinct captain in Brooklyn, still in pursuit of that defining moment for every cop—the next "big pinch." On Monday, June 27, 1966, Patrick Flaherty died in his sleep of a massive heart attack. He had never married, and so his legacy died with him.

Following a solemn Catholic funeral Mass at St. Michael's Church in Sunset Park, Brooklyn, Patrick Aiden Flaherty was interred just off the Jackie Robinson Parkway in Section 18 of Cyprus Hills Cemetery—the New York Police Department burial ground—where he would rest forever at peace with his brother officers.

SS Obersturbannführer Fritz Knöchlein

In August 1948, Fritz Knöchlein was arraigned before a War Crimes Court in Rotherbaum, a borough of Hamburg, on charges that "in the vicinity of Le Paradis, Pas-de-Calais, France on or about 27 May 1940, in violation of the laws and usages of war, was concerned in the killing of about 90 prisoners of war, members of The Royal Norfolk Regiment and other British Units."

His trial commenced on Monday, October 11, 1948.

On the very first day of the proceedings, the most damning evidence was given by an elderly French peasant, Madame Romanie Castel, who stepped out of the witness box and hobbled to the center of the courtroom. Turning slowly, she peered at the faces around her, at the assembled court officials, military, lawyers, reporters, interpreters, and clerks and, suddenly, pointing a thin, bony hand at Fritz Knöchlein she cried, "That's him! That is the man!"

Just before noon on a sunny morning in late October, the president of the court pronounced his verdict. Fritz Knöchlein was found guilty of all the charges before him and was sentenced to death by hanging.

The sentence was carried out on January 21, 1949, in Hamelin. Like so many others of his black-shirted ilk who had made their way down that uniquely dark and festering pathway of self-deception, his last words were predictable. He was "only following orders." Fritz Knöchlein was thirty-seven years old.

No other German soldiers or officers were prosecuted for their roles in the massacre.

SS *Haupsturmführer* Paulus Henschell

Honoring their part of the deal, the Western Allies ensured that in March 1946, Henschell went on to live in anonymity in Buenos Aires, Argentina, aided by a handsome financial package and false passport and papers that safely altered his identity. There were anxious whisperings in the German ex-patriate Argentine community about a past that might draw undue attention to others of "his kind" living there.

Soon after immigrating, SS Captain Paulus Henschell—or rather Rudolph Gersdorff as he came to be known in his new homeland allegedly a *Wehrmacht* ordinance captain who served in Norway for much of the war—started a boutique travel agency on a side street in the patrician *barrio* of Caballito. He married a local woman, had three children, and in the summer of 1988 died peacefully in his sleep. He never talked about the war. As far as his Argentinian family was concerned, he was just a simple German soldier who had the misfortune to honorably serve his Fatherland on the wrong side of history.

However, Henschell did have a number of "curious" customers.

Many of them had slunk out of the darkest corners of war-ravaged Europe using Franco's Spain as a springboard to subsequently settle en masse in Patagonia, a sparsely populated region in southern Argentina. "Curious," because they were invariably German men of an age where they would have held positions of import within the Third Reich in its halcyon years. And, more tellingly, they were also individuals prone to clandestine reunions on dates that coincided with Nazi triumphs in years past.

In the spirit of the agreement he'd entered into with Johnny Callison, Paulus Henschell was never called upon to testify against Knöchlein. He also never spoke of his once-beloved German wife Astrid, or visited his aging parents in Spandau, again.

Doctor Werner Beck SS
(Director of the Staatliches Institut für Gerichtsmedizin im Geneneralgouvernement [State Institute for Medical Jurisprudence and Criminology], formerly known as the Judicial Medicine Department of Jagiellonian University, Kraków, Poland)

In early 1945, with the vengeful hounds of Stalin's armies and Beria's NKVD hot on his trail, Doctor Werner Beck seemingly disappeared from the planet in the fog of war. It was largely believed that he traveled into Bavaria and melded into the local population.

Yet that did not stop emerging cries for justice, for the new Communist regime in Poland claimed to have strong and compelling evidence that Beck had been involved in war crimes and, through diplomatic channels, demanded his extradition to face those charges.

The Babinski psychiatric hospital near Kraków held over one thousand patients when the Second World War began. The occupying Germans began a three-stage liquidation of all patients through starvation, deportations of Jews to the camps, and finally, mass murder of those that remained.

To that end, on June 23, 1943, Doctor Werner Beck arrived with a detachment of SS troops under the command of SS-Sturmbannführer Karl Meyer and SS-Standartenführer Max Hammer. The Polish staff members were locked in an old theater building during the time of the action. Thirty patients temporarily on rehabilitation in a nearby

Catholic convent were transferred back to the hospital and were the first to be loaded onto a truck and delivered to the Swoszowice railway station. Later, SS troops opened the wards and counted patients, then herded the remainder to trucks that transported them to the railway station. In the evening, the train carried them to Auschwitz-Birkenau, where they were all subsequently gassed in the "little red school house," as it was known by the inmates and "Bunker One," as its official SS title.

As the head of the State Institute for Medical Jurisprudence and Criminology in Kraków, Beck had assisted in the investigation of graves at Katyn Forest and was the principal custodian of all material taken from the graves of Polish officers to be used as proof of mass murders committed by the Soviet regime—though the physical evidence was never recovered.

On Thursday, April 24, 1952, Doctor Werner Beck was called as a key witness to appear in Hamburg, West Germany before the US Congressional Select Committee to Conduct an Investigation and Study of the Facts, Evidence, and Circumstances of the Katyn Forest Massacre.

His testimony concerning such findings was both compelling and damning.

Thereafter, Werner Beck went on to live quietly at Roermonder Strasse 80 in Laurensberg, a leafy suburb of Aachen in what was then West Germany. He worked as a senior physician in the Städtische Krankenanstalten (municipal hospital) on Goethestrasse in Aachen and died peacefully in 1989. For all intents and purposes, he appeared a kindly and competent physician who cared deeply for his patients. Attempts to return him to Poland to face war crimes allegations failed. He was never extradited to Poland.

Klaus Emile Julius Fuchs

In 1959, after serving nine years and four months of his term at HM Prison Wakefield, Klaus Fuchs was unconditionally released. He immediately emigrated from the United Kingdom to the German Democratic Republic (Communist East Germany) where he was elected to the Academy of Sciences and became a member of the Socialist Unity Party of Germany central committee. He was appointed deputy director of the Institute for Nuclear Research in Rossendorf, where he served until retiring in 1979.

On January 28, 1988, Klaus Fuchs passed away in Berlin. His body was cremated and his ashes buried in the Pergolenweg of the Socialist Memorial in Berlin's Friedrichsfelde Cemetery.

It is alleged by his closest friends at the Institute for Nuclear Research that Fuchs's greatest frustration in life was intellectual, not political. He was never able to fully determine how to construct a fusion-able bomb. Throughout his time at Los Alamos and later in Communist East Germany, Fuchs lacked the mathematical formula that he so desperately needed to think through the fusion process—a method that would fuse two separate atoms to form a third, more volatile, one.

It was a formula that he knew existed; something Stanislaus Ulam, his colleague at Los Alamos, had let slip one time over a night of heavy drinking. Something alleged to be in mysterious calculations developed by Ulam and a group of his friends before the war at a café in Lwów. Something he knew that men had died attempting to discover. Fuchs had been so close and yet so far. Perhaps in the world he inhabited, not to have invented such an evil might be considered a blessing. But for Klaus Fuchs, it was intellectually a godless curse.

Even at the very end, Klaus Fuchs never knew who from within had betrayed him to the West. He would certainly never have guessed that it was Kim Philby.

Harold Adrian Russell "Kim" Philby, OBE
(awarded King's Honours list on January 1, 1946; awards officially stripped on August 10, 1965). Hero of Soviet Union, Order of Lenin, Order of People's Friendship

As the decade ended and Winston Churchill's infamous Soviet Iron Curtain thundered down over Eastern Europe, Kim Philby sensed leaden footsteps closing in on him. The world had dramatically changed. Fascism had been soundly defeated, and Soviet Russia was no longer considered an ally. So he now trod very carefully.

In 1949, Kim Philby was posted to Washington, officially as First Secretary to the British Embassy, but in reality as the chief British intelligence representative in the United States. He was a confidant of the CIA and oversaw the most urgent and top-secret communications between the Washington and London. Most critically, Philby became aware of *Venona* and the Pandora's box of secrets it was slowly but surely exposing—secrets that might soon implicate him.

Guy Burgess, an associate of Philby's and fellow traveler to the Party from university days (recruited by Philby in 1935), was posted to the British embassy in Washington in 1950. He was a walking disaster waiting to happen. A loud-mouthed, indiscreet alcoholic, Burgess all but placed a bull's-eye on his back for American counterintelligence operatives, buttressed by knowledge about his espionage for the USSR that *Venona* held in its decoded formulas.

Then the inevitable happened. Burgess's defection to the Soviet Union in 1951 with his fellow spy—Donald Maclean, who was also a close friend of Philby—led to a serious breach in Anglo-United States intelligence co-operation and caused long-lasting disruption and demoralization in Britain's foreign and diplomatic services. The "affair of the missing diplomats," and their long-time association with Philby, placed him squarely in the crosshairs of MI5.

It came then as no surprise that Philby was sent back to London, where he underwent MI5 interrogation aimed at ascertaining whether he had acted as a "third man" in the Burgess and Maclean spy ring. In July 1951, he resigned from MI6, pre-empting what would have been, at the very least, an all-but-inevitable dismissal.

After Philby's departure from MI6, speculation regarding his possible Soviet affiliations continued unabated. Interrogated repeatedly regarding his intelligence work and connection with Burgess, Philby continued to deny he had acted as a Soviet agent.

From 1952 onward, Philby struggled daily to find salaried work. In August 1954, he accepted a minor position with a diplomatic gossip sheet *The Fleet Street Letter*. Lacking access to material of value and out of touch with Soviet intelligence, he had all but ceased to operate as a Soviet agent.

On November 7, 1955, Philby was officially cleared by Foreign Secretary Harold Macmillan, who told the House of Commons as recorded in Hansard, "I have no reason to conclude that Mr. Philby has at any time betrayed the interests of his country, or to identify him with the so-called 'Third Man,' if indeed there was one."

Following this pronouncement, Philby gave a press conference in which he calmly and confidently, and without evidence of the stammer he had struggled with since childhood, declared his innocence: "I have never been a Communist."

Exonerated in the eyes of the general public in 1956, Kim Philby went to Beirut as a correspondent for British newspapers. He subsequently traveled frequently throughout the Middle East.

In 1961, a major in the First Chief Directorate of the KGB defected to the United States from his diplomatic post in Helsinki. He offered the CIA revelations about Soviet agents within the American and British intelligence services. Following his debriefing in the United States, the Russian was escorted to England for further questioning. The head of MI6 had suspected Philby as the "Third Man" for some time. Comprehensive debriefing of the Russian agent only confirmed those suspicions.

The CIA next sent a man named Elliott to "interview" Philby in Beirut. Confronted with the allegation of espionage and ongoing intelligence activities on behalf of the Soviets, Philby was unrepentant, almost defiant. He would not sign a statement of confession and requested a delay in the inquiry to get his personal life in order. For a reason known only to the fates, Elliott agreed.

On the evening of January 23, 1963, Kim Philby vanished from the Lebanese capital on the *Dolmatova*, a rust-bucket Soviet tramp steamer bound for Odessa. The ship had departed so abruptly that its cargo was left scattered over the docks.

Upon his arrival in Moscow in January 1963, Philby discovered that he was not a colonel in the KGB as he had been led to believe, but a mere mortal. He was paid 500 rubles a month. His family was not immediately able to join him in exile. Philby was placed under house arrest, with all visitors screened by the KGB.

It was not until July 1, 1963, that Philby's flight to Moscow was officially confirmed. On July 30, Soviet officials announced that they had granted him political asylum in the USSR, along with full Soviet citizenship.

Philby initially occupied himself by writing his memoirs that were published in 1968 under the title *My Silent War*. In the book, Philby states that his loyalties were always with the communists. He considered himself not to have been a double agent, but "a straight penetration agent working in the Soviet interest."

In the early 1970s, Kim Philby found employment—a minor role training KGB recruits. He also worked in the KGB's Active Measures Department, churning out fabricated documents. Using genuine unclassified and public CIA and US Department of State papers, Philby inserted "sinister" paragraphs regarding America's plans. The KGB would stamp these items "top secret" and begin their calculated circulation.

Harold Adrian Russell "Kim" Philby died of heart failure in Moscow in 1988. He was given a hero's funeral and posthumously awarded numerous medals by the Soviets: Order of Lenin, Order of the Red Banner, Order of Friendship of Peoples, Order of the Great Patriotic War, Lenin Medal, and the Jubilee Medal for "Four Years of Victory in the Great Patriotic War 1941–1945."

Marshal Georgy Zhukov,
Hero of the Soviet Union, 1939, 1944, 1945, 1956. Order of Victory (two times), Order of Lenin (six times), Order of the Red Banner (three times), Grand Cross of Legion d'Honneur (France 1945). Honorary Knight-Commander Order of the Bath, military division (United Kingdom 1945). Croix de Guerre (France 1945). Chief Commander Legion of Merit (United States of America 1945).

In 1955, Georgy Zhukov's star was once more on the ascent, and he was appointed Soviet defense minister. He immediately and successfully opposed the re-establishment of the Political Commissar system in the military—combat soldiers should be led by generals, not politicians.

A year later, on his sixtieth birthday, Zhukov became the first person to receive the Hero of the Soviet Union title for the fourth time. He became the highest-ranking military professional to also be a member of the Presidium of the Central Committee of the Communist Party. His prestige was higher than that of the KGB. Yet when Zhukov publicly demanded an official condemnation of Stalin's crimes committed during the Great Purge of the 1930s, he was once more deemed a threat to political leaders and again was accused of being a Bonapartist.

In 1956, at the 20th Congress of the Communist Party of the Soviet Union, Nikita Khrushchev was elected as First Secretary of the

317

Party. He immediately attacked Josef Stalin's legacy in a speech *On the Cult of Personality and Its Consequences*. To engage in such a startling performance, Khrushchev needed and received the full approval of the military, headed by the Minister of Defense, Georgy Zhukov.

In June 1957, Zhukov continued his spirited support of Khrushchev. On this occasion, against the Anti-Party Group, which had a majority in the Presidium and voted to replace Khrushchev as First Secretary. At that gathering, Zhukov stated: "The Army is against this resolution and not even a tank will leave its position without my order!" In that same session, the Anti-Party Group was condemned, and Zhukov was again made a member of Presidium.

Yet his ultimate fall from grace was as sudden as it was unexpected. On October 4, 1957, he left on an official visit to Yugoslavia and Albania. When he returned to Moscow at the end of the month, he was immediately ordered to a meeting of the Presidium and arbitrarily removed from that body.

Accused of "non-party behavior," conducting an "adventurist foreign policy," and sponsoring his own personality cult, he was expelled from the Central Committee and sent into forced retirement at age sixty-two. According to knowledgeable Kremlinologists, most Soviet politicians—including Khrushchev himself—had a deep-seated fear of "powerful persons." And Georgy Zhukov was deemed to be one such person.

After Khrushchev was deposed in October 1964, Zhukov was restored to favor—though not to power. His popularity was deemed good for the nation and, more critically, for its new political leadership. Zhukov was lionized for his role in the Great Patriotic War, and on May 9, 1965, the twentieth anniversary of the Soviet defeat of the Fascist forces of Adolf Hitler, Zhukov was invited to sit on the tribune of the Lenin Mausoleum and given the honor of officially reviewing a massive parade of Russian military might in Red Square.

But like the lion in winter, Zhukov slowly began to fade. He began writing his memoirs, yet his health steadily deteriorated. In 1969, he suffered a serious stroke, was hospitalized for seven months, and then returned to his home. He was paralyzed on his left side, his speech was heavily slurred, and he could walk only with great assistance.

On June 18, 1974, after being in a coma for some time while being scrupulously guarded by the KGB, Georgy Zhukov died in the Kremlin

Hospital, an exclusive medical facility for Russia's power elite and considered the best in the Soviet Union. Ironically, the place he passed away in was a mere forty-five-minute walk from the *dacha* where his nemesis, the Man of Steel, had spent the last hours of his life twenty-one years before.

Commander Charles Tiberius Vickery, aka "V."
Distinguished Service Order, Indian Order of Merit, Commander of the British Empire, Companion of the Most Distinguished Order of St. Michael and St. George.

For all intents and purposes, the Second World War was a very good period for Charles Vickery. Operating in the shadows, as was his nature, he had sent many truly remarkable men and women to their deaths in Occupied Europe without undue qualm or regret. For, as he occasionally reminded himself, such was the unspoken cost of victory over a ruthless and relentless enemy.

Until he retired in 1947 to take ownership of a coffee plantation in Kenya, "V" never stopped trusting his instincts and, for the most part, he'd been right to do so. But his instincts were honed in a time when only gentlemen played the "Great Game." And that time had passed.

Like so many Englishmen of his class, he had an ingrained condescension for all things American and, for that matter, foreign, and in that respect, he had badly misjudged both. He would never know after his first seemingly victorious salvo at Gordon's Club how Flaherty had shrewdly befriended the Polish colonel and thereafter had "played" "V," as only an expert in spy craft could.

Still, it mattered little in the scheme of things, for on New Year's Day, 1946, Charles Tiberius Vickery was fittingly rewarded for service to his sovereign king by being made a Commander of the British Empire. He was pleased that a close confidant and like-minded soul, Kim Philby, with the breeding that only time spent in Imperial India had produced when it was still the Raj, was also named on the list. Philby, a true gentleman of the old school, was even at the pier to see him off on his journey to a new and more restful life in colonial Kenya.

As he sat sipping a nightly gin and tonic on the broad porch of "Simla," the name he had given his plantation, magnificently nestled in

319

the sight of Mount Kenya, he occasionally thought of the loss of Antony Eskenzi. It still troubled him, but he always reminded himself of the words of George Patton speaking at an event in Boston Massachusetts on June 7, 1945: "It is foolish and wrong to mourn the men who died. Rather, we should thank God such men had lived."

On the cool morning of July 14, 1947, Vickery's manager drove him to the nearest train stop in the plantation Land Rover. He carried only an army surplus duffle bag filled with a change of clothing, toiletries, and the paperwork he needed for the journey. Under his safari jacket he had strapped a loaded Webley pistol, for he also carried a large sum of money for the journey and to buy provisions for the plantation, which he would purchase on the return trip.

After a grueling sixteen-hour train ride into Mombasa, Kenya's deep seaport on the Indian Ocean, Vickery taxied straight to the pier to take delivery of a brand-new cherry-red Hillman Minx drop-head coupe, offloaded from a Union Castle Line freighter inbound from Southampton.

Relishing his new toy as he journeyed into the bustling port city proper, Vickery shrewdly provisioned himself for the return trek to Simla, loading up with his quartermaster's list of foodstuffs and the usual "et ceteras," in addition to jerry cans of petrol and, of course, sandwiches and water for the trek homebound.

He planned to stop over for a few days near the midpoint of the journey in a hunting lodge maintained by an old school chum—a retired British army colonel and Desert Rat survivor of the duels with Rommel, who relished the splendid isolation that rural Kenya afforded. His mate's fee? A few bottles of whiskey and some fine Cuban cigars. All in all, well worth the price for the gracious company, airy rooms, and elegant views of distant Mount Kilimanjaro.

Vickery would never see his friend. For in the late afternoon en route to the hunting lodge, his tiny Hillman was attacked by a raging black rhinoceros on an isolated dirt road. The tin box, cherry-red sedan tumbled end-over-end into the nearby Tsavo River like a child's toy.

After not hearing from his boss for several days, the plantation manager contacted local authorities. Two days later, the Hillman wreck was spotted by a lorry driver heading northbound for Nairobi. Vickery's body was never recovered.

A month later, a discreet memorial service was held at St Luke's, a quaint parish church in Kipping's Cross, the Vickery ancestral home in County Kent. There was a spartan notification in the *Times*. Actual attendance was strictly controlled by several burly gentlemen who looked distinctly uncomfortable in their ill-fitting suits. License plates of all vehicles found within a 5-kilometer radius of the church were discreetly recorded, some more than once.

Most of the mourners were retired gentlemen with thinning hair, wearing crow-black Saville Row suits, with the occasional regimental tie added for color. The ladies wore designer-cut black dresses and the requisite somber expressions. There were several Very Important Personages in attendance, but discretion was not only a coined phrase but a way of life for those surrounding them in the hard-backed pews of the eighteenth-century church.

The actual prayers were as traditional and meaningless as were the eulogies that followed. A mandatory repast was then held in the parish hall with the usual meat, cheese, and sandwich trays, fresh fruits, tepid tea, and watery coffee. The small talk was just as petty and unimportant as their postwar world had become. A dutiful twenty minutes passed, then slowly, discreetly muttering their insincere goodbyes, they drifted off into the shadows where they had grown so comfortable living their entire adult lives. For they were the survivors.

Few of those present at St Luke's actually spoke of Charles Tiberius Vickery, his life and exploits, for few really knew him. "V" had lived a life in the shadows and had died in them.

Yet he had done what many of his carefully selected SOE agents had not—he had outlived the War.

Major General Leslie Groves,
**United States Army. Commanding Officer, Manhattan Project.
Distinguished Service Medal; Legion of Merit; Commander of the
Order of the Crown, Belgium; Companion of the Order of the Bath,
Great Britain.**

General Leslie Groves retained oversight for the Manhattan Project until 1947, when responsibility for nuclear power and weapons was transferred from the Project to the Atomic Energy Commission. After his retirement in 1948, he went on to become a vice-president at Sperry Rand and retired there in 1961 at age sixty-five. On July 13, 1970, Leslie Groves suffered a severe heart attack and died that night as he was rushed to Walter Reed Army Medical Center in Washington. He was interred at Arlington National Cemetery. He was seventy-three.

Captain Ryszard Franciczek Manel, aka Tadeusz

There is no mention of Ryszard Manel or the agent code-named Tadeusz in the files of the Polish government-in-exile, the SOE, the OSS, or any other Allied entity. For all intents and purposes, he subsumed his identity and lived in obscurity as hostile forces continued their occupation.

Lest we forget that democratic nations ultimately triumph over evil only through the unheralded bravery of tens of thousands of ordinary and, indeed, extraordinary souls like Ryszard Manel.

Squadron Leader John Paul
"Johnny" Callison, USMC.
China Service Medal, DFC with bar, DSO, RCAF (retired)

In June 1953, Squadron Leader J.P. Callison officially retired from the Royal Canadian Air Force on a full pension. His last posting was that of Base Commandant at RCAF Station Hamilton. His diverse responsibilities entailed shepherding an auxiliary squadron of World War Two veterans who flew sporty P-51 Mustangs. On weekends, these "gentlemen pilots" buffeted gleefully about over Lake Ontario as they tried to recapture the exciting memories of a recent past. On the other days of the week, they held dreadfully mundane jobs as sales-clerks, teachers, and insurance salesmen.

When he finally dropped off his uniform and equipment at Trenton Depot in July 1953, Johnny Callison retired to a homeland he hadn't seen in years, settling on a small spread on County Road 8, a few miles west of his birthplace in Elkhart, Kansas.

Callison went on to live the life of a solitary bachelor. He became somewhat of a recluse to his neighbors and the people of Elkhart. His home was set back from the main road, and he traveled into town only for groceries and, when necessary, to repair his rickety Ford pickup. His home was euphemistically called a ranch by the real estate agent, but was in truth, nothing more than a glorified sharecropper's shack. He rarely drove the pickup and only replaced it in the early 1980s with an updated version of the same pickup when its motor blew.

A loner. The mystery man on County Road 8. His place was identified by three flag poles set in separate rock bases at the dirt-road entrance to his home—the Stars and Stripes, and on either side, the Marine Corps colors and the Royal Canadian Air Force blue ensign. Still, he was renowned for one thing and that was for breeding the best West Highland White puppies this side of the Great Divide. A small hand-painted sign at the roadway advertised this fact to the travelers who chanced down the county road.

The man who knocked on the screen front door on a particularly hot July afternoon was middle-aged and muscular. He wore a Cubs baseball cap atop a razor-shorn head of salt and pepper hair. His face was deeply tanned, with the sustained ruddiness of someone who lived in the outdoors. There was a small scar on his right cheek; an industrial accident perhaps or was it the consequence of an edged-blade wound? His eyes were gray, almost feral, yet tightly controlled. The stranger was dressed in a tan, pressed t-shirt, khaki chino pants, similarly pressed, and combat laced Kodiak boots.

"You sell pups? Westies?"

"To the right person I do," Callison remarked guardedly.

The stranger smiled. An amicable smile that belied his hard appearance.

Callison opened the door and invited the man in.

"Noticed your flag poles. I respect that." The next words he uttered spoke volumes to the right listener. "Semper fi."

The response resonated with Callison. "Semper fi."

"Where? If I may ask," the stranger wondered.

"I was a China Marine in '37. Shanghai."

"You saw a lot." The knowing look.

Callison was silent.

"And the other flag? Royal Canadian Air Force?"

"Last war," Callison volunteered. "I began as a fighter pilot in North Africa. Spent time in a POW camp before I was repatriated in

323

a prisoner exchange. And then Europe"—he paused—"I recovered the bodies of those who didn't make it."

It was the stranger's turn to nod, a silent communication made only between those who had "been there," and somehow made it back.

They talked for a time about unimportant things. Callison about dogs and their upkeep. The stranger about how he and his wife, Angela, were visiting their son and daughter-in-law in Boise City, Oklahoma, and New Mexico, and how he'd been sent on a mission to find the perfect gift for their grandkids.

The terrier pup that Callison subsequently brought in from the kennel was somehow predestined to be that gift. A snow-white furball of mischief and mayhem, it was just what the stranger had in mind.

A deal was quickly struck. The stranger took out his wallet and hesitated, slightly embarrassed.

"I can give you twenty in cash. Will you take a check for the rest? My credit is good."

A grin slowly formed on Callison's weathered face. "Can't see why not. You look like an honest fellow—for a Marine."

He took the check, squinting at the personal information of the account holder. "Polish?"

"Yes." Again that open smile. "With a name like Startek, it's hard not to be. Second generation. Dad came over in the thirties; married an Irish girl. We lived in Chicago where he worked in the meatpacking industry. Dad served in the Pacific. Fought at Peleliu with the First Marine Regiment. He was wounded there but survived."

"And you?"

"'Nam," the stranger answered simply.

Callison nodded. The words left unspoken said it all.

"I knew some Poles once," Callison offered unexpectedly. "During the war."

"Oh."

"Brave bunch. Never knew when to quit. Even when everything was against them." He repeated the word, thinking back to the ill-fated Brindisi missions into occupied Warsaw and his final eventful meeting with Tadeusz. "Brave."

"Yes," the stranger agreed.

Callison wavered once more as if he were searching through some dark place deep within his soul. "It doesn't matter anymore. It was during the war—a long time ago and it never happened anyway." His voice drifted to some far-off place only he resided in. After a respectable period of silence, the stranger departed to leave Johnny Callison alone with his memories.

* * *

John Paul Callison died seven months later of heart failure. His personal physician said that, with all his underlying medical conditions, it was truly a miracle that he'd lived that long.

The old man never talked much to anyone in Elkhart about his war experiences. The doctor knew, though, and he was professional and kept mum. Yet somehow, others in the tightly knit community had pieced together portions of the life of John Paul Callison.

The funeral chapel was filled to standing-room only, with neighbors, members of the American Legion, aging Vietnam War vets, and much younger men and women who'd survived Iraq and Afghanistan, most without visible scars but all carrying within the lasting crucible of combat. And there were many more present. It seemed as if the whole county was there—out of respect, word of mouth, or just plain curiosity—it was hard to tell and, in the end, it didn't matter.

Callison hadn't been particularly religious and it showed as the rent-a-minister unsuccessfully tried to make allowances for it in his sermon, grasping at hollow platitudes about duty, honor, and sacrifice. But it was the presence of a full US Marine Corps honor guard led by a highly decorated Marine colonel that caused the congregation to pause and make some sense of the life that John Callison had lived in ways that the minister could never begin to understand.

As the honor guard stood to respectful parade rest at the rear of the chapel, the colonel made his way to the very front pew and took a seat normally reserved for the immediate family. He had a kaleidoscope of campaign medals hung stiff as sentries across his left breast and two rows of ribbon-only awards on his right. His dress blues were so pressed they appeared to have been starched. His gray eyes captured the rapt attention of those who dared gaze at them too long, for they held the hard look of a man who had confronted death more than once and stared it down. The colonel's name was Startek and, on this day, his honor party were there to pay their last respects to a brother Marine.

At day's end, John Paul Callison was laid to his final rest in the county cemetery outside town and beside the grave of his departed father. It was as close as they would ever be. Two warriors living their lives in solitary search of an ideal that perhaps never existed, but which somehow now bonded them forever in death in ways they had never been in life.

SOVIET POSTSCRIPT

The Soviets continued to deny their role in the Katyn massacre until April 13, 1990, when Russian President Mikhail Gorbachev admitted NKVD responsibility for the 1940 killings of 22,000 members of the Polish military and intelligentsia at various sites in the Soviet Union, the principal one being in the forest of Katyn.

On October 14, 1992, Russian president Boris Yeltsin released secret NKVD materials about the killings that included this one:

From: Headquarters of the NKVD.
Region of Minsk.
10 JUNE 1940
To: The Headquarters of the NKVD Moscow.
Official Report

By Order of the Headquarters of the NKVD on February 12, 1940, the liquidation of the three Polish prisoner-of-war camps was carried out in the regions of the towns of Kozielsk, Ostaschkovo, and Starobyelsk. The operation of liquidating the above named three camps was completed on 6 JUNE of that year. Comrade Burjanoff, who had been seconded from the Central Office, was appointed to be in charge.

Under the above-mentioned Order, the camp at Kozielsk was liquidated first by security forces of the Minsk headquarters of the NKVD in the area of the city of Smolensk during the period between 1 March and 3 May of that year. As security forces, territorial troops, in part from the 190th

Rifle Regiment, were employed.

The Second action under the above Order was carried out in the area of the town of Bologoye by the security forces of the Smolensk headquarters of the NKVD and was also covered by troops of the 129th Rifle Regiment (Velike Luki). It was completed by 5 JUNE of that year. The Charkow headquarters of the NKVD was entrusted with carrying out the third liquidation of the camp of Starobyelsk. It was carried out in the area of the Dergachi settlement, with the assistance of security forces of the 68th Ukrainian Rifle Regiment of the territorial troops on 2 JUNE. In this case, the responsibility and leadership in this action was entrusted to the NKVD Colonel B. Kutschov.

A copy of this report is being sent simultaneously to the NKVD Generals Raichmann and Saburin for their attention.

Russia's state archive has recently published formerly top-secret Soviet-era documents on the April 1940 Katyn massacre on its website. The documents include a key letter to then Soviet leader Josef Stalin from secret police (NKVD) chief Lavrentiy Beria dated March 5, 1940, and marked "Top Secret."

Some 22,000 members of the Polish elite were killed by Soviet forces and, for decades, the USSR claimed that it was the work of Nazi Germany. Russia gave the documents to Poland in 1992. Here are excerpts from the Beria letter:

To Comrade Stalin:

In prisoner-of-war camps run by the USSR NKVD and in prisons in western Ukraine and Belorussia, there are currently a large number of former Polish army officers, former officials of the Polish police and intelligence services, members of Polish nationalist counter-revolutionary parties, members of unmasked rebel counter-revolutionary organizations, defectors, and others. They are all sworn enemies of Soviet power and filled with hatred toward the Soviet system.

The POW officers and police in the camps are trying to continue counter-revolutionary work and are engaged in anti-

Soviet agitation. Each of them is just waiting for liberation, so as to actively join the struggle against Soviet power . . .

In total, in the prisoner-of-war camps (not counting soldiers and non-commissioned officers) there are 14,736 former officers, government officials, landowners, policemen, military police, jailers, settlers, and spies. More than 97 percent are of Polish nationality . . .

In total, the prisons of western Ukraine and Belorussia contain 18,632 detainees (of whom 10,685 are Poles).

Based on the fact that all of them are steadfast incorrigible enemies of Soviet power, the USSR NKVD deems it essential:

1. To propose that the USSR NKVD give special consideration to
   i.   the cases of 14,700 people remaining in the prisoner-of-war camps—former Polish army officers, government officials, landowners, policemen intelligence agents, military policemen, settlers, and jailers.
   ii. and also the cases of those arrested and remaining in prisons in the western districts of Ukraine and Belorussia, totaling 11,000 members of various counter-revolutionary spy and sabotage organisations, former landowners, factory owners, former Polish army officers, government officials, and defectors.

      Imposing on them the sentence of capital punishment—execution by shooting.
2. The cases are to be handled without the convicts being summoned and without revealing the charges, with no statements concerning the conclusion of the investigation, and the bills of indictment given to them."

[The letter is signed "L. Beria" in blue pencil under the title USSR People's Commissar for Internal Affairs.]

The first page of the letter bears the word *Za*—"in favor," scrawled in blue pencil with the signatures of Soviet leader Josef Stalin and of Politburo members K. Voroshilov and A.

Mikoyan, along with V. Molotov in ordinary pencil.

In the margin, added in blue ink, are the names Rosinsky and Kaganovich aides to Stalin, and also the word **Za**—"in favor."

Streljajte vo vse. "Shoot all."

U. Ganuy

Historically, the fourteen boxes allegedly holding the damning physical evidence of Soviet culpability at Katyn have never been recovered. It is said they were inadvertently destroyed in an Allied bombing raid conducted by a solitary Mosquito in the Dresden suburb of Radebeul. But that has never been proven. Another speculation was that they were intentionally burned by the retreating Germans to prevent their capture by the Soviets.

Yet there is another, far more intriguing theory, concerning this reliquary of Soviet culpability.

In 1991, workmen removing cracked supports in the false attic wall of the caretaker quarters at the Institute for Forensic Medicine in Kraków discovered a shoebox wrapped in heavy construction paper. It contained copies of highly sensitive documents authored by Doctor Werner Beck, the German director of the Institute and others working for him, in addition to original documents taken from the graves of Katyn.

The occupant of the attic has never been identified and is assumed to have perished in the Second World War. The Polish authorities now believe he might have been a prisoner of war or slave laborer working for the Institute when it was under Nazi control up to, and including, the tumultuous time of the Soviet "liberation" of the Royal City.

Among other items found in the building supports were tattered diaries of one Ryszard Manel, Captain Polish Army, ending abruptly during the invasion of Poland in 1939, and pages from a play: William Shakespeare's *The Tempest.*

There was also a torn and faded photograph of a well-dressed man standing in front of an obvious artificial forest backdrop, the kind one would find in any respectable studio of the period. The cut of the man's clothing is from the mid- to late-1930s. The person in the photo is not identified.

Captain Ryszard Manel is officially listed as among those Polish officers who were murdered by the KGB in the Katyn Forest in the spring of 1940. His remains were recovered, arbitrarily assigned a number—Body 865—and summarily identified by forensic authorities as Ryszard Franciszek Manel.

There is no record of a Polish Red Cross member officially attending the Forensic Institute in Kraków during the Second World War. There is also no record of any prisoners of war or slave laborers working there in various menial capacities having even the remotest possibility of access to the confidential files concerning Katyn maintained by the Nazi director of the Institute.

The individual's posture in the photo indicates that another male was standing next to him—a cavalry boot and a jodhpured uniform pant of the kind worn by a cavalry officer in 1939 are partially visible. Perhaps it was a Polish officer. Perhaps it was a man now known to history as Tadeusz and to those who truly knew him: Ryszard Manel, lover of strawberry trifle, houndstooth jackets, and the works of William Shakespeare.

ACKNOWLEDGMENTS

I offer my thanks and gratitude to the following people:

Doctor Albi Razak, whose medical knowledge and humanity help so many.

Dean Baxendale, my publisher and the driving force and genius behind so many timely and thought-provoking books.

Joe Reis, a dear friend and true visionary, who opened the door to enable this book to begin its journey.

Don Loney, Lea-Anne Solomonian, and Janice Weaver, editors most writers can only dream of having, who guided me through the arcane nuances of the printed word with remarkable patience and understanding.

Anne Konkel, my mother, who at 107 years is living proof that age and wisdom do go together.

My amazing wife, Robin, who has been, and will always be, at my side.

My daughter, Laura, whom we love beyond words!

My late father, Edward, who lived through the horrors that this novel attempted to capture—and survived.

A NOTE ON SOURCES

This is a work of fiction, but it's also based on facts gathered through years of painstaking research. I would especially like to note that the medical observations made in chapter 6 by Doctor Ference Orsos, a real-life professor of forensic medicine and criminology at the University of Budapest, are extracted from his written records. Orsos was one of twelve expert scientists sent in by the European Red Cross to determine the cause of death of the Katyn victims. His remarks can be found in *The Katyn Forest Massacre: Hearings Before the Select Committee to Conduct an Investigation of the Facts, Evidence and Circumstances of the Katyn Forest Massacre*, Eighty-Second Congress, First Session on Investigation of the Murder of Thousands of Polish Officers in the Katyn Forest Near Smolensk, Russia (Washington, DC: Government Printing Office, 1952).

In chapter 11, Johnny Callison sits reading *Wing Victory* at RAF Brindisi as he patiently awaits the return of the Warsaw supply mission bombers. This classic First World War novel, originally published in 1934 and republished since then many times, was written by Victor Maslin Yeates. The original was widely read and shared by British and Commonwealth flight crews during the Second World War because of its accurate depiction of the horrors and tragedy of aerial combat. The extract shown in these pages is from V. M. Yeates, *Winged Victory* (Brantford, ON: Arcadia Press, 2017), p. 135.

The information in the postscript about Werner Beck's later years was graciously provided to me in an interview with Doctor Richard Kuhl, of the University of Tübingen, who has made the pursuit of truth and accountability as it relates to Nazi war criminals a cornerstone of his academic work.

In addition to the titles named above, many other books and

documents were integral to my research for this novel. What follows is a selected bibliography of those I relied on most heavily:

Abarinov, Vladimir. *The Murderers of Katyn*. New York: Hippocrene Books, 1993.

Beevor, Antony. *The Fall of Berlin 1945*. New York: Viking Press, 2002.

———. *The Second World War*. London: Weidenfeld & Nicolson, 2012.

———. *Stalingrad*. New York: Viking Press, 1998.

Bessel, Richard. *Germany 1945: From War to Peace*. New York: Harper Perennial, 2009.

Bohlen, Celestine. "Russian Files Show Stalin Ordered Massacre of 20,000 Poles in 1940." *New York Times*, 15 October 1992. https://www.nytimes.com/1992/10/15/world/russian-files-show-stalin-ordered-massacre-of-20000-poles-in-1940.html.

Bruce, George. *The Warsaw Uprising*. London: Pan Books, 1972.

Churchill, Winston. *The Second World War*. 6 vols. Boston: Houghton Mifflin Company, 1953.

Conot, Robert E. *Justice at Nuremberg*. New York: Carroll and Graff, 1984.

Davies, Norman. *Rising '44: The Battle for Warsaw*. London: Macmillan, 2003.

Delgado, James P. *Nuclear Dawn: The Atomic Bomb from the Manhattan Project to the Cold War*. Oxford, UK: Osprey Publishing, 2009.

Dimsdale, Joel E. *Anatomy of Malice: The Enigma of the Nazi War Criminals*. New Haven, CN: Yale University Press, 2016.

Dobbs, Michael. *Six Months in 1945: From World War to Cold War*. New York: Vintage Books, 2012.

Dunmore, Spencer. *Bomb Run*. London: Pan Books, 1971.

Edwards, Robert. *The Winter War: Russia's Invasion of Finland, 1939–1940*. New York: Pegasus, 2009.

Finder, Gabriel N., and Alexander V. Prusin. *Justice behind the Iron Curtain: Nazis on Trial in Communist Poland*. Toronto: University of Toronto Press, 2018.

Foot, M. R. D. *SOE: An Outline History of the Special Operations Executive, 1940–1946*. London: British Broadcasting Corp. Publishers, 1984.

Fry, Helen. *The London Cage: The Secret History of Britain's World War II Interrogation Centre*. New Haven, CN: Yale University Press, 2017.

Goodchild, Peter. *Edward Teller: The Real Dr. Strangelove*. Cambridge, MA: Harvard University Press, 2004.

Grossman, Vasily. *A Writer at War: Vasily Grossman with the Red Army, 1941–1945.* Translated by Antony Beevor and Luba Vinogradova. London: Pimlico Press, 2006.

Hadaway, Stuart. *Missing Believed Killed: The Royal Air Force and the Search for Missing Aircrew 1939–1952.* Barnsley, UK: Pen and Sword, 2008.

Hastings, Max. *All Hell Let Loose: The World at War 1939–1945.* London: HarperPress, 2011.

———. *Armageddon: The Battle for Germany 1944–1945.* London: Macmillan, 2005.

———. *Bomber Command: The Strategic Bombing Offensive 1939–45.* London: Macmillan, 2010.

———. *The Secret War: Spies, Codes and Guerillas 1939–1945.* London: William Collins, 2015.

Horne, Alistair. *To Lose a Battle: France 1940.* New York: Little Brown, 1969.

Hughes, Jeff. *The Manhattan Project: Big Science and the Atom Bomb.* New York: Columbia University Press, 2003.

Kelly, Cynthia C., ed. *The Manhattan Project: The Birth of the Atomic Bomb in the Words of Its Creators, Eyewitnesses and Historians.* New York: Black Dog and Leventhal, 2020.

Kelly, John. *Saving Stalin: Roosevelt, Churchill, Stalin and the Cost of Allied Victory in Europe.* New York: Hachette, 2020.

Khrushchev, Nikita. *Khrushchev Remembers: The Glasnost Tapes.* Translated and edited by Jerrold Schecter. Little and Brown, 1990.

Kirchubel, Robert. *Operation Barbarossa: The German Invasion of Soviet Russia.* Oxford, UK: Osprey Publishing, 2013.

Kuniczak, W. S. *The March.* New York: Doubleday, 1979.

———. *The Thousand Hour Day.* London: Secker and Warburg, 1967.

Maresch, Eugenia. *Katyn 1940: The Documentary Evidence of the West's Betrayal.* Spellmount, 2010.

Mawdsley, Evan. *Thunder in the East: The Nazi-Soviet War 1941–1945.* London: Bloomsbury Publishing, 2015.

———. *World War II: A New History.* Cambridge, UK: Cambridge University Press, 2009.

McKay, Sinclair. *The Fire and the Darkness: The Bombing of Dresden, 1945.* New York: St. Martin's Press, 2020.

McKinstry, Leo. *Lancaster: The Second World War's Greatest Bomber.* London: John Murray, 2009.

McMillan, Priscilla J. *The Ruin of J. Robert Oppenheimer and the Birth of the Modern Arms Race*. New York: Viking Press, 2005.

Moorhouse, Roger. *Berlin at War*. New York: Basic Books, 2010.

Murphy, David James. *The Finnish-Soviet Winter War 1939–40: Stalin's Hollow Victory*. London: Bloomsbury Publishing, 2021.

Page, Bruce, David Leitch and Phillip Knightley. *Philby: The Spy Who Betrayed a Generation*. London: André Deutsch, 1960.

Paul, Allen. *Katyn: The Untold Story of Stalin's Polish Massacre*. Annapolis, MD: Naval Institute Press, 1996.

Pilecki, Witold. *The Auschwitz Volunteer: Beyond Bravery*. Translated by Jarek Garlinski. Los Angeles: Aquila Polonica, 2012.

Richie, Alexandra. *Warsaw 1944: The Fateful Uprising*. London: William Collins, 2013.

Roberts, Andrew. *Storm of War: A New History of the Second World War*. New York: HarperCollins, 2011.

Shepherd, Ben H. *Hitler's Soldiers: The German Army in the Third Reich*. New Haven, CN: Yale University Press, 2016.

Shirer, William L. *The Rise and Fall of the Third Reich: A History of Nazi Germany*. New York: Simon and Schuster, 1960.

Terraine, John. *The Right of the Line: The Role of the RAF in World War Two*. London: Hodder and Stoughton, 1988.

Thomas, Nigel. *World War II Soviet Armed Forces*. Oxford, UK: Osprey Publishing, 2010.

Ulam, S. M. *Adventures of a Mathematician*. New York: Scribner's, 1976.

Walker, Jonathan. *Poland Alone: Britain, SOE and the Collapse of the Polish Resistance, 1944*. Cheltenham, UK: The History Press, 2011.

West, Nigel. *Mortal Crimes: The Greatest Theft in History: Soviet Penetration of the Manhattan Project*. New York: Enigma Books, 2007.

———. *Venona: The Greatest Secret of the Cold War*. New York: HarperCollins, 1999.

Williams, Robert Chadwell. *Klaus Fuchs: Atom Spy*. Cambridge, MA: Harvard University Press, 1987.

Zaloga, Steven. *Poland 1939: The Birth of Blitzkrieg*. Oxford, UK: Osprey Publishing, 2002.

Zawodny, J. K. *Death in the Forest: The Story of the Katyn Forest Massacre*. New York: Hippocrene Books, 1988.